fool for love

BETH CIOTTA

St. Martin's Paperbacks

To my literary agent, Amy Moore-Benson.
My champion. My friend. Thanks for believing in me.
Together we persevered!

FOOL FOR LOVE

For information address St. Martin's Press, 175 Fifth Avenue, New York, NY 10010.

ISBN: 978-1-62090-377-3

Printed in the United States of America

St. Martin's Paperbacks are published by St. Martin's Press, 175 Fifth Avenue, New York, NY 10010.

ACKNOWLEDGMENTS

I write from my heart, my soul, and feel blessed and grateful to all those who inspire and support my creative efforts.

Thank you to my editor, Monique Patterson, who embraced my voice and provided me with this amazing opportunity. Creating the Cupcake Lovers and delving into their world has been a challenge and thrill. Here's to the future and more romantic, tasty adventures!

Holly Blanck, I thank you for your diligence, support, and constant cheer.

Barbara Wild, my copy editor, thank you for your meticulous and gentle touch. You're amazing.

My deep appreciation to the art and marketing departments, the editorial staff, and everyone at St. Martin's Paperbacks who poured their energy, talent, and enthusiasm into this series.

A very warm and heartfelt thank you to my critique partners on this project, Barb Justen Hisle (aka Elle J Rossi) and Cynthia Valero: I owe you! Thank you for *everything*.

Special thanks to Mary Stella, Heather Graham, and Julia Templeton for their friendship and avid support. No matter where I am in the writing process, in life, you are there.

To my friends (patrons and co-workers) at the Brigantine Library and my support system throughout the Atlantic

County Library System . . . To my friends—readers, book-sellers, and librarians—on-line and in life . . . thank you for your amazing support and enthusiasm.

Last but not least and first in my heart . . . My love and appreciation to my husband Steve—my hero, my friend. You make me laugh and keep me sane. You inspire happily-ever-afters.

AUTHOR'S NOTE

Though inspired by a northern region of Vermont, please note that Sugar Creek and the surrounding locations mentioned in this book are fictional. Welcome to my world!

On a fun note, while writing *Fool for Love*, I learned that many of my friends and readers were already avid cupcake lovers! In celebration of the book series and a mutual love of cupcakes I launched a cyber-club that's featured on my blog—Honorary Cupcake Lovers! Featured in the back of *Fool for Love* you'll find some of the honorary CL members' cupcake recipes. My heartfelt thanks to all who submitted. Some are original creations, some family favorites. Some easy, some challenging. Mix, bake, and enjoy!

ONE

Life is uncertain. Eat dessert first.

— Ernestine Ulmer

Manhattan, New York
Upper East Side

"How many years do you think I'd get for death by Cuisinart?"

"Chloe—"

"I'm serious, Monica. I want to kill him."

"With a hand mixer?"

"I don't want it to be quick."

"Or easy. How exactly would that work?"

Chloe didn't know—exactly. She wasn't thinking rationally. Her brain was choked with visions of Ryan licking vanilla-bean buttercream frosting from her beaters—frosting she'd prepared for a celebratory cake—right before announcing he was leaving her for a Parisian "tart." (Chloe's description of the other woman, not his.)

Heart full of equal parts grief and fury, Chloe squeezed back tears as she continued her long-distance tirade with her closest and oldest friend. "Maybe you're right," she said into her smartphone. "Maybe I should skewer his traitorous heart with my meat fork. Or pulverize him with my tenderizer."

"That's just grisly. And totally out of character. You're a pacifist, hon. Zero tolerance for gore. You threw up when we accidently ran over that squirrel on Route Twenty-two. Remember?"

Senior year of high school. Driving home from a rehearsal for *West Side Story*. Monica had swerved, but not enough. Chloe had screamed when she'd felt the thud, then, looking out the rearview window and seeing the furry roadkill, had puked all over the backseat of Monica's 1992 Camaro.

Remember?

"Sort of," she mumbled, letting out an aggrieved sigh. Monica was right. Violence and gore wouldn't do. Just thinking about that squashed squirrel turned her stomach and soured her killer instincts. Once she was depleted of rage, Chloe's knees buckled. She slumped onto the love seat she and Ryan used to cuddle on, misery pouring over her soul, slow and thick like the homemade maple syrup Monica had shipped from Vermont.

Two years. Chloe had invested two years of her life in this relationship—her longest serious liaison ever. She'd had a severe falling-out with her dad when she'd moved in with Ryan, and she'd lost touch with a contingent of her NYC friends when she'd given up partying for domestic bliss. She hadn't expected a conventional union, what with Ryan frequently traveling oversees for his job, but she hadn't expected this. She hadn't suspected an affair, hadn't felt Ryan's affections straying. She'd thought they were a solid couple, destined for marriage. She felt like the biggest freaking idiot on the planet.

"Listen, Chloe. I know you're crushed. The bastard cheated on you. That sucks. And he's leaving you for her. Sucks worse. But . . ."

"But what?"

Monica blew out a breath. "Okay. Here comes some tough love, sweetie. You had a comfortable relationship, lived a comfortable life, but did you seriously want to spend the rest of your nights with a guy who couldn't find your G-spot?"

Chloe flushed. "I had orgasms."

"With the shower massager. Doesn't count."

"I shouldn't have shared that with you."

"Why not? I told you about the time I got off sitting on top of the crazed washing machine."

"Are you trying to make me feel better? Because, news flash, you're not."

"I'm trying to tell you Ryan Levine isn't worth twenty-five to life in the state penitentiary."

"Don't worry. The murderous urge passed."

"Good."

"Now I just want to curl up and die."

"Oh, hon—"

Chloe burst into tears and poured out her heart. Maybe Ryan wasn't worth a stretch in the clink, but he was sure worthy of a good cry. "He ruined the happiest day of my life, Monica. After all these years, all the botched courses and careers, I finally followed through, finally excelled at one of my passions. After four hundred and forty hours of in-class training and a two-hundred-and-ten-hour externship, I not only earned a diploma from the Culinary Arts Institute; I graduated with *honors*."

"What? You're kidding! I mean, that's *fantastic*! Why didn't you tell me?"

"I just found out today. About the honors part, anyway. The happiest day of my life—*ruined*! The affair's been going on for months. He could've waited a day or two to dump me. Any day other than my proudest."

"Or," Monica growled, sounding like a provoked mother bear, "he could've broken off with you weeks ago, when the fling started."

"He said he didn't want to distract me from my studies."

"Big of him."

"Said he'd feel better leaving, knowing I was finally focused on a sensible career."

"Bastard."

"He's coming back at the end of the month to pack up his things. He's actually transferring to the company's resort in France so he can live with her. Said our apartment's paid up for the next three months. That gives me three months to find a roommate or to find a place I can afford on my own.

Both prospects are daunting. Not to mention I'll be job hunting at the same time."

"Maybe you could ask your dad—"

"No."

"Right. Dumb suggestion. Okay, then. Come stay with me."

Chloe blinked. "You live in Vermont."

"So what? Put your things in storage and fly up for an extended visit. It doesn't have to be forever. Just time enough to heal. To catch your breath and plan for your future. Who knows? Maybe you'll fall in love with Sugar Creek like I did and want to stay."

Chloe glanced around the living room and into the kitchen, her gaze drifting toward the bedroom. Every square inch of this apartment reminded her of Ryan and the life they'd shared. She couldn't imagine staying here for the next three months. What's more, she didn't want to.

"I don't feel right about imposing on you and Leo. You're trying to have a baby. I . . . I wouldn't feel comfortable." According to her friend, she and her husband of three years were doing it like bunnies every chance they got. Last week when he'd come home for lunch, she'd greeted him at the door naked.

"Potential for awkward moments," Monica said with a smile in her voice. "True."

"Plus, what would I do with my time? Sugar Creek is even smaller than the town we grew up in. I've been a city girl for fourteen years. I need culture. Activities and distractions." *Especially* now. The last thing she needed was empty hours enabling her to wallow in the breakup.

"We have activities and distractions in Sugar Creek," Monica said. "Just different than what you're used to. Hey, I know. Daisy Monroe is looking for a cook and companion."

"Who's Daisy Monroe?"

"You'll love her. She's just like you—charmingly off beat—only older. The town just celebrated her seventy-fifth birthday."

"The whole town? What is she, famous or something?"

"You could say that. She lives alone in a beautiful old colonial home. I bet if I asked, I could get her to include free board."

"Monica—"

"It's perfect! Time away. Time with me. Plus you get to cook. Let's put that diploma to use, honey!"

"I don't know."

"I do. Say yes."

She hugged Ryan's favorite toss pillow to her chest, breathed in his scent. Her aching heart pounded with renewed fury. What the hell. "Yes."

"Fantastic! I'll line everything up. You pack. Oh! Speaking of activities, you can join Cupcake Lovers. Hit us with some of those fancy recipes you learned in culinary school."

"No, thank you."

Monica had mentioned the local club in her e-mails. A small group that met once a week to swap recipes and ideas on how to make a difference in the world via cupcakes— chocolate, red velvet, banana walnut . . .

Chloe envisioned the devil's food cake she'd chucked in the garbage less than an hour ago. Thought about the way Ryan had sampled the frosting, the groan of delight just before the weary sigh. Remembered the way he'd raved about her cooking over the last few months, especially the dishes she'd created during her Contemporary Desserts course.

Equating confectionary with heartache, she wondered if she'd ever be able to mix up another dessert without feeling depressed or homicidal. "I'm swearing off sweets," Chloe said with a sniff. "Forever."

Monica snorted. "Now that's just crazy talk."

TWO

Devlin Monroe massaged his throbbing temple as his brother relayed troubling news. He shifted the phone to his left ear and scribbled a name on a notepad. "Thanks for the heads-up, Luke."

"If you would've accepted her invitation for breakfast you would've heard it from Gram herself."

"Backed up with work."

"You're always backed up with work. You need to get a life, Dev."

"So you keep telling me." He signed off with his brother and glanced at his watch. Nine fifteen a.m.

The store had been open to the public for fifteen minutes. Most of the employees had arrived fifteen minutes before that. Devlin, Chief Operating Officer of J. T. Monroe's Department Store—family owned and operated for six generations—had been on the property since 7:00 a.m. He'd already crammed three hours of work into two, focusing on a short, medium, and long-range report regarding the nineteenth-century retail store's ability to compete with the Walmart Supercenter opening two towns over, a short thirty-minute drive for anyone in or around Sugar Creek. A concern that had robbed him of a month's worth of decent sleep. Determined to bring J.T.'s into *this* century, he'd e-mailed the report to the CEO, his dad, who was in Florida enjoying the first year of his semi-retirement. Even though the old man had handed over the reins, he couldn't, or wouldn't, get out of the damned driver's seat.

Just after Devlin had texted his dad about the incoming high-priority document, Luke had called. Now Devlin stared at his phone contemplating who to wage war with first. His dad or his grandma.

Before he could decide, his sister, Rocky, blew into his office—unannounced—and dropped into the seat across from his desk. As always, she was dressed in jeans and layered T-shirts, her thick blond hair woven into two braids. Twenty-nine and still a tomboy. A tomboy with womanly curves and the face of a Hollywood starlet. Thankfully, she scared off a lot of men with her blunt talk and tough attitude; otherwise, given his overprotective nature, his big-brother role would be daunting. "Have you heard the news?" she asked.

"Most people knock."

"I'm not most people. I'm your sister. Besides, the door wasn't closed all the way."

"Ah." *As if that made all the difference.*

"Gram hired a companion."

"I heard."

"You don't look thrilled."

"I'm not."

"Why? You're the one who convinced Gram she needs help."

"I was hoping she'd rely more on us. Or hire someone local. Someone we know."

"We're lucky she hired anyone at all. You know how stubborn she is. Now we don't have to worry about her starting another kitchen fire or running over another fire hydrant. This woman can cook Gram's meals—I heard she's a gourmet chef, by the way—and drive her wherever she needs to go." Rocky crossed her arms and raised an eyebrow. "You're just pissed because Gram excluded you from the interview process."

"I'm concerned," Devlin said, leaning forward, "because we don't know this woman."

"Her name is Chloe Madison."

"Luke told me."

"Did he tell you that she's an old friend of Monica Smith's?"

Devlin nodded. "Doesn't mean she's trustworthy."

"I don't think Monica would hook Gram up with an ax killer." She frowned. "You need to loosen up, Dev. Seriously. This is good news. For all of us."

"You drive all the way here just to bust my balls?"

"No. That's a bonus. Actually, I came to ask a favor."

"You could've called."

"Too easy for you to say no over the phone. This way I can charm you by smiling and batting my baby blues." She proceeded to do just that.

In spite of his tense mood, Devlin smiled. "What do you want?"

"Your house."

"What?"

"For one night. Tomorrow night. It's my turn to host the meeting for Cupcake Lovers and my oven's busted."

"Since when?"

"Since this morning."

"I'll buy you a new one."

"I like my old one. I called a repairman, but it won't be ready in time. By the way, if I wanted a new cooking range, I'd buy it myself. That's the trouble with you, Dev. Always taking control. Sometimes people like to make their own decisions, take care of their own problems."

"Not helping your case here."

"So can I take over your kitchen and living room for about four hours? I'll make an extra batch of cupcakes just for you."

"Toss in a pot of your vegetable beef stew and you've got a deal."

Her mouth quirked. "You know, if you had a wife or even

a steady girlfriend, you wouldn't have to bribe me for the occasional home-cooked meal. Of course that would mean actually getting out and socializing so you could meet someone."

"I've met a lot of someones."

"Just not the right one. I swear you set yourself up for failure. Take Tasha for instance."

"Do you want my house for the night or not?"

"Cupcakes and stew it is." She stood and moved to the door, pausing on the threshold. "We missed you at breakfast."

Meaning "we miss you, period."

His family had always been close, and even though he and his sibs and cousins were adults with full lives and careers, they still got together regularly. Except for Devlin. With his multiple business interests and investments he spent more and more time at the computer. Seeing the genuine hurt in his sister's eyes, he offered a smile and a promise: "I'll see you at Sunday dinner." A running tradition at Gram's house.

Rocky rushed over and offered her pinky.

He crooked his own pinky around hers and squeezed. "Swear."

Smiling, she kissed him on the cheek, then rushed out, leaving the door open in her wake.

Shaking his head, Dev snagged his cell and, while moving to shut the door, dialed his best friend, a private investigator who'd relocated to Brooklyn, New York.

Jayce answered on the first ring. "Calling to shoot the shit or to raz me about the Jets?"

"Professional call. Need you to dig into someone's life."

"Must be serious."

"Concerns family."

"On it," Jayce said. "What's the name?"

He glanced at his notepad. "Chloe Madison."

* * *

In two days' time, Chloe had secured a job and lodgings in Sugar Creek, put most of her belongings into storage, and purchased a one-way ticket to Burlington, Vermont. She'd worked fast, refusing to second-guess her decision. The apartment was in Ryan's name and he'd purchased the majority of the furnishings. She suddenly felt like a kept woman, especially since he'd repeatedly pointed out her spastic work résumé. She needed to get her act together and, as Monica had suggested, take time to heal. Ryan had dinged her sense of security and blown a hole in her self-esteem. Was she really that much of a flake?

When her plane touched down in Burlington, Chloe vowed not to fall apart when she saw her best friend. Besides, Chloe was fairly sure she was all cried out. She'd gone through four boxes of tissues and two rolls of toilet paper in her two-day packing spree. Nope, she wasn't going to shed one more tear for Ryan-the-Cheating-Bastard Levine. She wanted to make the most of her time with Monica. Unbelievably, even though they frequently e-mailed and talked on the phone, they were lucky if they saw each other in person once every three years. In fact, the last time she'd seen Monica was when Chloe had flown back to their hometown in Indiana for Monica and Leo's wedding. That was also the last time Chloe had seen her dad.

"Oh, my God," Monica squealed as Chloe rushed toward her in Baggage Claim. "You're a brunette!"

"I didn't have time to keep up with the blond highlights when I was in school, so I went back to my roots, so to speak." Chloe hugged Monica and held tight. But she didn't cry.

The taller woman pushed her to arm's length and eyed her with a sympathetic smile. "You look good. A little thin, but beautiful as always. How the hell did you lose weight in culinary school? Don't you eat what you cook?"

"You end up tasting and sampling on the run rather than sitting down and lingering over a meal. Plus, between the heat of the kitchen and the anxiety and excitement . . ." She shrugged. "Watch. I'll put on twenty pounds in the next month."

"In these parts that would qualify you for curvy. As someone who could stand to lose an entire dress size, I, for one, appreciate the region's more generous views on the female form."

"I think you look wonderful," Chloe said honestly. Monica had always been on the "curvy" side, but she was tall and big boned and between her pretty face, signature pixie cut, and funky eyeglasses she made a bold, sexy statement while retaining a classy aura.

Wearing a mothering expression that Chloe knew well, her friend reached out and gently tucked Chloe's loose long hair behind her ears. "How do you feel?"

"Okay." She forced a smile. "But life will get better."

"Yes, it will." Monica squeezed her hand and tugged her toward the baggage carousel. "Come on. Let's get your luggage and get you to Sugar Creek."

Twenty minutes later they were loaded up and on their way.

Chloe rolled down the Suburban's window, enjoying the rush and smell of the cool fall air as Monica sped north on I-89. Instead of stark steel and glass skyscrapers, she was surrounded by lush valleys and wooded mountains. No wonder they called Vermont the Green Mountain State. She couldn't stop staring at the stunning landscape. Yes, she'd grown up in a small midwestern town, but in comparison this was the wilderness. "Feels like I'm in another country."

"You almost are. Once we get to Sugar Creek, we'll only be ten miles south of the Canadian border."

"I can't believe I'm doing this."

"I can't believe you only brought one suitcase. Didn't you agree to a three-month trial period with Daisy?"

"Yeah, but what do I need really aside from clothes and toiletries? I thought about bringing some of my new cooking appliances, but she said she has everything I'll need. I asked about bringing my own bed linens, but she nixed that as well."

"What about personal stuff?" Monica asked as she zipped past a slow-moving pickup.

"Like what?"

"Like your laptop, books, camera, CDs . . . I don't know. *Stuff.* You're the one who said you need distractions."

"Laptop's in the suitcase. Camera and music are on my smartphone. As for books . . ." She reached in her purse and fished out her Kindle. "Loaded with over a hundred novels and thirty-six cookbooks. So far."

"As a library assistant, I'm well aware of the explosion of digital books," Monica said, "but please tell me you still read the occasional print book; otherwise you'll break my old-fashioned heart."

"As an avid reader I indulge in both worlds," Chloe said with a smile. "Happy now?"

"Delirious. So," she said, gesturing to the Android and e-Reader, "when did you become a techno geek?"

"I'm not a techno geek," Chloe said. "Ryan bought me all that stuff. Christmas. Birthdays. I would've chucked it all, but I'm sort of used to it now."

"Yeah, well. Things move at a slower pace in Sugar Creek. I'm not even sure if Daisy has cable."

"That's okay. I'll connect at an Internet café."

"We don't have an Internet café."

Chloe gaped. "You're kidding!"

Monica smiled. "Nope."

"But . . . you said Sugar Creek attracts a lot of tourists."

"It does."

"How do they check their e-mail? Google directions and specifics for restaurants and attractions?"

"Chloe, in these parts, most of the people on holiday are too busy hiking, tubing, fishing, snow skiing, horseback rid-ing—"

"I get the picture."

"—to check e-mail." She glanced over. "If it makes you feel better, there's a computer with Internet access at the library."

"Thank God. So," she said, still amazed. "No Internet café. I'm guessing no Starbucks?"

"Nope. But they serve great coffee at Gemma's Bakery."

"I'll keep it in mind." Chloe sighed. "What about a grocery store? I told Mrs. Monroe I'd take care of the shopping. Plus I'm sort of picky about the ingredients for my recipes."

"Not too picky, I hope. One place to do your food shopping in Sugar Creek. Oslow's General Store."

"Seriously? A general store? What, something the size of Marlton's IGA? " The family-operated grocery in their hometown.

"Smaller, but better stocked. If you don't find what you want there, your best bet is the supermarket in Pixley. It's a thirty-minute drive on a clear day. If it's snowing, tack an hour or never."

"I'll only be here until mid-December."

"Last year we had our first big snow late October."

"Oh." When making her deal with Mrs. Monroe she hadn't considered the weather. "I haven't driven in the snow since I moved to Manhattan."

Monica cut her a look.

"Hello? Big city? Public transportation?"

"When were you last behind the wheel of a car?"

Chloe looked away, knowing Monica was well aware of her arrangement with Mrs. Monroe. "The day before I moved to Manhattan."

"Fourteen years ago?" Monica jammed on the brakes and squealed to the shoulder of the road. "Get out." She unbuckled her seat belt and shoved open the driver's door.

"Why? What are you doing?"

"Trading places with you. If you're going to chauffeur Daisy you need all the practice you can get. One fender bender and Dev will have my ass. Yours, too. "

"Who's Dev?" Chloe asked as she scrambled out the door. Heart pounding, she rounded the hood of the Suburban, passing Monica along the way.

"Devlin Monroe. Daisy's oldest grandson. Heir to the Monroe legacy. Runs J. T. Monroe's Department store and a few other local businesses. Watches over his family like a hawk. Mess with his family and you're dead meat."

"Sounds like a scary guy."

"Not scary, just influential."

They stopped talking long enough to climb back into the vehicle.

Monica buckled the passenger seat belt and sighed. "Listen. I didn't mean to make Dev sound like a tyrant. He's the brother of a good friend of mine. It's just . . . the man has a major stick up his ass. A shame really. Otherwise he's the perfect catch. Rich and frickin' hot."

"Good looking, huh?" Not that Chloe cared. It's not like she was looking to date anytime soon.

"Drop-dead gorgeous," Monica said. "You do know where all the important parts are, right?"

Chloe blinked.

"Steering wheel, gas pedal, brake . . ."

She smirked. "I know how to drive. It's just been a while."

"Okay then. Keep the pedal to the metal until the exit for 105." She glanced sideways and smiled as Chloe peeled onto the interstate. "Just watch out for squirrels."

THREE

By the time they reached Sugar Creek the sun was setting and Chloe was running out of steam. She'd been up since 6:00 a.m. and hadn't slept well for three nights running. She hadn't eaten much either, operating mostly on coffee and adrenaline. Now that they'd reached their destination, even the wonder of the forested peaks and the high of driving had worn off. All she wanted was to eat a sandwich and go to bed. So what if it was only five thirty?

Monica had other ideas. One block into the quaint town, she instructed Chloe to make a left, then pointed to a bright blue barn with white trim—*Leo's Auto Repair*. "Just pull in here and let me tell Leo about our change of plans."

"Honestly, Monica, ordering in pizza is fine."

"Forget it. After hearing you describe all the dishes you've made over the past few weeks, I'm jonesing for a full-course, professionally prepared dinner."

"I could cook—"

"Not on your first night here. I'm taking you out. The Sugar Shack has the best food in town. Great atmosphere. You'll love it. Plus we can order champagne and toast your special honors diploma."

"It's not that big a deal."

"It's a huge deal, and you know it."

Which was why she'd been especially crushed when Ryan

had peed in her Cheerios. Or rather her cake. "You're right," she said, sitting straighter and forcing a smile. "I deserve a celebration."

"Atta girl." Monica hopped out. "I'll be quick. I'd call, but if he's working on a car he won't answer. When the man focuses on engines, he's oblivious to all else."

"How late does Leo work?"

"Depends. Tonight the garage is open until six."

"What about Oslow's?" Chloe asked, eyeing the general store across the street.

"Same."

"Mind if I peek in? I'd like to get an idea of what they stock so I can plan Mrs. Monroe's meals for the week." She was staying with Monica and Leo tonight, but tomorrow Chloe moved in with her new employer. She wanted to impress the woman from the get-go. Sharing a well-thought-out menu seemed like a good start. She noticed then that Monica had a goofy smile on her face. "What?"

"I just love how you never do anything half-assed."

Chloe laughed. "Me? Up until the Culinary Arts Institute, I never followed through with anything. Just ask Dad or Ryan."

Monica waved them off. "I'm not talking about commitment. I'm talking about passion. Since I've known you, whatever your current interest, you pour your heart and soul into the project. Your enthusiasm is infectious. And admirable."

Chloe swallowed an emotional lump and smiled. "I'm really glad I came."

"Me, too." Monica squeezed her hand. "Now run over to Oslow's. If you're not back when I come out, I'll join you."

"Deal." Chloe slid out of the Suburban, smoothed the wrinkles from her mid-thigh dress, and crossed the deserted street.

Sugar Creek's sole grocery looked like something out of a Norman Rockwell painting. Like Leo's garage, it resembled a converted barn. Only it was bigger and varnished an appealing shade of maple brown. A big green sign announced in white letters: *OSLOW'S GENERAL STORE— established in 1888.* Swinging out from the top gable was a brightly painted rooster displaying a much smaller sign that simply read: *GOOD FOOD.*

Chloe hooked her handbag over her shoulder and entered the store, smiling when a bell tinkled to announce her arrival. *Cute.* She closed her eyes and breathed deep. *Heaven.* Spices and freshly ground coffee, scented soaps and fresh herbs. She caught a whiff of fried chicken and . . . apple pie? *Must have a ready-made food section,* she thought as she opened her eyes and took in the layout.

Monica was right. Oslow's was smaller than their hometown IGA, but not by much. Instead of a sprawling building, it was compact and three stories high. The hardwood floor creaked under Chloe's wedge-heeled boots as she made her way up and down the narrow aisles. Folksy Muzak floated softly from hidden speakers.

The shelves were crammed with stock—lots of local specialty foods, but a ton of basics, too. Deli counter, dairy section. To her amazement, she only spied a couple of shoppers. The markets in Manhattan were crowded every day at every hour. Here the sparse shoppers smiled and nodded in greeting but other than that didn't pay her much mind. Probably assumed she was just another tourist.

She was lost in thought, mentally cataloguing stock and sifting through recipes when she rounded the soda and chip aisle and rammed hard into another shopper. Half the contents of his wicker shopping basket tipped out and crashed to the floor.

"I'm so sorry," she squeaked, dropping to her knees to snag a runaway can of pork 'n' beans. A box of cornflakes, a bag of chips, frozen dinners. He had to be single. Or lazy.

"Don't worry about it," he said, stooping to help.

Their fingers connected around his Vermont smoked and cured summer sausage. Chloe froze—her skin tingling with sensual awareness—then flushed when she noted the devilish tilt of his mouth. She wasn't sure which was more disconcerting—his sexy smile or her reaction to his touch. Not to mention he was freaking gorgeous. Chocolate hair, blueberry eyes, a beefcake body clad in grey canvas khakis and a plaid oxford shirt, the long sleeves rolled midway up his muscled forearms. Not that she was checking him out.

Heat flooded her body as she realized she was doing just that and he was doing the *same!*

"My sausage—"

"Excuse me?" She followed his gaze and saw in horror that she was still clinging to his processed meat. "Oh." Cheeks burning, she scrambled to her feet, wishing he hadn't helped by grasping her elbow. She couldn't remember the last time she'd been so flustered by a man's innocent touch. "You should buy some fruit," she said, noting the contents of his basket. *Wow. That was lame.*

Again with the sexy half smile. "What would you suggest?"

"Bananas? Apples?" She glanced at the fresh-fruit cart to their left. "Melons?"

"I like melons."

She waited for his gaze to shift to her chest. It didn't. He was looking directly in her eyes. Somehow that was worse.

He snagged a small honeydew and put it in his basket.

"What are you doing?"

"Buying fruit?"

"But you didn't thump it."

He raised a brow.

Men. She moved in and gave the melon a squeeze. "Too hard."

"I can honestly say I've never gotten that complaint."

Okay. Definite flirting here. She should leave. But the image of Ryan canoodling with his tart caused her to stand her ground. Her wounded ego needed affirmation that she was still desirable to the opposite sex. Problem was she hadn't flirted in a long time. "Let me give you some tips on how to handle melons." *Oh, brother.*

"I'm all ears."

Just then his phone rang. He pulled an Android from his pocket, glanced at the incoming call. "Damn."

Obviously, he needed to take it. *Perfect.* This way she could exit before making a *complete* fool of herself. She quickly squeezed and thumped three melons, putting the second one in his basket. "Nice meeting you," she whispered as he tried holding off the person on the other end of the line.

"Wait," he called as she backed away.

"Remember. Four food groups," she said, then made a beeline for the front door. *Four food groups?*

Lame, lame, lame.

* * *

"If this is a bad time," Jayce said, "I can call back."

"No. Now is good. Now is . . . great." Devlin watched her sweet ass go, telling himself not to follow. To what end? A one-night stand? She didn't strike him as the type. She'd blushed too easily, and her attempt at flirting had been awkward. Not that his had been much better. He couldn't remember the last time he'd been inspired to flirt. But, Christ, seeing her in that short flowery dress and those knee-high boots, the long dark hair and that *face.* Like any man wouldn't be reduced to a drooling idiot.

Yet for all her sensual beauty, she seemed oblivious. An even greater turn-on. Melon Girl was a nice girl and, since he'd never seen her before, no doubt a tourist. Which meant she'd be gone in a day or two. He chalked up the encounter to the sexiest five minutes of the last three years and felt thankful for it.

Oh, hell. Maybe Luke was right. Maybe he did need to get a life, because damn, that was pathetic.

"Sure you don't want me to call back?" Jayce asked.

"What? No. Go on."

"I was apologizing for the delay. Wanted to be thorough."

"I appreciate that," Devlin said, balancing his food basket on a pickle barrel.

"I'll give you the basics and e-mail the full report. You're not going to like it."

"I'm not surprised." Today had been full of frustrations. His dad had refused to comment on Devlin's report until he'd slept on it. Gram had refused Devlin's offer to bring her dinner, saying she'd already committed to an evening of chili and Canasta with the Larsens. And when he'd broached the subject of her chosen *companion,* she'd brushed him off.

"Chloe Madison," Jayce began. "Thirty-one. Single. Never been married. Born and raised in Marlton, Indiana. Moved to New York City straight out of high school. No siblings. Mother died when she was fourteen. Father's loaded. Funded her education and picked up the bulk of her rent for, get this, ten years."

"Who studies to be a chef for ten years?"

"She didn't study to be a chef until this past year. We're talking two years at Juilliard, two and a half at NYU, a year—almost—at a fashion design institute, back to NYU for six months, different major, then a shitload of workshops and courses on various subjects."

"What the hell?" Devlin scratched his head, baffled by the inconsistency. "Did she flunk out? Get expelled?"

"Dropped out."

Even worse. "So what? She's unmotivated? Unfocused?"

"Fickle maybe. One of those people who can't decide what they want to do. So far she studied for and/or worked as an actress, a singer, a playwright, a fashion designer, fashion photographer, model, spokesperson, publicist, and food critic. You can read some of her critiques on a popular e-zine. I'll send you the URL. They're pretty good."

"Sounds like Gram hired an impulsive free spirit." The kind of woman who pushed a personal hot button.

"There's more."

"Naturally."

"Looks like her rich daddy cut her off two years ago, about the same time she moved in with a guy. Hold on. Ryan Levine. That's his name. Fifteen years her senior. Works for an international resort company. Efficiency expert. Big bucks."

"From rich daddy to sugar daddy." Gold digger—another hot button. "Let me guess. Levine covered her tuition for culinary school."

"She did, however, finish what she started this time. Graduated from the Culinary Arts Institute four days ago."

"Four *days*? So she doesn't have any practical experience as a chef."

"Doesn't mean she isn't a hell of a cook. Plus, Dev, you've gotta see this girl."

"Considering she once worked as a model and has the ability to wrap rich men around her finger, I'm guessing hot."

"Blond hair. Brown eyes. Kick-ass curves."

"Sounds right up your alley."

"She's up every man's alley."

Devlin was more interested in the sweet-faced brunette who'd essentially told him to eat healthier. Drop-dead beautiful—in an Ivory-soap-girl kind of way. He thought about the glimpse he'd gotten of her pink panties as she'd scrambled on her hands and knees for his pork 'n' beans and cursed a hard-on that wouldn't die. "Dammit."

"Here's the part you won't like."

"I haven't liked any of it."

"You'll hate this. Had to dig deep, since she had her record expunged."

"Record?"

"Arrested twice. Once for shoplifting. Once for disturbing the peace. Both times charges were dropped."

"That doesn't make me feel better."

"Implies innocence."

"Or not enough evidence."

"I knew you'd say that. That's why I called in a favor. Details forthcoming."

"Meanwhile Miss Madison is also *forthcoming*."

"For what it's worth, Dev, I don't have a bad feeling about this woman."

"I do." All told, Chloe Madison sounded like his worst nightmare.

"Want me to fly up and run interference?"

"My problem to tackle."

His friend laughed. "Lucky you."

"What about Levine?"

"Lover boy's transferring to France."

"Left her high and dry," Devlin guessed, "and now she coming to mooch off Gram."

"Overall, I got the impression she's a nice girl, well liked. Just restless and reckless."

"Translation: an irresponsible user. Twice arrested."

"Two sides to every coin, my friend."

"I'll keep that in mind. Send a bill with that report, Jayce."

"Treat me to dinner at the Shack next time I'm up and we're square."

No use arguing, since Jayce never took money from those he considered family. "You're on." Devlin disconnected and snatched his shopping basket. He'd meant to pick up a few basics, then grab a fried chicken from the take-out section. Unfortunately, between his encounter with Melon Girl and his discussion with Jayce it was now five minutes to closing.

Skipping the fried chicken, he zipped through the check-out, obsessing on Chloe Madison. Maybe she didn't have any ulterior motives. Maybe she just needed a job and because of her friend Monica she'd lucked into this one. Still, he intended to keep an eye on her and would tell Luke and Rocky to do the same. In fact, he'd swing over to the Sugar Shack right now and fill Luke in. Might as well have dinner there, too. Something including all four food groups. Hell, he was half owner of the restaurant. He should probably show his face more often. Given the Shack was a hot spot for locals and tourists, maybe he'd spot Melon Girl there having a drink.

Not that he had ulterior motives.

FOUR

By the time they reached the Sugar Shack it was seven o'clock. By 7:05, Chloe had her second wind. Revived by the sights and sounds of crowded tables and happy diners and the mouthwatering scents of baked bread, roasted meats, and hearty stews. The atmosphere was casual and lively, the décor country-inn rustic. Polished wide-planked hardwood floors, cobblestone fireplace, colonial wall sconces, and assorted paintings featuring American Folk Art. An Alison Krauss song played in the background—not too loud, just enough to flow through your brain and loosen your limbs.

If Chloe were writing one of her food critic articles, she'd give the Sugar Shack "Four Forks Up" for ambiance. No cheesy theme. No pretensions. Just a nice place to hang out for drinks and a good meal. Her favorite kind of restaurant. The kind she used to seek out with friends before she hooked up with Ryan.

Monica slid into one of the old-fashioned window booths. "What do you think?"

"I think it's charming."

"Wait'll you meet the owner. Part owner anyway. See that guy behind the bar?"

Chloe glanced to where Monica pointed. Hard to miss a guy like that. Even from several yards away, Chloe could see that he was handsome, in a rugged, boyish way. Shaggy sandy-brown hair. Sculpted features. Nice upper body. Dressed down in a dark-colored T-shirt, he was serving drinks while chatting up two redheads decked out in matching skintight dresses. Chloe figured if she moved a few feet closer she'd get devoured by his animalistic charisma. He was *that* charmingly intense. Not her cup of tea. She knew the type. She'd kissed a lot of frogs to get to Mr. Right, except he'd turned out to be Mr. Wrong. Trying not to despise all men in general, she nodded toward sexy bar dude. "Serial dater or incorrigible flirt?"

"Both." Monica smiled. "But he's also a nice guy. Name's Luke Monroe and he's the most sought-after bachelor in Sugar Creek aside from his older brother, Dev."

Chloe raised a brow. "The overprotective entrepreneur with the stick up his ass?" *Mess with his family and you're dead meat.*

"Not so loud. Jesus." Choking back laughter, Monica opened the wine list to hide her blushing face and surreptitiously surveyed the crowded room. "Luke manages this place, but Dev's part owner. Never know when he's going to drop in."

"Do you see him?"

"No."

"Good." Chloe slipped off her sweater and snapped open her dinner menu, intent on derailing further talk of Devlin Monroe. She hoped to avoid the man for, well, *ever.* She had enough on her plate without fearing his wrath should his grandmother so much as stub a toe while under Chloe's watch. Not that she'd been hired to care for Daisy 24/7. In fact, Chloe's duties were pretty light. In their phone interview the woman had made it clear she didn't need or want a nursemaid. But she did want her family to get off her bony patooty (her words, not Chloe's). Apparently they considered Daisy a menace in the kitchen and behind the wheel. All Chloe had to do was prepare her meals and drive her around. A cushy gig if there ever was one.

"You'll meet him eventually," Monica said. "A) This is a small town. B) He'll want to know who's living under his grandmother's roof."

"Fine," Chloe said, feigning a carefree shrug. "As long as he doesn't try to tell me what to do."

"Tall order."

"I mean it, Monica. I'm over it. First Dad manipulated my life, then Ryan." She stared hard at the appetizers—Rosemary Potato Chips, Garden Bruschetta—summoning calm and confidence via her love of food. "I refuse to answer to any man. From here on out I'm trusting my own instincts. I'm capable. Responsible. Mrs. Monroe and I will get along just fine."

"I know."

"I mean it."

"I'm glad."

She could almost *hear* Monica smiling. She looked up and, *yep,* huge smile. "What?"

"Just happy you're here."

Chloe was sure there was more to it but didn't press. She was tired and suddenly starving. "Ever had the Baked Onion and Apple Soup?"

"To die for. Everything on this menu is to die for."

"You've had everything on the menu?"

"Almost everything."

Hungry for the carefree spirit of her younger days, Chloe beamed at her oldest friend. "What do you say we order a little bit of everything? Remember when we sampled every dish at Rosie's Café?" They'd been sixteen and celebrating the fact that they'd both been chosen to sing in the All-State choir.

"As I recall, you threw up less than an hour after we rolled out the door."

A bad reaction to French fries smothered in chili *and* cheese, just after a downing a chocolate milk shake. Chloe had blocked out that part. "Honestly. Why do all your memories revolve around my puking episodes?"

Monica's eyes twinkled with mischief. "Good times, good times."

"What if we restrict the smorgasbord to appetizers?" Her mouth watered just thinking about the Roasted Garlic Shrimp.

"And desserts."

"No desserts."

"Aw, come on. You aren't seriously swearing off sweets!"

She thought about the way Ryan's eyes had rolled back after he tasted her Raspberry White Chocolate Mousse, just before he'd made love to her on the living room carpet—only two days after returning from the French Riviera. "Seriously."

"Fine. No dessert. Not tonight."

"Not ever."

"I'd be stricken if I didn't know this insane boycott wasn't temporary."

"You're not listening to me."

"No, I'm not. I don't listen to crazy people. Obviously, Ryan drove you insane. Temporarily."

Chloe sighed. "Okay. Fine. Realistically, I can't imagine swearing off sweets *forever,* but just now . . . this moment and who knows for how long . . . confections are poison to my soul."

"Noted." Monica motioned for the waitress. "We'll start with a bottle of champagne."

* * *

After lingering over a full-course meal and giving up on an appearance by Melon Girl, Devlin had slipped into his brother's office to escape the unwanted attention of the Kelly twins. He could have had his pick of the girls, or he could have had them both—at the same time. They'd been upfront about their adventurous streak. Which should have been a turn-on but wasn't. Katie and Krissy were cute as hell but too young and shallow for his taste. Not to mention they'd made the same offer to his brother and their cousin Nash last June at the Vermont Dairy & Maple Festival. Devlin was fairly certain his cousin had crumbled and indulged in the average man's twin-girl fantasy. Nash wasn't one to screw and tell, but he'd walked around with a dopey smile on his face for an entire week.

Devlin shook his head while checking his e-mail. Luke and Nash juggled women and relationships the way he juggled multiple business interests. Life was complicated enough without having to deal with the drama of multiple affairs. He'd always leaned toward monogamous relationships but had never been inclined to fully commit—not since Janna had ripped out his heart. Once annihilated, forever wary. Not that he was celibate, just cautious. His cynicism and habitual bad luck with women ensured his bachelor status, as did his obsession with work and various investments. He had too many people counting on him—the employees at J.T.'s and the Shack, his relatives—to dwell on what eluded him.

The love and devotion of a down-to-earth, family-oriented woman.

Restless and hopeful that the Kelly twins had zeroed in on another target, Devlin left the office intending to have a last word with Luke before heading home. When he neared the bar, he saw his brother enduring the attentions of Viv Underwood, a woman he'd dated and broken off with a year ago, while waving good-bye to Katie and Krissy and serving draft beers to the Brody brothers. Luke had an amazing talent for making everyone seem like the center of his world while he was actually tuned into something else altogether. Just now Viv appeared smitten while Adam and Kane seemed enthralled by whatever bullshit Luke was spewing. Luke was . . . distracted.

"You outta here?" he asked without making eye contact.

"Almost." Devlin looked where his brother looked. *Damn.* Melon Girl had shown after all. Luke was practically drooling. "Down, boy."

"Am I that obvious?"

"Yes."

"Can you blame me?"

"No. But keep it zipped." The intensity of the jealousy rippling through Devlin's blood took him by surprise. He didn't even know her name, yet he had the insane urge to tell his brother, *Hands off. She's mine.*

Luke laughed while serving Devlin a Dewar's on the rocks he hadn't asked for. "Admit it. She's hot."

"How many women are you seeing now?"

"On a steady basis? Three. *What?* They know about each other."

Devlin rolled his eyes, then, unable to help himself, glanced back to Melon Girl. She was still wearing her flowery dress and knee-high boots, but she'd twisted her long hair into a messy ponytail. His cock twitched and he'd swear his heart skipped. Something that hadn't happened since— *Christ—Janna*. He ignored the warning bells, sifted through old-as-dirt pickup lines. But then Connie, one of the six waitresses on the payroll, showed at Melon Girl's booth carrying a tray loaded with enough food for *two* people.

Damn.

"When you asked me to keep a close eye on Gram's new companion," Luke said, "I had no idea it would be such a pleasure."

"What do you mean?" But then Monica Smith slid into the seat across from Melon Girl and Devlin connected the dots. *"That's* Chloe Madison?" Jayce had painted a different picture—an in-your-face gorgeous blonde—whereas the woman affecting Devlin's pulse was a dark, subtle beauty. "Are you sure?"

"I'd say it's a safe bet. She walked in with Monica and they've been gabbing like women who've known each other for years. Thought I'd wait till they got to dessert before introducing myself. If she isn't Chloe Madison, I'd like the name and number that goes with that dish."

"To hell with waiting." Devlin pushed away from the bar, drink in hand. Working his way through the crowded tables, he assured himself Luke was wrong. The sweet-natured woman who'd knocked Devlin's food basket and guarded heart for a loop could not be the same reckless free spirit who manipulated rich men and snowed dotty old women like Gram. Curiosity warred with dread. Either Melon Girl was someone other than Miss Madison or Miss Madison was even more dangerous than he'd first assumed.

* * *

"All I know," Chloe continued in mid-thought as Monica returned from the ladies' room, "is that I'm fed up with bossy men."

Her celebration dinner had turned into a bitch fest, soon after they'd toasted her "special honor." All Chloe could think about was the graduation cake she'd baked and how Ryan had ruined her day with his betrayal. Yes, she'd spewed to Monica on the phone, but it wasn't the same as face-to-face. At least tonight she was calm. She didn't cry. Didn't even raise her voice. She even refrained from cursing the *other woman*. Mostly, she was bitter because she'd given up a life she'd loved, along with a good many friends, because Ryan had convinced her it was time to settle down and commit personally and professionally. Something her dad had been preaching for years, only it had sounded different coming from a guy she was crazy about.

"So you said, although I never really thought of your dad as bossy, hon. Even though he's always been distant, he caters to your whims. Or at least he did before you moved in with Ryan."

"My point exactly," Chloe said as they picked at the appetizer smorgasbord. "He thought he could bully me into walking away from the man I loved by cutting me off financially."

"Well, you showed him."

"I suppose." She hadn't missed the money, because Ryan had insisted paying the majority of their rent. But she had missed the weekly phone calls. They'd talk about his life in Indiana and her life in New York. They'd had an amiable long-distance relationship. Now they only talked once in a blue moon and it was always strained.

"When are you going to tell him Ryan split?"

"When I'm ready to hear a big fat *I told you so*."

"Which intimates never."

"I'll tell him. When the timing's right."

"Which intimates never."

"I'll call him in a few days," Chloe grumbled while

finishing her second glass of champagne. "After I'm settled in at Mrs. Monroe's. I just . . . I want to feel somewhat stable when he offers to fly out to help me pick up the pieces of my life."

"Spin it so that he focuses on the fact that you're putting your diploma to good use. You found something you excel at, something you love, and something you're sticking with. Right?"

The hesitance in that last word wounded Chloe, though she tried not to show it. Even her best friend questioned her ability to commit to a profession. "Right," she said, and she meant it. "Although I wouldn't call cooking meals for Mrs. Monroe a great use of a diploma from the Culinary Arts Institute."

"Think of it as a segue," Monica said with a tender smile.

Chloe smiled back and, eager to shift the conversation, sampled the Baked Onion and Apple Soup. The contrasting flavors danced on her tongue and initiated a sigh of pure bliss. "You're right. Beyond scrumptious."

Behind Monica's rectangular glasses, her brown eyes rounded. Leaning in, she whispered, "Speaking of scrumptious . . ."

"Ladies."

Chloe glanced over her shoulder and nearly spit soup at the shock of seeing Sausage Guy. He'd changed into a fresh shirt, but other than that he looked exactly as she remembered—handsome and thigh-sweat sexy. Embarrassed for ogling, she flushed head to toe. "Hi."

"Hi."

She opened her mouth to add something pleasant or witty, but nothing came out. Her brain clogged with a collage of erotic images and thoughts. *Good Lord.*

"Mind if I join you?"

Monica, who'd yet to say anything, slid over to make room, but he squeezed in next to Chloe. His scent—manly soap and spicy cologne—went to her head, nearly causing her to sigh like a swooning teen. The mere brush of his arm prompted breathless desire. Once again, his touch unnerved her. Normally sociable, charming even, she could feel herself morphing into the tongue-tied airhead who'd scrambled for his pork 'n' beans.

"You ran off before I got your name."

"You were on the phone and I, well, I . . ."

"You two have met?" This from Monica, who was still wide eyed and looking as flummoxed as Chloe felt.

"Not officially," he said.

"Oslow's," she said. "We were shopping and I, well, there was an incident."

"Which resulted in me buying fruit, then coming here for a meal consisting of all food four groups."

Was he teasing? Scolding? Flirting? She couldn't tell. It wasn't like before. He was . . . guarded. "I'm sorry I blurted that bit about the four basics. As if you don't know how to take care of yourself. You're a grown man. Obviously." *Shoot me now!*

"And you're . . . ?"

Hot to jump your bones?

"Chloe Madison," Monica said, filling the awkward pause. "Chloe, this is Devlin Monroe."

FIVE

Rocky Monroe kicked off her morning like every morning, with a glass of OJ and a four-mile run along Pikeman's Trail. The only difference was she was at it earlier than usual. By the time she got back to the Red Clover Bed-and-Breakfast— her home and place of business—the sun was just breaking over Thrush Mountain.

Lately, she'd been having trouble sleeping. Too much on her mind. Even though she tried to play down the increasing frequency of Gram's incidents, Rocky was truly worried about the woman who was too stubborn for her own good. Then again, most of the Monroes had a stubborn streak a mile wide, so Rocky shouldn't have been surprised by Gram's dogged determination to carry on as though she were twenty-five instead of seventy-five. Not that seventy-five was ancient, especially in this day and age, but she'd grown forgetful and accident prone and, God help them all, more adventurous.

She'd nearly turned Rocky's blond hair white when she'd "borrowed" her snowmobile last winter to take a joyride. Considering the damage to the Arctic Cat, it was a miracle Gram had walked away with no more than a broken wrist and unsightly bruises. Then there were the cooking-related accidents. Last month while hosting a meeting of Cupcake Lovers, Gram had put a teakettle on the burner and turned the gas flame full up, which wouldn't have been so bad except she forgot to put water in the kettle. There'd been a small fire, which Rocky and her cousin Sam had easily extinguished, but what if Gram had been alone?

That's why Rocky had been immensely relieved to hear Gram had hired a companion. That alone should've helped Rocky sleep easier last night, except she was also obsessing on her broken oven. She'd had to replace the washing machine last month and now her fridge was making funny sounds. Since she normally cooked meals for the B and B visitors, she relied heavily on her appliances. Not that she had anyone to cook for today or for the next two weeks. The Red Clover had been experiencing unusually sporadic bookings for months now. Her savings account was taking a hit at a time when she really needed to overhaul the nineteenth-century five-bedroom house to attract more business. All she had to do was ask Dev and he'd cover the expenses. Or . . . he'd suggest she sell. He'd been against her buying the Red Clover in the first place, calling it a money pit, but Rocky had had her eye on this inn and the attached several acres since she was a kid. She'd be damned if she'd let her big brother, or anyone else for that matter, dictate her life.

By the time Rocky showered and dressed, she'd worked up the stress she'd worked off with the run. She needed to get out and get her mind off of the inn for a while. She needed to do something physical. She thought about Dev's place. He'd told her she could borrow his house tonight, since her stove was on the blink and it was her turn to host Cupcake Lovers. He'd probably tidied up, but her idea of clean differed greatly from both of her brothers'. Men. The kitchen and bathroom could probably use a good scrubbing and she'd vacuum *under* the furniture. God only knew what lived there—dust bunnies, rogue pretzels. But first she'd stop at Oslow's and purchase the ingredients for her featured cupcake and the vegetable beef stew she'd promised to make for Dev.

She was midway to Sugar Creek when she heard an ominous clunking in the engine of her Jeep. *Damn.* "Whatever's wrong, *please* hold out until I get the oven fixed."

* * *

Dev blew out of his house at—*Christ*—8:37 a.m. and nearly barreled into his sister. "What are you doing here?"

"You said I could borrow your house."

"Tonight."

"I have to prepare. What are you doing here?"

"I live here."

"But it's"—she glanced at her watch—"eight thirty."

"Eight thirty-eight."

"You're always out of here by six thirty or seven."

"I overslept."

"You never oversleep."

"First time for everything." Anxious to be on his way, Devlin relieved his sister of three recyclable grocery bags. "Any more in the Jeep?"

"One more. I'll get it."

He hoofed it back up his porch stairs and whizzed into the kitchen. He dumped the bags on the counter, then turned to hurry back out.

"You look like shit," Rocky said with a scrunched brow.

Compliments of two hours of sleep. "Gee, thanks."

"Did you have breakfast?" she asked as she set down the last bag and opened his fridge.

"I'll grab something at work."

"Meaning a donut and a pot of coffee." Rocky snorted while pulling out a carton of eggs and half a loaf of bread. "Breakfast is the most important meal of the day, you know."

"What is it lately with women lecturing me about my eating habits?"

"Another woman lectured you?" Rocky asked wide eyed. "Who? Tell me. Any woman who tried to advise *you* must be something special."

She was something all right. Devlin was still fuming over his dinner chat with the enigmatic Chloe Madison. Getting her to reveal anything about her past without letting on that he already knew her background, thanks to Jayce, had been impossible. She'd been flustered when Devlin had first approached, which struck him as cute, but then as soon as she'd found out who he was she'd shut down completely. As if she knew he was savvy to her type and she wouldn't be able to sweet-talk or manipulate him. Monica had made things worse by trying to talk *for* Chloe, bragging about her culinary diploma, then focusing on their childhood in Indiana. No mention of her life in NYC or the endless school and career shifts or the sugar daddy boyfriend who'd left her high and dry.

It also bothered Devlin that they'd ordered several dishes and that Chloe barely touched the food. When he'd commented, she'd mumbled something about not being hungry. Why then had she ordered so much to begin with? Had she tasted the food and found it lacking? Was the former food critic, newly degreed chef, that critical of other people's cooking? Since he'd personally helped Luke interview chefs and since he considered the Sugar Shack's menu top-notch (as did everyone else), Chloe's snooty palate irritated the hell out of him.

"I smell Lysol," Rocky said, breaking in on his thoughts.

"I cleaned."

She inspected the counters, sink, and floor. "You scrubbed."

"You're having a houseful of women over."

"Don't forget about Sam. He's an official member of Cupcake Lovers now, so we're officially coed, so to speak."

Their cousin. Sam McCloud. Widowed for two years and opposed to meeting women in bars or via dating services. Sam had assured his brother, Max, and his various male cousins that he'd joined Cupcake Lovers in order to cozy up to one of its members, Rachel Lacey, but that had been six months ago and Sam had yet to ask Rachel out. Meanwhile, he'd developed a troubling fondness for baking as well as a curious addiction to cable cooking shows.

"I don't want anyone, including Sam, gossiping about the state of my house and how it would benefit from the touch of a lady."

"The owner would benefit from a lady's touch, too."

"Don't start on that." The only woman who interested

him just now was Chloe Madison, and no way in hell was he going to pursue that physical attraction—not knowing what he did about her fickle tendencies and questionable morals. Maybe she wasn't an outright gold digger, but she had no problem taking advantage of rich men. Not to mention her *expunged* record (Jayce had yet to supply details) and her penchant for bailing when things got tough or boring. Daisy had hired her for a three-month stint. Devlin would be surprised if Chloe lasted three weeks.

"We don't gossip." Rocky cracked six eggs into a bowl in rapid succession. "We discuss our lives—"

"And the lives of everyone else in Sugar Creek."

"—share cupcake recipes and thoughts on how we can benefit soldiers abroad and charities on the home front."

"You don't have to sell me on the club." The Monroe women had been involved in Cupcake Lovers since its conception in 1942. What had started off as a purely social gathering, a specified place and time to commiserate with other women whose husbands or sons were away fighting in WW II, had eventually evolved into a group of women shipping their cupcakes to soldiers overseas as well as organizing local charitable events. He supported the efforts of Cupcake Lovers 100 percent. That said, growing up he'd been privy to occasional meetings at his mom's and grandma's houses and the members of the club absolutely indulged in gossip. "Just saying, the club talks about more than cupcakes."

"Since we meet once a week every week, it would be sort of boring if we didn't." Rocky snagged a frying pan from his oven drawer and clanged it to the gleaming stovetop. "What do you want? Omelet or scrambled?"

He glanced at his watch. "The store opens in five."

"The store will open with or without you, Dev. Hate to break it to you, but you and Dad trained your people well. J.T.'s is a well-oiled machine. Sit. Eat. I need to talk to you."

Something in her voice. No, her *energy*. When stressed, Rocky tended to move at an accelerated pace. He'd been so wrapped up in his own thoughts, he hadn't noticed until now. "What's wrong?"

"Nothing's wrong." She tossed four pieces of bread into the toaster oven and whizzed back to the skillet, beating the eggs with ruthless determination.

"Guess we're having scrambled." He parked on the edge of a stool. "What do you want to talk about?"

"Chloe Madison."

"What about her?"

"Luke called me last night. Said Chloe stopped in for dinner with Monica and that they appeared to be having a fine time." She frowned. "Until you joined them."

"Just wanted to meet the woman, the *stranger,* who'll be living with our grandmother."

"You interrogated her."

"I tried to get to know her."

"You made her nervous."

"How would Luke know? He was across the room, behind the bar."

"Monica told him, just before they left, just after Chloe slipped into the powder room. She said, and I quote, '*Your brother is an ass.*'" Rocky wrenched open the pantry and cursed. "You're out of coffee filters."

"Use a paper towel."

She looked to the empty holder and raised one brow.

"Must have used them all when I cleaned."

"Never mind. I brought Earl Grey for tonight." She rooted through her stash and snagged a box of tea bags.

Devlin passed her the kettle he rarely used and plucked two plates from the cabinet. "Listen, I don't know what Monica thought she saw or heard—"

"She saw and heard you being yourself, Dev. Knowing you, I can imagine. You were bent because Gram hired someone without consulting you, someone you don't know. Rather than trusting her or Monica's judgment, you assumed there was something fishy or unreliable about Chloe Madison."

"I didn't *assume* anything." Now he was getting pissed. It wasn't like he'd been a bastard. He'd asked a few questions. Not his fault she was so easily intimidated. "I *know* she's unreliable. She also depends on the other people to support her flaky lifestyle."

"How could you possibly *know* that?"

Devlin cursed himself for losing his temper. He did *not* want to go here. Not with Rocky. He turned his back and snagged two forks.

"Oh no. Tell me you didn't call Jayce."

He couldn't, so he didn't.

"You *did*! Oh, Dev. That's just so . . . so . . ."

"Responsible? Proactive? Wise?"

"Slimy."

"You're only saying that because Jayce is involved." For reasons still unknown to Devlin, his sister and his best friend had had a falling-out over a decade ago. "And what's slimy about instigating a background check on an *employee*?"

"He snooped into her private life."

"He investigated. That's what PIs do."

"I don't want to talk about Jayce."

"You never do." Devlin noted her flushed cheeks and racked his memories and, as always, came up with nothing. "One day, one of you is going to tell me why."

"I need you to be nice to Chloe," Rocky said after loading their plates with scrambled eggs and buttered toast.

Devlin poured boiling water into their mugs. "Why?"

"Because I need some peace of mind. I'm worried Gram is going to seriously hurt herself if she's left unsupervised. I think she's going through some crisis and she doesn't want to confide in family or friends. Sometimes it's easier to work your problems out with people who don't know you well. People who won't try to influence you or judge you or out-and-out tell you what to do."

"We still talking about Gram?" Devlin asked as he sat across from his sister.

"Of course," she said without making eye contact.

Huh.

"I've known Monica for a few years now. She's as down-to-earth and trustworthy as they get. She loves Gram as much as everyone else in Sugar Creek. She wouldn't set her up with a total incompetent. No matter what Jayce told you, remember, there are two sides to every coin."

He could mention that Jayce had pointed out the very same thing but didn't. He did, however, flash on the woman he'd run into at the supermarket and the woman his friend had described. Last night, sitting beside her at the Shack, he'd gotten a peek of both sides—sweet and flaky. It was part of what had kept him awake all hours. Chloe was a tantalizing enigma. She was also a keen distraction to the possible Walmart disaster. He couldn't take action until his dad green-lighted his plans for J.T.'s, and the man was dragging his golf-cleated feet. Devlin glanced at his sister, the apple of her father's eye and able to sweet-talk the old man into almost anything. He flashed on Chloe, wondering if he'd learn more by taking a softer approach. They'd clicked before they'd known each other's identities. They could click again.

Slathering his toast with orange marmalade, he said, "You know my idea about remodeling and expanding the store?"

The tension between them evaporated with that neutral question. She glanced up from her plate. "Yeah?"

He smiled. "I'll ease off Chloe if you work on Dad."

She smiled back. "Deal."

SIX

Chloe stared at Daisy Monroe's mammoth three-story home with a combination of dread and awe. Colonial Revival, Monica had called it, one of eight popular historic architectural styles in Vermont. To be honest, it looked a little scary. Like a haunted house or the creepy house in Hitchcock's *Psycho.* "It must have a gazillion rooms."

"Close." Monica parked the Suburban and cut the engine. "I've been in the house several times—every member of Cupcake Lovers takes turns hosting meetings, including Daisy—and I still don't think I've seen every room."

"How does she keep up with it?"

"Devlin's dad, Jerome Monroe, Daisy's son, hired a professional cleaning service about ten years ago after Daisy refused to move in with them or into a smaller home."

"Is that how long she's been a widow? Ten years?"

"More or less."

Chloe remembered what it was like when her mom died. Heartbroken, Chloe's dad had never remarried and, as far as she knew, he didn't see anyone steady. If he had the occasional affair, she didn't know. She couldn't imagine. Or maybe she didn't want to imagine. Who wanted to think about their parent having sex? All she knew was that he, too, lived alone in their big old house in Marlton. "Must be lonely."

Maybe that's why it had taken Chloe so long to commit to a relationship. Subconsciously she couldn't deal with loving someone for years only to lose him to death.

Or a Parisian tart.

"I never met Daisy's husband, but I've heard he was domineering and stuffy. She doesn't talk about him much, so, I'm not sure how much she misses him. As for being lonely, the Monroe clan is huge, lots of uncles and aunts, nieces, nephews, and grandchildren. Plus they're related to the McCloud and Bentley crew. Plus Daisy has a lot of friends, although her closest buds starting dying off a few years ago."

Chloe's friends hadn't died off, but most of them had faded away. You can only turn down so many invitations before people stop calling. Crazy, she hadn't met Daisy, yet she felt a weird bond. "That's sad."

"Yeah, but nothing keeps Daisy Monroe down for long. She's a real pip. Funny thing is, folks say she used to be conventional and reserved."

"Probably because of her husband," Chloe said, thinking on how she'd curbed her enthusiasm because of Ryan's influence.

"Maybe," Monica said. "She really came out of her shell about three years ago."

Chloe's lip quirked. "At seventy-two."

Monica laughed. "Gotta watch out for those late bloomers." She squeezed Chloe's knee. "Ready?"

"Sure. No. Give me a minute."

"I'll give you several. Want me to drive around the block a few times?"

Chloe shook her head. "Just need a sec." She blew out a breath and swiped her clammy hands over the legs of her grey chinos. "I don't know why I'm so nervous. I've held dozens of different jobs, worked with and for all kinds of personality types. "

"I blame Dev. He made you self-conscious last night. I knew he was going to be a pain, but I didn't count on him being a jackass. What was with the condescending attitude?"

"I don't know."

"And *you.* I've never seen you so easily flustered. The old you would have won him over with bubbly charm."

Chloe flushed remembering how she'd morphed into an antisocial butterfly. Even after he'd left, she'd been unable to rally. More than anything, she'd been stunned that, even though he'd acted like a jerk, she was still attracted to the man. How pathetic was that?

Too pathetic to even share with her best friend.

"I know," Chloe said, feeling hollow. "I think I lost the old me somewhere in the first year after I moved in with Ryan. He was molding me into a more sedate, stable, well, adult, I guess. Only that wasn't really me, just his vision for me, and when I realized *his* potential . . . he dumped me." She glanced at her friend, panic fluttering in her stomach. "I'm not sure I know who I am anymore."

Monica grasped her hand. "Maybe today's not the best day to start a new job. Come home with me; stay another night or two. I'll square it with Daisy without sharing details."

Chloe squeezed her friend's hand and forced a smile. "No. I'm good. Really." She'd heard Monica and Leo going at it late last night and again early this morning. They were head over heels in love and trying for a baby. Chloe couldn't be happier for her friend, and at the same time it made her absolutely miserable. A reminder of what she didn't have and wouldn't have for a very long time, if ever. She pushed open her car door. "Let's go."

A few seconds later, she was rolling her mega-sized suitcase along the sidewalk and up Daisy's driveway. Monica led the way. Chloe inhaled the scent of freshly mown grass and admired the beautiful landscaped lawn. So different from the occasional tree and patch of grass in Manhattan. And instead of soulless skyscrapers, she was surrounded by majestic mountains. The sights and scents of nature reminded her of simpler times. The closer she got to the massive house, the calmer her nerves, and when the front door swung open she felt a bit of balance in her wobbly world.

"You're younger than I expected, Miss Madison."

"You're hipper than I expected, Mrs. Monroe." Chloe stared at the short, spry woman on the threshold. Betty White channeling Whoopi Goldberg. Daisy's silver hair was a halo of short, frothy curls and her cat-eye glasses were tinted pink and accented with subtle bling. Her attire was equally funky—faded jeans, a bohemian peasant blouse, and a pair of metallic gold sneakers. Compared to her—dressed in straight-legged chinos, a light pink knit tunic, and grey ballet flats—Chloe felt like a preppy sorority sister.

Daisy scrunched her penciled brows. "Is hip cool?"

Chloe smiled. "Very."

The woman extended a wrinkled, age-spotted hand. "Call me Daisy."

"Chloe."

"I'll leave you two to get acquainted," Monica said with a huge grin. "See you at the meeting tonight, Daisy."

"Did you get the call?" she asked. "Rocky's oven's busted. We're meeting at Devlin's."

"Got it," Monica said with a sympathetic glance at Chloe.

Chloe telegraphed a silent, *No problem.* She'd drive Daisy to the meeting, but she wasn't going inside, no matter where it was being held. She wasn't ready to meet an entire social club, especially a club devoted to baking cupcakes. Desserts equaled heartache and the urge to do bodily harm with assorted kitchen utensils. She imagined Rocky serving chocolate cupcakes and Monica having to tackle her to the floor as she lunged for a cast-iron baking pan and started swinging. Not a great first impression.

Daisy ushered Chloe inside. "Park your suitcase anywhere, kitten. We'll pick out your room when we get back."

"Where are we going?"

"Sugar Creek."

"But we're in Sugar Creek."

"No, I mean *the* creek. I'm in the mood for a picnic." She pointed to her left. "Kitchen's that way. Make us some sandwiches and nab a bottle of wine. I'll fetch my hat and purse."

She took off and Chloe sought out the kitchen, instantly charmed by the woman and her home. It might have looked intimidating from the outside, but the interior couldn't have been more warm and welcoming. A mix of colonial and Victorian décor. Exquisitely perfect. Like something out of *Better Homes and Gardens* magazine. Chloe soaked in the antiques, the collectibles, the perfectly arranged clutter.

She stopped cold on the threshold of the spacious kitchen. She could scarcely believe her eyes. State-of-the-art appliances and a gazillion culinary gadgets. A Cuisinart food processor, KitchenAid stand mixer, waffle baker, slow cooker, Breville Café Roma espresso maker. She checked her pulse, because she was pretty sure she'd died and gone to heaven.

* * *

Devlin was pretty sure he'd died and gone to hell. "What do you mean, a quarter of our employees put in applications at the supercenter?"

"You can't blame them, Dev." Chris Bane, his assistant manager, dragged a hand over his stubbled jaw. "Walmart's offering—"

"I know what they're offering." A better health plan and a generous benefits package. J.T.'s was an independent store. Small potatoes compared to a national chain. "Dammit."

"There's also a growing fear that the supercenter will put us out of business. Why shop here when—"

"I'm working on that," Devlin said. "Renovation and expansion should keep us in the game."

Chris angled his head. "Shame your dad's opposed to change."

"Working on that, too. Do me a favor and temper the gossip on the floor. Tell them we're in there swinging and have no intention of going down."

"I'll do my best."

"That's all I ask." Devlin drank the last of his coffee and texted his sister: *did u call dad?*

did u mk nice w/chloe?

will do after wk

now wd b better
"Dammit." *on it*
☺

* * *

"Why are you driving so slow?"

"I don't want to risk a ticket." Or a fender bender. Chloe was supremely uncomfortable in this four-wheeled boat. She had to sit on the same pillow Daisy usually sat on to see over the dashboard, and the gearshift wasn't even in the right place. It was on the freaking steering column!

Daisy leaned left and peered over the rims of her prescription Jackie O sunglasses. "You're going ten miles under the speed limit."

"The slower I go, the less damage I'll do if I hit a deer or squirrel or anything. Besides, this road is rutted with potholes." Chloe flexed her hands on the steering wheel of Daisy's 1964 Cadillac. *1964!* Chloe still couldn't believe it. This car had been made almost twenty years before she was born. Even so, it was in good working order and pristine condition. Sort of like Daisy. Chloe felt like she was transporting precious cargo in a priceless antique. *Hello,* pressure?

They were at least twenty miles from town in the fricking middle of nowhere driving through the middle of the fricking woods. According to Chloe's new boss, this one-lane dirt road was a shortcut to Sugar Creek—the river, not the town. Chloe didn't want to damage the car, and she certainly didn't want to damage Daisy. Either would prompt a visit from Devlin Monroe. Chloe hoped to avoid him for a week or two while she reconnected with her old self or discovered an enlightened new self, someone capable of handling an Alpha Manipulator.

"No offense, kitten, but you drive like an old lady." Daisy crossed her arms over her chest and grunted. "I would've been better off with Morgan Freeman."

It took a second, but then Chloe flashed on the award-winning movie they'd watched in one of her film classes. "I get it," she managed without rolling her eyes. *"Driving Miss Daisy." Ha.*

"Didn't you live in New York? On TV people who drive in big cities are fearless."

"That or insane."

"Overly cautious people cause more accidents, you know. Punch it, Scaredy-Cat. I'd like to have lunch before it's time for dinner. I'm starving."

Chloe's stomach grumbled in agreement. Last night, she'd lost her appetite after Devlin had crashed her party for two. This morning, she'd been too nervous about her new job to eat anything other than a piece of dry toast. She was starving, too. After raiding Daisy's refrigerator, Chloe had quickly prepared roast-beef sandwiches and spiced up a fresh but bland batch of pre-made potato salad. The food was stashed in the picnic basket on the backseat along with a bottle of chardonnay and two bottles of water.

Eager to reach their destination, Chloe accelerated, pushing the speedometer to 40 mph.

"Regular daredevil," Daisy said.

* * *

Thirty minutes and a picnic lunch later, the two women were sprawled on a thick blanket, staring up through the rustling treetops at the cloudless sky. It was a beautiful day. Unseasonably warm for mid-September, according to Daisy. Chloe toed off her flats and wiggled her toes. If she rolled up her chinos, she could walk along the shallow portions of Sugar Creek—which was more like a river. That would certainly cool her off and help to digest the food she'd wolfed down.

She turned to ask Daisy if she'd like to take a walk and noticed she'd fallen asleep. Not surprising considering the heat and how much they'd eaten. Plus Daisy had polished off two plastic tumblers of wine.

Knowing she had to drive them back in the monster Caddy, Chloe had stuck to water. Smiling to herself, she pushed up onto her elbows, absorbing the woodland surroundings and enjoying the silence. Daisy had talked all through lunch, asking Chloe about her life in NYC. She'd been especially keen to learn about Chloe's social activities.

Have you been to the top of the Empire State Building? Ever danced the night away in one of those famous discos? Taken a hansom cab ride through Central Park? Indulged in a speedboat ride on the Hudson River? At night?

Chloe had done all of those things, except the nocturnal speed demon ride on the Hudson. Given her moderate swimming skills and a terrifying childhood incident, she'd never been fond of water sports. To which Daisy had said, *If you live life ruled by your fears, you're not really living.*

Chloe had never considered herself cautious. If she wanted something, she went for it. Mostly. Although, if she was honest, these past two years she'd been so focused on "growing up," committing to a relationship and domestic tranquility, in addition to studying her butt off at the Culinary Arts Institute, she had, sort of, temporarily (she hoped) forgotten how to have fun.

"So what'd you put in my potato salad?" Daisy asked. "Had more zing than usual."

Chloe started. "I thought you were napping."

"Naps are for babies and old people." She sat up and stretched her arms over her head, yawned. "Thought I tasted dill."

"Fresh dill."

"And?"

"Ground cumin and chopped red onions," Chloe said. "Normally I would've added chipotle peppers, but you didn't have any in the fridge and besides, it might have been too spicy for you."

"Never know unless you try. Next time add the peppers."

"Yes, ma'am."

The older woman slid her sunglasses to the end of her nose and nailed Chloe with narrowed eyes. "If this, us, is going to work, you have to call me Daisy. I only hired you to get my grandchildren off my back. I'd prefer to do my own cooking and driving. I'm not an invalid, but I am . . ." She looked away as if embarrassed.

"Lonely?" Chloe asked while snagging her water bottle.

Daisy snorted. "With a big family like mine? Someone's always popping over or inviting me to some or another shindig. I've got commitments and engagements coming out of my skinny patooty. What I yearn for is adventure. I want to make the most of what time I've got left. I want a fuck buddy."

Chloe choked on a mouthful of water.

"Someone who'll say *'screw you'* to convention. Someone who's not afraid to take chances and embrace opportunities. After talking to Monica, I just knew you were the one. Passionate. Fearless. Was I wrong?"

Daisy was referring to the old Chloe Madison, pre-Ryan Levine. She felt a stab of regret, nostalgia, *something*. "I'm not sure I'd call myself fearless, but I've taken a lot of chances in my life. Followed my heart. My passions."

"Exciting."

"Risky."

"But exciting."

Again she felt conflicted between her old life and the life she'd created with Ryan. She hadn't hated the person she'd become because of him, but she'd definitely felt restless. She'd waited her whole life for something to click, to feel like, *This is who I am* and *what I'm meant to do. This is the life I was meant for.*

She was still waiting for that click.

"About your FB reference." It's not like Chloe had never said the *f* word, but she couldn't say it in the presence of, well, someone's grandma. "It doesn't mean what you think it means."

"What does it mean?"

"I'm not comfortable saying."

"Are you a prude, Chloe Madison?"

"No. Just respectful."

Daisy sighed. "I'd hoped for fun."

"I can be fun."

"Prove it."

"How?"

"Let's go tubing."

"What?"

"Inner tubing. Perfect day for it."

Chloe turned a wary eye to the rippling water. "Isn't that more of a summer sport?"

"It's not officially fall."

"But—"

"Think outside of the seasonal box, kitten." She sprang up and corked her wine bottle. "Bert Hawkins owns a year-round recreation shop ten minutes from here. We can rent a couple of tubes and float down the river. Oh, don't look so panicked. Sugar Creek's not that deep or wide and you said you can swim. Not that you'll have to. Just keep your butt in the hole, dangle your legs over the side, and let the current do the work."

Chloe scrambled to her bare feet when Daisy tugged at the blanket. Her heart pounded as a dozen awful scenarios exploded in her brain. "I really don't think . . . We just ate. You're supposed to wait an hour—"

"Old wives' tale. And besides, we're not going for a swim. We're going for a float." Picnic basket over one arm, the blanket over the other, Daisy hotfooted it toward the Caddy.

Chloe pulled on her shoes and hurried to catch up. "You've been drinking," she blurted.

"What are you? My FB or my mother?"

"I'm your companion and I'm concerned. What if you fall off?"

"Then I'll climb back on or grab hold and scissor kick my way to shore."

"Tube a lot, do you?"

"Used to. When I was a kid."

Great. "Once we float downriver, how will we get back to the car?"

"I'll tell Bert to have someone pick us up."

Chloe felt like she was talking to a stone wall. Talk about stubborn. She took the basket and blanket from Daisy and placed them in the backseat. "We don't have bathing suits."

"We'll improvise."

Chloe racked her brain for another argument, something other than, *I'm afraid you'll fall in and drown.* "Only if you wear a life jacket."

"Only kids and old people wear life jackets." Daisy braced her hands on her bony hips and raised those penciled brows. "Scaredy-cat."

The taunt sizzled and burned. Did everyone have an opinion on her character? She was either too reckless or too cautious. Didn't anyone think she was just right? Unreasonably ticked, Chloe wrenched open the heavy-ass driver's door. "Get in and buckle up."

SEVEN

Devlin stood in the middle of his grandmother's living room cursing himself for not acquiring Chloe's cell number. Prodded by his sister, he'd come to smooth things over. Only Chloe wasn't here and neither was Gram. The Caddy was also missing. He glanced at the blue Samsonite sitting next to the front door. Assumedly Chloe's. What had been so urgent that Gram hadn't even allowed her new companion to unpack?

His phone rang. He didn't recognize the number. "Devlin Monroe."

"Hey, Dev. It's Bert Hawkins. Sorry to bother. Called J.T.'s and was told to call you at this number, seeing this is about your grandma."

"Go on."

"I tried talking her out of tubing, but she was adamant."

"Tubing? As in tubing down the *river*?" He flashed on the days when he and Luke would tether their inner tubes to a small watercraft, usually piloted by one of their uncles or sometimes one of Bert's summer crew. They'd shared many a wild ride, bouncing in the wake of the boat, sometimes going airborne. Sometimes wiping out. Heart pounding, Devlin blew out of the house. "What the hell, Bert? Don't you have restrictions?"

"Sure. Age six and up and must weigh at least fifty pounds.

I had no legal ground to refuse her, but Daisy's had a lot of mishaps lately and, frankly, I'm not comfortable with this responsibility."

Devlin's blood pressure spiked as he sped out of town toward the river. "Tell me she's wearing a life jacket."

"Them's the rules."

That didn't mean Daisy wouldn't pitch the jacket once she was out of Bert's sight. "You've probably heard Gram has a new and aggravating habit of breaking the rules."

"That's why I'm calling."

"Did her companion at least try to talk her out of this stunt?"

"Miss Madison? Barely said a word, except to argue over swimwear."

Chloe in a bikini. An image Devlin could've done without. He floored the Escalade and glanced at his watch. "When did they leave?"

"Fifteen minutes ago, give or take."

If he hurried he could head them off at Grenville's Overlook. "What took you so long to call?"

"Daisy threatened to make my life miserable if I alerted any of her kin, but after careful consideration, I decided I'd rather risk her wrath than yours. Oh, and one more thing, Dev. Your grandma's tubing in her skivvies."

Fan-fucking-tastic.

He didn't ask about Chloe. All the same, the vision of her in a lacy pink bra and matching panties exploded in his brain. By the time he neared Grenville's he had a hard-on and a short fuse. A dangerous combination. He parked the Escalade and speed-dialed Rocky as he stepped onto the historic covered bridge and looked upriver. "You want me to be nice to Gram's new companion? Then you better talk me down."

* * *

Chloe couldn't believe she'd let Betty White goad her into doing something against her better judgment. Granted,

Sugar Creek wasn't all that wide, and as far as she could see there was nothing but flat water ahead. But that didn't mean something awful couldn't happen. Like someone spotting them in their impromptu bathing suits. Or getting sucked in and pulled under by unexpected crosscurrents or a powerful whirlpool. Sure, the latter was far-fetched, especially since, according to Bert, entire families free-floated down this section at the height of the season. But it was possible. Anything was possible.

"Relax."

Chloe glanced at her employer. Since her skinny patooty was wedged in the donut hole of the inner tube, no one could see her nude knee-length girdle. Her Playtex bra was also hidden thanks to the three-buckle nylon life vest. Her bony arms and legs dangled over the side of the tube, and her creamy white, softly wrinkled face was tilted to the sun. She looked blissfully peaceful. Happy.

Chloe couldn't help herself. She smiled. "Your family's going to kill me when they hear about this." She was talking specifically about Devlin but didn't want to bring up his name.

"No, they won't. I won't let them. Now relax and enjoy the ride."

Chloe sighed and settled deep into the tube. Since she wasn't wearing a body shaper and had refused to strip to her thong, she'd talked Bert into loaning her a pair of swim trunks. Never mind that they were men's trunks and three sizes too big. Could've been worse. Could've been a Speedo. She'd also refused to float down Sugar Creek in her bra, but then Daisy had called her a prude and Bert had shown her the life vest that would conceal her entire upper body. *What the hell?* Anything to appease her new boss on her first official day. She'd done crazier things.

"Been a long time since I floated down Sugar Creek," Daisy said. "Used to come here all the time with my brothers and sisters. Sometimes we'd swim, sometimes we'd paddle in a rowboat, and sometimes, when we snuck away from our parents, we'd jump off Grenville's Overlook cannonball-style."

Charmed by the story, Chloe allowed her fingers to trail in the rippling water and closed her eyes, basking in the warmth of the sun. "What's Grenville's Overlook?"

"An old covered bridge. Overlooks the river. We'll be passing under shortly. Years later," she went on, "I brought my own children here. Jessup—that's my husband, rest his soul—didn't want me parading around in a bathing suit when he wasn't with us, and since he was always busy at the store I settled on allowing the kids to join their cousins and uncles and I'd wait with my sisters at Willow Bend, gossiping and preparing for a family picnic."

"That must have been fun," Chloe said, sensitive to the wistfulness in the other woman's voice. "Hanging out with your sisters." As an only child, Chloe had always been envious of people with sibling relationships. The good ones anyway.

"Not as much fun as tubing or boating. Time raced by and before I knew it I was watching my grandkids' water shenanigans. They enjoyed tubing, too, although they preferred getting towed behind a motorboat. More of a thrill." She snickered. "Little daredevils. I remember the first time I caught Devlin and Luke jumping off Grenville's. My heart stopped. But then they broke the surface, laughing and hooting, and I remembered how it felt throwing caution to the wind."

Chloe remembered, too. She flashed back on all the chances she'd taken over the years. The thrill of the unknown. The rush of flying by the seat of her pants. Going for it. Sometimes she failed. Sometimes she soared.

Her memories evaporated when she realized Daisy had fallen silent. Chloe glanced over just as the woman shrugged out of her life vest and hurled it away! "What are you doing?"

"Throwing caution to the wind. Never wore those pesky things back in the day."

"But . . ." Chloe sat up so fast she almost fell overboard. "Dammit, Daisy."

"Stop being such a worrywart."

"If anything happens to you—"

"I'll die a happy woman." She giggled and paddled with her hands, pulling ahead of Chloe. "I feel like a kid again!"

"You're certainly acting like one." Chloe debated whether to retrieve the castaway life vest or catch up to her runaway boss. She spied the bridge up ahead and a sharp bend beyond. If Daisy drifted out of sight . . . Chloe paddled for all she was worth. "Put this on," she said as she closed in.

"No, thanks."

"I'm not asking; I'm telling." A desperate need to take charge of a potentially dicey situation made Chloe's tone and actions clipped. She unbuckled the last strap and thrust her vest at her crazy boss. "Swear to God, if you don't put this on, I'll latch onto you or your tube and somehow muscle you to shore."

"Your bra's showing," Daisy said with an ornery grin.

"I don't give a flip about modesty just now." In the past, she'd performed as a party motivator, sometimes wearing beaded corsets or bras as part of her costume. It's not like she'd never shown some skin, and besides, her pink and red floral demi-bra could almost pass as a bathing suit top. *Almost.*

"Glad to hear that, kitten." Daisy snatched the life vest, but just as she shoved one arm through, a male voice bellowed from shore. "Bert must've snitched," Daisy grumbled under her breath. "The rat." Then she yelled, "Don't bust a blood vessel! I'm coming!"

Chloe looked to where Daisy looked and yelped. Just ahead, striding down a rocky slope and toward the edge of the lapping water: Devlin Monroe. *Of all the* . . . Her skin burned and her heart pumped. Two thoughts hijacked her brain.

He's going to kill me.

He's seeing me in my bra.

The latter caused her to fling herself over the tube into the river. A knee-jerk reaction.

The splash caused Daisy to look over her shoulder.

"I'm fine!' Chloe told her, clinging to the tube, her scantily clad body hidden safely beneath the murky water. "Keep going!" The sooner Daisy reached shore, the sooner Devlin would stop worrying, the sooner his temper would cool. She hoped.

Daisy paddled and kicked toward her grandson while Chloe frantically explored her options. How was she going to emerge from this fiasco with her pride intact? Once on dry land, she could hold the inner tube in front of her, hiding her bra. Although that seemed kind of childish. Not to mention she couldn't get in a car like that. She could brazen it out and pretend her bra was a bathing suit top. Why was she being so neurotic?

Because you're attracted to the man.

Another source of embarrassment. She'd been single less than a week and she was already hot to trot? She wasn't a prude, as Daisy had suggested, but she wasn't promiscuous either.

"Get the hell over here!" Devlin shouted to Chloe just as he pulled his grandma out of the water.

Chloe snapped out of her daze, realizing she'd floated under the bridge and was gaining speed. She could feel a difference in the current. Up ahead the river took a sharp turn. Was that Willow Bend? Bert had pleaded with Daisy to end their ride at Willow Bend, nixing the whitewater portion of the ride. She'd agreed, but Bert hadn't looked convinced. Although as soon as they'd pushed off, Daisy had reassured Chloe—no rapids. Except Daisy wasn't with her now and she had no idea how close or far she was from the more challenging part of the course.

Her pulse raced remembering when she'd vacationed in Florida with her dad and mom. She'd only been eight at the time. Her swimming skills extended to dog-paddling, so she'd been using one of those old inflatable donuts, something like an inner tube only flimsier, when the undercurrent had swept her far from the beach and . . .

"Oh . . . my . . . God." She scissor kicked with a vengeance, frantic to get to shore. She felt the oversized trunks slipping down her legs but refused to let go of her two-armed strangle grip on the tube. All she could think about was those rapids somewhere up ahead. Were they as fierce as some of the ones she'd seen on television? What if she went under?

She broke into a sweat even though she was chilled to the bone. Her vision blurred. She couldn't see Daisy or Devlin. Why wasn't she getting any closer to shore? She heard her name, heard a splash. She whipped around and saw someone swimming toward her in strong, easy strokes.

Devlin.

In a heartbeat, he was there. With her. Surrounding her.

She felt his arms close around her trembling body. She felt his warmth, his strength.

"You're swimming against the current," he said, maneuvering her around and guiding her toward shore. Which really wasn't all that far, although in her panic it had seemed like miles. It reminded her of how her dad had dove into the ocean and rescued her, but not before a wave had taken her under. She'd been so sure she was going to drown.

Overwhelmed by a flood of emotions, Chloe choked on tears.

"You're okay," Devlin said, tightening his hold. "Almost there."

She wanted to thank him. She wanted to apologize for freaking out. But her throat was clogged with embarrassment and relief and the thrill of his touch. If he held her any closer, they'd be one. His masculine scent made her dizzy and the feel of his warm breath on her neck as he continued to talk her down drove her wild. Moments ago she'd gone cold with fear and now . . . now every fiber of her body burned with desire. How could she be terrified one moment and turned on the next? Were her emotions that out of whack?

Apparently so.

Devlin half-carried her out of the water, before letting her go and easing away.

She swung around to face him, clinging to the inner tube while catching her breath and wits.

He stared.

She stared.

He'd shucked his shoes and socks before diving in, but other than that he was fully clothed. And soaked. His khaki Dockers clung to his muscled thighs and his white oxford shirt melded to his chiseled torso.

Wow.

Frowning, he raked his wet hair from his face—a sexy move that knotted her stomach—then started unbuttoning his shirt.

Face burning, she blurted, "What are you doing?"

He raised a brow in answer, his blue gaze sliding down her trembling body. She realized suddenly that she'd lost Bert's trunks in the river and that she was standing there in her thong and demi-bra. The inner tube pretty much covered her front, but Devlin had seen her backside when he'd carried her out of the water. Just now said backside was exposed for the world to see—should anyone happen by.

Shoot me now.

He moved in behind her, concealing her bare butt, and helped her into his shirt.

She dropped the tube and hurriedly buttoned up. Although his shirt was soaked and probably see-through, it was better than nothing.

She started to thank him, but Daisy emerged from a thicket of trees, hurrying toward them in her bra and girdle. "Are you all right?" she asked Chloe.

"I'm fine. You?"

"Dandy. Except for my killjoy grandson here. I—"

"We'll talk about this when everyone's dry and decent." Stern-faced, he guided them through the trees, up an incline, and toward the covered bridge.

Even though his bare torso was glorious to behold, it was difficult to enjoy when his mood was so prickly. Chloe fell into sullen silence while contemplating the best way of defending her actions without blaming the entire mess on Daisy.

Daisy pouted from the time Devlin loaded them into his Escalade to the moment he dropped them at Bert's, where they retrieved their clothing and the Caddy. Once the two women were alone in the old car, Daisy let loose with her gripes and concerns about her uptight, controlling grandson, then lapsed into an excited ramble about tonight's cupcake meeting. She had a new recipe that she was dying to share and hoped Tasha—whoever that was—didn't rain on her parade, again. The conversation was mostly one sided. Partly because Daisy wouldn't stop talking, partly because Chloe was obsessing on the man who'd insisted on following them home.

Unsettled and dreading a showdown, Chloe was beyond relieved when she parked the Caddy in Daisy's driveway and, after pausing to make sure they headed directly inside the house, Devlin kept driving.

Maybe he'd decided there was nothing more to talk about. He'd pretty much said it all with his hard looks and stony silence. Chloe had screwed up and he wasn't happy about it.

She could live with that. Now if she could just erase the image of those wet clothes clinging to his hard body and the memory of his strong embrace, she would be, as Daisy was fond of saying, dandy.

Desperate for a shower and some downtime, Chloe grabbed her suitcase. "If you could show me to my room—"

"Later." Daisy grasped her arm and tugged her toward the kitchen. "I don't know about you, but I could use a cocktail. While we're at it, I want your opinion on my Cinnamon Applesauce Cupcakes. By the way," she added before Chloe could get a word in, "I think my grandson has the hots for you."

EIGHT

"I can't believe Dev allowed you to borrow his house," Monica said. "For the meeting, I mean. He's so private. Wasn't he worried we'd poke around?"

"Worried enough to scrub the bathroom and kitchen," Rocky said as she poured her friend a cup of Earl Grey. "He must've really gone at it. The toilet bowl's gleaming."

"You checked the toilet?"

"Are you serious? You know men."

"I know Leo. He's usually pretty good, but once in a while he splashes the rim. What's so hard about aiming their willies for the middle?"

"Did you just say 'willy'?"

"Leo and I made a pact to clean up our potty mouths. You know, for when the little one comes."

Was that a hint of thrilling news? Rocky grinned. "So you're—"

"Not yet. Hopefully soon. You'd think after three months of doing it every day, twice a day . . ."

"Wow."

"Yeah, well, Leo's starting to wear on stamina . . . and patience. Don't get me started." Monica sipped tea, regrouped, then smiled. "So, why'd you ask me to show early? What's up?"

"My curiosity. Maybe you know something I don't."

"About?"

Jazzed for juice, Rocky leaned in. "Did Chloe call you about today?"

"You mean the tubing incident?"

"Dev called me before everything played out. Then after to let me know everyone was okay. No freaking details. He sounded pissed, broody even. I'm guessing he blames Chloe for indulging Gram's whim. I'm guessing he gave her hell when just this morning I begged him to be nice to her. So did he?"

"Give her hell?" Monica shook her head. "More like the silent treatment."

"Sometimes that's worse. Means he's stewing. If and when he blows . . . yikes."

"I actually think there's more to it." Monica leaned forward as well, an ornery gleam in her eye. "Did Dev tell you that he met Chloe yesterday at Oslow's and that they shared a *moment*?"

"What kind of moment?"

"A brief flirtation."

"Dev doesn't flirt."

"Chloe was pretty certain, which is why she was so surprised when he acted like a dick, *crap,* wiener last night at Luke's. Of course, Dev didn't know *who* he was flirting with at Oslow's. Chloe ran out before introductions."

"Huh." Sometime between Oslow's and Luke's, Jayce had filled Dev in on Chloe's background. Information that led Dev to believe Chloe was unreliable. Someone who took advantage of people to finance her *flaky* lifestyle. Rocky was dying to know what constituted flaky? She wanted to ask Monica about Chloe's past but didn't know how without revealing Dev had had her investigated. Instead she said, "I can't wait to meet Chloe."

"Well, it won't be tonight."

"What do you mean? She'll be with Gram, right?"

"She's dropping her off and picking her up. She begged off the meeting."

"As a chef, I thought she'd be into talking shop and swapping recipes."

"She has an aversion to desserts just now." Monica waved off Rocky's next question. "Not for me to explain. However, for what it's worth I totally understand. It's been a big day and she's wiped."

"Guess I'll have to rein in my curiosity until tomorrow when I stop over at Gram's for a visit." Rocky sipped tea, sighed. She was totally intrigued with Chloe Madison. Dev flirting? She couldn't imagine. But then she did and it made her smile really big. Was it possible that a woman had finally broken through her brother's defenses and truly bewitched the cynical, infuriatingly grounded man? Unreliable and flaky, huh? As in someone who lived life to the fullest? No regrets? That could be good or bad for Dev. Depending.

She *had* to meet this woman. When she did, as a keen judge of character, she'd know right away if Chloe was trouble or a blessing.

Someone pounded on the door. Before they were out of their seats, the pounding sounded again. "Someone's impatient," Monica said as she cleared their teacups.

"Probably Tasha. She was horrible before. Now she's a bitch on wheels. Who died and made her president of Cupcake Lovers?"

"Her mom."

"Oh, right. I try so hard to forget." Rocky cursed under her breath. "I'll get the door."

"I'll get the cupcakes. They smell scrumptious by the way."

"Thanks." Whenever someone hosted, they provided a featured beverage and cupcake. This week Rocky had gone with Earl Grey and Strawberry Jam Tea Cakes. Normally she looked forward to the meetings. A chance to catch up with friends. A chance to sample someone's new recipe or a favorite old recipe and to swap ideas on how to channel their fund-raising efforts. Sure. Cupcake Lovers was kind of old-fashioned, but that's what Rocky loved about it. The roots. The history. The combined efforts of locals to make a difference in and beyond Sugar Creek. There was only one thing about Cupcake Lovers she didn't like.

Tasha Burke.

Rocky's archenemy since high school, she didn't fool Rocky one bit with her new and enthusiastic plan to raise awareness about Cupcake Lovers' decades-old cause by compiling a recipe book and securing a major publisher. This wasn't about "their charitable efforts." This was about Tasha's ten minutes of fame and glory. Unfortunately, she'd snowed the rest of the members.

Pasting on a welcoming smile—because, hey, what if it wasn't Tasha?—Rocky opened the door. "Gram!"

"Wait'll you get a load of my new recipe," she said, waving a blue index card as she breezed inside. "Chloe says it's a winner! And *she's* a professional. This one will make our book for sure! If it doesn't, she said Tasha's a pinhead."

Smiling, Rocky watched as the Caddy zipped away from the curb. She *had* to meet this woman.

Before Rocky closed the door another car pulled into the drive. Her cousin Sam. Several other members trickled in over the next few minutes. Ethel Larsen, Helen Cole, and Judy Betts, three of the senior members aside from Daisy. All of whom had husbands, brothers, sons, or grandchildren who'd fought overseas in one or another war. Rachel Lacey, the day-care assistant who'd moved into town at the beginning of the year, and Casey Monahan, a local artisan who'd introduced Rachel into the club. They both had siblings stationed in the Middle East. Most but not all of the members had a personal tie with someone in the military. Just as the original members who'd started Cupcake Lovers back in the Forties had. To this day, one of the club's steady projects was to send cupcake care packages to various military troops. Tasha had introduced her recipe book project as a fundraiser as well as a way to inspire people to bake cupcakes for good causes. Noble. Too bad she had ulterior motives. Too bad she'd infected the membership with her visions of glory.

Traditionally, meetings opened with casual gossip. Some of it long distance. Much of it local. "Have you heard from so and so or how's so and so doing? Did you hear about this person or that organization and their troubles? How can we help?"

If tonight had been typical, someone would've inquired about Ethel's recent battle with insomnia. Or asked Rachel about the status of the day-care school grant. Someone definitely would've asked Daisy how she liked her new companion! But this meeting opened with, "Did you see the burly guy from that specialty bakery in Connecticut and his amazing creation on *Cupcake Wars*?"

Rocky blamed Tasha.

To think Dev had actually dated the self-absorbed manipulator. Granted, Tasha had seduced him at a vulnerable time. Still, even thinking about that short-lived affair made Rocky shudder. If Tasha had had her way, she would've finessed Dev into marriage. "Ick."

As if on cue, the curvy, cosmetically enhanced, brunette blew into Dev's house with only the briefest of knocks. "All right, people. You are *not* going to believe this. I was flipping through two of the newest dessert books at the library and what do you think I found? A recipe for Pumpkin Spice Cupcakes with Butter-Cream Frosting!"

Helen, who'd been baking cupcakes since the outset of the Vietnam War, perched her plump hands on her chunky hips. "Are you saying I submitted a poached recipe to the club?"

"I'm saying your recipe isn't original enough, Helen. Not for our book. If we're going to keep it, you're going to have to punch it up. A unique ingredient or a whimsical design. Did any of you catch this week's episode of *Cupcake Wars* where that fat hairy guy—"

"Who wants tea?" Rocky interrupted, desperate to interject some portion of the club's normal routine.

Everyone raised their hand but fell over one another talking about the latest episode of the cable food show. Even Sam! "The use of blueberry jam and tequila was inspired," he said.

"And what about the presentation round?" Casey asked.

"*That's* what I'm talking about," Tasha said.

"Style over substance," Rocky mumbled under her breath as she escaped into the kitchen. *Typical of the mayor's new trophy wife.* Once she'd lost her grip on Dev, Tasha had trolled for an even more influential and affluent man. She'd landed Randall Burke, a match that generated more local gossip than a national political sex scandal. A textbook narcissist, Tasha reveled in the notoriety.

Rocky put a kettle of water on the stove, then zipped around the kitchen, trying to blow off steam. Just now, she had to tread softly where Tasha was concerned. And, truth told, if done right the book *would* benefit the club's charitable efforts. Rocky didn't want to ruin a potentially profitable project based on an old grudge against their new president.

As if on cue, the witch poked her head in. "When you come back, would you bring some jam and butter with you? Your tea cakes are a *teensy* bit dry," she said with a fake smile, then blew back out.

"Killing her would be bad," Rocky said through clenched teeth as she loaded a tray with sugar and cream for tea and jam for her perfectly moist cakes. But that didn't mean she didn't think about maiming the woman as she pasted on her own fake smile and rejoined the group.

* * *

Devlin ate his dinner in Luke's office because he didn't feel like talking to anyone. He multi-tasked, devouring Anna's Tuscan Beef Stew while assessing the restaurant's bottom line. Business was good. Great. In spite of Chloe's snooty appraisal of the food. He hated that he couldn't wipe that episode from his mind. He hated that he couldn't wipe every episode, since the moment they'd collided at Oslow's, from his mind. Especially, specifically, today.

He'd been so damned relieved to see the women free-floating instead of bouncing behind a watercraft, but then he'd noticed neither was wearing a life vest. Not that huge of a deal, except Gram was accident prone. Ironic that his seventy-five-year-old grandmother had made it swiftly and safely to shore while Chloe had flipped off the tube and drifted past them, seemingly ignoring his order to come ashore.

Then Gram had mentioned Chloe's inexperience with water sports: *Got pulled under when she was a kid. Never outgrew her fear of drowning.* And there she was drifting toward the rapids. Without a life vest.

Suspecting she'd panicked, he'd raced along shore to catch up and, seeing her frantically kicking against the current, dove in. When he was growing up, Sugar Creek had been his second home in the summers. He knew every stretch. Every bend. He didn't have an ounce of reservations regarding that river, but it was the fear in Chloe's expression that had caused his heart to pound.

He'd concentrated on calming her down and getting her to shore. The fact that her petite body felt like the perfect combination of toned muscles and soft curves barely registered.

Until they were on dry ground. He'd thought getting a glimpse of her pink panties the day before had been a turn-on, but it was nothing compared to the sight of her bare ass. The fact that she was wearing a threadbare thong only intensified his arousal. He'd been torn between, *What were you thinking?* and, *Happy Birthday to me!*

Instead of ogling, he'd covered her. But seeing her in his shirt, his *wet, thin* shirt, had only amped his desire to kiss her stupid.

Not that he'd been happy to see Gram stalking toward them in her underwear, but he'd sure as hell welcomed the interruption.

Unlike now.

"Want to talk about it?" Luke asked as he barged in.

"Talk about what?"

"Whatever's causing your shitty mood."

No. He did not want to talk about the fact that he'd seen Chloe practically naked or the fact that all he could think about all day was jumping her beautiful bones. "Dad's stonewalling renovations."

"Not surprised."

"I asked Rocky to work her magic."

Luke smiled. "Normally, I'd say, 'Smart move.' She pours it on and the old man melts. But in this case . . ." He shook his head. "When it comes to the family business, Dad's—"

"Stubborn?"

"Traditional. You'd do better to take an ass-backward approach to progress."

"Meaning?"

"Go back, not forward."

Devlin angled his head.

His younger brother settled on the corner of his desk, looking at Devlin like he was a moron. "Instead of expanding and renovating J.T.'s so that it looks like a modern superstore, expand and restore based on its original design. How many times have you heard the old man say that the reason Sugar Creek attracts tourists is because of its quaint charm? Expand your merchandise. Compete with the big boys. But do it under the roof of a pseudo-nineteenth-century structure."

Devlin's lip quirked. "When did you get so smart?"

"I've always been smart. You just think you're smarter."

"Sorry to interrupt," a young woman said, after poking her head through the partially opened door, "but they need some help at the bar, Luke."

"Be right there, Nell."

She smiled and left.

"Do I know her?" Devlin asked.

"Our newest waitress."

"Did we need another waitress?"

"No, but she needed a job and she's cute."

"Don't fuck the help."

"Mixing business and pleasure. Recipe for disaster. Yada yada." Luke pushed off the desk. "There's a local-history section at the library. Official documents. Blueprints. A collection of daguerreotype portraits, views and street scenes of Sugar Creek that date back to the early eighteen-hundreds. Hell, Monica works there. Ask her. If it's her day off just get someone to point you in the right direction." He slapped

Devlin's shoulder on his way out. "You can thank me by showing for Sunday dinner at Gram's."

"I'll be there." He'd already promised Rocky he'd show, and now he had even more incentive. To see Chloe in action as Gram's personal chef. To sample her cooking. He couldn't imagine her talent exceeding Anna's. But he could imagine Chloe in a sexy French maid uniform serving up something spicy.

Devlin blew out of the office needing immediate distraction. That or a good lay. If the Kelly twins intercepted him on his way out, this just might be their lucky day. Or his lucky day. Depending.

He made it outside without spying the identical sex fiends. Plan B. The library.

* * *

Chloe couldn't believe her miserable luck. Yes, the library was open late on Thursdays. And yes, the public venue had public Internet access, but both computers were reserved up until closing and there was no free Wi-Fi. Monica had failed to mention that part. Chloe had just assumed. Wasn't that a standard perk these days?

Frustrated, she'd packed up her laptop and stalked outside. All she wanted to do was check her e-mail. All evening she'd clung to the possibility that Ryan had written her a long sappy note explaining that he'd been a stupid bastard, going through a life crisis or something. That he didn't really love that Parisian tart. That he loved *her* and wouldn't she, please God, take him back, because he was miserable, *dying,* without her.

She wasn't sure how she'd react if he did write such a note or something even close. She was still hurt and angry. But at least it would be a valid excuse to leave Sugar Creek pronto: *I'm going to try to work things out with my fiancé.* Although Ryan had never proposed, he'd led her to believe it was only a matter of time. She was certain Daisy would accept that reason for her sudden resignation easier than *I don't trust myself with your grandson.*

Chloe rested her trendy tote on the old-fashioned bench near the library's main entrance, then whipped out her phone. Even though she'd gotten a horrible signal at Daisy's, maybe she'd fare better here. Even if she got two bars on her Android, it would be enough to check e-mail through her Yahoo app. She thumbed on power. "Seriously? Half a bar?" She walked to the left. Then moved a few steps to the right. She held her phone higher, walked the length of the library, then across a portion of manicured lawn. "Unbelievable."

"What are you doing?"

Oh no. It couldn't be. Her luck could not be that freaking awful. She'd hoped to make it three days at the very least without crossing paths again with Devlin Monroe. Their river encounter was scorched on her brain. Even a cold shower hadn't doused her steamy thoughts. And, for the first time in two years, a high-pressure showerhead had held no appeal.

She turned to face him, her stomach coiled tight with sexual tension. Even under the subtle glow of the gaslight-style street lamp, she could make out every delicious detail. He looked almost as sexy in his dry jeans and pullover crew as he did in his wet Dockers and unbuttoned oxford. *Almost.*

"Trying to get decent signal on my phone so I can check e-mail," she blurted, cheeks burning.

"There's Internet access inside."

"Computers are all booked up. All *two* of them. I brought my laptop but—"

"No Wi-Fi. Is it important?"

"Yes. No." She cleared her throat. "It'll wait."

He angled his head, studied her. "I make you nervous."

"Circumstances make me uncomfortable."

"How so?"

Was he kidding? Chloe shifted her weight. Glanced back to make sure no one had stolen her laptop. Although this was Sugar Creek, not Manhattan. Ten to one the crime rate was so low, people slept with their doors unlocked.

"Thought you'd be with Gram tonight. Given your vocation—"

"Not my thing." *Not right now.*

"Too provincial?"

"Sorry?"

"You'd be surprised by some of the complex recipes that have originated with Cupcake Lovers."

"I didn't mean—"

"I need to talk to you."

"Aren't we—"

"In private."

He grasped her elbow and before she knew it he'd guided her out of the glow of the street lamp to a shadowed area of a massive tree. Her skin burned beneath his touch. Her heart pounded with dread as the afternoon fiasco exploded in her mind. He was going to lecture her about her lack of good judgment. About putting an old woman at risk. About parading around in public half-naked. She was a disappointment. An embarrassment.

She was spitting mad.

She was sick and tired of men judging her and making her feel like a screwup just for being her.

"I need to get something off my chest, Chloe."

She hiked her chin. She'd show him. "Let me have it."

He backed her against the massive tree trunk . . . and kissed her!

Hard!

She didn't think. *Couldn't* think. She threw her arms around his neck and melted against his smokin' hot body. She kissed him back.

Hard.

Her brain shut down as sensations overwhelmed. Sizzling skin. Knotted stomach. Thumping heart. Quivering thighs. Full lips. Warm tongue.

Heaven.

Hell.

He broke away and she struggled to breathe. Her knees

threatened to buckle. She shored up against the tree as he hung back.

The silence, the distance, was sobering. She struggled to find her voice and wits. "That was—"

"Uncalled for."

She was going to say, *Amazing.*

"And unwise."

She felt even worse.

"I don't fraternize with employees."

Now she was mad. "I don't work for you."

"You work for my grandmother. Same thing."

"Not in my world."

"You're angry."

"Ya think?"

"Let's approach this as adults, Miss Madison."

"By all means, Mr. Monroe." She wanted to sock him. Hard.

"Something sparked between us in Oslow's and again at the river. We scratched the itch and now we can move on."

"*Waaay* past you," Chloe said.

"If you'd feel more comfortable moving back to New York—"

"I wouldn't dream of reneging on my agreement with Daisy." *Asshole.*

"Glad to hear it."

Liar. It occurred to Chloe that she made Devlin as uncomfortable as he made her. Just now that thought brought her incredible joy. Knowing Daisy expected him for a traditional family dinner, she plunged the knife deeper. "See you Sunday?" she asked as she brushed past him.

"See you Sunday."

Chloe stalked away, telling herself he wasn't worth ten to twenty in prison. Poisoning his food wouldn't do. But she could make it taste bad. Really, really bad.

NINE

"Holy shit. That was intense even for you."

Exhausted and muscles burning, Rocky went limp and fell against Adam Brody's gloriously sweaty, amazingly awesome, and naked body. "I didn't hurt you, did I?"

He laughed under his catchy breath. "Only in a good way." Heart thudding in his chest, he stroked a gentle hand down her tense back, a soothing gesture that should've been welcome but wasn't. "Want to talk about it?"

"What?"

"Whatever's got you all worked up."

She wasn't sure. Part of what bothered her was damn personal, revolving around love and relationships, marriage and babies. Hot topics tonight because of Monica's baby-making talk, Rocky's big brother's possible attraction to Chloe Madison, and the way her cousin Sam kept sneaking lovelorn looks at Rachel all through the damned meeting. (When the hell was he going to break down and ask her out?) Things Rocky yearned for—someday, only as time crept by she wasn't sure that day would ever come. She didn't talk about stuff like that with Adam. It went too deep, and they'd agreed to keep things light. They were friends. Friends who had sex.

Fuck buddies.

Two people who liked each other, who enjoyed hot sex, but without the messiness and drama of commitment.

She hated the urban moniker, but it sure did apply. She'd known Adam a long time. He'd been a classmate of Luke's. She used to think Adam was kind of geeky, but then he'd relocated to Alaska for a while and, when he'd moved home, he'd morphed into a buff hottie—ten years older and ten times more confident. A sports fanatic, he freelanced for various local resorts, instructing tourists on everything from skiing (water and snow), to horseback riding, to snowmobiling. He was outgoing and good hearted and sucked at maintaining serious relationships.

A perfect match for Rocky.

The perfect alternative to celibacy—as long as they kept their rendezvous secret.

"Still awake?" Adam asked.

"Just thinking." As good as he felt, she rolled off his body and stared up at her moonlit ceiling. "Oh, hell. Is that a crack?" *Great.* Something else she'd have to shell out money to fix.

"It's an old house, Rocky. Bound to shift and settle."

"It's a *really* old house. It should've settled a long time ago."

Adam reached over and turned on the bedroom lamp. Braced on his elbows, he squinted up at the source of Rocky's irritation. "Easily fixed with spackle, a putty knife, and sandpaper. I'll stop over tomorrow."

She shot him a look.

"Yeah, yeah. You're capable of handling it on your own, but look at it this way. . . ." He rolled on his side and playfully nipped her lower lip. "Gives me an excuse to be here in the middle of the day."

"Afternoon delight? The big, strong handyman and the helpless, horny innkeeper?"

He waggled his brows. "I'll let you play with my tool."

She rolled her eyes and smacked his shoulder. "I need a drink of water."

What she really needed was distance. Because her emotions were a little out of whack and because Adam was so damn nice, she really wanted to curl into his arms and cuddle. That would be bad. Either it would scare him off or . . . he'd expect it to become part of their routine and that would scare *her* off.

Not wanting to ruin a good thing, she pushed out of bed and tugged on lounging pants and a tee.

"Clothes on. Night over," Adam said matter-of-factly.

She trotted downstairs, trying not to feel guilty about kicking him out of bed so soon. Not that he ever slept over. It was one of their rules. Wherever they hooked up, they always parted before morning.

Rocky moved into her kitchen and, without flipping on the light, crossed to the fridge. She ignored the loud hum and the random clank. Maybe if she ignored it long enough it would go away. She could *not* afford a new refrigerator just now on top of everything else. Nerves taut in spite of just having great sex, she wrenched open the door and nabbed two beers. The least she could do was offer Adam a drink before sending him off.

"Fridge sounds funny."

"I know." She shut the door and turned to find him on the threshold buttoning his shirt. "Beer?"

"Sure." He relaxed against the doorjamb and took a deep pull off the longneck.

"Sorry if I'm a little bitchy tonight."

"No apology needed."

"So I am bitchy."

He just smiled.

"It's just . . ." She grappled for something she didn't mind sharing. "Things are a little tense just now and the one activity that always brings me joy is fast becoming a total stress factory."

"Talking about us? Or Cupcake Lovers?"

She almost laughed. "The latter, smart-ass."

"Glad to hear it."

"Tasha's making waves by putting too much emphasis on that damned recipe book."

"Thought everyone agreed it's a smart venture. All proceeds going to charity."

"That part's great. It's putting the book together that sucks. Tasha keeps harping on the fact that whatever recipes we include have to be extraspecial. Otherwise we won't get the interest we need or the notable sales to make a difference."

"Sounds reasonable."

Rocky glared.

"Just sayin'."

She took a swig of beer, then set aside the bottle. "We need forty to fifty recipes. Which shouldn't be a problem between our archives and the current members' input. Do you know how many we have after three weeks of suggestions?" She held up six fingers.

Adam raised a brow, sipped more beer.

"Pathetic, huh? All because Tasha keeps shooting them down for one or another reason. She even nixed Gram's latest submission. Called it too ordinary. Gram called her a pinhead, then let it drop."

"Don't you guys vote?"

"Tasha influences the vote. I'm telling you she could sell Speedos to an Eskimo."

Adam moved past her to set his bottle on the counter. "Sounds like someone needs to take Tasha down a peg."

"If you mean me, no can do. Not just now. She's playing the sympathy card."

"Her mom?"

"Mmm." She noted his tender expression and resisted the urge to move into his arms. She could sure use a hug. *What's wrong with you, Monroe?* "Everyone knows Tasha and I have been at odds since high school and everyone knows I was angling to be appointed as the new president of the club. If I don't handle this right, it'll just look like an old grudge or sour grapes."

"Or both."

"Also, if Dev convinces Dad to let him expand, he'll need the city council's approval. They're influenced by the mayor, who's influenced by—"

"His wife."

Rocky's oldest rival had married into her family's oldest rivals. The Monroes and Burkes had been at odds for eons.

Adam tugged at her messy braid. "You'll figure it out." Instead of kissing her good night, he swatted her butt. "Be back tomorrow to spackle your crack."

"Somehow that didn't sound right." In spite of her cruddy mood, Rocky grinned as he breezed out the back door. She polished off her beer, cursed the fridge, then headed back upstairs. She thought about Gram and the way she'd called Tasha a pinhead after the woman had nixed her recipe. She thought about Chloe Madison—gourmet chef, former food critic. "I wonder. . . ."

Did Chloe have the grit and wit to take down someone like Tasha?

Rocky nabbed her laptop and, sitting cross legged on her bed, Googled "Chloe Madison" and "Food Critic" and came up with a link for an e-zine called *Out and About New York*. She located Chloe's archived articles . . . and read.

TEN

Considering the intensity of the "river" incident and the "kissing" incident, Chloe was surprised and impressed with her ability to stifle thoughts of Devlin Monroe (mostly) for (almost) forty-eight hours. Whenever he popped into her brain, she asked herself if she really wanted to waste one second of her life obsessing on a controlling, infuriating man.

No, she did not.

She used that same tactic to vanquish thoughts of Ryan, replacing "man" with "cheating bastard."

It also helped that she kept busy, spending a large portion of her time getting to know Sugar Creek. The streets. The businesses. The people. Since she'd be doing so much shopping at Oslow's General Store, she'd made a point of meeting the owner, Vince Redding, and his son Marvin, who referred to himself as the store's lifelong manager, since his dad, who had to be in his early seventies, refused to retire.

"Doin' what I love keeps me young," Vince had said with a crooked smile.

Chloe couldn't be sure, but she thought the amiable old guy had tender feelings for Daisy. He'd been a little too relieved when Chloe had mentioned she was working as the woman's new companion.

"About time someone took Daisy under their wing. She hasn't been the same since—" He bit off his words, looked away, and scratched his snowy beard. "It's good she's not alone."

He'd piqued Chloe's interest big-time. The same since what? Her husband's death? The snowmobile catastrophe Chloe had heard so much about?

Near as Chloe could tell, Daisy was loved and revered by her family and if she said the word, any one of them would take her in or under their wing. All the more reason Vince's statement struck Chloe as strange.

Also, Daisy had assured Chloe she wasn't lonely, saying a day rarely passed without a visit or phone call from one of her kin. Sure enough, between Friday and Saturday Daisy received calls from her sister Rose, her brother-in-law Spike, and her friend Ethel Larsen. And that's not counting other calls initiated by Daisy.

Devlin's siblings, Rocky and Luke, had dropped by as well as his cousins, Nash Bentley (a charter pilot) and Sam McCloud (a master furniture maker). After the initial introductions, Chloe had excused herself, not wanting to intrude on "family time" even though they'd been eager for her to stay and chat. Although they'd all seemed genuinely warm and friendly (unlike Devlin), she'd felt awkward (because of Devlin). So each time she'd begged off, saying she was up to her neck reorganizing Daisy's kitchen and shopping and planning meals. Oh, and the Cadillac had needed an oil change, too. All true.

Chloe's goal was to minimize Daisy's chances of a mishap. Reorganizing her shelves and pantry, so that she didn't have to use a step stool to get to the things she needed most, seemed like a no-brainer. Keeping her old car in top-notch condition so that it didn't break down on one of the many "scenic" drives she had planned seemed proactive. One thing was certain: Daisy, as Monica had pointed out, was a pip and had a mind of her own. Even though the woman had promised her family she'd rely on Chloe to do the cooking and driving, that didn't mean Daisy wouldn't "bend" that promise when she saw fit.

Chloe swished pink gloss over her lips, the finishing touch to her subtly applied makeup, while her mind continued to wander. She'd met a lot of eccentric people in her vast and colorful circles, but no one quite compared to Daisy. Though she maintained a chipper persona, Chloe sensed a stifled touch of sadness. Or anxiety. She couldn't be sure. Then again, she'd known the woman less than a week.

A rap on the door jerked Chloe out of her musings. "You ready, kitten?"

"Just a sec!"

Chloe moved across her new bedroom, a lovely room decorated in varying shades of yellow and red. The custommade furnishings, featuring hand-painted floral arrangements, intricate scrolls, and dainty birds, were stunning. She'd been shocked to learn the elegant furniture had been made by Devlin's cousin Sam. Not so much that he'd mastered woodworking but that he'd painted such delicate scenes. A rugged man of few words, he hadn't struck her as the artistic type. Learning he belonged to Cupcake Lovers was a double whammy. If Daisy hadn't told her he was a widower and the father of two, she would've jumped to an obvious assumption.

Focusing on the moment, she cracked open the door and smiled at her boss. "Wow. Gloves and everything." *Everything* included a pink pillbox hat that matched her two-inch patent-leather pumps, and short-sleeved silk shantung A-line-style dress. Chloe had studied fashion design for six months, and that part of her brain revved as she assessed Daisy's retro ensemble. Nineteen-sixties. A cross between Jackie Kennedy and Audrey Hepburn. Trendy chic.

"My Sunday-go-to-meeting clothes." Daisy sniffed and tugged at the ruffled hems of her dainty gloves. "One old habit I've yet to shake."

She sounded downright miserable, yet Chloe thought she looked fantastic. "Why shed perfection?"

"Keep saying nice things like that and I might start feeling bad about talking you into accompanying me to church."

"I don't mind."

"I don't believe you, but I'm not going to let you off the hook. I'd appreciate your company."

"I'll be down in five minutes."

"I'll be waiting in the car."

She spun away and Chloe held her breath listening to those high heels clattering down the stairs. "Please don't trip or fall." Not that Daisy was sickly or fragile, but when her mind wandered, and it did that a lot, mishaps occurred. Last night while helping Chloe clear the dinner table (and pondering a radical change in hair color) Daisy had put the sugar bowl in the fridge and the leftover roasted asparagus in the pantry. Earlier that day, she'd nearly pruned her rosebushes to death while having an imaginary bitch fest with Tasha-the-Pinhead Burke, a woman Chloe had no interest in meeting anytime soon for fear of giving her an earful. She'd called Daisy's recipe ordinary. Honestly? Chloe had thought the apple brandy drizzle inspired.

Not hearing any shrieks or thuds, she assumed her boss had descended safely. Chloe scrambled to her dresser, desperate to spruce up her daffodil-yellow shift. She pulled on a three-quarters-sleeved black cashmere shrug and accentuated it with a lime-green flower pin, then swept her hair off her face with a matching lime-green headband. Last, she traded her ballet flats for black pointy-toed pumps. She studied her reflection in a full-length mirror and declared herself more Sunday-go-to-meeting suitable.

Still . . . her stomach fluttered with dread. She hadn't been to church in a long time. She wasn't all that crazy about attending now. It conjured memories of her mom and dad and the way things used to be. Sunday had always been their special day. Family day. Church. Dinner. Snacking on bowls of buttered popcorn while watching their favorite TV shows.

Chloe used to love Sundays. But then her mom had died and everything, *everything*, had changed.

Squashing down morbid thoughts, Chloe hurried downstairs. When she reached the garage, Daisy was sitting in the driver's seat.

Crap.

Rolling back her shoulders, Chloe opened the driver's door and jerked her thumb. "You know the deal, Daisy."

The old woman bolstered her own shoulders. "Deal, schmeal."

"You cannot drive to church," Chloe said reasonably. "You told me yourself a good portion of your friends and family attend. If you drive and anyone sees you . . ." She narrowed her eyes. "Do you *want* me to get grief?"

"We're not going to church."

"We're not?" She nearly wilted with relief. "Then where are we going?"

"A Sunday drive," Daisy said with a smile. "Usually I save that for after. But I've decided to buck tradition."

"What about Sunday dinner?"

"Keeping that part." She arched an already comically arched penciled brow. "You okay with that, kitten?"

"Sure." She could handle a couple of hours of Devlin's company. That's if he even showed. "But I'm not okay with you driving."

"I'll make you a deal. I'll relinquish the wheel, if you promise to let me drive once we're out of town."

Chloe raised a brow. "You'll have to do better than that."

"Give me fifteen minutes. Open stretch of road. No potholes. No sharp curves."

"Sounds . . . uneventful. What do you get out of it?"

"Fifteen minutes of being in control."

"What do I get out of it?"

"Fifteen minutes of bliss."

"Not sure what that means."

"You'll have to take a leap of faith. Or . . . we can go to church."

The woman was shrewd. Chloe blew out a breath. "Slide over."

Daisy shimmied to the passenger side, then, as Chloe

took the driver's seat, pointed the remote at the garage door. The door swung open with a slow grind, allowing sunshine to spill in and over the Caddy. "See there," Daisy said. "Beautiful day for a drive."

No argument there. Clear blue skies. Mild temp and lots of sunshine. "Won't your family worry when you don't show for church?"

Daisy opened her pink and white handbag and pulled out a cell phone designed for seniors—big numbers, big buttons. She speed-dialed and a heartbeat later she smiled. "Yes, Rocky, dear, it's me. . . . No, nothing's wrong. It's just . . . it's Chloe's first Sunday and she's feeling jittery about dinner. We're driving to Pixley. Oslow's didn't have the fresh herbs she needed for the . . ." She looked to Chloe.

"Cornish hens."

"For the Cornish hens. . . . Mmm. Yes. I know. Well, she did study culinary arts. . . . Sure thing, sweet pea. See you then." She snapped shut her phone and looked at Chloe. "Happy now?"

"That your granddaughter thinks I'm some sort of anal herb freak? Delirious." She keyed the ignition and, after gripping air where the gearshift *should* have been, maneuvered the shift on the steering column and stepped on the gas. "Wish I wouldn't have traded my flats for heels."

"If they're a hindrance, kick 'em off."

"Drive barefoot? I think that's against the law."

"Law, schmaw."

Chloe pushed on her sunglasses before rolling her eyes. "Where am I headed?" she asked as she pulled out of the garage.

"Same route we took out of town to get to the river. Only when we get to that fork in the road, veer right instead of left." She donned her own sunglasses, the big black classic Jackie O shades. "I've been watching you the past couple of days."

"Oh?"

"You're wound tight, kitten."

"Something I've never been accused of." People typically

referred to her as carefree. Reckless even. Depending on who you asked. Although, granted, she hadn't been the same since Ryan's betrayal. Maybe even before.

"I'm thinking you need a boyfriend."

"I had a boyfriend."

"Was he a rat?"

"A cheating rat."

"Then you're better off without him." She patted Chloe's arm with her gloved hand. "Don't worry. We'll get you a new one."

"I don't want a new one."

"What about Sam?"

"I'm sure he's a very nice man, but—"

"He has eyes for Rachel."

"Well, then—"

"And Luke." Daisy sighed. "Luke has eyes for every woman over eighteen and under forty. I love that boy, but he's a Casanova. He won't do at all."

"I'm really not interested—"

"Of course, Devlin—"

"No!" Chloe's body burned with the memory of his four-alarm kiss. "I mean, no, thank you. I'm really not interested in dating right now."

"Still pining for the rat?"

"No. Yes. I mean . . . It's only been a week. I'm just . . . confused."

"And frustrated."

She squeezed the steering wheel, imagining Ryan's neck. He'd landed her here. In this . . . moody funk. In this freaking antique car with the ill-placed gearshift and impossibly stiff brake pedal. She sweated bullets every time she had to slow or stop. "Definitely frustrated."

"What about a sex toy?"

Chloe nearly clipped a mailbox as she turned onto Main Street. *"What?"*

"I had a vibrator once. Had two speeds. *Oh, My* and *Oh, God.* Big Al, I called it. Seemed more subtle than Big Dick."

"For the love of—"

"If you don't have one, I know a place—"

"Could we not talk about this?"

Daisy shot her a look over the rims of her big shades. "I thought you said you weren't a prude."

"I'm not. But you're . . ." *Someone's grandma.* "Jackie-freaking-Kennedy."

She narrowed her eyes. "Is that your way of saying I look antiquated or sophisticated?"

Chloe smiled. "*Très* Retro Chic."

"*Merci.*" Daisy smiled back, then, after easing back in her seat, adjusted her pillbox hat. "I can't imagine talking about sex toys with Jackie either."

"Maybe we shouldn't talk at all for a while." She fumbled with the old-fashioned knob on the radio, trying to dial in a strong station. "Maybe we should crank up some music. Set a tone for our Sunday drive." She stopped when she got to an easy-listening station. Barry Manilow? Oh, well. At least he was mellow. Mellow music for a mellow drive.

Daisy shook her head. "You're worse off than I thought."

Several minutes and five disgustingly sappy songs later, Daisy said, "Pull over."

"Here?"

"Here."

Chloe pulled onto the shoulder of the two-lane concrete highway. No potholes. No sharp curves. As far as she could see. Just open road yawning toward beautiful mountains and endless trees—their random colorful foliage bursting with the first hints of fall. She got out and, as agreed, traded places with Daisy, who, after popping a couple of latches, started retracting the convertible's roof. Chloe lent a hand, following the other woman's lead, since she had no clue as to how to "pop the top." "Hope it doesn't start raining."

"Or hailing," Daisy quipped in a tone that made Chloe feel like an uptight worrywart.

A few minutes later the roof was folded away and se-cured. Daisy kicked off her heels and threw them in the backseat. Sliding behind the wheel, she adjusted the pillow beneath her butt, buckled her seat belt, and dialed the radio to a rock station. She cranked the volume and yelled, "Fasten your seat belt!"

Oh no. Oh, God.

Daisy floored the Cadillac and Chloe held her breath. *Please don't let me die.* No potholes. No hairpin turns. But the passing landscape blurred. Her loose hair whipped fast and furious about her face as they raced along the open highway. Buckled in, she couldn't lean far enough over to see the speedometer, but they had to be going . . . seventy? With the top down.

"Feel the wind, the sun, the surge of adrenaline!" Daisy yelled.

She felt it. How could she not? Senses reeling, Chloe glanced over at the silver-haired hellion behind the wheel. "How in the world is your hat still on your head?"

"Hairpins!"

Naturally.

Chloe busted out laughing. She threw her head back and reveled in the perfect fall day and the rush of adrenaline.

"Just like Thelma and Louise!" Daisy shouted as she deftly steered the Caddy around a wide curve.

Chloe's heart pounded. "Except for the driving off the cliff part, right?"

"Pa-leeze. I've got a lot of living to do!"

Something clicked inside Chloe's heart and mind. Something that had once burned bright but had been snuffed and contained for several months.

The desire to live in the moment.

Inspired by Daisy and a burst of spontaneity, Chloe toed off her heels and unbuckled her seat belt. Pulse racing, she maneuvered herself to her knees and gripped the edges of the windshield with all her might, her face taking the full force of the wind. Fear and excitement pulsed through her veins, making her giddy. She felt like Rose in *Titanic,* dangerously perched at the tip of the ship, soaring, only without stretching her arms wide. The rock music blared and her injured heart sang. She closed her eyes and screamed, "Woo-hooooooo!"

Almost in tandem with the *woot-woot* of a police siren.

ELEVEN

Devlin had spent the past two days meeting with the store's employees who planned to jump ship. He'd asked point-blank what it would take to keep them on board; then he'd listed those needs in a succinct report to his dad. Presently, they weren't in a position to match the perks of a chain supercenter, but they could be. *If* the old man gave up his old ways, which entailed taking some financial leaps.

While waiting yet again to hear back on yet another report, Devlin tempered his frustrations by studying materials he'd checked out of the library the day before. Luke had been dead-on about the wealth of historical material stored in the archives, and Monica had pointed out the few books available for circulation.

Devlin had found the local research fascinating, taking special interest in the Monroes' contribution to the town's growth. His dad had always preached about the family's role in developing Sugar Creek, but it had always come across as arrogant and exaggerated. The Burkes had also played a central role. The two families had been at odds for decades, and now Randall Burke, Devlin's dad's contemporary and long-time foe, was the town mayor. Devlin suspected the election had nudged his dad into relocating to Florida for the better part of the year. It was that or suffer a heart attack. He got *that* worked up about Randall and his sudden seat of power.

Devlin on the other hand had always practiced discretion where Randall was concerned. Considering Devlin's multiple business interests and his plans to expand J.T.'s, it wasn't wise to alienate someone who could stonewall his efforts. Even before he'd been elected mayor, Randall, a former practicing attorney and member of the town council, had been a powerful force in Sugar Creek. So, unlike his dad, Devlin had taken a diplomatic approach whenever dealing with the man. Given Devlin's new plans for the store and the fact that he'd have to get approval from the town council, he was glad to be on decent terms with the mayor. The less hassle the better, especially since Devlin still had to win over his dad.

Devlin had been consulting old photos and revising the floor plans when he'd gotten the call from Sheriff Stone. Gram and her, companion, Chloe Madison, had been hauled in for various traffic violations and, most troubling, assault.

What the hell?

Devlin blamed Chloe. Even though Gram was the one facing charges, Chloe was the one with the criminal history. Fuming, he dropped everything and raced over to the police station, an innocuous building flanked by the vintage firehouse and library. As he pushed though the station's front doors he wasn't sure what fueled his anger more: that Gram was in jail or that she'd assaulted a law officer. After five minutes with Stone, a man Devlin knew on friendly terms but didn't consider a friend, he was still undecided.

"I realize Daisy's getting up there in years, Dev, and I'm willing to overlook her eccentric behavior and a minor infraction here and there, but I can't tolerate her striking an officer of the law."

"Nor should you." Devlin sat in the sheriff's office, trying to make sense of his grandma's latest debacle. He couldn't. She wasn't a violent person. Not even on her most irrational days. "She must have had a reason—"

"*Thought* she had a reason," Stone interrupted. "That's why I contacted you instead of granting Daisy's demand to phone her attorney. I don't want this to mushroom. I want it to go away."

Devlin felt as though he was missing something. "Want *what* to go away?"

"Daisy's misassumption that Deputy Burke got *fresh* with Miss Madison when in fact he was just doing his job." He held up a hand, warding off questions. "Since I'm not acquainted with Miss Madison or her character, I'm not sure if she's a prig who overreacted to a routine frisk or a player who decided to manipulate the situation to weasel herself out of trouble. One thing I do know: Billy Burke is a decent married man, an upstanding citizen, and a respected law official."

He was also the number two son of the town mayor. Of all the police officers for Gram to bean with her purse. The son of the freaking mayor. The son of her son's rival. Devlin knew Billy, and he knew Stone. Billy had a roving eye. Stone had his nose up the mayor's ass. As for Chloe, she'd studied acting. She'd dodged a criminal record. Devlin still didn't know the details, but a few scenarios played out in his mind. None of them good.

"Why was it necessary for Deputy Burke to frisk Miss Madison?"

"He had reason to believe she was intoxicated. When she got belligerent he took precautions. If anyone was out of line it was your grandma and Miss Madison. Speeding, seat belt violation, reckless endangerment, assault—"

"Were charges filed?" Devlin asked. "Do I need to post bail?"

"So far everything's off-the-record. Can we keep it that way?"

Meaning could he count on Devlin to silence Gram's so-called false accusation? "I'll make things right."

"Then the ladies are free to go."

"I appreciate your flexibility and consideration." Devlin stood, initiating the end of the discussion. The longer he sat here, the more he wanted Daisy and Chloe out of here. He wanted the women's take on what had happened, but in private. His objective was to avoid pressing Stone's buttons and risking a legal hassle for Gram. Accusing someone of sexual misconduct was a serious matter. Accusing a Burke complicated matters to the extreme. One thing Devlin knew for certain: If Billy *had* stepped over the line, Stone would cover his tracks. In which case Devlin would be forced to handle the offense privately. Off-the-record—mano a mano. It wouldn't be the first time he'd knocked heads with Billy over a woman.

When Gram and Chloe were released into Devlin's care, he greeted them with a disappointed glare. "Later." Just as he'd hoped, he shamed them speechless, although on the way out Gram did shoot Stone a furious look.

Deputy Burke was conspicuously absent.

Seeing the women decked out in dresses and heels, Devlin had a hard time imagining them speeding along the highway on a reckless joyride. Although Chloe's windblown hair proved they'd been driving with the top down.

His balls tightened as his mind took a prurient turn. Tousled and flushed, she looked like she'd just had sex. As if conscious of his thoughts, she twisted the long tangles into a loose bun. It didn't help. She still looked sexy as hell. Maybe it was the dress. Just tight enough to hint at her compact curves. Just short enough to accentuate her toned legs. Or maybe it was stiletto heels. Just an inch shy of Fuck-Me Pumps. He could easily imagine Billy having sinful thoughts. Hell, *he* was rolling in them. But if the deputy had touched her inappropriately, he'd kick the man's ass. Abusing his position to take advantage of *any* woman was reprehensible.

"What about my car?" Gram groused as Devlin ushered the women into his Escalade.

"I'll send Luke for it." He handed Gram up into the front passenger seat, then moved to help Chloe. The minute he grasped her arm, he relived their brief but torrid kiss in vivid detail. The feel of her lips, her tongue, her hands. Her taste. Her scent.

Christ.

He'd purposely avoided Chloe all weekend, furious with himself for losing control. Some warped part of him had thought if he kissed her, if he unleashed the lust he'd stored up since crashing into her at Oslow's, he'd get her out of his system. *Right.* Instead of slapping him, she'd responded with equal passion. Instead of falling flat or satisfying his hunger, the red-hot union had only stoked his desire.

Given their abrupt parting that night, he expected Chloe to shrug off his touch as he helped her into the backseat. She didn't. But she didn't make eye contact either. He could hear her wheels turning but couldn't guess her thoughts. It made him insane.

Evasive or embarrassed? Instigator or victim?

Once behind the wheel, he took back control of his renegade lust. "I have some questions."

"You're actually interested in our version?" Chloe asked from behind.

He couldn't tell if she was being sarcastic or if she was genuinely shocked. Either way, her reaction chafed. "I'm interested in the truth."

"Sheriff Stone's a brownnosing skunk," Gram said. "As for Billy Burke—"

"What do you want to know?" Chloe asked.

Devlin pulled out of the parking lot and headed for Daisy's house. He told himself to keep an open mind. To focus on the road and not the appealing reflection of Chloe in his rearview mirror. "Did you let Gram drive?"

"I did."

"I tricked her into it," Gram said.

"I'm not that gullible," she said. "Next question?"

"Were you speeding, Gram?"

"Heck if I know."

"Probably," Chloe said.

He glanced over his shoulder. " 'Did you unfasten your seat belt and—"

"I did. I know it was dangerous, but it just happened. A spontaneous act of . . ."

"Derring-do," Gram said. "That's what Errol Flynn would call it."

"What's Errol Flynn got to do with this?" Devlin asked.

"He had a sense of adventure. Like Chloe and me." She adjusted her pink hat and sniffed. "You only live once."

"I wish I could say I'm sorry," Chloe said, "but I'm not."

He let that one go and cut to the chase. "Was Deputy Burke out of line?"

Gram slapped a gloved hand to her thigh. "He accused Chloe of being under the influence! Why else would she pull such a crazy stunt, he said. He made her walk a straight line. Which she did. Twice! He just wanted to stare at her butt."

"Daisy."

"You know I'm right, kitten. *Then* when she had the gumption to refuse to jump through more hoops, Billy accused her of being contrary and ordered her to place both hands on the hood of the car. Said he didn't know her, didn't trust her, and that he'd have to frisk her. It was just an excuse to feel her up!"

"For the love of—" Chloe sighed. "It wasn't *that* obscene."

Devlin clenched his jaw. *"Was* his touch inappropriate?"

"I've never been frisked, but I don't think his hands were supposed to brush up my thighs, *under* my skirt. I cursed and jerked away."

"That's when I belted him with my handbag," Gram said, looking enormously proud.

Devlin glanced in the rearview mirror and locked gazes with the woman who'd either suffered injustice or feigned it. Asking her out-and-out if she'd manipulated the situation would only earn him a slap from Gram. God knew how Chloe would respond. Instead, he gave her the benefit of the doubt. "Could you have misjudged Burke's intention?"

"Are you calling me a liar?"

"I'm asking if it's possible that you were rattled because you'd been pulled over and accused of being intoxicated. I'm asking if, under pressure, it's possible you overreacted to the frisk?"

"Stop badgering her," Gram said.

"Wanna go head-to-head with the Burkes?" he asked. "With the law? Better be damn clear on the facts."

"It's a fair question," Chloe said, red faced. She looked out the window, then after a tense minute sighed. "I don't think I misjudged, but . . . I can't be sure. Between the thrill of the ride and the shock of being busted, I was unnerved."

More acting? Another ploy? It griped the hell out of him that he couldn't read this woman.

"Well, *I* wasn't unnerved," Gram snapped. "I know what these old eyes saw."

"I need you to let me handle this, Gram."

"Of course you do."

"Do you want the Burkes to make your life miserable?"

Chloe reached forward and squeezed his grandma's shoulder. "Let it go, Daisy. I overreacted."

She snorted. "I still think Billy's a jerk."

"No argument there." He'd never liked the guy, and not just because he was a Burke. "But unfortunately you're not guilt free in this matter. Speeding. Assault. Goddammit, Gram."

"Don't you cuss at me, Devlin Monroe. And *don't* tell me how to live."

"I'm not . . . Forget it." He'd said enough. At least to his grandma. He glanced back at Chloe—arms crossed, eyes narrowed, lips compressed. For once, her mind-set was clear. She was pissed.

Tough shit. So was he.

He pulled into Gram's driveway, rounded the car, and handed her out. "I need a private moment with Chloe," he whispered into her ear.

"It wasn't her fault," she whispered back, poking him in the chest for emphasis.

"Noted."

She peeked around him and smiled at Chloe. "See you inside, kitten." After another indignant poke at Devlin, Gram tottered toward the house in her pink heels.

"Didn't want to read me the riot act in front of her, huh?" Smirking, Chloe stepped onto the SUV's running board in those sexy heels.

This time when he tried to help her down, she dodged his touch. He waited until she stepped semi-gracefully to the ground—trying not to stare at her shapely legs—before unleashing his frustration. "What were you thinking? You're supposed to chauffeur Gram, not the other way around."

"I—"

"And that *derring-do* stunt you pulled. What if Gram had swerved or slammed on the brakes? If you have no regard for your own safety, think how she would've felt if you'd been hurt."

"Message received. Are we done here? I have a dinner to prepare."

No apology. No excuses. Just damned evasion. "Because of you," he barreled on, needing to cement his point, "my grandmother, a seventy-five-year-old upstanding citizen with suddenly questionable judgment, was *arrested*."

"Not formally. Charges were dropped."

"They always are where you're concerned. How do you swing that, Miss Monroe? Oh, wait. By crying foul. In this case, sexual misconduct."

If looks could kill, he'd be six feet under. He waited for her to ask how he knew there'd been other arrests. Waited for her to plead innocence and spew some hard-luck story. Waited for her to lose her tightly controlled temper, to make a scene. Something overdramatic. Something worthy of an ex-actress, ex-publicist, ex–party girl (among a dozen other things)—a woman who manipulated men and situations via tears or seduction or some other calculated measure. Jayce's report burned in his brain, and the sheriff's suggestion that Chloe had lied in order to weasel out of trouble had burrowed under his skin.

Instead of ranting or bursting into tears, she crossed her arms and regarded him with quiet scorn. "Monica was wrong about you," she said in a low, steady voice. "You don't have a stick up your ass. You have a whole tree jammed up there."

He blinked.

"For your information, I didn't *cry foul*. I know when I'm being groped."

"But you said—"

"I wanted Daisy to let it go, you obtuse . . . jackass. When we were sitting in the jail cell, she told me how Deputy Burke's related to the mayor. Mentioned there's bad blood between the Burkes and Monroes. Then you said the Burkes would make her life miserable. I don't want to risk that, especially when I can't prove anything. A cop's word against mine. I certainly know who Sheriff Stone believed."

Devlin's already-burning temper flared. Billy *groped* her?

"As for my former arrests," she plowed on, "I assume you learned about them from Sheriff Stone, although I don't know how *he* learned about them, since my record was . . . I thought . . . whatever. It doesn't matter. Obviously he chose to think the worst in spite of the facts."

"Those facts being—"

"None of your business."

He moved in, backing her against the Escalade, torn between shaking her and kissing her. Both urges sparked by her fiery defiance. "You're living with and supposedly taking care of my grandmother. Everything you do, everything you've done, that may adversely affect her is *my* business."

She jutted out her chin, taking him on. "I don't answer to you. I don't answer to any man."

"No," he said, caging her between his arms and leaning in, "I suspect they usually answer to you." He thought about the rich daddy who'd supported her irresponsible lifestyle, then the sugar daddy who'd put her through culinary school. He imagined her working her charms, wrapping them around her dainty fingers. Did she always use the same ploy or switch it up? How did she plan to win him over?

He was so close he could smell her shampoo and the light scent of jasmine perfume wafting from her dewy skin. He could see the green flecks in her wide brown eyes, and the rapid pulse at the base of her throat. When her delectable mouth turned up into a coquettish grin, he thought he knew her weapon of choice. Manipulation by flirtation.

She leaned in and he braced himself for the brush of her lips. "If you treasure your nuts, Sausage Boy, you'll back off. Literally."

Not what he'd expected. Easing away, he regarded her with curiosity. "What happened to the sweet, flustered girl who voiced concern about my eating habits?"

"What happened to the charming gentleman who tried to put me at ease with a smile?"

Touché.

Raw sexual energy pulsed between them as they stared each other down. Conflicting emotions charged the air. Frustration. Temptation. Anger.

"Your attempt to physically intimidate me is as insulting as Deputy Burke's unwanted attentions."

The verbal slap struck hard. She was right. *Fuck.* He started to apologize, but she plowed right over him.

"I know you're worried about Daisy. I am, too. You're right. She's reckless and forgetful. I'm trying to process the best way to handle that without making her feel like I'm taking control. Question her every impulse and decision, squash her passionate spirit, and she'll eventually lose her sense of self."

The fire and vulnerability in those beautiful eyes pricked his curiosity and conscience. *Two sides to every coin,* he heard Rocky say. "That last part sounded personal. Speaking from experience?"

She glanced away. "Let's just say Daisy and I have a lot in common."

"So I should worry about you, too?"

She snorted. "Right. You don't even like me. Which blows my mind, since you don't even *know* me."

He knew enough to make him wary, thanks to Jayce. Plus he couldn't get a clear read on her. Shy or feisty? Manipulative or misunderstood?

"I have enough going on in my life without obsessing on what went screwy between our first run-in at Oslow's and our second at the Sugar Shack. Our relationship, for lack of a better word, has been on the downslide ever since."

As if that were solely his fault. Increasingly uncomfortable with being declared an intimidating jackass where this woman was concerned, he defended his actions. "Excuse me for not showering you with praise and flowers for putting Daisy in jeopardy. *Twice*."

"Some people would see the humor in those situations."

"Some people would own up to their irresponsible actions."

"I'll just chalk it up to your overprotective nature where family's concerned. Which should be charming. But isn't." With that she brushed past him. "See you for Sunday dinner?"

"Wouldn't miss it."

As she stalked toward the house, Devlin watched, questioning his sanity as he envisioned those shapely legs locked around him, in bed. He'd never been so hot for a woman in his life. Chloe Madsion rattled the foundation of his stable world, tangled his emotions, messed with his family, invited trouble and chaos, and all he could think was, *Bring it on*.

TWELVE

Chloe mentally blasted Devlin the moment she stormed into Daisy's house. It was that or scream. That or smash something. He was the most infuriating man Chloe had ever had the misfortune of meeting, and all she could think about was rolling around in bed with him for a day or three.

Naked.

Every time he touched her, she relived that torrid *uncalled-for, unwise* kiss. His lips. His tongue. His hands. No doubt he excelled at lovemaking the way he excelled at business deals. She groaned, thinking about all that ego, power, competence, and charm (something he doled out with an eye-dropper) focused on giving her the ultimate orgasm. Devlin Monroe—controlling overachiever.

"You okay, kitten?" Daisy popped out from behind a set of heavy floral drapes. Clearly she'd been spying and, from her casual demeanor, felt no remorse.

Chloe, on the other hand, was mortified. Not because Daisy had witnessed the heated showdown, but because Chloe had just been imagining the woman's grandson as a sexual paragon. "I've been better."

"I blame my son."

"For what?"

"For making Devlin grow up too fast. Too much responsibility, too soon. Too much emphasis on the family legacy.

Too much pressure to be the smart one, the responsible one. The price for being a firstborn."

Even though Daisy had issues with her grandson, apparently she still felt compelled to defend him. Sweet. Not that it softened Chloe's present opinion of the man: *bossy, judgmental bastard.*

"Although, truth told, Jerome took his cue from Jessup." Daisy's husband.

"I feel like a cocktail," the woman said a little too brightly. "Join me?"

Chloe's brain hurt. Daisy had the habit of changing topics mid-conversation. Devlin exhibited hostility one moment and concern in the next. She needed a break from the both of them. "Maybe later," she said with a weary smile. "I need to change into something more casual. Time to start dinner. There's a lot to do and—"

"I'll help!" The old woman's face lit up as she kicked off her heels and padded toward the kitchen barefoot. "Just tell me what to do."

Chloe smothered a beleaguered sigh and hoped Daisy didn't detect sarcasm when she mumbled, "*Great.*"

* * *

Barring Daisy from her own kitchen had felt incredibly rude, but it was the only way Chloe could prepare dinner. The woman kept rearranging the countertop, lining up ingredients and hauling out cookery in a way that defied logic—or at least Chloe's personal routine. Daisy's nonstop chatter was distracting, and Chloe was nervous. Yes, she'd already cooked two days' worth of meals for her boss and yes, Daisy had applauded her efforts. But this was different. This was dinner for eight. Though Daisy had assured her it was a casual affair, Chloe assumed the guests would be expecting something extraordinary.

According to Monica, Rocky had told everyone in Cupcake Lovers that Chloe was a gourmet chef. It was not a title she felt comfortable with. Gourmet chefs specialized in fine, often foreign, cuisine and typically worked in upscale establishments. This was her first job as a professional cook and she was still honing her skills, yet this was a small town and word spread like wildfire. Rocky's moniker stuck. Even though Chloe had corrected Vince Redding twice, he kept referring to her as a gourmet chef, saying he hoped Oslow's stock was up to snuff. She'd assured him his small store met all of her needs and hoped he didn't hear about her phantom trip to Pixley to purchase special herbs. The last thing she wanted was to insult Sugar Creek's sole grocer.

Nor did she want to disappoint Daisy's family.

Hence booting the woman out of the kitchen so she could concentrate on the meal. Nothing too fancy, but she hoped something that assured everyone she was—at the very least—deserving of the title *personal* chef. She especially wanted to impress Devlin. He'd made it clear he considered her a screwup. She wanted to prove she was capable of attending Daisy's needs. That she was capable, period. Not just to him, but to the whole damned universe, including herself. She blamed Ryan and her dad for her unwelcome issues with self-confidence. She cursed Devlin for meddling in her attempt to reclaim her identity.

She'd show them.

She'd excel at cooking and become the best damn, most reliable "companion" on the planet!

Another reason for throwing herself into the fine art of cooking was to forget the embarrassment of being thrown into jail. For Daisy's sake, Chloe had chosen to bury the frisking incident, but that didn't mean she wouldn't have her say with Deputy Burke. In private. At some point. She'd suffered frustration and humiliation the other two times she'd been hauled in by the law, but this was different. This time she'd been personally violated. Burke's fingers had actually brushed her inner thighs, something she'd kept to herself, because at the time she'd been too stunned (*Did he just . . . ?*) then embarrassed (*He did!*). She'd known by the smirk on his weasel face, the cocky glint in his squinty eyes, that no one would believe her. As she'd told Devlin, she had no proof.

Daisy, who'd been standing on the other side of the car, hadn't even witnessed the violation, just Chloe's reaction.

She'd been hurt by Devlin's suggestion that she'd somehow overreacted or misjudged the situation. Then she'd gotten angry. Did he think she was an idiot? Or that she'd somehow *asked for it*? Why did he think the worst? Sure, her former arrests were a stigma, but he'd been pissy with her long before today. Calling him names and threatening his family jewels probably hadn't been the best way to elevate his opinion of her, but dammit, the man pushed her buttons! Instead of suppressing her anger, like she used to do with Ryan (something she didn't want to contemplate just now), she'd stood up to Devlin, spoken her mind and stuck to her guns. He didn't want her working for his grandma. He didn't want her in Sugar Creek at all. Well, too damn bad. She was exactly where she wanted to be.

For now.

Pulling that derring-do stunt earlier today might have been reckless and crazy, but it had unleashed her repressed adventurous spirit. It had made her question her choices and actions over the past two years.

"Who are you, Chloe Madison? Really? And what are you doing with your life?"

Culinary school hadn't been a mistake, but she hadn't felt that "click" either. And if she was brutally honest with herself, she hadn't "clicked" with Ryan either. But she'd wanted to. So much so, she'd relinquished a part of her soul. Examining the reasons now was too painful. She was too raw. Too unstable. The only thing she knew for certain, this moment, was that she'd been afforded a new opportunity. Instead of looking at her time in Sugar Creek as a time to heal, as Monica had suggested, Chloe would take an aggressive approach, embark on journey of self-discovery. She'd live in the moment and embrace the adventure. She'd stop worrying about living up to anyone's expectations except her own. As soon as she figured out what they were.

"I declare this *the season of me!*"

Water splashed her shirtfront and she realized suddenly

that instead of rinsing a Cornish hen, she'd almost scrubbed off its skin. *Oops.* Sighing, she placed the poor bird alongside the others and vigorously washed her hands.

"Focus, Chloe, focus."

Placing her life musings on the back burner, she tightened her apron strings, cranked the volume on the portable radio, and concentrated on wowing her guests with a memorable meal.

One challenge at a time.

THIRTEEN

Patience had never been one of Rocky's strengths and she'd been anxious to spend quality time with Chloe Madison for days. First Gram's companion flaked out on Cupcake Lovers; then when Rocky stopped over for a visit the woman made herself scarce. She was supposed to be at church today, in which case Rocky could've started up a casual chat afterward while Gram gossiped with her friends. But no. She and Chloe had skipped church in favor of grocery shopping in Pixley!

All Rocky wanted was some one-on-one time with Chloe. Hell, fifteen minutes would suffice. Time enough to plant a seed, enticing her to come to the next Cupcake meeting. After reading her witty food critique column, Rocky was certain Chloe could go head-to-head with Tasha while giving others, like Gram, a dose of confidence with her professional Forks Up on some of their recipes. Rocky just needed to educate Chloe about the club's core mission and Tasha's misguided attempt to launch them to fame. She'd only met the woman briefly, barely spoken, but she was pretty certain Chloe was a good egg—contrary to Jayce's report and Dev's assumptions.

Fifteen minutes. That's all she needed. Fifteen stinking minutes.

She'd be lucky if she got two.

Sunday dinner at Gram's usually topped out at four or five guests. Rocky and Luke were pretty much the mainstays while assorted other relatives revolved through. Tonight Nash had opted in as well as Dev. Not wanting Chloe to feel overwhelmed by family, Gram had also invited Monica and her husband, Leo. Including Chloe, that made eight people, which pretty much eliminated a stretch of private, uninterrupted conversation.

A woman of action and determined to have her moment, Rocky showed up at Gram's an hour ahead of schedule. Unfortunately, she wasn't the only one. Cursing under her breath, she parked her Jeep behind Nash's pickup just as Luke rolled past in Gram's Cadillac and pulled into the garage.

Rocky hopped out and met her cousin curbside. "What are you doing here so early?"

"Luke called and said he needed a lift to the police station."

"What for?"

"To pick up Gram's car."

"I'm afraid to ask."

"I'm not. But Luke didn't have details. Something about reckless driving and Billy Burke. Dev said he'd fill us in later."

"Billy called Dev?" Bad enough Gram and Chloe had landed in another mess, but of all the dozens of family members who could've come to the rescue . . .

"Billy made the bust. Stone called Dev. Whatever you do, don't bring it up once we're inside."

"Why not?

"Something about damage control."

Luke trotted across the yard and joined them just before they reached the house. "Nash give you the scoop?" he asked Rocky.

"Details were sketchy."

"Dev said he'd fill us in later."

"So I heard. Okay. Gram's car aside, what's with the early arrival? "

The two men looked at each other and shrugged. "Thought we'd help out," Nash said.

Rocky smirked. "Doing what?"

"Setting the table," Luke said. "Or something."

"Eight people. That's a lot," Nash said. "Chloe's got her hands full cooking. The least we could do is . . . offer to make the salad."

"Or something," Luke added.

Rocky snorted, then rolled her eyes. "You two are so freaking lame."

"What?" they asked, feigning innocence.

"You want to impress Chloe."

"I'm wounded," Nash said.

"No, you're not. You're a dog." She jerked a thumb at her brother. "Just like Snoopy here."

Luke flashed a cocky grin. "Arf."

"There's a new girl in town," she continued.

"A pretty girl," Nash added.

"And you're both sniffing after her. Do me a favor and don't. I'm pretty sure Dev likes her."

Nash looked crushed. "Really?"

"I picked up on that," Luke said with a devilish gleam in his eye. "Thought he could use a shove. A little brotherly competition. You know Dev."

"Picky," Nash said.

"Cautious."

"Uptight."

"Whatever." Rocky huffed a breath. "Can I trust you clowns to behave yourselves?"

"Seriously?" Nash asked.

Rocky whacked him in the back of the head.

"You three coming inside anytime soon?" Gram called out the front door. "The neighbors are starting to talk."

"The neighbors always talk," Nash said. "Sugar Creek. Home of the busybody."

"Coming!" Rocky called.

"What are *you* doing here early?" Luke asked her.

"Unlike you two, I'm actually useful in the kitchen. Like

you said, eight people, that's a lot. Figured I'd lend a hand. Plus," she added, feeling a little guilty about ribbing them when she had an ulterior motive of her own, "I need to talk to her about Cupcake Lovers."

"What about it?" Luke asked as they neared the front porch.

"I want her to join."

"Why?" Nash asked. "She's only here for a couple of months."

"So what? Given her background, she could prove a dynamic force in a condensed amount of time."

"I heard she has something against desserts," Luke said.

Nash stopped in his tracks. "No dessert tonight?"

"I'm sure Gram has some cookies in the pantry or something," Rocky said. "Don't look so stricken."

"How can a gourmet chef have a beef with sweets?"

"Let it go, Nash." Although Rocky wondered the same thing. She also hoped it didn't prove a barrier once she explained to Chloe how Cupcake Lovers would benefit from her two cents.

Just as they reached the door a horn blared. All three turned as Leo and Monica's Suburban pulled in behind Rocky's Jeep.

"Bet Monica's here to lend Chloe a hand, too," Luke said.

"Perfect," Rocky said. "There goes my fifteen minutes."

FOURTEEN

The longer Chloe toiled in the kitchen, the lighter her mood. She lost herself in the rhythm of cooking and the classic rock tunes blaring from the radio. Regarding her ability to impress the Monroes as a chef, any lingering anxiety faded the moment she mixed the ingredients for the apple sausage stuffing. She'd prepared a Cornish hen entrée similar to this in class and it had received high marks and rave reviews. She reflected on that moment and several other successful dishes as she lightly stuffed the birds and secured the opening with skewers.

Into the roasting pan. Into the oven.

Her confidence swelled like a perfect soufflé as she prepared the garlic mashed potatoes and a green bean and mushroom medley. She didn't even mind when Monica and Rocky invaded her domain. Unlike Daisy, they didn't try to take charge. The helping hands were welcome, the banter light and fun, centering mostly on the Food Network. They even timed their efforts when they prepared the Apple-Fennel Salad as if they were competing on *Iron Chef*.

"If heaven has a scent," Luke said, bursting in for the second time in thirty minutes, "this is it. You're killing us, Chloe. Nash started drooling ten minutes ago. Garlic?" he asked, reaching for the deluxe mixer's potato-glommed beater.

She gave his hand a playful smack.

"Gram always lets me lick the beater."

"I'm not Gram."

He gave her a smoldering once-over. "You can say that again."

Chloe quirked a brow. "Is this the part where I'm supposed to get all weak kneed?"

"You mean you're not?"

"No."

"Damn."

Monica laughed.

Rocky snapped his butt with a kitchen towel. "Would you get out of here?"

He sauntered to the fridge. "Just came in for a couple of brewskies." He grabbed four. "Something to wash away the taste of Gram's cocktails."

"What was it this week?" Rocky asked.

"Long Island Pucker."

"Most disgusting ingredient?"

"Watermelon schnapps."

Chloe *ewwed* along with the other women.

"Plus she's on a scrapbook kick. Dev, Nash, Leo, and I are ODing on family photos. Please, God, tell me dinner's almost served."

"About fifteen minutes," Chloe said.

"You're a goddess." He winked, flashed a killer smile, then after a seductive pause raised a brow. "Nothing?"

"Sorry."

"Guess I'm having an off night."

"Or something," Rocky muttered with a grin.

As soon as he left, the women shared a laugh.

"That was priceless," Monica said.

"He's actually very charming," Chloe said as she tugged on a pair of oven mitts. "In a shallow, disconnected, womanizing kind of way."

"Ouch," Rocky said.

"I didn't mean . . . I'm sure Luke's really sweet—"

"He is," Monica said.

"But you're right," Rocky said. "He's a player."

"I'm sorry. I'm just overly aware of potential heartbreakers these days. Although at least Luke's obvious. Never saw it coming with Ryan," Chloe said.

"Cheating bastard," Monica blurted, then, red faced, glanced at Chloe. "Sorry, hon."

She shrugged. "That's okay." After all, she'd opened the can of worms, by mentioning the slimy sucker. "Ryan's my ex-boyfriend," she told Rocky as she cracked the oven door. "We lived together for over two years. I thought marriage was in our future, but then, well, it wasn't."

"Broke up with her on the day she learned she graduated with honors," Monica snapped.

"You graduated with honors?" Rocky asked, sounding impressed.

"No big deal," Chloe said, testing the tenderness of the hens.

"Huge deal," Monica said. "She baked a special cake for an intimate celebration and—"

"Tell me that's when he broke up with her," Rocky said.

"Insensitive bastard."

"No wonder she's adverse to desserts."

"Oh no," Chloe said. "Everyone will be expecting dessert. I didn't think . . . Well, I did, but then I blocked it out." Her face burned from the oven's heat as much as her faux pas. Even so, she relished the camaraderie of the moment. A woman amongst friends. She never felt more alive and happy than when enjoying a good meal with good company. "No, worries," she said, channeling a vibrant hostess. "I'll whip something up." The pantry was stocked. At the very least she could serve instant pudding topped with whipped cream. Yeah, *that* would impress.

"Don't worry about it," Rocky said. "You've done enough."

"Mark my word," Monica said, "everyone will be too stuffed from this incredible meal to even *think* about dessert."

"And if they do," Rocky said with a sly smile, "Gram always keeps a stash of cookies from Gemma's Bakery." She moved to the fridge, nabbed an imported beer and a chilled bottle of wine. "I don't know about you, but I think we deserve a cocktail, too. And not the toxic swill Gram's serving the boys." She poured two glasses of wine, then screwed off the cap of a longneck.

"Not a fan of chardonnay?" Chloe asked when Rocky opted for the beer.

"Allergic." She clinked her bottle to Chloe's and Monica's wineglasses and toasted their combined efforts. "Here's to a delicious dinner."

"And friendship," Monica said.

Heart lighter than it had been in days, Chloe nodded and smiled. "To friendship."

* * *

Dinner was a hit. Chloe accepted every compliment (and there were plenty) with subdued grace, but on the inside she was happy-dancing like a loon. Even Monica, who'd known her forever, was impressed.

The only glitch was that Daisy had seated her next to Devlin. Hard to relax when the tension between them was palatable. Did he have to sit so close? Did he have to smell so good? He'd spared her few looks and fewer words, but she'd swear she had his full attention—if not his approval. Unlike everyone else, he hadn't raved about the food. Since he sampled every dish and ate heartily, she assumed he didn't hate her cooking. More likely he hated that he loved it.

Chloe had smiled to herself more than once, thankful that she'd strived to impress rather than torture. It would have been so easy to sabotage his hen. The wrong combination of spices. Overcooking—dry and tough instead of moist and tender. But that would have been petty. Much more satisfying for him to eat crow and admit she rocked in the kitchen. Not that he'd admitted squat. Not that she expected him to. That would require applauding her efforts instead of finding fault. The man seemed intent on disliking her. It must have galled him that the rest of his family thought she was the best thing since Starbucks coffee.

Nash and Luke had complimented everything from her cooking to her taste in music and books. Daisy bragged that she'd hired a culinary genius and Rocky asked if Chloe minded sharing her stuffing recipe, something she'd like to try out on her B and B guests—although she didn't have any bookings for the next two weeks.

Chloe took that opportunity to shed the spotlight on someone else, expressing interest in the Red Clover as well as the Sugar Shack. Talk turned to business and she relaxed and absorbed as the conversation bounced from Rocky's seasonal slump, Leo's heavy workload, and Nash's chaotic flight schedule to a staffing issue at the Sugar Shack and renovations at J.T.'s. Daisy, bless her heart, had an opinion on everything, as did Devlin—although they rarely agreed. But even the occasional flareup was tempered with respect and good humor.

If Chloe closed her eyes she could imagine herself at any one of her favorite haunts in Manhattan enjoying a good meal and energized conversation with any one of her circles of colorful friends. Something Ryan had referred to as a frivolous waste of time and money. Looking back, he'd never felt comfortable with her artistic friends and little by little he'd pulled her away and into his own social scene—which boiled down to stuffy business dinners and the occasional "date" night. What peeved her most was that she'd allowed that to happen. She'd abandoned a precious part of her life to make *him* happy. To be the kind of woman *he* preferred. Although in the end, he'd preferred another woman altogether. Why had he turned her life inside out, only to leave her high and dry? "Bastard."

Her mind glitched when she felt Devlin squeeze her thigh. *What the—?* But then she realized he wasn't being fresh; he was stilling her bouncing leg—a brief, under-the-table squeeze that scorched her senses.

Then Nash asked, "Got a beef with that bird?" and she realized she'd been sawing at her hen's leg with a little too much zeal. No way was she going to admit she'd had the fleeting urge to cut off Ryan's cheating wanker. *Good Lord.* Loosening her grip on the knife, she joked, "A little tough."

"Really?" Leo asked. "Mine's perfect."

"Mine, too," Luke said. "And Rocky's right. This stuffing's amazing. We could use a gourmet chef like you at the Shack."

"I'm not a gourmet chef," Chloe said, "and you've already got a perfectly wonderful culinarian on staff."

"True," Luke said, "but we could always use another."

"No, we couldn't," Devlin said.

Chloe bristled. Was that his way of saying she wasn't good enough to cook for the restaurant he partially owned?

When Luke balked, Devlin cut him off with a raised brow. "Do you *want* Anna to quit?"

"Of course not. But—"

"He's right," Chloe said, not wanting to side with Devlin but acknowledging his wisdom. Anna wouldn't welcome another chef into her kitchen. She'd consider it a slight or intrusion. Egos were as rampant in the culinary world as the entertainment industry. "Ever heard the cliché 'too many cooks in the kitchen'? Besides, I have a job."

"Darn straight!" Daisy pointed her fork at Luke. "You're not stealing my cook and chauffeur."

"Speaking of driving," Leo interjected. "Heard you two had a run-in with Deputy Burke."

Everyone at the table shot him a look.

"What? It's a small town. People see things. People talk."

"Home of the busybody," said Nash.

Daisy snorted. "Billy Burke's a pinhead and a scoundrel."

Luke grinned. "Don't hold back, Gram."

"He got fresh with Chloe!"

Monica gaped. *"What?"*

"A misunderstanding," Chloe blurted.

"I'm handling it," Devlin said.

Which implied Billy *had* been out of line. True. But not a truth she wanted unleashed. She didn't want to be the talk of this table, let alone the town. And the *last* thing she wanted was for Devlin to handle *her* problem.

"Maybe I should be the one to take this on," Luke said to

his brother. "Considering you need the city's approval on renovations—"

"And considering the deputy is the mayor's son," Nash said. "Not a good time to piss off a Burke."

"Part of the reason I'm walking on eggshells with Tasha," Rocky said. "Not that Billy shouldn't get an earful."

"Just not from Dev," Nash said. "You're too close, too, Luke. Let me handle Billy. Trust me. My pleasure."

"Not up for negotiation," Devlin said. He nabbed a newly opened bottle of chardonnay. "Who wants more wine?"

Chloe gawked, stunned by his insistence to be her champion. Did he actually believe she'd been wronged or did he simply relish an opportunity to knock heads with a Burke? She shot him an irritated look that said, *Butt out,* at which point he had the nerve to grace her with his first smile all evening. A smile that should have burned her butt and instead stoked a sensual fire. Flustered, she drained the last of her chardonnay, hypersensitive to the sudden lull in conversation. As for the rest of the family, having everyone rise to her defense was humbling and weirdly wonderful, albeit unwanted. Managing her own mess was vital to bolstering her self-esteem. Plus the offense, though smarmy, wasn't worth risking a legal hassle for Daisy. Nor did Chloe want to jeopardize Devlin's store renovations, since, financially, that affected *all* of the Monroes.

"I'll have more wine," she said, with a forced smile. "And I'm respectfully asking everyone at this table to forget my clash with Deputy Burke. It was nothing. Really." Her cheeks burned with the lie. Devlin glanced her way and she burned even more. Was that a glimmer of respect she saw sparking in his bluer than blue eyes, or censure?

Monica, bless her soul, came to Chloe's rescue. "Speaking of Tasha," she said, although they weren't, "I overheard her bragging about how she's going to pose for the cover of the Cupcake Lovers' recipe book."

"Over my dead body," Rocky said, stirring sweetener into her iced tea.

"Ten bucks says she plans on wearing something skimpy," Nash said. "Sex sells, right?"

"No one's a pro at peddling her wares like Tasha Burke," Leo added. "Even Dev—ow!" He frowned at Monica, who'd apparently pinched or kicked him under the table.

Had Devlin and Tasha been an item? Chloe made a mental note to ask Monica later. Just now she blurted a burning question, delirious that the conversation had taken a new turn. Anything to keep the focus off of her. "I'm confused. *How* is Tasha related to the Burkes?"

"She married Randall Burke," Monica said. "The newly elected mayor of Sugar Creek."

"Thirty years his junior," Rocky added. "A match made in hell."

"She wanted an influential husband."

"He wanted a trophy wife."

"Meanwhile," Rocky said, "she's creating havoc in Cupcake Lovers with her stupid book project."

"But if the book's a hit, the club's cause will benefit," Nash said, "right?"

"I'm not questioning the desired goal," Rocky said. "I'm questioning Tasha's judgment. And influence. There's no reason in the world that Gram's latest recipe should have been nixed. Am I right, Chloe?"

"I confess, I don't get it. I thought Daisy's recipe was delightful." She hadn't been keen on tasting a dessert, but she'd been even less keen to hurt the old woman's feelings.

"What we need," Rocky said, "is someone who can be objective. Someone who isn't afraid to make a statement and stand by it. Someone with experience in the culinary world. If you ever feel like sitting in on a meeting, Chloe . . ."

"I'm not an authority on cupcakes."

"Think about it," Rocky said.

"We'd love to have you," Monica said.

"I'm counting on it," Daisy said. "I've decided to submit my special secret recipe. If Tasha turns up her reconstructed nose, I need you to convince everyone else she's doesn't know nutmeg from curry powder. I've been a member of the club for fifty years. I deserve to be in that book!"

Chloe, who knew all about passion and the desire to succeed, couldn't resist the woman's heartfelt determination. Though Chloe wasn't planning on creating a dessert herself anytime soon, she wasn't opposed to being Daisy's champion. "When you put it like that . . ."

Monica and Rocky high-fived. Daisy pumped a scrawny fist. Luke winked his approval while Nash gave her a thumbs-up.

Chloe smiled but fidgeted under Devlin's quiet regard. What was he thinking? Typically she was pretty good at reading men, but not *this* man. It made her nuts.

"Speaking of cupcakes," Leo said. "What's for dessert?"

Monica punched him in the arm.

"What?"

Chloe cursed the fact that, once again, she was the center of attention. Half the table expected her to follow up with a fantastic dessert. The other half knew she'd dropped the ball. But even more disconcerting was the sexual energy rolling off of Devlin and crashing over her in erotic waves. She wanted to drown in it almost as much as she wanted to flee. There was something incredibly warped about being attracted to a man bent on finding fault with her every move. "As it happens . . . ," Chloe said, red faced.

"As it happens," Daisy said, "*I* made dessert. Needed to try my special secret recipe on *someone*." She sprang from her seat with a smile. "Consider yourselves guinea pigs." She shooed them up and away from the table. "Let's not waste a beautiful sunset. Dessert and coffee on the back porch. It's a little nippy out there, but you'll live."

"I'll brew the coffee." Chloe hurried after Daisy with panic in her heart. "When," she whispered with vehemence as they crossed the kitchen's threshold, "did you bake cupcakes?"

"Yesterday morning when you were at the library."

Chloe had made a habit of arriving at the library when the doors opened, snagging the first public Internet access appointment of the day. An hour to check e-mails and to surf her favorite cooking blogs, then she was good for the day. "You told me you'd been burning coconut and caramel candles!"

"I lied."

Chloe nabbed a bag of coffee beans from the fridge as Daisy produced her secret stash of secret recipe cupcakes. "I can't believe I fell for that. I can't believe you duped me. You're not supposed to bake or cook or . . . why didn't you ask me to help?"

"Because I didn't *want* your help. Or Rocky's. Or any other of my well-meaning relatives and friends. I needed to do this on my own." Eyes glittering behind her metallic blue cat-eye glasses (the fourth set of funky glasses she'd worn this week), Daisy set the three-tiered cupcake carrier on the counter and unlatched the lid. "I've been baking cupcakes for decades. I remember sifting flour with my mom and grandma when I was five. Learning icing techniques from my aunt Pearl when I was seven. I owe it to them and the founding members of Cupcake Lovers to earn a place in this recipe book on my own."

Chloe was speechless. How could one argue with such divine motivation?

Daisy pointed to the tall Shaker-style cabinet standing against the north wall. "Would you grab me that crystal serving platter on the third shelf, please?"

"Sure." Rising to her toes, she reached back and scored the dish. "I just wish you would have . . . Wow." Her thoughts jumped track as Daisy lifted the lid to reveal two dozen edible works of art. "Those look incredible. What kind of frosting is that?"

"Caramel Buttercream topped with toasted coconut."

"Rich?"

"Unsalted butter. Heavy cream. Brown sugar. White sugar. Powdered sugar."

"Decadent."

"The chocolate ganache filling is decadent," Daisy said while transferring cupcakes from Tupperware to crystal. "This calls for my favorite china. Cups, saucers, matching sugar bowl and creamer—same cabinet as the platter, top shelf."

"Right." Chloe plucked a folding step stool from the corner, climbing to the third platform to search through the crammed and cluttered shelves. "I'm sure they're delicious, Daisy, and I understand why you wanted to make them on your own. I just wish, please, don't bake or cook without . . . an assistant. Someone, specifically me, to help if . . . well, if you need it. What if there was a kitchen fire? What if you slipped on a banana peel? I don't want that on my conscience and I certainly don't want Devlin up my . . . patooty."

"I'll keep that in mind."

Chloe winced at the male voice, nearly bobbling six china saucers and the sugar bowl as she slipped on the stool. Her heart skipped as strong hands caught her by the waist, then eased her to the ground. She didn't have to turn to know it was Devlin. She knew his voice. His touch. His scent.

"Came to help with the coffee."

"Don't make it too strong," Daisy said. "And don't make the flavored stuff. I don't want anything competing with the taste of my cupcakes."

Trapped between an immovable cabinet and a tall, hard man, Chloe cautiously turned just as Daisy whisked over the threshold with a tray of cupcakes. *Damn.* Before she could say anything, Devlin relieved her of the china.

"What else do you need?"

That's a loaded question, she thought as her body hummed in response to his touch. "Two more saucers, eight cups, and the creamer." She sidled past him and made a beeline for the coffeemaker. She filled the water tank, loaded a filter, and packed the grinder all the while waiting for a lecture. Surely he'd overheard enough to know Daisy had baked when Chloe wasn't in the house. Instead, all she heard was the clink of dishes and the soft *snick* of the cabinet doors closing. Anxiety built as the silence stretched. She could feel him watching her. Could smell his cologne as he moved closer. On pins and needles, she jumped when the grinder jammed. "For cryin' out . . ." She froze as Devlin pressed against her, reaching around to solve the problem with one easy maneuver. "Thank you," she said.

"You're welcome."

Neither one of them moved. Caged between his arms, she focused on the grinding beans, her mind whirling with questions: *What did you think of dinner? Why are you feuding with the Burkes? How was I supposed to know Daisy would bake behind my back?* Instead, she blurted a demand: "Don't confront Deputy Burke on my behalf."

"Don't underestimate Daisy's reckless mind-set. Not that she's always been reckless. Rocky thinks she's going through a crisis."

His mild and caring tone caught Chloe off guard. Turning, she looked up and met his earnest gaze. "I do, too. Not that she's said anything specific. It's just . . . a feeling."

"I'm worried about her. If she confides in you—"

"I can't make any promises. What if she swears me to secrecy? What if it's something really personal and none of your business?"

His mouth quirked. "I can respect that. On the other hand, I consider anything having to do with the emotional and physical well-being of my family my business."

No anger. No arrogance. Just a simple heartfelt decree . . . and a hint of the charming man she'd first bumped into at Oslow's. "I can respect that," she said, wary of the swift turnabout. "Still . . ."

"That doesn't give me leave to act like an overprotective, overbearing jackass."

That prompted a smile out of her. "You said it, not me."

He eased back and offered his hand. "Truce?"

She couldn't imagine what had inspired this cordial attitude and she didn't entirely trust it. But with the rest of her life in chaos, she welcomed one less headache. "Truce." She grasped his big hand, willing herself not to blush as heat stole up her arm and flared throughout her body. "About Deputy Burke . . ."

"I can't make any promises, except that I won't seek him out."

"That's something, I guess."

"If you knew me, you'd know that's a lot."

She realized then that he was still holding her hand. Or was it the other way around? When he brushed his thumb over her wrist she tingled from head to toe. "I'd like to," she rasped. "Know you, I mean." *Don't babble!* "That is, I can't figure you out."

"Same here. Maybe that's the attraction."

"That was . . . direct."

"Not as direct as kissing you."

"You're going to kiss me?"

His eyes sparked with something she couldn't read, damn him. Still stroking her wrist, he said, "That would be . . ."

"Uncalled for?" she said, throwing back his previous summation. "Unwise?"

"Dangerous."

How so? she wanted to ask, but didn't. She snuffed every flirtatious volley that came to mind. She wasn't prepared to follow through to whatever end. Not tonight. Not for a while. Too much was happening too fast. Too many changes. Too many unknowns.

One challenge at a time.

Instead of pushing the moment, she retreated. Severing their physical connection, she turned to check on the coffee. "I've had my fill of derring-do stunts for today."

"Sorry to hear that," he said with a smile in his voice, then deftly changed the subject. "I can't imagine Gram's dessert trumping your dinner. Nevertheless, she's waiting."

"We should get out there," Chloe said, anxious to rejoin the others. She wasn't sure she could withstand another five minutes alone with Devlin. Even though they'd cooled the flirtation, the air sizzled with awareness. Another five minutes and they could be doing horizontal mambo vertically in the broom closet. Java wasn't the only thing brewing. "I'll bring the coffee if you . . . Wait." She glanced over her shoulder. "Did you just compliment my cooking?"

"I did." He smiled while arranging the coffee service on

a large serving tray. "You realize of course that you've dazzled my family."

"With my cooking skill?"

"With your people skills."

Another compliment? "Does that bother you?"

"It intrigues me. *You* intrigue me."

That, she thought as he disappeared over the threshold, tray in hand, was the sexiest thing any man had ever said to her.

Don't go there, her wounded heart cautioned even as her inner Errol Flynn urged, *Jump!*

"Let's compromise," Chloe told herself, heart racing as she snagged the pot of coffee and ventured into risky territory, "and live in the moment."

FIFTEEN

The sun beamed over Thrush Mountain, yet the temperature had yet to break fifty. Rocky breathed in the brisk air as she jogged along Pikeman's Trail. Instead of shorts, she'd opted for capri sweats. Instead of a tank, she'd slipped on a T-shirt and hoodie. Her ponytail slapped at her back, and her heart rate increased at a steady pace. A lot of joggers listened to music as they ran, but she preferred the sounds of nature. Leaves rustling, birds chirping. The distant rush of Sugar Creek.

After a lousy night's sleep, she'd dragged herself out of bed, dressed, swigged OJ from the carton, and dashed off to kick-start her day. She struggled to quiet her mind and lost. Mounting bills. Lack of business. Gram's shenanigans. Rocky's beef with Tasha. Her envy of Chloe. Two days after Sunday dinner and Rocky was still marveling at the woman's culinary skills, not to mention her effect on Devlin. So much so that it dominated the conversation when Adam surprised her and joined her midway through her run.

"I'm telling you, the chemistry between those two was palpable and I wasn't the only one who felt it. Luke, Nash, Gram, Monica, and Leo." They'd burned up the phone lines later that night and again the next morning. "Everyone's buzzing about what they observed and we all came to the same conclusion."

"They're hot for one another."

"Not in an obvious way. I mean there wasn't any flirting, not that we saw anyway, but there were lots of stolen looks and enough sexual tension to get a rise out of a eunuch."

"Whoa."

"Tell me about it." Rocky had been torn between being thrilled for her brother and feeling sorry for herself. She hadn't felt that kind of searing attraction for a man since . . . It had been a long time.

"Think they'll act on it?"

"I don't know. Chloe's fresh from a bad breakup and Dev is—"

"Cautious."

"Suspicious."

"He *has* been burned a few times. First Janna—"

"We don't talk about her. Ever." Rocky's heart iced over at the mention of her ex-sister-in-law. Not that she was a bad person, just a person who'd behaved badly . . . and broken Rocky's big brother's heart.

"Fine. Then there was Fiona and Cory and, at the risk of being punched, Tasha."

Each one more enamored with Dev's wealth and prestige than Dev himself. Rocky sighed. "I know. But at least he approached those relationships with an open mind. Not this time. Thanks to Jayce."

"Jayce Bello? What's he got to do with this?"

Shit. "Nothing. Forget I said anything." Rocky cursed her loose tongue and picked up her pace. They'd all grown up in the same small town. Adam knew Dev and Jayce were best friends. He knew Jayce lived and worked in New York.

Undaunted, Adam jogged a few paces ahead, then turned to face her, jogging backward without missing a step. "Did Dev have Chloe investigated?"

"Why would he do that?"

"Because he's cautious. Suspicious. Because he'd want to make sure that the woman living with his grandmother wasn't a psycho or swindler."

Rocky didn't know whether to confess or lie. Feeling the

need to tread lightly, she straddled the fence. "I'm not saying he did, but if he did, he wouldn't want anyone to know. So let's just drop it."

"You're the one who brought it up."

He fell in beside her and they jogged in silence for the next few minutes. Rocky's brain, on the other hand, kept turning.

"I just . . . I'd like to see them get together. She's fun. Dev could use some fun in his life. All he does is work and talk about work. When he's not doing that, he's trying to micromanage everyone else's life."

"Still trying to get you to sell the Red Clover?"

"Says it's a money pit."

Adam didn't respond and she knew he agreed. When he'd helped her spackle the ceiling the other day, the repairman had arrived to work on her stove. While installing parts, the man had commented on her groaning fridge. In addition to the appliances, her back porch was also in need of repair. Even though Adam hadn't said anything, she knew he thought the shed where she stored the recreational equipment for the guests was unsuitable. He'd merely raised a brow at the buckets she'd distributed to catch rain that dripped through the leaky roof.

"You think I should sell it, too." She knew she sounded surly. She couldn't help it. She'd tossed and turned all night, and what should have been a stress-relieving run was now officially ruined.

"No, but I do think these are tough times. For a lot of people. I think you could use some help."

"I'm not asking Daddy for money and I'm not *taking* money from Dev." Every time he offered, she wanted to scream. It made her feel like a failure. Incapable. Even though she knew his intentions were good.

"What about taking on a partner?"

"Someone who'll try to impose their ideas and will on me?" She snorted and ran faster. "No thanks."

"Someone willing to invest time and money. Someone

who shares your love of the land and appreciation for tourism."

The sounds of their Nikes hitting the worn dirt trail pounded in tandem. Her heart raced, and not just from exertion. Something in Adam's voice jangled her nerves. "Just where would I find this perfect partner?"

"You're trying to outrun him."

To her credit she didn't stumble or trip over her feet when she came to a knee-jarring halt. She did, however, walk in small circles, hands on hips, trying to avoid cramping up. Trying to avoid his gaze while she assembled her blown-to-bits thoughts.

"I've been thinking about this for a while," Adam said. "I've spent the last two years freelancing, offering my services to three different tourist facilities. Which was fine. I built a reputation, socked away a lot of money. But now I want to get involved on a deeper level. I thought about investing in my own lodge, but given the economic climate, I'd be taking a hell of a risk on a start-up business. The Red Clover is an established regional bed-and-breakfast."

"Established, yes. Popular, no."

"We can make it popular."

The word "we" should have triggered a full-out run in the opposite direction. But she'd been maintaining the inn on her own for three years now, and despite her enthusiastic efforts to make a profit, she was miserably in the hole. With each passing day she could feel her dream slipping away. Heart pounding, she finally met his gaze. "Have some ideas, do you?"

He smiled. "Yes, I do."

"I have to admit, I'm curious."

"Curious enough to listen to a proposed plan over breakfast?"

A good judge of character, she sensed nothing but sincere enthusiasm at the prospect of uniting for a business venture. Adam was one of the most grounded, trustworthy men she knew. Competent, too. He was also sinfully good in bed.

"You do realize that if we went into business together we'd have to stop sleeping together."

"Why? Aren't you capable of separating business and pleasure?"

"Are you?"

"Sure."

She should have felt good about that, but instead her ego took a hit. Didn't he have any tender feelings for her at all? Not that she wanted him to. "I just think it could complicate matters."

He moved in then. Close enough that she could smell the combination of sweat and shampoo. Close enough that she could see every wrinkle in his Sling Blade snowboarding T-shirt. Close enough to admire his imperfect nose and the scar just above his upper lip. He grasped her shoulders and squeezed, the affectionate, supportive touch of a friend and lover.

"I'm not asking you to marry me, Rocky. I'm not even asking to move in. I'm hoping for what we have and . . . more. If it isn't working, we'll make adjustments. If it's a disaster, we'll call it quits."

"As fuck buddies?"

"Or business partners."

The perfect arrangement. Maybe. All she knew was that for the first time in months, she didn't feel like a total stress ball. Giving him a half smile, she turned and sprinted toward the Red Clover. "You better have some damned spectacular ideas, Brody."

He caught up with her in a heartbeat. "Brace yourself, Monroe."

"Last one back to the house makes breakfast."

"I can already taste your blueberry pancakes," he said with an ornery grin, then commenced to kick her ass.

SIXTEEN

Devlin considered himself a calm, rational man capable of handling any crisis that came his way. Early on he'd developed a talent for taking everything in stride, never panicking, rarely losing his cool. Even when his marriage to Janna had fallen apart, he'd kept it together. But when his dad called, threatening to fly home in order to *save* the family business, Devlin blew a gasket. "What do you think *I'm* trying to do?"

"Between the cost of your proposed renovations and an enhanced employee benefit package, you're setting us up for financial ruin."

"The hell I am." He'd researched, calculated and projected. "What I'm proposing entails minimal risk."

" 'Risk' being the key word."

"Nothing ventured, nothing gained."

"You're not playing the stock market, Son. You're playing with people's lives. Our family's future income."

"I know that and I know what I'm doing." Ticked, he pushed away from his desk and paced the office occupied by every senior male Monroe since the 1800s. He'd never aspired to this role, not as his sole purpose in life, but he'd never considered turning his back on the job either. Now that he was in charge . . . except he wasn't. "Did you even read my report?"

"Which one? Over the past two weeks you've bombarded

me with more paperwork than the health insurance company. You're both a pain in my ass."

Devlin paused in his heated tracks. "Why are you getting hassled by VT Med?"

"It's nothing. Some . . . hitch in the eye-care plan. Point is there's no need to panic and instill massive changes just because we're facing a little competition."

"Nothing little about a Walmart Supercenter, Dad."

"Nothing wrong with staying the course. Slow and steady wins the game."

"What if you're wrong?"

"What if *you're* wrong?" The older man sighed. "I know you have a master's in business administration and finance. I know you're a visionary. But if you're so desperate to overhaul a business, turn your attention to one of your other investments. Or invest in something new. But leave J.T.'s alone."

By refusing to discuss his plans or even debate the issues, his dad had reduced him to little more than a puppet. Devlin was no man's yes-man. "If that's how you feel, maybe you *should* come home. Take over as COO as well as CEO."

"Don't be an ass."

"Like father, like son." Devlin hung up before the conversation turned brutal. Yes, they'd argued in the past, but never like this. Jerome Monroe had always been conservative and stubborn, but he'd never been irrational. Lately his behavior, like *semi*-retiring at fifty-five and moving to Florida in the *summer,* had been as questionable as Gram's. What the hell was going on with everyone?

After a sharp knock, the office door swung open and Devlin's assistant manager stepped in. "Met with the liaison for VT Med like you asked," Chris said. "Got the stats on enhanced employee benefit packages." He placed a bulging folder on the desk. "Even if J.T.'s matches the supercenter's benefit plan, we still lack the varied opportunities for advancement and/or relocation."

"I know. I don't expect everyone to stay, but I can reward

those who do. High employee morale results in a highly effective team and premium customer service and that's one area we can definitely excel at." In spite of his dad's decree, Devlin had made a progressive decision. "Schedule a mandatory employee meeting for next Monday just after closing. Book Gemma's to cater the event. Pastries. Coffee."

"Topic of discussion?"

"Upcoming changes and perks."

"That'll have them flocking," Chris said on his way out.

And buzzing with presumptions and guesses for the next six days. Word would get back to his dad within that time unless Devlin got word to him first. Either way, he'd just betrayed both his parent and boss in one fell swoop. Frowning, he picked up his phone and hit autodial. "Hi, Mom."

"Funny you should call, Devlin. I was just getting ready to phone you."

"About?"

"Fighting with your dad."

"It's about to get worse."

"What do you mean?"

"I can't wage this war over e-mails, faxes, and the phone. I need to speak with dad face-to-face. If I can't book a commercial flight for tomorrow, I'll have Nash fly me down."

"Don't do that, honey. Please."

Her brittle voice put him on edge. "Why?"

"I'm not supposed . . . I promised your father . . ."

Wary now, Devlin eased into a chair. "What's going on?"

"He doesn't want to see you. He doesn't want to see anyone in the family. Not right now."

"Why?"

"This goes no further."

"For Christ sake, Mom, what is it?"

"Your dad was diagnosed with prostate cancer."

His heart thudded slow and hard. Of all the things she could have said, he hadn't expected a health crisis. Vacillating between disbelief and shock, he took a steady breath and tried not to think the worst. He'd already lost two family members to various forms of that son-of-a-bitch disease, one of them being his Granddad Jessup, Daisy's husband, his dad's dad.

"Devlin?"

He reined in his emotions and focused on facts. "What stage?"

"Stage Two, but he's winning the battle."

"You say that as if he's been fighting for a while."

"Three months."

The dull buzz in Devlin's ears intensified to a roar. "You've both known about this for three *months*?"

"Hear me out," she said, hardening her tone. "It's your father's body. His choice who he tells and when—if ever. He didn't want his family and close friends to worry and he didn't want pity. You know what a proud man he is. He wanted to fight this on his own terms, which entailed radical treatments with a specialist here in Florida. We've seen tremendous improvement, but the treatments take their toll. He should be focusing his energy on recovering, fighting the disease, not you."

Guilt and anger pummeled his senses. "If I'd known—"

"You would have dropped everything to help. He needs you . . . *we* need you in Sugar Creek, honey, watching over the family and the family's interests. He's never had faith in Rocky's B and B and Luke runs the Sugar Shack with his heart, not his head. The one constant, the only proven security, in the immediate family's lives is J.T.'s. I know you want to make big changes, but now's not the time. Wait until your dad's stronger, until he's cancer free. When he comes home—clear mind, strong body—I'm sure he'll be more open to your ideas."

Devlin rubbed his throbbing temple. "Semi-retirement was a ruse."

"Running the store is in his blood. He's not ready to throw in the towel, but he did need a break."

Several things came together in that moment, recent comments and actions that hadn't made sense to Devlin before.

"Trust me when I tell you, he's beating this thing."

"If anyone can, Dad can." Even though he wasn't happy that his dad had kept the diagnosis secret, Devlin understood his motivation. Knowing the toll cancer took on a victim's loved ones, he would've made the same decision. "What about you, Mom? How are you holding up?"

"I'm okay. Better, now that I've shared the news with you. Although I have a strong support system down here, it helps to share concerns with family. But as I said, this goes no further. Say nothing to Luke or Rocky or, God forbid, Daisy. Nothing to the cousins or your aunts and uncles. If they hear it from anyone, let it be your dad."

"Understood." Just as his dad wanted to spare them heartache and worry, so did Devlin.

"And don't let on to your father that I confided in you. I'll try to convince him to come clean, with you at least, but until then . . ."

"Soul of discretion." The last thing he wanted to do was add to his mom's anxiety.

"I have to go. I'll call you tomorrow and fill you in on treatment specifics or anything else you want to know."

"I appreciate that, Mom, and rest easy. I won't hassle Dad with additional reports."

"Knowing you, I don't entirely trust your wording. Should I be concerned?"

"Absolutely not." He said his good-byes, barred visions of his dad's physical suffering, and focused on how he could help. Clearly the man was concerned about the future security of his wife and children.

Turning to his laptop, Devlin keyed in the password to his personal business accounts, his mind churning with calculations and projections. "No worries, you proud bastard." He couldn't wish away disease, but he could work magic with finances.

SEVENTEEN

The only difference between this morning and every other morning Chloe had spent in Sugar Creek was that she hadn't gone to the library straightaway. A cable guy had knocked on the door announcing he was there to fill a work order. An order initiated by Devlin. The upgraded service combined cable television, phone service, and high-speed Internet. Since Daisy didn't own a computer or any wireless devices, Chloe assumed the Internet service was intended for her benefit. She could've refused the gesture but didn't. Now she could check e-mail and research recipes at her convenience without having to worry about leaving Daisy alone for too long. Not that Chloe wanted to be her shadow, but ever since she'd lied and baked behind Chloe's back, she didn't trust the woman not to pull a harebrained solo stunt.

Chloe was especially concerned since Daisy's secret recipe cupcakes had tasted less than spectacular. Clearly, Daisy had screwed up the ingredients or the measurements. Chloe had studied Daisy's recipe card, and theoretically the cupcakes should've tasted insanely good. In a private moment, Chloe had offered to assist Daisy or to at least observe as she made a second batch. The proud, stubborn woman had refused. Chloe wouldn't have cared except Daisy had seemed even more distracted and even a little depressed all through Monday.

This morning in a desperate attempt to rekindle the woman's confidence, Chloe had begged *her* assistance. "If I'm going to offer my two cents at Cupcake Lovers, I figure I should invest some time in the art. I'd really love to swing this decoration," she said, flashing a photo she'd found in a magazine, "but I have no experience with fondant."

"I'd love to help you, kitten, but I have a date."

On cue, Vincent Redding knocked on the door. "Here to take Daisy on a country drive," he told Chloe.

She couldn't have been more surprised. Or thrilled! Maybe *he* could charm Daisy out of her funk. More than ever Chloe was certain Oslow's owner had a crush on her employer. On their way out, Daisy had presented Chloe with "a mission," after which Chloe had immediately called and enlisted Monica's help. Even though she and Devlin had struck a truce, she hadn't seen him since Sunday night and felt awkward about her appointed shopping excursion.

Pulling into Monica's drive, Chloe tapped the horn, then checked her makeup in the mirror. Not that she wanted to impress Devlin, but . . . oh, who was she kidding? Since he'd addressed their attraction, she'd been unable to think of little else.

The passenger door wrenched open and Monica plopped inside. "Ready when you are."

"Thanks for breaking away on such short notice."

"A welcome distraction, trust me. I plan on doing major damage to our credit card. It's not like I'm saving up for a nursery or anything."

"Whoa. Whoa." Chloe shifted back into park and took a good look at her friend. Clearly, she was upset. "What's wrong?"

Staring straight ahead, Monica sniffed. "This morning Leo informed me that he wants to stop trying for a baby."

"Forever?"

"For now. Says we've been at it for three months and since I haven't conceived . . ."

Heart in throat, Chloe reached over and squeezed her friend's hand.

"As if it's my fault."

"I'm sure he didn't mean it that way. He's probably just . . . frustrated."

"And I'm *not*?" She blew out a breath. "Sorry. Not your fault."

"It's not anyone's fault." Chloe dug deep for the right words. Instead of getting her friend more worked up, she decided to play it cool. Hopefully, no, definitely this was a temporary glitch. "You know three months isn't really all that long."

Monica cast her a look that said, *Put yourself in my shoes,* in which case three months probably felt like forever.

"Sometimes," Chloe tried again, "when you want something too bad, when you try too hard . . ."

"Yeah, yeah. Sometimes the best things happen when you're not expecting them." Monica quirked a small smile. "You sound like Leo."

"No, I don't. His voice is much deeper."

Monica rolled her eyes. "Okay. Let me see Daisy's shopping list."

Smiling now, Chloe plucked the folded paper from her purse and passed it over.

Monica scanned the full page of the older woman's chicken scratch while Chloe backed onto the street. "Must've been in a hurry," she said. "Normally Daisy has beautiful handwriting." She squinted, then whistled. "Everything from garden supplies to guest towels. Wait. What's Big Al?"

Chloe blushed. "Nothing I'll find at a local department store. Trust me."

"Five new Sunday frocks, including handbags and shoes?"

"She's determined to overhaul the last of her conservative wardrobe."

"No more hats and gloves? No matching shoes and purses? I always thought she looked so regal."

"Good-bye, Queen Elizabeth, hello, Lady Gaga."

"That's sort of sad." Monica shivered. "And scary."

"Don't worry. I'll find a moderate compromise. As it happens, we wear the same size. I can try on everything and match up accessories. Just have to keep in mind I'm standing in for a senior. Hemline appropriate and all that."

"Don't recall 'personal stylist' being part of your job description."

"It wasn't, but last night Daisy got me talking about some of my past jobs and I mentioned my brief stint in the fashion world."

"Ah, yes. You wanted to be the next Vera Wang."

"Until I learned I had no real talent for design. Then I caught the photography bug, but sucked at that, too."

"At least you tried," Monica said. "Lots of people have special interests, but never pursue them. Take me for instance. I've always wanted to play the fiddle, but have I ever taken a lesson? *You* would have bought the instrument and signed up for personal instruction with a renowned violinist."

"Yeah, but if it didn't come naturally, if it turned out to be more stressful than fun, I would've dropped out."

"Sounds smart to me. Why invest time and money in something that doesn't bring you joy or at least satisfaction? My point is, you'll never have to look back and wish you would have pounced on an opportunity. You pounced plenty and you're a fascinating person because of it."

Chloe smiled. "Stop or I won't be able to get my head out the door when we stop."

"Sure you will. Plenty of room." She glanced around the car. "This thing's a freaking boat. How do you even see over the hood? It must stick out twenty feet."

Chloe laughed. "Believe it or not, I'm sort of used to it now." She'd been driving Daisy all over town and then some. They'd been in and out of several artisans' shops, Oslow's, the drugstore, the library, the hairdresser's, Gemma's Bakery, and the Sugar Shack. The only place they hadn't been was J.T.'s Department Store. Chloe hadn't stopped in on her own because she didn't want Devlin to think she was looking for him or snooping around his business. Even though, admittedly, she was curious about the place that dominated his life.

Then this morning, Daisy had presented Chloe with "the

list," instructing her to shop exclusively at J.T.'s and to charge everything to her account. Chloe had changed her clothes three times before settling on slim-cut jeans, wedge-heeled boots, a scoop-necked tee, and her vintage leather jacket. She'd fluffed her hair, plumped her lips with gloss, and spritzed on her favorite perfume. All the while reminding herself why it was bad to encourage Devlin's attention.

As if reading her mind, Monica shot her a sly grin. "So how are things between you and Dev?"

"Fine. I guess. I haven't seen him since Sunday."

"From the way you're sexed up, I guess you're hoping to see him today."

Cheeks hot, Chloe focused on the road. "I'm not sexed up."

"It's okay, you know. Being attracted to the man. He's single. You're single."

"Newly single."

"Have you heard from Ryan?"

"No." She was torn between relief and outrage. "Goes to show what I meant to him. Not a call, text, or e-mail. I could be dead for all he knows. Or cares."

"Maybe he feels bad. Maybe he's too embarrassed to check up on you."

"Whatever." The longer she was away from him, the more she wondered what she ever saw in him. The longer she was away from Manhattan, the more she felt like a woman caught between two worlds and not wholly belonging to either.

"Tell your dad about the breakup yet?"

"You asked me that yesterday."

"And?"

"Same answer as yesterday. No. Although I did try to call him last night. Got his voice mail. Left a message, nothing specific. I'm waiting for a callback."

"You'll feel better once you tell him."

"I doubt it."

Monica smiled. "Don't you want to move on with your life?"

"I *am* moving on with my life. New motto: Embrace the adventure. Live in the moment."

"So if Dev asks you out—"

"He won't."

"But if he does, you'll embrace the adventure, right?"

"He's totally wrong for me." Which was probably why she was so drawn to him. Another controlling alpha male. *Hello, heartache.*

"So he's not Mr. Right. Doesn't mean he can't be Mr. Right *Now*."

Chloe laughed. "You're such a bad influence!"

"You love it."

"I do."

They shared geeky, sappy, best-girlfriend smiles; then Monica gestured to the upcoming intersection. "Maple Street dead ahead. Make a right. That's it," she said, pointing to a multi-level building that took up half the block. "Doesn't look like there's a parking space on the street, so you'll have to swing around to the small lot on the side."

"It's not as quaint as some of the other buildings in town," Chloe noted as she followed Monica's instructions, "but it's not very modern looking either." Frankly, considering the vibrant personalities of the Monroes, J.T.'s Department Store was surprisingly unimpressive.

"From what I understand, Devlin's dad and grandfather and even his great-grandfather put most of their time and energy into the workings of the store. I think the last time this building had a major exterior overhaul was in the nineteen-fifties."

"I can see why Devlin's keen on renovating," Chloe said as she nosed into a parking space. "It's not much to look at."

"Maybe not, but J.T.'s stocks quality items for reasonable prices. The staff is friendly and efficient, and they have a kick-butt no-hassle return policy. As the saying goes, don't judge a book by its cover."

Chloe breathed in the crisp, cool air as she and Monica rounded the building. Her senses buzzed with anticipation as they neared what appeared to be one of three front entrances. She eyed the old-fashioned white cursive penned across the green-and-blue-striped awning: *J.T. Monroe's Department Store—established in 1885.* Three years prior to Oslow's. Clutching Daisy's shopping list, Chloe pushed through the glass doors with the same excitement as when she'd first entered Manhattan's historic Macy's. She couldn't explain the immense wonder and joy she experienced when she spied the old-fashioned candy counter and the display featuring moose socks, moose mugs, and moose stuffed animals in three distinct styles and sizes. Charming!

"Shoot."

Chloe looked over and saw Monica checking text messages.

"It's Leo. He wants me to call. I'm going to step outside for this. You go on. I'll meet up with you when I'm done."

"Take your time. I need to assemble five Sunday ensembles, remember? Including handbags and shoes!"

"I still want to know about Big Al," Monica said as she backed toward the door they'd entered.

"I am so crossing that off the list," Chloe mumbled to herself. "I am *not* shopping for a vibrator."

"Can I help you?"

Chloe glanced up into the sparkling eyes of an overeager salesclerk—an older woman with a fondness for overprocessed hair and excessive makeup—praying she hadn't heard her grumbling about a dildo. Blushing, Chloe stuffed the list in her jacket pocket and smiled. "Why, yes . . . Mitzi," she added after glancing at the woman's name tag. "Could you direct me to the ladies' fashion department?"

Three seconds later, as she trailed after Mitzi trying not to think unkind thoughts about the woman's overly tight pants and overly swishing hips, Chloe's own phone chimed with an incoming text.

" 'Leo wants to make up,' " she read aloud. " 'Now.' "

"Excuse me?" Mitzi asked.

"Nothing. Sorry." According to the text, Monica was sorry, too. She was skipping shopping in favor of a kiss-and-makeup quickie with her husband, leaving Chloe on her own. She tried not to feel bad about her friend's good fortune. So what if she had to shop alone? So what if she bumped into Devlin? As much as she'd fantasized about tearing his clothes off and doing it against a tree or in a closest or under a covered bridge, she could resist temptation.

With luck, she wouldn't see him at all. In and out. Shop and go. She had a list and she had a good eye. Her fashionista background roared to life as they skirted the shoe department and neared multiple racks of clothes. For a small store, J.T.'s had a decent selection of quality merchandise. She spotted two perfect Sunday dresses right off and mentally matched them with a pair of yellow pumps she'd spied two aisles back. In and out. Shop and go. "Embrace the adventure."

EIGHTEEN

"Should've known I'd find you glued to the computer."

Devlin glanced over his shoulder as Jayce Bello sauntered into his office. As if his oldest friend had sensed a personal crisis and magically appeared. Pleased yet surprised, Devlin rose to greet the man. "What are you doing here?"

"Told you I'd have this report to you by noon today." He tossed the thin file onto Devlin's desk, clasped his hand in a warm shake, then dropped into an opposing chair.

"Expected a fax or an e-mail," Devlin said, reclaiming his own seat. "Not a personal delivery."

"I needed to fly up anyway. The Ashfords informed me they're not renewing the lease on my parents' house. Sudden job opportunity in Arkansas."

"Who relocates to Arkansas?"

"My former tenants. I'm here to assess the condition of the property. Don't know that I want to rent it out again. Maybe it's time to sell."

"And sever all ties with Sugar Creek?"

Jayce shrugged. "Unlike you, I'm not bound by family."

"Nice to know where we stand." As far as Devlin was concerned, Jayce was a second brother. They'd grown up together. Tight friends since grade school. An only child, Jayce had spent countless hours at the Monroe house and had joined them for family affairs and even on a few vacations.

When Jayce's parents had been killed during his senior year of high school, Devlin's parents had stepped in to help him through the transition. Even after he'd moved to New York, the deep bond remained. Or so Devlin had thought.

"I was referring to blood." Jayce crooked a taunting grin. "Since when did you get all sappy-ass sentimental?"

Since about a half hour ago. The shaky state of his dad's health only intensified Devlin's devotion to friends and family. The urge to preserve and protect those bonds had never been more fierce.

"Bad day?"

"Had better." He closed two accounting programs, rose, and crossed to the refreshment sidebar installed by his grandfather more than fifty years ago. "Coffee?"

"Sure."

Devlin poured two cups—one black, one with sugar.

"That file's been sitting on your desk for five minutes now and you've yet to open it. Last we spoke you were anxious for details regarding Chloe Madison's former arrests."

Right now it was the last thing on mind, but since he couldn't discuss his dad's condition . . . "Since you're here," he said, locking the file in a secured drawer, "just spill."

Jayce drank from his cup, then shifted into PI mode. "Since Chloe's record was expunged, I couldn't obtain detailed specifics, but some matters were part of public record. I got enough information to track down parties involved, but even their stories were sketchy, not to mention one sided."

"Go on."

"First arrest was ten years ago—shoplifting. She left a Fifth Avenue boutique with a designer coat she didn't pay for."

"A coat? Not easy to hide. What, did she stuff it in another shopping bag?"

"She was wearing it."

"So she casually walked out of the store wearing stolen merchandise." Devlin shook his head. "Can't decide if that's stupid or ballsy."

"Actually, she didn't walk. She ran. She was midway

down the block before the salesclerk who gave chase stopped her with the help of a cop. Chloe claimed she'd gotten an emergency call from a friend on her cell phone and she'd been so flustered, she'd blown out of the store without thought. Since the clerk had been in the other room looking for a similar coat in a different size, she didn't hear the call, just caught sight of Chloe tearing out the door."

"Couldn't they verify her story by calling the friend in need?"

"Apparently the friend's story was suspect, though, yes, it eventually proved strong enough to cast doubt on Chloe's guilt. And, no, I don't know details of the friend's so-called crisis. Arrest number two," Jayce said. "Two years ago. Disturbing the peace. Chloe got into a verbal row with a chef she'd dissed in an online critique for the e-zine I told you about. The dude she was dining with interceded. Punches were exchanged, between dude and chef, not Chloe, although she was in the thick of it. I didn't speak to the friend because I didn't want it getting back to Chloe, but I did speak to the chef. He blamed the row entirely on Chloe and her friend. If you want Chloe's side, you'll have to ask."

Except he didn't want to let on that he'd pried into her background. "That would be tricky."

"Is it even necessary? Obviously, she's not a dangerous criminal, just someone with bad timing or shitty judgment."

"Either/or resulted in another run-in with the law a few days ago." He had started relaying the reckless driving fiasco when his desk phone rang. "Devlin Monroe," he answered on speaker.

"Dev, it's Chris. Need you in my office. We've got a security issue involving the woman who works for Daisy."

He raised a brow. "Chloe Madison?"

"I stopped the department manager from calling the police. Thought you'd want to keep this quiet."

"Be right down." He disconnected, glanced at Jayce, who, damn him, was grinning. "Don't suppose you'd consider waiting here."

"Right." He blew out of the office on Devlin's heels.

"One thing's for sure: That girl adds color to your dull-ass life."

"Why is everyone under the misconception my life is dull?"

"Are you seeing anyone? When's the last time you got laid? Have you been out with friends lately? A ball game? Poker night? Did you boat or tube on Sugar Creek even once this summer?"

Devlin didn't answer.

His friend snorted as they cleared the stairs and hit the main floor. "Dull."

Devlin tuned him out as he navigated the first floor—not particularly bustling, then again this was Tuesday afternoon and in between the summer and winter high seasons. Past cosmetics and perfume, specialty gifts, handbags and accessories, and, last, women's fashion. He stepped into Chris's small office and into a heated storm.

"She's blowing this out of proportion!" Chloe shouted. "If you'd just—"

"Are you calling me a liar?" Mitzi turned her outrage on Chris. "Why aren't you sticking up for me? Why—"

"What's going on?" Devlin felt Jayce slip in behind him, heard the *snick* of the door as he afforded them privacy. His attention, however, was on the two women who whirled to face him. Mitzi Hall, a fairly new employee, a woman who'd recently lost her husband and seemed hot to replace him as soon as possible. Twice she'd flirted with Devlin, though he'd pretended not to notice.

Then there was Chloe. Her sweet face burned with embarrassment, or maybe it was fury. From his experiences with her so far, probably both.

"There's been a misunderstanding," she said.

"She ran out of J.T.'s," Mitzi said to Devlin, "wearing things she didn't pay for. I knew there was something fishy about her when she said she was shopping for your grandma." She pointed at Chloe. "As if your grandma would wear *that*."

Actually, Devlin thought as he took in the bright blue and green floral dress with the matching green shoes and purse, *she would.* Up until a few years ago, Daisy Monroe had been conservative in most matters. But just as her behavior had turned unpredictable and outrageous, so had her taste in clothing. Not that this particular outfit looked outrageous on Chloe, but on his seventy-five-year-old grandma? On second thought, it could've been worse. At least the hemline was modest and the heels two inches shy of sexy.

Jayce cleared his throat and Devlin forced his gaze from Chloe's shapely calves to her sparking eyes. "I assume you can explain."

"Of course I can explain. First, I didn't run; I walked."

Mitzi gasped.

"Okay. I *race*-walked. But that was because I was frustrated. I got a phone call."

Devlin could feel Jayce's eyes burning into his back. Could feel his amusement. "Go on."

"It was important. I needed to hear and I couldn't. What is it with the reception around here? So I moved around, seeking better signal, and suddenly I found myself outside."

"Likely story," Mitzi grumbled. "She bolted because I scoffed when she told me to charge everything—about three hundred bucks' worth of merchandise—to Daisy Monroe's account. That's when I stepped away to call a supervisor and *poof* she was gone."

"I told you, I got a phone call," Chloe snapped. She turned her attention to Devlin, her big eyes pleading innocence, her body language softening from defiant to earnest.

"I believe you," Devlin said.

Mitzi gaped. "What?"

"You do?" Chloe looked stunned, then grateful, then leery.

For once Devlin read her perfectly. She'd been the victim, in Jayce's words, of bad timing and shitty judgment. Not malicious, just unfortunate. And just like that, Devlin's foul mood lifted, leaving him exposed and vulnerable to an attraction that grew stronger with every Chloe mishap. Instead of running from trouble, he edged closer. "Thank you for being so diligent, Mrs. Hall, but I'll vouch for Ms. Madison. I'd appreciate it if you'd follow her direction regarding billing. Chris, see that the merchandise is delivered to Daisy's home."

"Will do." Chris guided the blustering salesclerk from the office.

Jayce followed, but not without sarcastic commentary. "A veritable rainbow."

Devlin nudged him out, then locked the door. When he turned, Chloe crossed her arms and squared her shoulders. He smothered a smile, knowing she expected a lecture. Instead he asked a question: "Where's Daisy?"

"On a date."

"Excuse me?"

"Mr. Redding took her for a scenic drive."

"Vince Redding?"

The wary glint in her eye turned ornery, just like the tilt of her luscious pink lips. "I'm not sure, but I think he might have a crush on her."

"Vincent Redding," Devlin repeated. "Owner of Oslow's."

"You don't approve?"

"I don't believe it."

"Because they're too old to have romantic urges?"

"Because they've known each other for years and I've never once witnessed an infatuation on either side."

"Maybe you weren't looking at the right time." She shrugged. "Whatever. I'm glad he stopped by. She needed a distraction. That last cupcake failure tanked her spirits."

"Shopping would have been a distraction. Gram loves to shop. Hard to believe she chose a leisurely drive over an opportunity to embellish her increasingly peculiar wardrobe."

She frowned. "You think this outfit's peculiar?"

"Not on you."

"Well, it's not for me; it's for Daisy. I'd show you the shopping list she gave me, but it's in my jacket pocket, which is in the dressing room along with my purse. My actual purse," she clarified, acknowledging the price tag and sensor device dangling from the handbag on her arm.

"I believe you."

She narrowed suspicious eyes. "If Sheriff Stone told you about my record, you probably know I was arrested once for shoplifting."

He didn't confirm or deny.

"So why do you believe me?"

He couldn't say.

"It was a crazy mistake. Poor judgment on my part. I don't think the sanest when I'm frazzled."

"Who frazzled you this time?"

"My dad. He wants . . . We don't . . . Things aren't the best between us."

He flashed on his own dad, not knowing if, by defying him, he'd just done their relationship more harm than good. Knowing he had some explaining to do either way. "Try to amend that."

"But—"

"Is he a decent man?"

"Yes, but—"

"Life's short, Chloe."

She studied him for a long moment, either struggling for a response or wondering how to make a diplomatic escape because, hell, he'd just made this conversation personal. *Intimate.* She could've made a flip remark or segued into a quick good-bye, but she stood her ground and, as he acted on instinct and moved closer, her gaze sparked with anticipation. *Desire.* An invitation or a dare to seize the heated moment.

Aside from the obvious physical attraction, he acknowledged a need to connect with her vibrant spirit. To act recklessly, spitting in the eye of fate. His social life wasn't dull. Worse, it was dead. Right now he needed to feel alive. Strong. *Impassioned.*

He realized suddenly that he'd backed her against the faded wall of Chris's cramped office. Inappropriate. Possessive. Sexual. The professional, sensible part of him screamed, *Back off!* But her imploring gaze and shallow breathing beckoned him as a man.

He kissed her. Softly. Thoroughly. Holding her sweet

face captive between his hands. Suckling her tongue. Pressing his hard body against her pliant form and reveling in her eager acceptance and soft moans. The simmering heat raged into an inferno and in turn the kiss grew wild. Rainbows exploded behind his closed lids, arced through his dull-ass world, and warped his normally logical senses. Pent-up urges trampled better judgment. He wanted this woman here, now, naked, writhing beneath his touch. Screaming out his name.

Stunned, he broke off.

Sex on company time? In the family store? Nothing between them and scores of people aside from thin walls and a locked door?

Well, hell.

Eyes bright, hair tousled, she quirked a loopy, perplexed grin. "What was that about?"

Even though they were no longer touching, the inferno raged, the rainbow lingered, making him feel like a besotted teen. Reckless. Alive. "Color."

She blinked in confusion, then launched herself against him. He landed in a worn wing chair with Chloe straddling his lap. She kissed him. Hard. Deep. Holding his face captive between her hands. Suckling his tongue. Wiggling against his arousal. More rainbows. *Christ.* He palmed her ass through the voluminous floral skirt, itching to peel off the thong beneath, dying to touch bare skin. He'd heard about people getting off on the thrill of possibly getting caught in the act. His cousin Nash was one of them. Devlin wasn't, but he was seriously contemplating a fast and furious fuck.

As if reading his mind or coming to her senses, Chloe eased back, eyes wide, cheeks flushed. Her hands flew to her kiss-swollen lips, her expression somewhere between dazed and mortified.

Striving for casual, he teased her with her own words. "What was that about?"

"Living in the moment."

"Huh."

"Probably not the best choice."

"I'm not complaining."

Breathless, she searched his gaze, causing his heart to race, or maybe that was an aftershock of that earth-rocking kiss. As swiftly as she'd tackled him, she scrambled off his lap. "I can't do this. Whatever this is. Not now."

"Bad timing," he conceded. "Public place."

"It's not that." She paused when he raised a brow. "I mean that doesn't help. But mostly, bad timing overall."

Logic cut through the rainbow haze, tempered the sexual heat. "Same here." He needed to focus his energies on the store, the family.

"As of two weeks ago—almost—I was living with some-one. A man. I'm not . . ."

"Over him?"

"Myself. If I followed through with this . . ."

"Attraction?"

"I wouldn't know if I was acting out of revenge, a need to reaffirm my desirability, or a sincere animal urge to burn up the sheets with you."

"I vote the latter," he said while tucking in his shirttails.

"Which would be as disastrous as the first two, because, no offense, you're totally wrong for me."

"You're not my ideal either." His dream girl was grounded, stable. "But here we are."

She backed toward the door. "Not to mention I don't want you or anyone else to think I used sex to beat a shoplifting charge."

"We established you weren't shoplifting."

"I know. I just don't want there to be any doubt."

"There isn't."

"Good. Great." She tamed her hair with one hand while struggling with the dead bolt.

He moved in, resisting the urge to kiss her, resisting . . . her. He released the lock. "So we're not going to pursue this."

"Doesn't seem wise."

Succumbing to a small temptation, he tucked a hunk of her tousled hair behind one ear, lightly caressing her lobe, smiling when she shivered. "In that case, we should proba-bly keep our distance."

"Probably," she croaked, fumbling for the doorknob.

"See you for Sunday dinner."

"See you then." She held his gaze a moment longer than she should have. A moment that betrayed sincere longing, before she scrambled out the door. "Oh, and thank you for the high-speed cable service," she blurted nervously over her shoulder. "That was really thoughtful."

He watched her go, marveling at her complexity. Nice girl? Bad girl? Confused? Conniving? For better, for worse, that kiss had sealed it. Melon Girl was in his blood.

NINETEEN

Chloe waited until she'd parked the Caddy in Daisy's garage before dialing Monica. All the anxiety and frustration she'd been stuffing down since she'd bolted from J.T.'s erupted when Monica answered with a cheery, "So how was shopping?"

"How could you desert me like that?" she screamed into her cell.

"What? You texted back that you understood. You said no worries."

"That was before I got accused of shoplifting. Before Devlin and I went at each other like two dogs in heat!" Her blood and body still burned from the spontaneous, passionate interlude. She'd never been so turned on, so close to an orgasm, while still wearing all her clothes!

"*What*? You and Dev had sex?"

"No! But we may as well have. I mean it was heading there. We were all over each other!"

"Before or after you were accused of shoplifting?"

"After. A total misunderstanding by the way."

"The groping or the shoplifting?"

"The shoplifting." Chloe still couldn't believe how fast a blissful excursion had soured. She'd enjoyed shopping for Daisy, coupling her past fashion education—albeit brief— with her present employer's taste, however unique. Chloe had been pulling together the last of five outfits when her phone had chimed. Her dad. That's when things had gone from heavenly to hell-in-a-handbasket. "Anyway," Chloe said, shaking off the upsetting call, "first Devlin kissed me; then I kissed him."

"You're freaking out over a measly kiss?"

"There was nothing measly about it. It was . . . orgasmic!"

"Wow."

"I know. It was *awful*."

"Awful?"

"It only made me more hot for him. Brain-melting, thigh-quivering, do-me-now-or-I'll-die *hot.* "

"I'm trying to figure out why that's bad."

"The timing's off. *We're* off. He even admitted it. I'm not his ideal."

"He's totally wrong for you. Yeah, yeah. I gotta say, Chloe, I don't get it. You're both single. Both adults. Whatever happened to healthy, guilt-free sex?"

"But what if I fall for him? Really fall for him? He's a control freak."

"And you're a loose cannon. Maybe you'd even each other out."

"Maybe we'd drive each other crazy."

"Maybe you should give it a try."

"Not gonna happen. We agreed to keep our distance."

"Which will only make it worse." Monica snorted. "Wake up and smell the apples, Eve."

"What?"

"Human nature. We always want what we can't have or shouldn't have. Deny yourself something and you'll only crave it more. You've just made Dev the forbidden fruit."

Chloe fell forward and thunked her head against the steering wheel. She recognized the wisdom in Monica's words; she just didn't want to admit it. Admitting gave the observation weight. She needed to shrug this off as if it were nothing. "I have to go. Daisy might be back and . . . I should get inside."

"Chloe—"

"I'm glad you and Leo made up. Talk to you later."

* * *

Rocky pushed the Jeep to sixty-five, ignoring the speed limit and the intermittent troubling sound from the engine. She rolled down the window, welcoming the rush of cool air, willing serenity. Her brain was crammed with finances and legalities, pros and cons. After listening to Adam's impressive proposal over pancakes, she'd driven into town to speak with her lawyer, then loan officer. She'd questioned them about a possible partnership and what that would and could entail. Both men had listened; both had advised. Both, though striving to stay neutral, had seen the advantage in a joint venture. Probably because they both knew she was struggling. Which probably meant they thought, if she stayed the course, her dream was doomed. Even so, the desire to solely own and operate the Red Clover was intense. She feared giving over an ounce of power. Or was it that she feared a business alliance would ruin her personal alliance with Adam? Why mess with perfection? And their casual sexual relationship *was* damn near perfect.

"No rash decisions," she told herself. Even Adam had told her to live with the idea a couple of days before giving him an answer. Logical, sound advice. "Damn him." He really was the perfect business partner, *if* she decided to go that route.

The wooded landscape blurred as she buzzed down the highway. Caught up in a cyclone of thoughts, she answered her trilling cell without screening.

"What are you doing tonight?"

Rocky grunted. "If any man other than my big brother had asked me that question, I'd be intrigued. Since it's you, I'm leery. What do you want, Dev?"

"I need to talk to you."

"About?"

"The Red Clover."

She tightened her one-handed grip on the steering wheel, steeled her spine. Dev had a way of knowing everyone's business, especially family, but surely he hadn't heard about her back-to-back visits with Tommy and Joe. She'd shown up and walked in—no appointment. All told, she'd spent less than an hour in Sugar Creek and was now on her way home. Dev couldn't know. Unless her business associates had betrayed her confidence.

Paranoid much? she could hear Adam say.

Getting a grip, Rocky chalked up this call to her control freak brother's freaking annoying sixth sense. "I'm not going to sell—"

"You've made that clear and I appreciate your commitment."

"So give it a rest."

"I can't. I have some ideas—"

"Forget it." She stepped on the gas, desperate to see the inn. *Her* inn. The property she'd coveted. The property she'd saved for and, with the help of her dad, had bought dirt cheap. She knew he'd been pacifying her, affording her a hobby. But she hadn't cared because she'd had big plans. Big plans based on a childhood dream. Admittedly, she'd hit roadblocks and experienced disappointments and maybe, just maybe, she was going to have to alter her plans, but she still had her frickin' *dream*. "Shouldn't you be concentrating on J.T.'s?"

"I am. So about tonight—"

"I have plans."

"Tomorrow then."

"I'm sorry. What? You're breaking up," she lied. "Dev?" She feigned static, then disconnected. She tossed her cell on the passenger seat, cursing her well-intentioned brother, crummy luck, and the economy. Her engine made a clunking sound and she cursed her Jeep, too. Chest tight, she rolled down her window even more, needing fresh air. Needing air, period. Breathing was suddenly a chore.

Her phone chimed again. "Dammit, Dev." But then she saw it was Monica. "Hey, Mon. What's shaking?"

"My conscience."

"What?"

"Part of me feels guilty for betraying a friend's confidence, but the other part screams it's for her own good. Something wonderful is staring her in the face and she's shoving it away."

"The 'friend' being Chloe and the 'it' being my brother?"

"Exactly."

"Did you promise to keep whatever Chloe told you to yourself?"

"No."

"Well, there's your loophole, hon. Plus, don't think of it as a betrayal so much as a mission of mercy."

"It's just we all saw it, the chemistry between those two."

"And we all agreed they'd probably be good for one another. So what happened and how can I help?"

Monica sighed. "It all started when Chloe went shopping at J.T.'s."

Rocky listened while her friend told a tale that had her shaking her head. She turned onto a side road that led to the Red Clover, certain there'd just been a shakeup in the cosmos. "I could've sworn you just said my brother, my usually conservative, by-the-books, always-in-control brother, *lost* control in a mega-hot make-out session with Chloe."

"You heard right," Monica said.

"In J.T.'s."

"Yup."

"Where? In his office? On the floor? In front of people?"

"I don't know. I don't have details. I just know it rattled the hell out of Chloe."

"That's awesome!"

"Her word was 'awful.' "

"Kissing Dev was awful?"

"Orgasmic, actually. Apparently."

"And that's awful because?"

"She's worried about falling for him."

"News flash: Dev's already fallen for *her*."

"He told you that?"

"His actions did. Making out in the middle of the work-day? On work property?"

"I see what you mean."

"This is fabulous!" Rocky said. "Dev's head over heels. Someone else to obsess on aside from family!"

"Except they agreed to keep their distance."

She frowned. "That would explain his phone call."

"What phone call?"

"Never mind. Just . . . Don't worry about it. I'll get them together."

"How?"

"Family."

"Not sure I follow, but go for it. Keep me advised, will you?"

"Sure thing."

Rocky signed off and dialed Nash. "Need a favor."

"Shoot."

"Ask Chloe out."

"Thought you said Dev's interested."

"He is. Just do it."

"Why?"

"For Dev. For me."

"This is screwy."

"Pretty girl. New in town. Kick-ass cook."

"Well, when you put it like that."

"Thanks, Nash."

"Anytime."

She disconnected, called Luke. "Remember the other night when you said something about giving Dev some broth-erly competition?"

"You want me to ask Chloe out, too?"

"What do you mean, *too*?"

"Nash just texted me."

"Holy . . . I just hung up with him!"

"Hot news travels fast. So I assume our goal is to make Dev jealous?"

"I have reason to believe he's fallen big-time for Chloe, which, in addition to possible long-term bliss for him, could mean big-time freedom for you and me. Unfortunately, he's resisting the attraction."

"You want me to shove?"

"Hard."

"My pleasure."

She imagined the cocky grin on his face when he disconnected, and couldn't help feeling a little arrogant as well. She knew Dev well enough to know any seductive move on Nash's part would shake his resolve. Luke's pursuit would push him over the edge. The two biggest players in Sugar Creek after the woman who'd inspired him to get hot and heavy in J.T.'s? His ego wouldn't stand for it. And if he was truly, deeply taken with her, neither would his heart.

Rocky refused to feel bad about pushing his buttons. In fact, she had additional plans to throw the reluctant would-be lovers together. She liked Chloe and, unlike the other women Dev had been attracted to, sensed she'd actually be good for him. She swerved to miss a pothole and dialed another cousin. "Hey, Sam."

"What's up, sweetheart?"

"Cupcake meeting's at your house Thursday, right?"

"Last I knew."

"Create some kind of excuse. Bail. Not totally. Just make your house taboo and ask Dev if you can borrow his."

"Why would I ask Dev? Why not someone else in the club?"

"Because I want Dev there and we stand a better chance if it's at his house."

"Couldn't we just invite him?"

"Just do it, Sam. It's for the family's good. I'll explain later."

She disconnected, confident that she'd set critical wheels in motion when the Jeep's engine stopped cold. "What the . . ."

She coasted to the side of the road, the Red Clover in sight a half mile away. Frustrated, she whacked the steering wheel hard with the flat of her hand. "Dammit!"

Her oven, the fridge, the porch, the shed, her ceiling.

Now her damned transportation? She was torn between crying and screaming. Resisting both, she blew out of the Jeep
and kicked the tire—twice—before throwing open the hood.
She knew a little about engines but not a lot. She'd probably
have to call Leo, ask him for a tow. She estimated charges
and cringed. Maybe Adam could help. Not seeing any hiss-
ing, steaming or obvious broken valves or wires, she back-
tracked for her phone, pausing when she heard a car drawing
near. Maybe it was someone with a knack for mechanics.

She stepped out to wave down the driver, not recognizing
the make and model as belonging to anyone she knew. The
dark-blue sedan slowed and suddenly Rocky's skin prick-
led with dread. Living in a secluded area for years, inviting
tourists into her bed-and-breakfast as a norm, she'd never
been squeamish about encountering strangers. This moment, though, her heart pounded as though she'd just
flagged down the devil.

In the next moment, a tall, well-built, golden-haired
Adonis unfolded from the car. Even though his hair was
longer and he'd grown a goatee . . . even though his eyes
were hidden behind a pair of aviator sunglasses, her mind
and body recognized him in an instant, responding with a
familiar firestorm of emotions.

Of all the freaking people on the damned planet.

She would have preferred *Lucifer*.

Rocky stood frozen as Jayce Bello strode toward her, an
enigmatic expression on his absurdly gorgeous face. She
hated him for being so incredibly good looking, so confident,
so charismatic. She hated herself for being so affected, even
after, even still. She shoved down traitorous yearnings and
conjured ancient resentment. She hardened her heart and
will, relaxed against her Jeep, and feigned a casual demeanor.

Even though they hadn't spoken in over five years, he
bypassed formal greetings. "You okay?"

She raised a brow, lacing her tone with more sarcasm
than intended. "Don't I look okay?"

He slid his sunglasses on top of his head and raked his
bourbon gaze down her body.

She ignored the tightening of her belly, the sensual tingle between her legs. There was nothing sexy about her attire—faded jeans, layered tees, worn Nikes—yet his silent assessment betrayed a primal appreciation. Was he imagining the body beneath the clothes? She'd filled out in the bust and hips since he'd last seen her naked.

"Something wrong with the Jeep?" he asked, dragging his gaze from her curves to the open hood.

"Some detective you are." Twice now he'd asked the obvious.

"Just trying to keep it civil, Rocky."

So his deductive skills were indeed intact. He sensed her anger, knew without asking that all was not forgotten. Definitely not forgiven. She wasn't sure she could manage civil, especially when her second-greatest urge right now was to punch him. She crossed her arms over her chest and frowned. "What are you doing in Sugar Creek?"

He slid his hands into the deep pockets of his black cargo pants and rocked back on the thick rubber soles. "Personal business."

She thought about his background check on Chloe and smirked. "Regarding Dev?"

"Regarding my parents' house. I'm thinking of selling."

"Oh." She should've been thrilled. Instead, she was shocked and more than a little sad. She'd known Jayce all her life. Even though they were at odds, she had a mental scrapbook of incredible childhood memories. He'd been like a brother until she'd hit her teens and then . . . She looked away, gathered her wits. She didn't want him living in Sugar Creek, but she didn't want him gone for good either. *Well, hell.*

"Either way," he went on, "renovations are in order. I'll be in town a week or two. Need a place to stay. Dev suggested the Red Clover."

That snapped her head back around. "What?" Was he *insane*? "Why not stay with Dev? He's got two spare bedrooms."

"It's complicated."

She frowned. Complicated because Jayce had investigated Chloe and once she learned he was a detective and that he and Dev were best friends she might somehow put two and two together? Beyond that, Rocky realized that if Jayce stayed at Dev's it might cramp her brother's style and jeopardize her matchmaking plans. Still . . . "There are several other inns and lodges in the area, Jayce."

"Dev said you have plenty of room; plus you're only fifteen minutes from my folks' place."

"You mean he said I could use the business. Or is it that he wants you to help me fix up the place? He said he had some ideas." She spun off and paced the length of the Jeep. "He's determined to take control. As if I'm incapable."

"I just need a place to sleep, Rocky."

And she needed Jayce in her home like she needed a hole in the head. At the same time . . . maybe she could work this to her advantage. "Fine. Just . . . don't offer any help or advice or try to make nice. Oh, and keep out of my way. "

"Anything else?"

"Yeah. See if you can get the Jeep running."

His mouth quirked. "Sure, Dash."

"And don't call me Dash!" she ordered as he inspected the engine. The childhood nickname conjured better times. Before their blowout. If Jayce was going to be living under her roof, sleeping a mere few rooms away, she needed to nurture resentment in order to combat desire. Nerves taut, she reached through the open window, snagged her cell from the passenger seat, and called Adam. Logical, reliable, good-hearted, safe Adam.

"I'm with a client," he answered. "Can I call you back in a half hour?"

"No need. I just wanted . . . I thought about it," she said in a low voice. "The partner thing." She massaged her chest, blew out a breath, and took the plunge. "I'm in."

TWENTY

It was six in the evening before Daisy got home. A scenic country drive had turned into an all-day event. Chloe would have been frantic except she'd broken down and phoned the woman around 3:00 p.m. Daisy had assured her she was fine—although she didn't sound like it—and that she'd be a while longer.

Three hours later . . .

"I'm glad you had a good time," Chloe said as Daisy took off her wide-brimmed bonnet and hung it on the hat-filled coat tree.

"Vincent is excellent company."

"He seems like a very nice man."

She fluffed her silver curls. "He's the best of friends."

"Just friends?"

"We've known each other a long time." Which wasn't really an answer. Peeling off her rhinestone-studded denim jacket, Daisy plopped down on the living room's floral sofa. "How was shopping?" she asked, turning the spotlight on Chloe.

"I got everything on your list. Almost." She wasn't about to bring up Big Al, and she wasn't sure how much to share about the entire shopping fiasco. "Chris Bane had everything delivered. I put the packages in your room. I hope you like the outfits I put together. "

"I'm sure I will. Thanks, kitten."

Normally, Daisy would've bounded up the stairs, eager to try on her new clothes. The fact that she remained on the sofa, head relaxed against a toss pillow, sneakered feet crossed at the ankles, concerned Chloe. Was Daisy still depressed? Even after spending the entire day with her "friend"?

"Did you run into Devlin?" she asked, after closing her eyes.

Chloe fidgeted. "You could say that."

Daisy squinted her way.

"There was a misunderstanding. He intervened. I thanked him. We're good. J.T.'s is a great store, by the way."

"I've always thought so." She smiled and allowed her lids to drift back shut.

Chloe frowned. "Would you like something to eat?"

"No, thank you. Vincent treated me to a chili dog and ice cream."

Knowing her own reaction to such combinations, she cringed. "Would you like an antacid then?"

Daisy smiled. "No need."

"A cocktail?"

"No, thank you."

Maybe she should call Devlin. Something was definitely wrong.

"You know what I *would* like to do?"

"No, what?"

She pushed to her sneakered feet. "I'd like to take another crack at my secret recipe cupcakes. Would you like to help?"

"You bet!" Not that Chloe was eager to bake a dessert, but this was a sign that Daisy was bouncing back, albeit without her normal pep and vim. Maybe she was just worn out from the long day.

When Chloe was midway to the kitchen, her phone rang. "Shoot."

"Go on and take it," Daisy said. "I'll assemble the ingredients."

Chloe returned to the living room, dug her cell out of her purse, and stepped out on the back veranda. She'd been expecting a return call from her dad all day. They'd argued, just like she knew they would, after she told him about the breakup with Ryan. He'd followed up *I told you so* with *take my advice,* only she'd cut him off with *don't tell me how to live my life.* Nothing had been resolved due to poor reception, then being confronted by a security guard. Chloe wasn't keen on picking up where she and her dad had left off, but at the same time she felt sick about the wider rift. She took a deep breath of cool evening air. "Hello?"

"Hi, Chloe. It's Nash."

She blinked.

"I hope you don't mind. I got your number from Rocky, who got it from Daisy in case of an emergency."

"This is an emergency?" She dropped into a patio chair. "Did something happen to Monica?"

"No. No, sorry. Didn't mean to alarm you. Actually this is a social call."

"Thank God. I mean . . . how so?"

"You know I run a charter service. Well, I also freelance with a hot-air balloon tour company. There's nothing like drifting along the Vermont skyline as a way of getting a feel of the land. Since you're a Flatlander—"

"A what?"

"A newcomer from out-of-state. Local term. Sorry. Anyway, since I have some flight time racked up, I thought you might enjoy a personal tour."

"In a hot-air balloon?"

"Ever been up in one?"

"Never."

"Once-in-a-lifetime experience."

She thought about the way Daisy had quizzed her during their picnic by the river. Had she ever done this or that? She remembered the wistfulness in Daisy's tone and her excitement when they'd tubed. Her exuberance when she'd raced the convertible Caddy down the highway. If anything put a spark in Daisy's eyes and a spring in her step, it was a thrill. "Let's do it."

"Great," Nash said, sounding vaguely surprised. "What about Friday? Unless the weather forecasts changes, it'll be a perfect day for skimming the clouds."

Skimming the clouds. Daisy would love it. "Friday's great."

"Perfect. Wear warm layers, a hat, sturdy shoes. I'll pick you up around nine a.m."

"See you then."

"Looking forward to it."

They disconnected and Chloe did a happy hop. If a ride in a hot-air balloon didn't lift Daisy's spirits—*ha!*—nothing would. Chloe would surprise her with the news Friday morning. She probably should've warned Nash that she was bringing along a guest, but he might've balked at the thought of taking up Daisy. Devlin wouldn't like it. Actually, chances were good that the entire family, including Nash, wouldn't like the idea of their grandma floating thousands of feet over the earth. But from what Chloe had heard, hot-air ballooning was perfectly safe when the balloon was operated by a licensed pilot, which Nash was.

Better to spring it on him. He'd have a hard time denying Daisy with her standing in front of him and raring to go. Thrilled with the opportunity to cheer her up, Chloe hurried back inside and into the kitchen.

"Everything okay?" Daisy asked as she arranged her mixing bowls and measuring spoons.

"Great." Chloe took in the ingredients lined up on the kitchen counter. Everything they needed to make coconut cupcakes with Daisy's special filling and frosting. The woman's movements were slow but methodical, as if she was concentrating hard, determined to get it right this time. Suddenly Chloe itched to bake. *We'll get it right.*

Her own troubles faded far and away as she moved to the sink to wash her hands. She cursed under her breath when her cell phone sounded a second time.

"Might be important," Daisy said when Chloe ignored it.

Sighing, she plucked the phone out of her sweater pocket, eyeing the nearest door in case it was her dad.

"Hiya, Chloe. It's Luke."

* * *

"What are you doing here?"

Dev raised a brow at his brother as he slid onto a bar stool. "What kind of welcome is that?"

"It's just when you called earlier I told you tonight wasn't a good night for a business meeting."

"I'm not here to talk business. I'm here for a drink." He'd worked late, more juggling of investments, making notes regarding his meeting with the staff on Monday. Once home, he'd nuked a frozen dinner, picking at processed meat loaf and tasteless mashed potatoes while researching prostate cancer on the Internet. Mood darkening, he'd tossed the dinner and snagged a beer, trading his computer for television. Channel surfing led him to the Food Network, which made him think of Chloe. A beer and a half later, he realized he was lonely, depressed, and getting a buzz on alone. *That* was a low he never wanted to experience.

"Dewar's?"

"Beck's."

Luke poured him a draft, served three more customers, then returned to top off his half-empty mug. "What's wrong?"

"Why do you think something's wrong?"

"Nine o'clock on a weeknight. Sitting at the bar, slamming back suds. Even if it was *Saturday* night that would be unusual for you."

"It's been an unusual day."

"Heard Jayce is in town. Surprised he's not here with you."

"He had other plans, plus he's settling in."

"At Rocky's. I know. She called me a couple of hours ago, venting about her not-so-welcome guest." He shook his head. "You know there's bad blood between those two, Dev. What possessed you into pushing Jayce to stay with her?"

"Bad blood." He sipped more beer. "Whatever happened,

over a decade ago, they need to get over it. We're family, dammit."

"I'd tread lightly on this one."

"You know something I don't?"

"No, but I have my suspicions."

"Which are?"

"My own." He flashed a grin while pouring Dev another beer. "Also heard about the shoplifting incident."

"From who?" Chris had contained the mess and Devlin had swept up the pieces. It chafed that a trusted employee had turned a misunderstanding into fodder for gossip. Then it dawned. "Ah, hell. Mitzi Hall?"

"She was in here for happy hour. The woman was half-soused and obviously exaggerating. I cut her off and sent her home in a cab. " Luke offered him a bowl of spicy party mix. "So what really happened?"

Devlin waved off the snack and filled him in, minus the part where he and Chloe had ravaged each other in Chris's office.

"So what gives with her dad?"

"Don't know." He hadn't asked. He'd been too worried about *their* dad. Too swept away by an urgent need to lose his misery in Chloe.

Luke slid a menu under his nose. "You should eat something."

Devlin glanced from his frosty mug to his warmhearted brother. Luke's caring nature was his best quality and worst enemy. If he knew what their dad was going through . . . "Trying to keep me sober?"

"Trying to figure out why you want to get drunk."

If he met his brother's gaze he just might slip, divulging their dad's condition. When Devlin had promised his mom to keep the diagnosis secret, he hadn't realized he'd feel like this much of a traitor to his siblings. What if she was wrong or what if she'd sugarcoated his dad's progress? What if Devlin was robbing Luke and Rocky of quality time? Robbing himself? Suddenly he couldn't live with that promise. Or at least one part of it. "I'm flying down to Florida this weekend."

"What? Why? Oh, wait." Luke gestured to the beer mug. "Is that what this is about? Dad stonewalling your renovations?"

"I need to talk to him face-to-face." *Need to assess his condition.*

"Guess that would drive me to drink, too. When the old man's got his mind set on something . . . Or against something . . ."

"We'll come to terms."

"This weekend, huh?"

"Friday to Sunday should do it. That a problem?"

He shrugged. "Just surprised you're willing to leave Chloe unattended that long. Thought you didn't trust her with Gram? Although, you won't have to worry about a chunk of Friday and Saturday. Then Sunday's the family dinner, so that's covered. On second thought, your timing's great. Go. Haggle with Dad. Hug Mom."

"What's up with Friday and Saturday?"

"Rocky wanted some one-on-one time with Gram this weekend."

"And?"

"That means free time for Chloe."

"So?"

"So Nash invited her on a hot-air balloon tour and I offered to escort her to the food festival in Burlington."

Devlin cursed a pang of jealousy. "When did this happen?"

"A couple of hours ago."

After their passionate encounter. After she'd refused to pursue the attraction between them due to feeling vulnerable in regards to her recent breakup. Yet she was willing to spend time alone with Nash and Luke? Sugar Creek's most notorious hounds? Devlin tried to give her the benefit of the doubt, tried not to read into it. *Jesus.* They weren't even in a relationship and she had his emotions in a tailspin.

Luke raised a brow. "You did ask us to keep an eye on her, remember?"

"That didn't include hooking up."

"Who said anything about hooking up? Just welcoming her into the community and keeping her out of trouble. You have to admit she's prone to misfortune."

"Similar to Janna." In their on-and-off two-year high school romance and even during their short six-month marriage, it always seemed like he was rescuing her from one or another predicament.

Luke swept away Devlin's half-empty mug and replaced it with a cup of steaming black coffee.

"You're cutting me off after two beers?"

"You just brought up Janna," he said in a low voice. "Someone you haven't talked about in years. And," he said, looking aghast, "you compared her to Chloe. You must be sloshed. They're nothing alike, Dev."

"You don't know her background."

"You do? Not for anything, but you two haven't seemed all that chummy to me. When and why did she confide . . . Oh, hell. Jayce?"

"I have a right to protect my family."

"She has a right to her privacy. Jesus, Dev."

"She'll never know. She'll be gone in two months. Probably sooner. As you pointed out, it's been one misfortune after another, plus Gram's more of a handful by the day. Chloe's not one to stick when things get tough."

"Like Janna."

The name stung like salt in an open wound. "Forget I brought her up."

"I wish I could."

Devlin pushed off the stool. "Stop looking so glum. I'm fine. Everything's fine."

"Wish I believed you." Luke shouted for Anna to cover his shift, then catapulted over the bar and nabbed the keys out of Devlin's hand. "I'll drive."

* * *

"I'll walk you to the door."

"I'm fine."

"No, you're not. You're blitzed."

"You're screwy." Rocky shrugged off Adam's hold, then fell back against his SUV. "Oops."

"Like I said." He looped an arm around her waist and practically carried her across the lawn. "You should've slept over at my place."

"Against the rules." Unable to hold her head up, she lazed against his broad shoulder and squinted up at the night sky. "Moon's moving. Cool."

Adam groaned. "I'm putting you straight to bed."

"Can't come in. Jayce."

"Is rooming here for a week. You told me. So what?"

"Won't approve."

"Of me taking care of you?"

"Of me in this connition. Ca-di . . ." She pinched her tongue. "Numb."

"Come morning, babe, you're going to wish your whole body was numb."

Just as he swooped her up the porch stairs, the front door whooshed open.

Busted.

She felt like a teen breaking curfew. A teen who'd been caught sneaking in. "Uh-oh," Rocky mocked, then lapsed into a fit of giggles. She tried to stop, couldn't stop, and finally gave in. She hadn't felt this good in a long, long time.

"Everything okay?" Jayce asked.

Rocky snorted. "And he calls himself a detective."

Adam tightened his hold as her knees gave way. "I don't know what happened," he said to Jayce. "I've watched her drink three beers without getting buzzed. Two glasses of champagne and . . . this."

"She's allergic."

"What?"

"White wine, champagne. It's the sulfites."

"I didn't know."

"Rocky knows."

She heard the censure in Jayce's voice and smirked. "Fuck you." Then she turned in Adam's arms—*strong , de-*

pendable Adam—and smiled up at him. "Thank you for a lovely evening."

He smiled back. "I'll see you upstairs."

"I've got her." Before she knew it, she'd been hauled into Jayce's arms—the honorable bastard who'd annihilated her young foolish heart. "Good night, Adam," he said.

"Make sure she drinks lots of water and give her some ibuprofen."

"I know what to do."

Rocky mimicked Jayce, then blew Adam a kiss. "See you in the morrow, I mean tomorrow . . . *partner.*"

Her good humor fled the moment Jayce carried her inside and shut the door. She'd met up with Adam for a late date, needing to escape, feeling smothered by Jayce's presence, bombarded with memories and feelings that wouldn't die. Even now, even though she wasn't thinking straight, her body responded to this man with a clarity that shook her core. "Need a drink."

"You've had enough." He swept her limp body into his arms and scaled the stairs. "How long have you been seeing Adam Brody?"

She rolled her eyes. "We're not *seeing* each other. We're just sleeping together."

"Dev didn't mention—"

"Dev doesn't know. No one knows."

"Just me. Huh."

"Jealous?"

"That what you were hoping for?"

"Ashfully," Rocky said, head spinning. "That just schlipped, I mean sipped out."

He smiled down at her, causing her heart to race. *Damn him!* "Champagne? What were you thinking, Dash?"

She was thinking that she didn't want to think . . . or feel. Revisualizing one dream and facing a broken dream in the same day had been rough. "We were celebrating."

"Celebrating what?" He nudged open her bedroom door with his shoulder.

She wanted him to throw her on the bed, to make slow,

hard love to her, which in turn made her want to drive him away. "Our partnership."

"You're getting married?"

She snorted. "That what you were hoping for?" If she married someone else, he'd know that she'd healed and moved on, alleviating his guilt.

He laid her gently on her bed. "You've shut me out for almost thirteen years. We're not going to talk about it now."

"Why not?"

"Because you won't remember this discussion tomorrow."

"What do you care?"

"I care."

She stared up at him, her heart thudding slower and harder. A monstrous noise roaring in her ears, her vision blurring. "I don't feel so well."

"I know." He squeezed her hand. "Hang tough, sweetheart. I'll get aspirin and water."

She could feel herself slipping, falling into a dark, chaotic oblivion. She grasped his shirt and tugged him close. "Jayce?"

"Yeah?"

"I hate you."

He brushed his mouth over hers. If only she could've felt it. "I hate you, too, Dash."

TWENTY-ONE

Wednesday blew by quickly, followed by most of Thursday. The weather had turned ugly, cold and rainy, keeping Chloe and Daisy inside and impromptu visitors away—although many had checked in by phone. While some had lamented the unexpected thunderstorms, the "Soul Sisters" (as they'd begun to refer to themselves) had embraced the isolation, exploring their specific culinary interests. They'd searched magazines and surfed the Internet for recipes. Chloe got Daisy addicted to her favorite food blogs and Daisy hooked Chloe on the TV show *Cupcake Wars*.

They talked about things they'd done in their lives and things they'd like to do.

They baked.

Bread. Cookies. Biscuits. Cupcakes. Daisy had even taught her how to make homemade marshmallow fondant, which tasted a lot better than the store-bought variety. To her amazement, working with sweets hadn't soured Chloe's mood. She'd been prepared for feelings of anger or depression when she mixed up a batch of devil's food cupcakes. She'd braced for a mental replay of presenting Ryan with her celebratory cake only to receive the news of his betrayal. Instead, her brain fixated on the rock music blaring from the radio and Daisy's instructions regarding the espresso meringue frosting. Part of Chloe felt like she was back in culinary school—exploring, learning. She got the same buzz off of Daisy's teachings as she did off Chef Avery's. Every lesson was couched within a story, making the recipe more memorable and poignant. Another part of Chloe spun wistful scenarios. If she hadn't lost her mom, if she'd ever known Grandma Vine, or if Grandma Madison would've been more demonstrative, maybe they would have shared similar moments. Connecting with Daisy, hearing her nostalgic stories, sharing a love of cooking, filled a void in Chloe's life—as did the anticipation of hanging out with Luke and Nash this weekend, joining Rocky and Monica for the meeting tonight, and, on Sunday, cooking dinner for all of them with the addition of Sam and his two children and Devlin's friend Jayce. Even though Chloe was at odds with her dad, even though Ryan had dumped her, even though she ached for Devlin's touch, she'd never been happier. In her heart, she'd adopted a family.

Sitting cross-legged on the sofa with her laptop, Chloe surfed the Net, skimming various recipe books, specifically those featuring cupcakes. Not that she planned on offering any suggestions or advice during her first Cupcake Lovers meeting, but she wanted to be prepared should anyone ask. Given her short stint in PR, her brush with photography and her experience in culinary school, she definitely had some ideas.

"How that boy couldn't know better is a mystery to me," Daisy said as she joined Chloe in the living room.

"What boy?"

"My great-nephew Sam. Just got off the phone with him," she said as she plopped next to Chloe. "He started refinishing his hardwood floors two days ago, the same week he was supposed to host Cupcake Lovers. He's a furniture maker for crying out loud. Works with sanders and stains all the time. How could he not know that the floors wouldn't be completely dry by tonight? And the toxic *smell*? For crying out loud!"

Chloe frowned. "So the meeting's canceled?"

"No, no. Just moved. I told Sam he could host the meeting here, but he'd already asked Devlin. That's two weeks in a row. At this rate, my grandson will become an honorary member by virtue of loaning out his house."

"Why would Sam ask Devlin? Why not another club member?"

"Why indeed?" Daisy thought about it, then leaned close as if she had a secret to share. "Here's a thought: Devlin doesn't have much of a social life. That boy's a workaholic."

"I've heard."

"Serious minded, too."

"I've noticed."

"Maybe Sam's trying to get him to join the club."

Chloe's lip twitched. "I can't imagine Devlin baking cupcakes. I'm not sure he even knows how to cook. I've seen him shop. He's all about convenient, processed foods."

"That's because, like most men, he never took the initiative to learn his way around the kitchen. Which is usually fine, because usually the wife handles that end of the partnership, except Devlin married a girl who didn't know a Dutch oven from a skillet. Then she was gone and . . ." Daisy trailed off and looked away. "Maybe you could give Devlin some cooking lessons."

Chloe barely registered that last part. She was fixated on the wife part. "Devlin was married?"

"Never mind about that. In fact, put it out of your mind completely. And for heaven's sake never mention it. To anyone. Ever." She bounced off the sofa and beelined up the stairs.

Chloe blinked in her wake. Obviously, Devlin's marriage, however long or brief, was a sensitive subject and Daisy had spoken out of turn. Was he divorced? Widowed? How long ago and why was the topic taboo? It must've happened a long time ago, before Monica moved to Sugar Creek. Taboo or no, if Monica knew about a Mrs. Devlin Monroe, she would've have mentioned it to Chloe.

Via the Kindle app on her PC, she sat there staring at a page of *The Sweet Little Book of Cupcakes*. Staring but not absorbing as her brain circled around one thought.

Devlin had once been married.

She didn't feel jealous or betrayed because he hadn't told her—why would he, given they barely knew each other? She was just a little stunned and a lot curious. She wanted to know more, but Daisy had warned her not to ask. "Damn."

Rain pelted the windowpanes, lightning flashed, and two minutes turned to ten. Unreasonably spooked, Chloe ditched her laptop and ran up to check on Daisy. The past two days, she'd been her talkative self, still changing thoughts mid-sentence every now and then but not nearly as forgetful. Just now she'd blurted a secret, and from the way she'd hurried off, she was upset about it. Chloe suddenly burned with the urge to assure the woman that her secret was safe. The last thing Chloe wanted was to spur another depression. Granted, sometimes Daisy's incessant chatter was tiring, but at least it was cheery.

Chloe scaled the last step, noted the closed bathroom door. She knocked. "You okay, Daisy?"

The door swung open and the woman stepped out, bright eyed and red cheeked as if Chloe had caught her doing something wrong. "I'm dandy, kitten." She pushed her pink cat-eye glasses up her nose and hurried down the hall toward her bedroom. "Come help me pick my outfit for tonight. I want to look my best when I present my secret recipe to the club."

"Be right there. Just need to pee." Chloe stepped into the bathroom and closed the door. She noted the dripping faucet, the squished Dixie cup in the trash, and the slightly ajar door of the medicine cabinet. Curious, she peeked inside. She used this bathroom all the time but hadn't paid much mind to the medicine cabinet, since she kept all of her toiletries in a hanging cosmetic bag. She noted the shelves, crammed like every other shelf in Daisy's home. Toothpaste, dental floss, mouthwash, talcum powder, nail polish, lens cleaner . . . and assorted bottles of pills. Mostly over-the-counter remedies—pain reliever, allergy relief, nasal spray—but there were also several vials of prescription drugs. Not that that was odd. As an older woman, she probably battled high blood pressure or arthritis or any one of a dozen other maladies. Thing was, she also drank a lot of *cocktails*. Was it safe to mix these drugs with liquor? How many pills was she taking a day? What were the side effects, if any? Did they affect her mood? Her memory? Her judgment? What if she forgot and missed a dose? Or forgot and doubled up?

Concerned, Chloe skimmed the names of a few of the prescriptions as well as the name of the doctor. Make that *doctors*. She closed the cabinet, flushed the toilet, and washed her hands.

As she hurried toward Daisy's room, Chloe's mind whirled with the recent revelations: Devlin had a former wife. Daisy had possible health issues *possibly* complicated by medication. With every step, Chloe remembered something else she'd heard over the past couple of weeks: Rocky's issues with Tasha. The lifelong feud between the Burkes and Monroes. Luke's questionable management skills. Sam's struggles as a single parent. Devlin's present battle with his dad. Rocky's financial problems. Nash's weakness for gambling.

The list went on.

If she had a lick of sense, she'd mind her own business, concentrate on solving her own problems. After all, even though they were her dream family, she wasn't *really* family— just their grandmother's hired companion. A tight-knit group, they'd probably balk at a meddling outsider. Still . . . all she could think as she entered Daisy's cluttered room and found her rooting through a wardrobe that would have made Cher proud was . . . *How can I help?*

TWENTY-TWO

Dress sleeves rolled to his elbows, Devlin was scrubbing the inside of his microwave when his cousin Sam barged in through the side door, shaking off rainwater like a dog and tracking in mud.

"For Christ's . . . I just mopped."

"You did?" Arms full of Tupperware and a zipped canvas tote, Sam glanced around the whole of the kitchen. "You did. Scrubbed the sink and stove, too. Is that Lysol I smell? I'm impressed."

Devlin flipped him the bird and returned to scouring dried eggs and sausage.

"What exploded?"

"My breakfast burrito."

"From this morning?"

"Hence breakfast."

"And you're just now cleaning it?"

"I was in a hurry and, at the time, wasn't expecting a houseful of women."

"And me."

Devlin glanced at the triple-tier cupcake carrier his cousin set on the counter. "Like I said." He moved to the sink and rinsed the glob-caked sponge. "You couldn't give me more than a few hours' notice?" He could've said no, but at the same time this was the perfect opportunity to see Chloe before he left for Florida without seeking her out. Agreeing to keep his distance had been a bonehead move. Avoidance only heightened the attraction.

"I thought the polyurethane finish would be dry," Sam said, shrugging out of his soaked blue slicker. "I miscalculated."

"So you said."

"About that 'women' crack—"

"I know. You joined the club to *meet* women. Except it's been, what, six, seven months now and, even though you're supposedly hot for Rachel, you haven't made a move."

"Timing hasn't been right."

Would it ever be? Sam had been crazy in love with his wife of ten years and devastated when she died. Paula had been gone for two years now. As much as Sam professed wanting to get on with his life, Devlin sensed a profound resistance in the romance area. He commiserated, hence let the subject drop. "I've got a lot of work to do, so I'll be holed up in my den. Do me a favor," he teased. "Don't let the ladies trash the place. I know how wild things get after a few cupcakes and sips of tea."

Sam grinned. "Go ahead. Joke. But A) things *have* gotten pretty heated lately, and B) my beverage of choice for the night is *not* tea." He unzipped the canvas tote and pulled out two bottles.

Devlin raised a brow. "Red wine?"

"Dessert wine. Sweeter, as is recommended, than the dessert." He unlatched the lid of the top tier and revealed a dozen white cupcakes topped with white frosting. "Vanilla almond cupcakes with salted caramel buttercream frosting." He waggled his eyebrows. "Perfect combination."

Sam McCloud—master furniture maker. Retired military. Fluffy cupcake baker. Devlin shook his head, then smiled. "You, Cousin, are an enigma."

"Just exploring new horizons. I owe it to myself as well as my kids. Feel free to follow my example and shake up your own mundane world." He spread his hands. "Wineglasses? Small plates?"

"I'll get them. You clean up the mud. Mop's in there."
They both took action and, although Sam worked in silence,
Devlin couldn't restrain his thoughts. "If I were a suspicious
man, I'd think the family was conspiring against me."

"Meaning?"

"Every time I turn around one of you comments on
my—in the words of Jayce—dull-ass life."

"I don't know why we care," Sam quipped.

"Neither do I. And I am not joining Cupcake Lovers. As
Gram's fond of pointing out, I don't know shit from shortening."

"I find that hard to believe," Sam joked as he rinsed and
returned the mop to the closet. "Nevertheless, you do know
finance and business. This book venture, it's a worthy cause,
but, given Tasha's lofty goals, what if we get in over our
heads? She's determined to pursue a major publisher. What if
she nails a contract? Do we need to incorporate? How do we
ensure proceeds go to the charity of our choice?"

"You need to consult a lawyer."

"Or someone with a degree in finance. Come on, Dev," he
said while artfully arranging his cupcakes. "Three of your
kin are active members of the club. Factor in friends, associates, ancestors and your belief in our cause? You've already
got a vested interest."

"You should have been an attorney. Or a salesman."
Shaking his head, Devlin carried several wineglasses into
his living room while considering the man's case. Even
though Devlin had multiple responsibilities, taking on another project stoked his interest. Maybe because the busier
he was, the less time he'd have to worry about his dad. Or
maybe because this particular project would give Devlin an
excuse to spend time with Chloe. There was also his unwill-
ingness to see a good organization burned by bad business
decisions. He returned to the kitchen, snagged forks, and
pointed Sam to the napkins. "I'll listen in tonight. But beyond that—"

"No promises. Got it."

Thunder boomed, the door slammed open, and Rocky

blew in, soaked and scowling. "Could it be any more miserable out there?"

"Thought you were laid up with a stomach bug," Devlin said.

"Ran its course," she said, grimacing when she spotted the bottles on the counter. "We're having wine?"

"Dessert wine," Sam said. "Not you. You get whacked on wine. If I'd known you were coming—"

"I'm sure Dev's got coffee. He practically lives on the stuff."

"I'll make you some tea," Sam said, snagging her soggy coat and hanging it next to his. "You're flushed."

Devlin frowned. "You should've stayed in."

"I'm not feverish, if that's what you're thinking. I'm pissed because I had to rely on Jayce for a ride. Leo's backed up at the garage. Who knows when he'll get to my Jeep?"

"If it makes you feel better," Devlin said, "you can use my wheels this weekend while I'm in Florida." He felt a little guilty about pushing Jayce into staying at the Red Clover. Instead of mending bridges, his friend and sister seemed to be burning the remnants. Had the tension contributed to her ill health?

"You know what would make me feel even better?" she asked while wringing rain from her drenched braids. "Coming with you to Florida. Sunshine. Sand and surf. Mom and Dad."

Taken off guard, Devlin stalled, seemingly giving the matter thought while unrolling his sleeves and buttoning his cuffs. Actually, he was scrambling for a good lie because, according to their mom, the truth wasn't his to tell. Then he remembered. "You can't come with me. You and Gram have plans this weekend, remember? You can't bail and leave her to God knows what mischief."

"Won't Chloe be around?" Sam asked while uncorking the wine.

"Thanks to Luke and Nash," Devlin said, trying not to sound churlish, "she's otherwise engaged Friday and Saturday."

Sam quirked a wry grin. "Beat you to the punch, did they?"

Rocky smirked while filling the teakettle. "He wasn't even in there swinging."

Before Devlin could comment, loud knocking announced the arrival of another club member. Not wanting to discuss his attraction to Chloe or the green-eyed monster gnawing at his gut, he welcomed the interruption. "Whatever happens," he said, heading for the front door, "don't let Tasha sit next to me."

"You're sticking around?" Rocky asked with a smile in her voice.

"Apparently so."

* * *

By the time she and Daisy reached Devlin's house, Chloe's nerves were shot. Driving the retro Caddy in a torrential downpour had been a nightmare. The headlights had seemed too dim, the windshield wipers too slow. She'd hydroplaned once even though she'd only been going 25 mph. Another time, she'd pulled over because she couldn't see through the blinding rain. All the while Daisy had been oblivious, rambling about all the recipes she had in mind for the book project, fretting over which were the best, and bemoaning Tasha-the-Pinhead. Chloe could think of a dozen ways to deal with that cupcake tyrant, most of which she pushed from her mind in order to focus on the road. When Daisy complained about her cautious driving and how they were already ten minutes late for the meeting, Chloe blocked her out, too.

Chloe's stressed-out body wilted with relief when she pulled safely into Devlin's driveway. But five seconds later, as she was standing on his porch, knocking on his door, her anxiety returned tenfold. She hadn't seen him since that searing-hot kissing session. Had he thought about the way they'd been all over each other? Had he dreamed about the clash and mesh of their hands and tongues? Fantasized about what might have happened if they hadn't come to their senses?

She had.

So much so that she wondered why in the world she'd cooled the heat by pushing him away. Monica was right. Temptation was an überaphrodisiac.

The door swung open and the devil invited her inside. "We were worried."

"You'd think she'd never driven in the rain." Ditching her umbrella, Daisy relieved Chloe of the precious samples of her secret recipe cupcakes, then disappeared into the next room.

Devlin leaned close to Chloe's ear. "I'm glad you took it slow."

She didn't answer—rendered speechless by his confident and charismatic presence. Mesmerized by his good looks and scrumptious physique. Luke, though a seductive force, had nothing on his older brother.

"You okay?"

"Just happy to be here." *In one piece. With you.* She took a deep breath—*get a grip, Madison*—and smiled. Her gaze darted past him, into his home. Richly painted walls, maple-planked floors, old-fashioned braided rugs. Warm and welcoming—like the man helping her out of her wet leather jacket. "It was nice of you to host the meeting," she said. "Again."

"I had an ulterior motive."

She made the mistake of looking into those blueberry-blue eyes. Her heart skipped, then raced, then pounded. She shifted her weight, a reality check, since it felt like she was floating on air.

"I'm leaving for Florida tomorrow."

"Daisy told me. I know we agreed to keep our distance, but that's a bit extreme, don't you think?"

His lip twitched. "When I get back—"

"So *you* must be Chloe." A formidable energy blasted into the foyer, hijacking the conversation. "Sam and Rocky have been singing your praises for the last ten minutes. A professional chef. Aren't we lucky to have you as a guest to-night?" The slender, buxom woman with dark bobbed hair and model-perfect makeup slipped her arm through Dev-lin's, a possessive move meant to put off Chloe, not that it did, mostly because Devlin looked annoyed. "And speak-ing of lucky," she rushed on, "I don't know *what* we would have done if this generous man hadn't opened his doors to us tonight."

"You would have met at another member's house," he said, slipping her touch and stuffing his hands in his pant pockets.

Ignoring the diss, she nailed him with a thousand-dollar smile. "Modest as always." Tearing her gaze from their host, she extended a manicured hand to Chloe. "Tasha Burke, *wife* of the *mayor* of Sugar Creek, *president* of Cupcake Lovers."

Even if she hadn't introduced herself, Chloe would've known who she was. The family had been dead-on in their description. Plus she was one of those people who com-manded attention. Of course she emphasized her *titles.* Ev-erything about her was pretentious and fake, from her 36C breasts and acrylic nails to her collagen-injected smile. Chloe had met a hundred Tasha Burkes in her lifetime. She was neither impressed nor intimidated.

"I've heard a lot about you, too," Chloe said with a pleas-ant smile. "As well as the charitable efforts of Cupcake Lov-ers. No wonder you're inspired to share their recipes and goodwill with the world." She lowered her voice for dra-matic effect and leaned in, feigning collusion. "I don't know if anyone mentioned it, but in addition to my culinary de-gree, I also worked for a Madison Avenue PR firm and wrote food articles and reviews for a prominent New York City e-zine." Amazing how impressive that sounded when it really wasn't. "Between my experience and connections, if I can do anything to help . . ."

"That's generous of you." Though Tasha's smile was in-tact, her unnaturally apple-green eyes shot venom. "We should join the others. Especially since we're already off to a late start." *Thanks to you* hung unspoken in the air as she spun on her designer heels and strode toward the sound of voices.

Devlin squeezed Chloe's elbow as he guided her into his home. "You realize you just made an enemy."

"What a relief. Who'd want to be friends with her?" Chloe knew she'd come off strong, but she also knew Tasha's type and hated the way they manipulated people and situations for their own benefit, usually without regards to anyone's feelings. Knowing how she'd crushed Daisy with negative appraisals of her cupcakes was enough to cause Chloe to draw her verbal sword.

"You were quick to see through her façade. You'd be surprised by how many people she bullshits."

Chloe didn't comment, but she wondered plenty. Had Tasha managed to fool Devlin over a certain period of time? Had she cast a spell? Hooked him with her physical charms? Chloe was almost certain, by things said and from the jealous vibes rolling off the woman, that they'd been an item. Not that Chloe cared, but it certainly intensified her curiosity. Was Devlin one of those people who excelled at professional matters but sucked at personal relationships? It made him less than perfect and all the more intriguing.

They stopped short and Chloe absorbed the living room in one sweeping glance. Cobblestone fireplace, burgundy leather sofa, large-screen plasma television. Tidy, simple, cozy. A small room made all the more intimate by the seven people crowding up the comfortable-looking furniture.

"Thanks for driving Gram over in this crappy weather, Chloe."

Spying Rocky, Chloe busted into an ear-to-ear grin. "Didn't expect to see you here."

"I'm feeling a lot better. Even if I weren't, I'd drag my sorry butt here. Wouldn't miss this meeting for the world."

"Unfortunately, not everyone shared your dogged commitment," Tasha said to Rocky. "Of all the meetings for anyone to miss. *I* have exciting news!"

"Ethel, Helen, and Judy are as committed as any of us," Monica said, breezing over the "exciting news." "They're also older and not as willing and able to drive in inclement weather."

Tasha smirked. "*Daisy's* here."

"I had young eyes," Daisy said in defense of her senior friends. "And even *she* had trouble driving in this deluge." Daisy sniffed at Tasha, then smiled at Chloe. "Take a seat, kitten."

Feeling like the new girl in class, something she'd experienced a lot, Chloe sat on the sofa, in between Daisy and Monica, while Sam introduced her to Rachel Lacey, a day-care assistant, and Casey Monahan, a jewelry maker. Rachel looked twentysomething and Casey maybe a decade older. From what Daisy had said, Chloe knew they both had brothers serving in the military. She also knew Sam, who she guessed was in his late thirties, had eyes for the sweet-looking, if not plain, Rachel.

"Now that everyone knows everyone," Tasha barreled on, "I officially call this meeting to order."

"Mind if I listen in?" Devlin asked.

Tasha looked surprised yet pleased. "It's your house." She motioned him to join her on the love seat.

Monica scooted over at the same time, and Chloe's heart pumped when Devlin sat next to her instead.

"Curious about your news," he said to Tasha. "Also jonesing to try one of Sam's cupcakes."

"He got a whiff when I first arrived," Sam explained. "Vanilla almond with salted caramel buttercream frosting."

"I brought cupcakes, too," Daisy piped up.

"Traditionally," Tasha said, "we feature one recipe per meeting."

"Yes, but it's not written in stone," Rocky said.

"I'm feeling adventurous tonight," Casey said.

"Me, too," Rachel said. "Otherwise I wouldn't be here. Anyone else hydroplane on their way over?"

"I did," Chloe said.

"Maybe I should drive you home," Sam said to Rachel.

A hush fell over the group as the blond-haired, brown-eyed girl shifted in her seat and looked everywhere but at

Sam. Chloe assumed everyone, except maybe Rachel, knew about Sam's crush. She wondered if everyone else was on pins and needles like her, because that sure as heck sounded like a move. *Say yes!* her mind screamed at Rachel. *He's nice and handsome and amazingly talented with his hands. Plus he likes to bake!*

"That's sweet of you, Sam," she said. "But I'll be fine."

Damn, Chloe thought.

"Of course you will," he said with a quick smile. "I'll get the cupcakes."

"Me, too," Daisy said, following him into what Chloe assumed was the kitchen.

There was an awkward pause, one of those oh-crap-my-friend-just-blew-it moments.

Devlin broke the tension. "Speaking of adventurous, Sam brought a dessert wine."

"What fun," Monica said.

"I wondered about those," Casey said, motioning to the long-stemmed glasses on the mahogany coffee table.

"I'll pour," Devlin said.

"Just half a glass for me," Chloe said. She also cut him off at the halfway mark when he poured a glass for Daisy. When he raised a questioning brow, Chloe shot him a look that promised she'd explain later. And she would. She couldn't help worrying about Daisy mixing liquor with medications, especially since she had no idea what combination of pills Daisy had taken today or how many. Maybe Devlin knew about her meds. Maybe he could ease Chloe's mind.

Sam and Daisy breezed back into the room along with their cupcakes and served them up, side by side, on Devlin's cobalt-blue dessert plates. Almost everyone *oohed* and *ahhed* when sampling the dual creations. Sam's cupcakes weren't fancy looking in the least—white frosting on white cupcakes—but the combination of sweet and salty was distinctly unique and exceptionally pleasing along with the dessert wine.

Four Forks Up, Chloe thought.

Daisy had utilized caramel buttercream icing as well,

although, after piping on the frosting in a circular motion, she'd dipped the frosted cupcakes into a bowl of toasted coconut. What took everyone by blissful surprise was the chocolate ganache filling. "I used an apple corer," she explained when Rachel asked about her method. "Cored out the center of the cupcake and used a pastry bag to fill the pocket with the ganache."

"They're delicious, Gram," Rocky said with a smile, and Chloe knew she was thinking about the awful first batch a few days before.

"Semi-sweet dark chocolate," Tasha said, "right?"

Daisy spared her a stiff nod.

"But there's something else. Something other than chocolate and coconut."

"My secret ingredient."

"Which is?"

Daisy smiled. "A secret."

Everyone except Tasha chuckled as they continued to sample the tasty treats. "You mean you're not going to tell us?"

"Depends."

"On?"

"Whether or not my special secret recipe cupcakes are good enough for the Cupcake Lovers' recipe book."

Everyone stopped mid-bite and looked from the scrappy senior to the pretentious prez.

Chloe mentally prepared her defense, although it was difficult to think straight with Devlin sitting so close—thighs touching, arms brushing, as they ate and drank. If she didn't know better she'd think Daisy and Monica, who sat on either end of the sofa, were crowding them together. All she knew was that he smelled great and felt great and all she wanted to do was straddle his lap and kiss him senseless. Embarrassed, she focused on Tasha's words.

"I can't speak for everyone," the woman said, "and of course we'd have to vote, but I think this creation is divine, Daisy."

"Really?" the group chimed in unison. Obviously, like Chloe, they'd expected a thumbs-down from Tasha.

"Yours, too, Sam," she went on with a dazzling white smile. "Both would be a stunning addition to *Cupcake Lovers' Delectable Delights—Making a Difference One Cupcake at a Time.*"

Rocky's brows shot up. "To what?"

"It's just a working title," Tasha said. "I needed to call our recipe collection *something* while pitching it to that editor in New York."

"What editor?" Sam asked.

"*That's* my exciting news!" Tasha set aside her plate and pulled a leather organizer from her purse. "Randall recently reached out to some prominent friends regarding my idea. After all, if we're published and successful, the recipe book would draw attention not only to Cupcake Lovers but to Sugar Creek. Potentially, it could have a positive effect on tourism. Anyway, someone knew someone who knew someone—you know how *that* goes—and next thing I know, I'm having a conference call with Brett Pearson, a senior editor at a publishing house that specializes in nonfiction books!"

"When did this happen?" Casey asked.

"Monday."

Daisy frowned. "And you're just now telling us?"

"I wanted to research the company first—they're legit by the way—and I also wanted to make sure I had all of my notes in order. As you know, cupcakes are the rage right now, so every baker from here to California is pitching a book. Brett was intrigued by the club's history and what we do for soldiers as well as select charitable functions. Said that's our platform."

"Our what?" Rachel asked.

"Angle," Chloe said. She glanced at Devlin and saw that, like her, he was intrigued. As much as she didn't like Tasha, Chloe very much liked the idea of sharing the concept of Cupcake Lovers with the world. Their history *was* interesting and their efforts through the decades commendable. Imagining the thrill Daisy would get out of seeing her recipes in print, in bookstores, and online made Chloe's heart swell.

"So what's next?" Monica asked. Clearly the question on everyone's mind.

Bursting with excitement, Tasha opened her organizer and started reading a list of all the things they'd need for a proposal. "The history of the club and a partial list of members throughout the decades. Personal stories about some of the members, past and present, including their ties with the military and maybe the one charity event that touched them the most. At least ten recipes, photos of the finished product, and candid photos from past events as well as a few professional shots of us."

"I'm not comfortable having my picture taken," Rachel said.

"Don't worry," Tasha said. "We'll fix you up. A little makeup does wonders."

As if Rachel needed a lot of help. Chloe marveled at Tasha's insensitivity.

Rocky opened her mouth, but Sam beat her to the punch. "Not everyone gets their beauty out of a jar," he said to Tasha. "Some people are naturally born with it." He looked to Rachel. "You don't need makeup."

She blushed. "Thank you. But that's not . . . I'm just not comfortable."

Casey turned the conversation away from her shy friend. "That list of yours," she said to Tasha. "That's pretty involved."

"Sounds more like a memoir than a recipe book," Monica said. "Who's going to convert all that information into interesting prose?"

"If we get the company on board, Brett said they'd hire a ghostwriter."

"I don't like the idea of putting our story in a stranger's hands," Daisy said.

"Maybe Chloe could do it," Rocky said. "She was a professional writer and reviewer."

Chloe tensed as all eyes turned to her. Not exactly what she'd had in mind when she'd come here this evening. She'd never written a book—fiction or nonfiction. Plus it was a lengthy process and who knew if she'd be in Sugar Creek beyond her three-month trial period with Daisy?

"Let's not get ahead of ourselves," Tasha said, saving Chloe from answering.

"Ten recipes to start," Sam said. "Forty if we land the contract." He raised a brow. "As of tonight only eight have made the cut."

"I know," Tasha said, "and on reflection I think I may have been a bit harsh in my judgment." She shrugged and gave an apologetic laugh. "I was so concerned about collecting the most unique and incredible recipes, thinking that's what would set us apart, but now, thanks to Brett, I know we're about so much more than the cupcake itself."

Devlin subtly bumped his knee to Chloe's as if to say, *There it is. The bullshit.* Chloe wasn't falling for Tasha's sudden "we" mentality either, but clearly some of the others were. She didn't blame them. Tasha talked a good game and, truth told, this *was* an exciting project. The only reason Chloe refrained from jumping into the conversation was because she wasn't a member. She'd come prepared to defend Daisy's baking, but Tasha had pulled that rug from beneath her by applauding Daisy's secret special recipe and by reversing her decision regarding another recent submission. Instead of an avenger, Chloe felt like a rebel without a cause.

Her cell phone chimed with an incoming text just as the club started debating who was going to take what responsibility as far as preparing materials for the proposal went. "Sorry."

She nabbed the phone from her purse, intending to shut it off, but then saw the text was from Ryan. Blindsided, she pushed off the couch, cheeks burning. "I need to take this."

She walked out of the room without making eye contact with anyone, especially Devlin. Up until two weeks ago, she'd been living with another man, a man she'd assumed she'd marry, and now the only man she ached to make love with was a veritable stranger. Her emotions spun as she sought privacy. Over the past few days, she'd managed to push Ryan and the hurt he'd inflicted further and further from her mind. She'd been on the mend, on the move. Her new life came to a screeching halt with this intrusion of the old. She ended up in the kitchen, of all places, which reignited memories of that awful moment when Ryan had stomped all over her heart and pride. Legs shaky, she slumped onto a kitchen bar stool and triggered the "messaging" app on her smartphone.

Delayed overseas. Talked to the condo super. Said u moved out. Where r u? U ok?

She stared at the backlit text, heart pounding. She thumbed in: *Fine.*

Find a job?

What the hell? She thought, but typed: *Personal Chef.*

That's great.

I know.

She took deep breaths. In and out. In and out.

I only wanted what was best 4 u.

F U. F U. F U, she ached to type. *How's France?*

Dont b bitter.

F U. F U. F U, she thought. *Not bitter. Grateful.*

She shut off her phone before he could respond. She realized then that her leg was bouncing. *Damn.* She willed it to stop, willed herself to relax.

She couldn't.

I only wanted what was best 4 u? What did *that* mean? And why had he texted instead of called? It felt so impersonal. So detached. Was his Parisian tart in the same room? Was he texting because he didn't want *her* to overhear? And why text her now, three weeks after leaving her, ruining an otherwise perfect evening? Once again his timing couldn't have been worse. All the anger Chloe had shoved down welled and brewed. She hugged herself, suppressing murderous impulses.

"You all right?"

She wanted to puke. She glanced up at Devlin, torn between crying on his shoulder and spewing her venom. "Considering there are dangerous utensils within my reach, you may want to leave."

He raised a brow.

"Sorry." She blew out a breath. "It's not you. It's . . ."

"Him?"

Either Devlin was very astute or she was extremely transparent. Probably both.

"Want to talk about it?"

"Even if I did"—she inclined her head toward the living room and the ongoing meeting—"now's not the time." Her anger receded as she noted the genuine concern in his eyes. He stepped closer and obliterated all thoughts of Ryan-the-cheating-bastard. Devlin's presence soothed and excited, a heady mix. "I'm sorry I rushed out like that."

"I'm sorry he upset you." Devlin reached out and tucked a hank of hair behind her ear, a tender, intimate gesture that caused her to stomach to flutter. "Do you love him?"

The question took her by surprise, but not as much as her gut answer. "No." She pressed her palm to her forehead. When had *that* happened? Had she fallen out of love a little at a time or had his betrayal squashed her feelings in one swift stomp? Had she ever been truly *in* love with Ryan?

One thing for certain: He'd never ignited her senses the way Devlin did with the simplest touch. What would it be like if he touched her intimately? The possibilities caused her to shiver. She met his gaze and her pulse raced. He wanted to kiss her. She willed him to. Needed him to. *Make me burn.*

Arguing voices cut through the sensual haze, reminding Chloe they weren't alone.

Devlin eased back, frustration sparking in his eyes. "When I get back from Florida—"

"We'll talk." She pocketed her phone and eased past him. She wanted to do a whole lot more than talk. She wanted to fall into bed with him, to explore whatever burned between them. One night with him would surely trump a thousand with Ryan. She wouldn't allow herself to think beyond succumbing to temptation. She wanted to move on, to rediscover passion in all its forms. *Holding back is for sissies,* she could hear Daisy saying.

"Wait." She turned to Devlin before they crossed the kitchen threshold. "I need to ask you something about Daisy. About all the medication she takes."

His expression hardened. "What medication?"

TWENTY-THREE

Rocky wrenched open her groaning fridge's door, nabbed a bottle of water, and downed a Tylenol PM. She'd been tossing and turning for the past three hours. Two in the morning and Jayce still hadn't returned to the Red Clover. When he'd dropped her off at Dev's, he'd told her he had plans for the evening and wouldn't be back until late, to which she'd answered, *Whatever.*

She hated that he'd seen her drunk two nights before and even more that he'd held her hair back from her face and massaged her shoulders as she puked her guts up in the toilet that next morning. The worst was the fact that she couldn't remember that night clearly. Everything that transpired between Adam driving her home and her waking up the next morning with a monstrous sick headache was a blur. She knew Jayce had tucked her into bed because he'd told her so, and she knew she'd blabbed and told him she was sleeping with Adam because he'd made a not-so-subtle reference. Other than that, they hadn't spoken about that night. They'd barely spoken in two days. He'd spent most of his time at his parents' house consulting with a contractor about renovations. She'd wasted an entire day recovering from a hangover, then committed a good chunk of today to meeting with Adam to coordinate their plans to merge. Since her Jeep was in the shop, she'd been counting on Adam for a ride to Cupcake Lovers, but then he'd been called away by a client.

That left Jayce. Considering they were at odds, she should've shown a little gratitude when he'd offered to drop her at Dev's. Instead, she'd been resentful and flip. Guilt rippled through her blood as she imagined that exchange being their last. *Ever.*

Thunder rumbled and rattled the kitchen panes, intensifying her already-ominous thoughts. Two days of scattered, severe storms. There was talk of potential flooding. Roads were slick with rain and mud. What if Jayce had spun out and slammed into a tree? Or what if an oncoming car had lost control and hit him head-on?

She heard the front door open and close and, in spite of herself, nearly tripped over her feet hurrying from the kitchen to the outer sitting room. "Where have you been?" She cringed at her slightly hysterical tone, smoothed her clammy hands over her baggy striped boxers.

"I told you I'd be late."

"It's two in the fricking morning!" She was torn between hugging and slapping him. Flicking on a table lamp, she looked him over for scrapes or broken bones, but all she saw was a superfit, superfine man who made her blood boil and burn.

He raked his damp, longish hair from his face and angled his head. "Worried or jealous?"

She realized then that he smelled of perfume. While she'd fretted about him being dead in a ditch, he'd been boinking some woman. She hadn't expected that. Throat thick with resentment, she turned on her bare feet and returned to the kitchen for her water. Unfortunately, he followed. "How was your *date*?" she gritted out.

"Great. How was your meeting?"

"Interesting."

"Want to talk about it?"

"The meeting or your date?"

"About why you can't let it go."

He was referring to their blowout thirteen, going on fourteen, years ago. That night exploded in her mind as if clearly as it were yesterday. Anger and hurt merged and intensified, causing her stomach to turn and her hands to tremble. She balled them at her sides.

"Hating me for doing the right thing is warped, Dash."

The right thing had shattered her heart. "Don't call me that."

Thunder and lightning boomed and flashed as they faced off in the kitchen, an ancient storm brewing between them. "You're just as stubborn and unreasonable now as you were then. Maybe more so. God help Adam if he actually falls for you."

Before she could rally, a crack of lightning blinded and a loud crash shook the house. Acting on instinct, Rocky rushed toward the sound, bursting out the back door onto the rickety back porch. The motion detector light flicked on, flooding the grounds and tripping her panic button. "Oh no!"

"Hold on," Jayce ordered, but she was already bolting toward her damaged shed.

Her bare feet slipped on the sodden grass and she went down hard on her knees. Pain shot up her thigh, but she ignored it and scrambled upright.

Jayce snagged her arm and hauled her back. "What the fuck?"

Lightning had struck a huge sugar maple near the base of its trunk, splitting it through. The bulk of the huge tree had toppled and crashed into the roof of the shed that housed the recreational gear she rented to guests. Bikes, snow skis, croquet sets, lawn tennis equipment, two motorized scooters, the Arctic Cat snowmobile . . . The entire shed was listing. "I have to get my things out of there!" she shouted over the thunder and driving rain.

"Are you insane? The roof and walls could give any minute!"

"That's why I need to get my gear out. At least the big-ticket items. I can't afford to replace everything!"

She tried to tug free, but he held firm. "It's not worth risking your safety, Rocky."

"Yes, it is!" He didn't get it. No one aside from Adam did. This wasn't just her home, business, and livelihood. This was her *dream*. She heard an ominous creak of wood. Heart pounding, she swung hard and clipped Jayce's jaw.

"Son of a—"

Another wild swing connected with his eye. She yanked free and bolted forward, screaming when he lunged and tackled her to the ground. At the same time, the roof buckled and the walls gave way under the mighty sugar maple—her recreational equipment crushed under the weight and ruin of timber, metal, mass foliage, and thick branches.

Tears she'd been damming up for weeks burst free, coupled with rage—old and new. She twisted under Jayce's body, and when he eased off she knocked him flat on his back in the slick grass and pummeled him with her fists. She blamed him for stealing and shattering her heart and innocence. For her warped views on love and her wrecked shed and gear. She hated him for doing "the right thing" then and now.

If she'd thought for one second Jayce was going to lie there and withstand her fury, she'd been sorely mistaken. In a swift move that made her head spin, he deflected her blows, sprang upright, and whisked her into his arms. The storm raged around and inside them as he carried her into the house and dumped her soaked, aching body into a kitchen chair.

"Don't ever scare me like that again," he warned in a dangerously low voice. His gaze flicked over her, his breathing shallow. A muscle ticked in his jaw as he thumbed a tear from her cheek. He opened his mouth, closed it. Pushed off and swung away. *"Fuck!"*

Her chest ached, his anger crashing over her in suffocating waves. Was he pissed because she'd acted recklessly or because she'd punched him? She was too heartsick to care. She gritted her teeth to keep them from chattering, aware that her boxers and tank top were soaked and plastered to her body. The last thing she needed was pneumonia. The last thing she wanted was for Jayce to notice she was chilled and do the *right thing* by trying to warm her. She couldn't bear it if he wrapped her in his arms or, worse, placed her in a hot bath. It had been torture enough when he'd pinned her under his hard body. Even in her anxious state, she hadn't been numb to his sexual pull. Physically aching for a man who'd resigned himself to marriage on *principle* made her want to bash her head against the wall.

Disgusted with herself and knowing there was nothing to be done about the shed and its contents until the morning, she swiped away tears, dug for control and headed for her bedroom. "I want you out of this house," she said in a quiet voice, not caring if she was being irrational or unfair. *Life* was fricking unfair. "The sooner, the better."

* * *

Devlin gave up on sleep around 2:00 a.m. He was too damned revved, his brain racing with multiple issues, possible solutions and outcomes. For the most part his hands were tied until tomorrow. Some things, like the possible employee crisis at J.T.'s, couldn't be broached until Monday at the earliest.

Tomorrow, he'd get a personal handle on his dad's state of health. Tomorrow, he'd contact Daisy's second doctor, the one he knew nothing about, in order to learn if she had health issues he knew nothing about. He'd researched the few prescriptions Chloe remembered and was relieved to find most had to do with common ailments like high blood pressure and arthritis. Still, the fact that Daisy was seeing a mystery doctor was troubling. Also troubling, the fact that Devlin had unspoken business with Chloe. He'd thought it could wait until he returned from Florida, but it was actually the one thing within his control tonight. He fought a knee-jerk impulse for close to twenty minutes.

"This is insane."

Caving, he rolled out of bed and pulled on jeans and a wrinkled T-shirt.

Ten minutes later he'd crossed Sugar Creek and pulled into Daisy's driveway. Using a spare key, he let himself inside and, without turning on any lights, quietly moved into the kitchen at the opposite end of the house, away from the stairway that led to the upstairs bedrooms. He felt like he was back in high school, sneaking in late and trying to filch a beer from the fridge on top of it all. Only he wasn't here for the beer.

Slaking his wet hair from his face, he rolled back tense shoulders, then palmed his phone and pulled up his newest contact.

"Hello?"

Her voice was hushed and husky and tripped every sensual wire in his body. "Sorry to wake you, Chloe."

"I wasn't sleeping. Too much on my mind."

"I know the feeling."

"What's wrong? Is it Daisy?" she asked in a worried whisper. "The medications?"

"No. It's me." *I'm crazy about you.* "I need to speak with you."

"Okay."

"In person. Come downstairs. Meet me in the kitchen."

"*Daisy's* kitchen?"

"Try not to wake her." He signed off, thumbed the phone to vibrate, then slipped it in his pocket. Whatever reservations he'd had about Chloe had muddied and waned over the last few days. Desire trumped suspicion and apparently rational thinking. Otherwise he would've tempered this incessant yearning with a cold shower or a stiff drink instead of driving across town in the middle of the night like an obsessed lunatic.

Before he could second-guess his actions, Chloe sailed into the moonlit kitchen, a vision of innocent beauty in her short pink robe and silky pink bottoms, her dark hair pulled back from her sweet face in a loose, lopsided ponytail.

Oh yeah. Instant hard-on.

"What is it?" she whispered, looking him up and down as if she expected broken bones or a bloody wound. "What's wrong?"

"It can't wait until I get back from Florida."

"What can't wait?"

He grasped her wrist and pulled her against his body.

Their gazes locked and a split second later they launched into a frenzied kiss. A tangle of limbs as they each shifted, vying for control. A jolt of sensations as they touched and claimed. Sampling, savoring.

She matched his fervor, her hands moving up and under his damp tee, smoothing over his abs, then around to his back.

He pushed open her robe, palmed her ass through her silky pajamas. He lifted and her legs instantly wrapped around him, her pelvis grinding against his arousal as they kissed each other senseless.

A kiss. He'd come for a kiss. A scorching kiss that would brand his senses, staying with him over the next two days, satisfying him enough until he could return and seduce her properly. Except in the midst of this white-hot kiss he couldn't think beyond his dick. He knew she'd fried his good senses when he laid her back on the kitchen table, his fingers loosening the drawstring at her waist.

She palmed his shoulders, caught her breath. "Not here."

"The guest room." Across the house, but downstairs. Behind locked doors.

"What if the floor creaks? What if the *bed* creaks?"

At least she was thinking along the same lines. He swept her off the table, his brain shorting when she locked her arms around his neck and nailed him with another mind-blowing kiss. The more she gave, the more he wanted.

Next thing he knew he'd carried her through a side door from the kitchen into the garage. "Feeling adventurous?"

"Living in the moment."

Between the dark and the various stacked boxes, somehow he managed to make it to the Cadillac without tripping. Outside thunder boomed and rain pelted the metal garage door—not exactly soulful jazz but mood-setting ambiance all the same. Intense. Primal. He opened the back door without bonking Chloe's head on the car and suddenly they were in the backseat making out like two horny teenagers.

"This is so wrong," she rasped as she pulled his T-shirt over his head.

"Not as wrong as the kitchen table."

"Right."

He pushed up her silky cami and brushed his lips over her taut belly while cupping her firm breasts. Her soft moans driving him toward the edge of carnal bliss. Squeezing and plucking her pebbled nipples, he kissed and licked his way up her smooth, creamy skin, his dick throbbing when he tongued and sucked her erect, rosy tips.

He was halfway to heaven when bright light flooded the interior of the car, jolting him like a bucket of cold water. With a muttered curse, he shifted to shield Chloe, certain they were no longer alone.

"Show yourselves or I'll shoot!"

Devlin dropped his forehead to Chloe's. "Gram."

"She owns a gun?"

"Not that I know of. But to be on the safe side . . ." He pushed himself up enough to look out the rear side window at the silver-haired woman wearing moose pajamas and wielding a baseball bat. "It's me, Gram."

The woman marched forward and peered in.

Chloe, who'd managed to pull down her top, blushed and smiled. "Hi."

"You should be ashamed, Devlin Monroe!" Daisy blasted. "You couldn't take her to a ritzy hotel?" With that she turned away, shut off the light, and slammed the door.

After a stunned moment, they both laughed.

"A bit of a mood killer," Chloe said.

"Not a bad thing," Devlin said. He smoothed his thumb over her cheek, still aroused but thoughtful. "She's right. You deserve better." He kissed her then, a sweet, soulful kiss. *This* he would carry with him to Florida. "When I get back," he said, "we're going to pursue this."

"Okay."

"No argument?"

She smiled up at him and his damned heart skipped. "No argument."

TWENTY-FOUR

Chloe woke up to the sound of Devlin's voice. It didn't matter that it was over the phone. She was still in bed, still basking in the aftermath of their late-night rendezvous. Still gloriously and wondrously under his spell. The fact that he'd called from the airport proved she hadn't dreamed the entire episode.

"Get any sleep?" he asked.

"Not much. You?"

"Hard to sleep when my mind's full of you."

She closed her eyes, reveling in the sexy sentiment even as she doubted his sincerity. "Use that line a lot, do you?"

"Never."

White-hot desire blazed through her body. His voice, so sexy. His words, so romantic. She snuggled deeper beneath her blankets, resisting the urge to touch herself. *Ever had phone sex?* she wanted to ask. She suppressed an embarrassed giggle. "This is crazy."

"What?"

"I feel like . . ."

"Tell me."

"I feel like I'm in high school. A teenager dealing with her first major crush. All those intensely wonderful and insane sensations. Logically, I know it's a case of textbook infatuation. Accelerated heart rate. Weak-kneed adoration."

"Sounds like something out of *Cosmo*."

"I definitely read it somewhere. Intense yearnings," she continued. "Obsessive sexual fantasies."

"If I weren't about to board, I'd ask you to elaborate on that fantasy aspect."

Her mouth quirked. "Anyway, you see my point."

"Actually, I do."

"Frustrating."

"Yet stimulating."

"Can we not talk about stimulation?"

He laughed, knocking her further off balance before jostling her with a dose of reality. "Seen Daisy yet this morning?"

"Not yet. I'm sort of dreading it. Knowing her, she'll ask for details regarding our backseat tumble."

"Fortunately, or not, depending on your viewpoint, the details are tame."

"Yes, but if I tell her we didn't get beyond, uh, second base, I worry she'll lecture me on how to get *home*."

"Gram talks that frankly to you about sex?"

"Pretty much."

"That's awkward."

"To say the least."

"I'm sorry I lost control last night, Chloe."

"I'm not. It was exciting. *You're* exciting."

"Tell that to my friends and family. They think I'm boring as hell."

"I don't know about boring as much as uptight." She grinned, remembering how Monica had described him as having a stick up his ass. "You've been lovingly described as a workaholic and control freak."

"Lovingly, huh?"

"Impressive if you ask me. People adore you even though you tick them off."

"It's a gift," he joked.

But she sensed he wasn't really laughing. Chloe snuggled under the covers, the phone pressed to her ear, wishing Devlin were here beside her. Amazing how much their relationship had changed between yesterday and this morning. "Good luck with your dad," she said. "Hopefully he's more reasonable than mine and once you talk face-to-face about your renovation plans he'll honor your wishes."

"At the very least we'll strike a compromise. Maybe you should try that route with your dad."

"He'd have to be talking to me to strike a compromise," she said, trying not to feel bitter and failing. "I've left two messages since our last blowout and he's yet to return my calls."

"You could follow my lead. Fly out and resolve things in person."

"You don't know my dad. Once I was home he'd do everything in his power to dictate my future. He's convinced I can't take care of myself and now that Ryan's out of the picture . . ."

"So he's a good man, but controlling."

Like Ryan. Like you. That thought pricked a hole in her pretty pink bubble. "Can we not talk about this?"

"So what are your plans for the day?"

She pushed up to her elbows and peered out the window. No rain, but no clear blue skies either. "I was supposed to meet Nash this morning for a hot-air balloon ride, which you probably knew, but he called last night soon after the Cupcake Lovers meeting and canceled due to the crummy weather."

"Can't say I'm sorry."

Something in his voice. She raised a brow. "Because you're jealous about me keeping company with your cousin or because you were worried about us navigating stormy skies?"

"Both."

His honesty boosted her dreamy mood. Smiling, she decided not to mention she'd planned on taking Daisy along for the ride, knowing it would only rattle his chains. Selfishly Chloe wanted to cling to this knee-melting flirtation for as long as possible. "For what it's worth, I'm not attracted to Nash. Or Luke," she added, assuming, because this family talked about *everything,* that Devlin also knew she was meeting up with his brother tomorrow.

"Good to know," he said with a smile in his voice. "Although they'll have a hard time believing it."

She laughed at that. "They are indeed . . . confident in their charms."

"That's a nice way of putting it." He paused as a woman's voice shrilled over a loudspeaker.

Chloe sighed. "Your flight?"

"Boarding now," Devlin confirmed. "I'll call you if I learn anything about Gram's meds."

"I appreciate that."

"Have a nice weekend, Chloe."

She closed her eyes and imagined his handsome face, his heart-pounding kisses. "Have a safe and productive trip." *And hurry back.*

She'd barely disconnected when a loud knock startled her into a sitting position. "Yes?"

Daisy blew into the room dressed in a long-sleeved grey pullover, denim overalls tucked into bright pink rubber rain boots. "Get dressed, kitten. Family emergency."

Her heart pounded as she threw off her blankets. It couldn't be Devlin. Then . . . "Who? What?"

"Rocky. Tree crashed into her utility shed. The shed collapsed, burying all her sports equipment. Luke rallied the troops. We're all meeting at the Red Clover. It's wet and muddy out there. Dress accordingly. Not that we'll be doing any of the heavy work, still."

Chloe scrambled out of bed and rooted through her drawers. "Does Devlin know?" Surely not or he would've said something.

"That boy's got enough on his mind. Besides"—she glanced at her watch—"he's in the air by now."

Or at least close to it. Chloe wondered if she should text him, then thought better of it. Daisy was right. He had enough on his mind and, since he was already in Burlington and soon headed for Florida, there wasn't much he could do aside from worry. Instead, she'd just pitch in and do whatever she could in his place.

Daisy turned on her neon-pink soles. "Meet you downstairs in ten."

Chloe threw on jeans, a worn tee, and high-top sneakers. She scrubbed her face and teeth, brushed her hair into a high ponytail, and, two minutes later, was sitting alongside Daisy in the Caddy. Shoving erotic thoughts of last night's liaison from her mind, she hit the garage door remote and keyed the ignition.

Daisy buckled up and, after a teasing glance at the backseat, grinned at Chloe and snickered. "Guess you won't be needing Big Al, after all."

* * *

Rocky ignored the pounding at her brain, pulled her pillow over her head, and willed the day to go away. At some point she'd have to deal with her collapsed shed. Not wanting to impose on family, she'd have to hire help. She'd also have to buy a new shed. Just now she couldn't bear thinking about the impending cost, so she shut it all out. She'd deal in an hour or so. After the groggy effects of two Tylenol PMs, too little sleep, and too much anxiety had worn off.

Unfortunately, someone yanked her pillow away. Temples throbbing, she squinted at the obnoxious daylight and an unwanted guest. "I thought I told you to leave," she rasped, voice hoarse from lack of sleep.

"Rise and shine," Jayce said, looking infuriatingly refreshed. "Luke coordinated a friends and family rescue team. They're on their way."

It took a second to absorb his words. When they sank in, she sprang out of bed and rushed toward her private bathroom. It was that or punch him. "I suppose you called Dev, too!" she blasted as she splashed cold water on her face. "It's why he coerced you into staying here, right? To keep an eye on me and to take charge if things went wrong. As if I can't take care of myself, which I can! What's he going to do when you go back to Brooklyn? Hire a babysitter?"

"I didn't call anyone," Jayce said, moving in and crowding up the threshold. "Your boyfriend did."

"What?"

"Adam showed up early to check on you and the property. He was worried because of last night's storm. Apparently there was wind damage at the Spruce Lake Lodge."

Very close to where Adam lived. "Was he okay?"

"Get dressed and you can see for yourself. He's walking the grounds, looking for damage beyond the shed."

Probably regretting his offer to invest in her ill-plagued B and B. She'd have to give him an out. He didn't deserve getting dragged into her financial woes.

She realized suddenly that Jayce was staring and in a heartbeat absorbed what he'd really meant when he'd said, *Get dressed*. Last night she'd peeled off her soaked boxers and tank and pulled on clean, dry underwear—lace-trimmed boy shorts and a sheer cotton cami. She was practically naked. She willed herself not to blush or to grab the chenille robe hanging on the back of her bathroom door. She decided to let him drink his fill of her long, toned legs, taut stomach, and full breasts. She worked hard to keep fit, especially since she'd been blessed (or cursed, depending on her mood) with a generous bustline and booty. *This is what you're missing!* her mind screamed, a warped message, since she was the one who'd sent him packing in the first place.

"And he's not my boyfriend," she blurted while squeezing toothpaste onto a brush. "Just a *good* friend."

"With benefits."

Was he jealous? Judgmental? She couldn't tell. But the longer he stared, the more she ached. Intimately. *For him.* Panicked, she rinsed her mouth, then, without making eye contact, finger-combed her messy blond waves. "If you're not going to leave," she snapped, "make yourself useful and brew some coffee."

In the blink of an eye, Jayce nabbed her hand and pulled her roughly against him.

She nearly died from the feel of his hard muscles, the proximity of his gorgeous face. When his mouth brushed her ear, she suppressed a lusty groan.

"Keep pushing, Dash," he said in a low, threatening voice, "and you'll be sorry."

"Problem?" asked another male voice.

Adam.

"No problem," Jayce said in an even tone, then stepped back and wordlessly brushed past the other man as he left the room.

Now Rocky blushed. From head to toe. In her barely there underthings.

Adam moved forward and regarded her with injured eyes. The first indication that he actually *did* harbor tender feelings. "Are you and Jayce—"

"No. I know that looked bad, but—"

"You don't owe me an explanation, Rocky. We're just fuck buddies, right? No strings."

Her stomach cramped. Everything was falling apart. Her dreams. The property. And now her secret but stable relationship with this generous and terrific guy who'd never been anything other than kind and supportive.

"Adam—"

"I'll be outside. The shed. There's a slew of people headed over to help." His disappointed gaze raked over her skimpy attire and she knew he was thinking about her in Jayce's arms and thinking the worst. "You might want to get dressed."

* * *

Instead of skimming the clouds, Chloe spent the morning driving through puddles. First in town, when they'd made a stop at Oslow's, then later, as she navigated a lush valley in order to get to Rocky's B and B. The thunderstorms had abated, but the evidence of torrential rains and heavy winds was aplenty. Downed branches, overturned lawn furniture, partially flooded roads. Apparently lightning had wreaked havoc, too. Specifically, zapping the tree that had felled Rocky's shed.

Chloe felt awful about that, as if the woman didn't have enough problems already. It warmed her heart knowing family and friends were pulling together in a big way. Even though it was a Friday, a common workday, apparently several people had committed to an all-day cleanup, including Luke, Nash, Sam, Devlin's friend Jayce, and a friend of Rocky's named Adam. Leo was also making an appearance along with Monica. Also dropping by to lend a hand a few people Chloe had yet to meet—two female cousins and three senior members of Cupcake Lovers.

Daisy had asked Chloe to stop at the grocery to stock up on food in order to contribute to the smorgasbord everyone would pick on throughout the day. Apparently, in addition to cutting away the tree and salvaging what they could of Rocky's gear, they planned on erecting a new shed. Being from the Midwest, Chloe equated the affair to a barn-raising event. She'd only been to one and could still remember the overwhelming sense of community.

Day by day, the longer she was in Sugar Creek, the more she embraced small-town living. Although it wasn't just the town. It was the Monroes and their extended clan. It was being included in a family rescue mission and being able to meet up with Monica any time she wanted. She not only saw more of her best friend; they talked on the phone more often, too. It was about being invited to participate in the Cupcake Lovers' recipe book project even though Tasha had made it clear she wasn't an official member until she'd attended a month's worth of meetings and contributed to at least two charitable functions. Until then she was a *guest consultant* in charge of formatting their proposal. Fine by her.

Last, it was about being attracted to a man who, although obsessed with work, put family problems first, going so far as to fly to another state to settle a disagreement with his dad. Even though there were assorted personality issues and varied crises, getting drawn in and tangled up with this old-fashioned yet unconventional family filled Chloe with a sense of wonder and joy.

"I'd give anything to belong to a big, awesome family like yours," she said, thinking aloud while noting a sign advertising *The Red Clover Bed-and-Breakfast—2 miles ahead.* Like most everything in this region, the sign looked like a remnant of the 1800s.

"Stick around long enough," Daisy said, "and you might get your wish."

Chloe glanced from the passing scenery—dairy farms, apple orchards—to the woman wearing bib overalls and blingy cat-eye glasses. "I'm afraid to ask."

"Obviously, Devlin's crazy about you. If that doesn't work out, maybe we can match you up with Sam. He's a good man and though he's set on courting Rachel, you saw how *that's* going."

"I'm trying to figure out which one of those bizarre comments to address first."

"You don't think my grandson's crazy about you? Then what were you two doing fogging up my back windows?"

Chloe focused on the narrow road and rolling hills. "Let's not go there."

"All right then, let's talk about Sam."

"I'm not attracted to Sam and he's not attracted to me. A girl knows these things. Trust me. Not an ounce of zing."

"But there's zing with Devlin?"

Enough to light up the Manhattan skyline. "I'd appreciate it if you wouldn't mention last night to the family," Chloe said. "I mean it was sort of . . . embarrassing."

Daisy snorted. "Only because you got caught."

She smiled. "Only because we got caught."

"I won't mention it. Not on purpose anyway." The older woman shifted in her seat. "Sometimes things just pop out."

Chloe sensed an opening to pry into Daisy's state of mind and health and carefully wiggled in. "Why do you think that is?"

"Part of growing old," she said with a shrug. "Loss of

memory. Lack of focus. The mind starts to go. Among other things."

Chloe was pretty certain that was a broad and not wholly accurate generalization. She'd known a few seniors whose minds were as sharp as tacks and who, through daily exercise, remained physically fit. One of her favorite teachers at the culinary institute had been in his early seventies and spry and smart as a whip. "I read somewhere that crossword puzzles and other brainteasers help to keep one's mind strong," Chloe said. "I think vitamin supplements help, too. Although I'd have to research—"

"Ginkgo biloba. Been taking it for years."

"Anything else? Other medications, I mean."

"Lots of medications. For various, sporadic ailments," she elaborated, though not enough. "Part and parcel of aging. Not that you have to worry about that anytime soon."

"Maybe not. But I do worry about *you*."

Daisy reached over and patted Chloe's arm. "That's sweet, but don't. Believe you me, I'm enjoying what's left of this life." Before Chloe could comment, the woman pointed out the front window. "Look at all those cars. We're late for the party. Punch the gas, kitten."

Chloe noted the Red Clover, a sizable Victorian home with a wraparound porch and a magnificent view of a not-so-distant tree-covered mountain. Her first impression was, *Beautiful, remote, and in need of a paint job.* But other than that, even as she tried gearing up for working and socializing with the people who'd already arrived, Daisy's words monopolized her thoughts.

I'm enjoying what's left of this life.

As if she knew the end was near.

Chloe prayed heart and soul Daisy was wrong.

TWENTY-FIVE

Once they'd toted all the groceries inside the Red Clover, Daisy hunkered down in the kitchen with her friends Ethel and Helen, telling Monica to give Chloe the nickel tour, since Rocky was outside with "the boys."

"It's really amazing, what she did with the place," Monica said as she led Chloe toward the central sitting room.

Behind them, laughter flowed from the kitchen, and Chloe relaxed, suppressing her concerns about Daisy's enigmatic statement about life. Probably she only meant it as the cliché it was. Life is too short. Live life to the fullest, and such. Maybe, no, most likely, that was why she'd been throwing caution to the wind, cramming in as many thrills as possible. No matter how old you were, you never knew when it could all end. Chloe's own mom had died at thirty-five. So many unrealized dreams. One of the reasons Chloe had always followed her passions no matter where they took her, no matter how brief the experience. No missed opportunities. No regrets.

Although, in hindsight, she could see now that some of her choices had been made out of fear: *What if this opportunity never comes again? What if I wait or say no, only to die tomorrow?*

Chloe shook her head. She'd never had that thought before. Why now?

"Earth to Chloe."

"What?"

Monica frowned. "I was trying to give you a heads-up about the situation out back, but you were zoning." She sighed, "What a mess," then whisked Chloe into the downstairs guest suite.

Snapping to the present, Chloe took in the eclectic décor, somewhat surprised by the romantic element, given Rocky's tough-as-nails persona. "I'm sure the men will have that tree cleared away in no time," she said, admiring a hand-painted armoire that just *had* to be a creation of Sam's.

Monica shook her head. "I don't mean that. I mean Rocky. This really knocked her for a loop. Generally she's a rock. Today? Totally stressed out. I swear I saw her hands shaking."

"She's probably worried about the cost of replacing the shed and the damaged gear. You heard her at dinner last week. Business is down. Has been for a while. Diminished income, yet she's been shelling out to repair and replace appliances."

"And now her Jeep's in the shop," Monica said. "Leo's scrounging for the best deal on a few parts so he can essentially build her a new engine. He can't work for free, but he's trying to cut her a break."

Chloe smiled at her friend. "You've got a good man."

Monica smiled back. "Yes, I do. Hoping we can say the same for you someday soon."

Chloe opened her mouth, closed it.

"What?"

"I shouldn't. . . ." Chloe shook her head as her thoughts centered on her own situation. "Now's not the time. I feel bad about being so . . ."—she grappled for a word that didn't sound immature—". . . happy when Rocky's so . . . miserable."

Monica shut the guest room door and leaned against it, ensuring Chloe couldn't get past her. Her eyes sparked with curiosity. "Spill."

Alone with her best friend, the only person who knew

everything about her—good and bad—it was all Chloe could do not to break into a silly dance. "Devlin kissed me."

Her friend looked disappointed. "I know. In J.T.'s. It was awful in an orgasmic kind of way."

"No. Last night. In the backseat of the Caddy, and it was . . . *incredible*." She briefed Monica on the nocturnal liaison without sharing graphic details, which meant she pretty much told her everything. "He said when he gets back we'll pursue this and I said, 'Okay.'"

"You did?" Monica pushed off the door and jammed a hand through her pixie cut, making the shorter layers stand on end. "Wow."

"I know, I know. I'm on the rebound and this is probably a really bad idea for several reasons. But I'm living in the moment and going with that *Mr. Right Now* premise."

"I'm not judging, Chloe. I think this is great. I'm just . . . surprised."

"From the first moment I plowed into him at Oslow's there was this . . . spark. And then an itch. No matter how much we scratched or resisted, it wouldn't go away. Then when he called me this morning from the airport . . ." She trailed off, feeling like an idiot for rambling.

"Oh . . . my . . . *God*." Monica gawked at Chloe as if she were an alien. "Are you in *love*?"

Chloe's hand flew to her racing heart; her eyes widened. "What? *No*." She laughed, but it sounded nervous even to her ears. "How could I . . . I barely know him. We've never even been on a date. It's just infatuation. A crush."

"Sounds like love at first sight."

"That's crazy."

"Why? Leo and I fell head over heels the first time we laid eyes on each other and look at us now. Married and trying for kids."

Flustered, Chloe forced a smile. "How's that going anyway?"

"Don't change the subject."

"Then I'll end it." She'd just accepted the fact that she was hopelessly infatuated with Devlin. *Love*? She wasn't sure she'd know real love if it bit her on the butt. But this wasn't it. Couldn't be it. He was all wrong in the long-term scheme of things. Frowning now, she breezed past Monica and out into the hall, nearly barreling into Daisy.

"I was just coming to get you," she said. "We made some iced tea. If you girls wouldn't mind taking the jug and tumblers out to the men—"

"Our pleasure," Chloe said, grateful for the distraction. She hurried toward the kitchen with Monica on her heels, trying to ignore the teasing love ditty her friend was singing under her breath. "Honestly," Chloe huffed.

Monica just laughed.

Five seconds later, they were navigating a rickety back porch, refreshments in tow. "As beautiful as the interior is," Chloe said, "the exterior could sure use some work."

"I know for a fact Devlin offered to put some money into the place, but Rocky refused his help."

"Pride. I get that." Chloe eyed the men hard at work. Some with chain saws. Two others heaving debris into the back of a pickup along with Leo. "That's Jayce, right?"

Monica nodded. "I just met him this morning. Close friend of the family. I know he grew up here and still owns a house here, but I don't think he visits much. Seems nice enough. Kind of quiet. Intense. Handsome if you go for the bad-boy type."

Chloe pointed toward the only other man she didn't know. "Who's that?"

"Adam Brody. Also a native of Sugar Creek, though I understand he moved away for a few years. I guess you'd call him a freelance sports instructor. Hires out to various lodges and gives lessons in everything from horseback to snowmobile riding. I thought he and Rocky were just friends, but . . ."

"But what?"

"I don't know. When we first got here, I noticed them sneaking looks at each other and I sensed . . . tension."

"Maybe they had a disagreement."

"Caught some other looks, too. Between Jayce and Adam, and Rocky and Jayce."

"What are you saying?"

"I'm not sure."

Chloe gestured. "Looks like she's giving Luke hell just now."

They fell silent as they reached the disaster area, just as Nash and Sam cut the motors of their chain saws, allowing Luke's words to carry loud and clear. "Chill out, for Christ's sake, Rocky! We've got it covered. Take a walk or something. *Damn.*"

She spun off in a fury, blond braids swinging, jeans smeared with mud.

Monica cleared her throat to draw attention away from their stressed friend. "In case you guys are thirsty," she said, holding up a jug of tea.

"Is she all right?" Chloe whispered when Leo joined them.

He simply raised his brows and relieved Monica of the jug. "Maybe you girls should join her."

Sam took the plastic tumblers from Chloe. "At first I thought it was pride." He frowned over at Adam. "Now I'm not so sure."

"We'll look after her," Monica said, grasping Chloe's elbow and hurrying after Rocky, who was jogging toward a distant patch of trees. "I told you. Something's up between Rocky and Adam."

"And Adam and Jayce," Chloe whispered. "Just after Rocky split, I caught them trading a look."

"Was it hostile?"

"It wasn't friendly."

"Oh, boy. All right, well, Rocky's pretty tight lipped about her private life and she suffers from control issues, so whatever you do, don't push."

"Me? You're the pushy one."

"True."

They followed the younger woman into the woods and found her pacing back and forth along a skinny trail. "I can't breathe," she blurted as if she'd been waiting for them to hurry and catch up.

214 **BETH CIOTTA**

"Are you hyperventilating?" Chloe asked.

"Maybe you should sit," Monica said. "Put your head between your legs."

"No. I need to walk it off."

"Would it help to talk about it?"

Chloe glared at Monica and mouthed, *Pushing.*

"I don't know. I don't . . ."

"You don't have to say anything," Chloe said gently, prodding Monica to sit next to her on a flat-topped boulder. She thought about how frantic she'd been when Ryan had shattered her world. How alone she'd felt with her closest friend hundreds of miles away, even though she was only a phone call away. It wasn't the same as being in the same breathing space where you could reach out and touch and hug, if that's what you needed. "Just know we're here for you," Chloe said. "That's all."

The women sat quietly as Rocky continued to pace and after a minute or two she started spewing. "I just . . . I feel like my life is spinning out of control. Nothing's going according to plan, and if that's not bad enough, I think . . . I know I hurt Adam."

"Does it have something to do with Jayce?" Monica asked.

Chloe kneed her just as Rocky stopped in her tracks. "Why would you say that?" she asked, wild eyed.

Chloe swallowed hard, struck by the misery in the younger woman's tortured gaze. "We just . . . we saw them trading looks and you seemed to be the cause."

Rocky sank down on a log across from them, although one leg bounced nervously as she chewed on her thumbnail. "Do you think any of the guys noticed?"

Chloe and Monica shared a look. Sam and Leo had. They shook their heads.

"I doubt it," Monica lied.

"They were too busy sawing wood and pitching trash," Chloe said.

"Plus, you know men," Monica added. "Oblivious."

Rocky blew out a breath, stared at the ground. "Adam and I have been seeing one another for a few months now. Actually, we've just been sleeping together. And not overnight. It's just about sex."

"Friends with benefits?" Monica asked.

"Fuck buddies." She shrugged. "Same difference."

Chloe instantly wondered if Daisy had picked up that term from Rocky. Although it could have been Luke, who also seemed to have a relaxed attitude toward sex.

Monica whistled. "Wow."

"It was perfect," Rocky plowed on. "The perfect arrangement. No promises. No expectations. No grief from anyone, specifically my brothers, since we kept it secret."

"What happened?" Chloe asked. *So much for not pushing.*

"Adam offered to invest in the Red Clover. To partner up professionally. Which was perfect, actually, given his interests and skills."

"But that complicated the personal end," Monica ventured.

"From my point of view," Rocky said, "there was that potential. But mostly, I wasn't willing to give up full ownership. It made me feel like a failure and threatened my dream."

"I get that," Chloe said. "So you turned him down and now he's hurt."

"I took him up on the offer and then he caught me in Jayce's arms this morning. In my underwear," she added. "*Now* he's hurt."

Chloe and Monica swapped gazes. *What the hell?*

"Is there something between you and Jayce?" Chloe asked. Only because she sensed Rocky wanted or needed to get this out. That's not to say she wasn't curious herself. As was Monica. This was juicy stuff.

"No," Rocky said, leg bouncing. "Yes. Once. A long time ago."

"How long ago?"

"I was seventeen. Just."

"Twelve, thirteen years ago," Monica said. "Jayce is the same age as Devlin, which means . . ." She did the math. "He was . . . twenty-one? Two? *Damn*."

"Your first?" Chloe guessed, blowing over the jailbait issue.

Rocky dropped her face into her hands. "I was so freaking in love! Had been for *years*."

Puppy love. First love. At least on her end. But what of Jayce? Forbidden love? Talk about powerful stuff. Still . . . "He should've known better," Chloe said. "Not to mention he's your brother's best friend and, from what I've heard, adored by the entire family."

"Not Jayce's fault," she said. "Not that part. I seduced him."

Monica blinked. "You knew how to seduce a guy at seventeen?"

"I had two older brothers and a pack of male cousins," Rocky said. "And eyes."

"Enough said."

Chloe tried to make sense of it all. "Do you love Adam?"

"No. Although, I do care. I think. Just not in the way I love Jayce."

"So you love Jayce," Monica said.

"What? No!" Rocky bolted back to her feet and resumed pacing.

Chloe scrambled. "But you said *love*. Present tense."

"Loved," Rocky said. "Past tense."

"Yet he's here and coming between you and Adam," Chloe pointed out. "Does *he* love *you*?"

Rocky snorted. "Yeah, right. If that were true, I would've married him when he asked."

Wide-eyed, Monica looked over her shoulder, making certain they were still alone, then blurted in hushed amazement, "Jayce asked you to *marry* him?"

"When?" Chloe asked.

"The day after we . . . did it."

"Thirteen years ago," Chloe clarified.

"I thought he loved me," Rocky said in a choked voice.

"The way he . . . he was so gentle. It was so perfect. Then he ruined it the next morning by saying we should get married."

"*Should*," Chloe said, beginning to put things together.

"Because it was the *right thing to do*," Rocky spit out, more angry now than upset.

"So he offered more out of a sense of duty than love," Monica said. "Ouch."

"Still," Chloe pointed out, "there's honor in that." She was trying desperately not to judge. She didn't know Jayce. Didn't know his side of the story. And Rocky was drawing on the naïve and melodramatic emotions of a teenager.

"Devlin married for honor," Rocky blurted, "and look what that brought him."

Monica cast Chloe a glance that verified she knew nothing about Devlin's previous marriage. Chloe played dumb, because she'd promised Daisy she wouldn't bring it up. *Ever.*

Talk about an awkward moment.

Chloe cleared her throat. "I don't mean to pry," she said, redirecting the focus back to Rocky, "but are you certain there's nothing between you and Jayce?"

"Just a decade of resentment."

"You resent him for offering marriage out of duty," Moncia said.

"And he resents you for rejecting his proposal," Chloe finished. "Not to minimize what must have been an exceedingly intense moment in your lives, but . . ." *Tread lightly, Madison.* "After all these years, you haven't been able to . . . get past this?"

"We've never really addressed it."

Monica gawked. "What?"

"I told him to fuck off and he obliged by keeping his distance."

"But he's Devlin's best friend," Chloe said. "He owns property here. Surely your paths have crossed before now. He never tried to smooth things over?"

"He brought it up." Hugging herself against the cool, damp weather, Rocky turned her back on them and stared at her mud-caked Nikes. "I shut him down."

"Oh, honey," Monica said in a nurturing voice Chloe knew well, "you need to resolve this with Jayce. Let it go. Move on."

"I don't know if I can."

Chloe ached for the woman. She denied it, but obviously she was still in love with Jayce. An idealistic love born of youth and nurtured by repression. In the words of Monica, *what a mess.* "What are you going to do about Adam?"

"I don't know." She whirled then and nailed them with frantic eyes. "No one knows about Jayce and . . . what happened between us. *No one,*" she reemphasized. "Promise me you'll never repeat this. If it ever got back to Dev . . . he'd never forgive Jayce for sleeping with me, for being my first, for keeping it secret. . . ." She blinked back tears. "He thinks of Jayce as a brother. I can't, I *won't,* come between them. I can't live with that, too. Promise me."

"Of course," Monica said.

Chloe shifted uncomfortably, feeling as if she was sabotaging her relationship with Devlin before it even got off the ground. At the same time, she empathized with Rocky and respected her desire to protect her brother's lifelong friendship. Stomach knotted with yet another family secret, Chloe forced a smile and nodded. "I promise."

TWENTY-SIX

Chloe stared at her laptop. She'd read the same Food Network blog twice and still didn't know what it said. She couldn't focus. Not with her brain buzzing around a dozen different concerns. Daisy's meds. Rocky's dilemma. The Cupcake proposal. Devlin's return.

The weekend had passed in a blur.

Devlin had called Friday night to check in. No luck in his efforts to glean insight from Daisy's mysterious second doctor. A confidentiality issue. Overall Devlin had seemed distracted, and truth told, Chloe had felt uncomfortable, struggling with Rocky's secret. He did, at least, know about the collapsed shed, thanks to Luke, and though Devlin was frustrated about not being around to take charge, he trusted his brother and cousins to handle the situation. *Thank God Jayce was there when it happened,* he'd said. *I knew my instincts were right when I asked him to stay with her.* Chloe had wanted to argue that point but didn't. She couldn't. Thanks to her *promise.* Their phone call had been short and lacking in any flirtation, putting a kink in her already-convoluted mood.

Because the cleanup and installation of Rocky's new shed extended into Saturday, Luke had asked Chloe for a rain check regarding their plans to attend the Burlington Food Festival.

Fine by her.

Ever since Rocky had unburdened her soul, Chloe had dreaded spending one-on-one time with anyone in the family, especially Rocky's brothers. Knowing how protective and fierce Devlin was about his kin, Chloe could only imagine how he'd react to his best friend's betrayal. Would Luke rise to his sister's honor as well? Probably. Would a face-off merely result in ugly words and broken trust? Or would it get physical? It would have been better if Rocky and Jayce had come clean years ago. Better for them. Better for everyone. Now it was a buried dirty secret putting everyone who knew about it in an awkward position. Although part of Chloe was flattered that Rocky had confided in her, the other part resented the knowledge. Monica seemed to be taking it in stride; then again, Monica wasn't primed to pursue an intimate relationship with the person Rocky wanted the least to know.

"The girls just called," Daisy said, tottering into the living room. "They'll be here in five minutes. How do I look?"

Chloe moved her laptop from her knees to the coffee table and made a show of checking out Daisy's Sunday frock. Ironically, she'd chosen the blue and green dress Chloe had been wearing when she'd been accused of shoplifting. Which made her think of Devlin and the kiss they'd shared in the office. Which made her giddy and melancholy at the same time. That promise to Rocky hung over her head like an ominous cloud. "You look great."

Daisy pushed her blue-tinted glasses up her nose and clicked her apple-green heels. "Thanks to you."

"I'm glad you like it."

"Sure you won't join us?"

"Us" being Daisy and the other senior members of Cupcake Lovers. Tasha had assigned them the task of coming up with three of the most sentimental and successful charity events from their earliest recollections, stories they'd pass on to Chloe, who'd type them into a word document. *So many wonderful memories,* Daisy had said. The ladies had decided

to discuss their choices over Sunday brunch. Directly following church.

Chloe fidgeted. Brunch might be fun. But church? It made
her think of her mom and dad, of what had been and what
Chloe hadn't had for very long time. A deep connection with
family. *Her* family. Logically, she knew she should've let go
of those wistful notions years ago, but being at odds with her
dad only made her cling to the good times all the more. "Not
that I wouldn't enjoy the company," Chloe said.

"But you'd rather have some time alone."

"As of last night, I've received e-mails from most everyone in the club regarding the tasks Tasha assigned for the
proposal. Once I have the stories you're collecting today, I'll
have everything I need. With the exception of the pictures."

"Which we'll have by Tuesday," Daisy said.

"Right."

Tasha had booked a session with a local photographer for
Monday and had used her influence to pressure him into
providing digital prints by the next morning. A publicity
shoot that everyone in the club, with the exception of Tasha,
had insisted Chloe attend.

She knows food and media, Rocky had said.

And PR and photography, Devlin had added with a sly
smile.

Daisy had crossed her arms over her scrawny chest, a defiant glint in her eye. *She can offer valuable perspective. Beside, as my driver, she'll be there anyway.*

Tasha had relented, but because she wanted to get on
with the meeting, not because she agreed. She'd told Chloe
so by way of an annoyed look.

"Anyway," Chloe said, shaking off the uncomfortable
moment, "since Tasha wants everything formatted and in
the mail by Thursday, I should probably use this morning to
get started. Plus there's Sunday dinner to prepare and—"

Daisy cut her off with a raised hand. "Say no more."

A car horn announced the arrival of Ethel, Judy, and
Helen. Chloe honestly *was* looking forward to some free

time and not having to worry about her soul sister pulling some derring-do stunt. Chloe had met Daisy's cronies over the weekend and, though fun, they didn't strike her as the Errol Flynn type. Besides, how much trouble could they get into at the Pine and Periwinkle Inn? "Have fun," Chloe said with a smile and a wave.

Daisy waggled her fingers, then spun on her shiny new heels. "One of these days you're going to tell me what you have against church," she called over her shoulder.

"One of these days you're going to tell me what's really going on between you and Mr. Redding!"

Daisy shocked her as she sailed out the door. "Deal!"

* * *

Rocky usually joined Daisy and a portion of the family for morning services, but today all she could think about was her many faults and sins and how she'd wronged some very good people. Asking the Lord for forgiveness, then doing nothing to atone would only make her a hypocrite, so she decided to stay away until she'd cleaned up her act.

Apologizing to family for her irrational and rude behavior the past two days would be a piece of cake compared to having a heart-to-heart with Adam. As for Jayce, she wasn't sure how to "let go and move on," but she knew she had to do something. The one thing she couldn't do was come clean with her brothers or parents about why she'd been at odds with Jayce all these years. The more she thought about it, the more she fretted. She wasn't exactly an innocent in this matter, and he had, after all, asked her to marry him. Her parents and Dev were big on *the right thing*. Luke would probably cut her some slack, but she wasn't even sure she could tell him. On top of everything, by keeping her teenage indiscretion a secret she'd been lying to her family for years. And what about Adam? She'd kept their relationship secret, too. Their purely *sexual* relationship. How many times had she concocted a tale or dodged questions to keep everyone in the dark about her fuck buddy? Maybe her family would forgive the liaisons, but could they forgive the lies?

All she knew was that she had to address the future with Adam and resolve the past with Jayce. If she could at least accomplish that, maybe she could breathe. Since the moment Adam had offered to invest in the Red Clover and Jayce had returned to town, she felt like she was suffocating.

Chest tight, she massaged her aching heart and sipped coffee. As soon as she had enough caffeine in her, she'd get out of her ratty pajamas, into some decent clothes, and take action. She glanced at her half-empty cup. It might take a pot or two.

Feeling sorry for herself and horribly alone, she fell forward and banged her forehead on the kitchen table.

In tandem the back door swung open and Luke strode in. "I was going to mind my own business, but I can't. So," he said when she cast him a pathetic gaze, "whose ass do I need to kick? Jayce's or Adam's?"

* * *

Since there were no direct flights from Miami, Devlin's morning flight landed at the Burlington airport just shy of 2:00 p.m. Normally, he would've resented the layover in D.C., but in light of the circumstances, he welcomed the additional downtime to decompress. Meeting with his dad had been a bear. Not because the old man had given him shit about flying down or shit about pushing revised health benefits, but because he'd refused to talk about his battle with cancer.

I'm fine.

Thankfully, because Devlin's mom was forthcoming and the oncologist a compassionate, no-nonsense man, Devlin trusted that his dad was indeed gaining ground on that bastard disease.

But he was not *fine*. "Fine" implied nothing was wrong. Due to chemo, he'd lost weight and most of his hair. It had taken all of Devlin's resolve not to verbally or physically react to his dad's appearance. Show no pity. Imply normalcy. Which entailed a strong façade that screamed, *You'll beat this*.

After two days in the trenches, Devlin was exhausted. How did his mom find the strength, the resolve? Where did his dad dig up that unwavering faith and courage? Not one spoken word of doubt. Not one complaint. In one weekend Devlin's admiration for both of his parents had tripled.

Leaving hadn't been easy, but it had been a relief. The entire time he'd been with his parents, he'd felt like he was choking on fear. What if things went bad? What if his dad suffered? Since he refused to discuss the disease, Devlin had felt useless. He needed to get back to where he could make a difference.

After tossing his overnight bag into the rear seat of the four-door rental, he leaned back against the trunk, breathed in the clean, crisp air, and collected his thoughts. Once home, he'd hit the ground running. He snagged his Android, intending to check in with Jayce, a follow-up that would help him decide where to concentrate his immediate efforts—Rocky or Gram. But instead he dialed Chloe.

"You're back!"

Her enthusiastic greeting warmed him more than two days of intense Florida sunshine. "Almost," he said. "Getting ready to leave the airport. Just wanted to let you know I'll definitely make Sunday dinner."

"That makes three of us then."

"What do you mean?"

"Calls have been coming in all day. Rocky canceled first, saying she wouldn't be good company. Then Luke bailed due to a previous engagement he forgot about. Sam canceled about an hour ago. His daughter came down with a stomach bug."

"Sorry to hear that."

"Oh, and Jayce canceled," she said in a rush. "Though he didn't give a reason."

"Huh." Since Devlin had spent next to no time with his visiting friend, he was sorry about that, too. On the other hand, a quiet dinner with Chloe and Gram might be the perfect time to subtly pick his grandma's brain: *Why are you seeing a doctor in Pixley? What's behind your sudden need for reckless kicks?* "How's Daisy doing?"

"As far as I can tell, great. She was an inspiration all weekend at Rocky's, a shining example of a tireless caretaker. Other than that, she's totally jazzed about the Cupcake Lovers project. She's spending today with Ethel, Helen, and Judy, compiling stories for the recipe book."

"Sounds encouraging." Knowing his grandma hadn't pulled a crazy stunt in his absence, knowing her spirits were good and her mind focused, relieved Devlin of an immediate source of tension. He was still curious about that second doctor, but maybe there was no real need for concern. Maybe there was a simple explanation based on Gram's recent quirky nature. Trying to channel his mom's and dad's optimism, Devlin chose to think positive, relaxing enough to focus on Chloe. "So you're alone right now?"

"I am," she affirmed with a seductive smile in her voice.

"Maybe I'll swing by early."

"Something to look forward to." She paused and he knew they were both thinking about their last steamy interlude. After a moment she cleared her throat. "How did it go with your dad?"

"We struck a compromise."

"So things are good."

"Improving. See you in a couple of hours, Chloe."

"See you then."

Mood lighter than it had been in two days, he slid behind the wheel and keyed the ignition.

Twenty minutes into the drive, he got a call from Luke. "Just heard from Ethel Larsen," his brother said, voice tight. "There's been an accident. They're taking Gram to the hospital in Pixley."

* * *

Rocky steered Devlin's Escalade, her weekend loaner, into Adam's driveway and parked. She sat there for a moment, staring at his two-bedroom rental, gathering her wits and nerve.

She hadn't meant to spew her guts to Luke, but she wasn't sorry. He'd listened patiently and he hadn't judged, although he wasn't pleased to learn she'd lost her virginity to Jayce on her seventeenth birthday.

Something told me you two had hit the sheets at some point, but I never guessed you were so young. At least now I know whose ass to kick.

Please don't.

Request noted.

She'd managed to divert the conversation to Adam. If Luke had been shocked that she'd engaged in a friend-with-benefits relationship, he'd kept it to himself, merely saying, *At least Adam's a stand-up guy.*

Which was part of the reason Rocky felt so awful. Which was why she'd taken Luke's advice to heart regarding their personal and professional relationship.

The conversation had ended with a comforting hug and Luke asking if she was going to confide in Devlin about Adam, to which she answered, *Yes.*

What about Jayce?

I can't, and after explaining why she'd asked, *Will you keep my secret?*

Yes. But I'm not happy about it.

So here she sat, trying to get up the nerve to do the right thing with Adam. Mostly it was about finding the right words. She didn't want to hurt his feelings. But partly, it was because she couldn't help worrying, *What if I'm making a mistake?*

Just then the passenger door opened and Adam climbed inside. "Since you're wrestling so hard with it, thought I'd save you the anxiety of knocking on my door."

Chest tight, she regarded him with teary eyes. "I did you wrong, Adam."

"If this is about Jayce . . . I had no right acting like a jealous ass. We had an agreement. No strings. For what it's worth, my reaction surprised me as much as it did you."

"I just want you to know, I haven't been with anyone, sexually, since you and I paired up."

"You don't owe me—"

"Yes, I do. As my friend. As someone I care about. As someone . . . as someone I'll miss."

He blew out a breath. "So you're breaking off with me."

"My head's in a crazy place right now, Adam. I need to step back and reassess."

"Alone?"

She nodded. "Alone."

"What about the Red Clover?"

She swallowed hard, feeling like a reneging bitch. "I need to do that alone, too. That is, without a partner. I said yes to your offer in a moment of panic. I appreciate everything you've done," she blurted in a nervous rush, "especially with, God, the way you organized my family and erected a new shed—"

"It's all right."

"No, it's not. But it's my dream and—"

"I'm not part of it. I get it, Rocky. Honestly, knowing you like I do, I never should have crossed that line."

"Adam—"

"It's okay." He reached for her hand, kissed her palm. "No strings." Then he was gone.

Heartsick, she gripped the steering wheel, eyes burning. Had she just written off the one good thing in her life? She grappled for her ringing phone, saw the incoming call was from Luke. Maybe he had some wise brotherly advice to add before she faced off with Jayce. "What?" she croaked.

"It's Gram."

TWENTY-SEVEN

By the time Devlin blew through the front doors of Pixley General Hospital, the waiting room was crowded with family and friends. Luke and Rocky, two of Daisy's sisters and their spouses, her Cupcake cronies Ethel, Judy, and Helen, and Chloe—who looked nervous as hell, sitting apart from the others, her leg bouncing as she read something on her Android. She glanced up and met Devlin's gaze and he knew she felt guilty about the accident.

Luke stepped into his line of vision. "Gram's sleeping comfortably, knocked out on painkillers. I called the rest of the family, told them the doctor's discouraging visitors until tomorrow." He gestured to their great-aunts and uncles. "Some people don't listen. As for Ethel, Judy, and Helen, they feel responsible. Refused to leave until they had a word with you."

Before Devlin could acknowledge his relatives, he was rushed by his grandma's friends.

Ethel spoke first. "We're so sorry, Devlin. It was the craziest thing. One minute she was bicycling next to us on a wide, even path and the next she'd veered off."

" 'Bike paths are for kids and old people,' " Helen huffed. "That's what she said. 'We *are* old,' I reminded her."

"That's what set her off, I think," Judy said.

"No," Ethel said, "it was reminiscing about our younger

days in Cupcake Lovers that set her off. Talking about all
the things we used to do or that we wanted to do but never
did. That's when she got riled."

"We never should have let her talk us into an after-brunch
bike ride," Judy said. "Two of us were wearing dresses, for
goodness' sake. Not to mention most of us haven't been on a
bicycle in two decades."

Ethel sighed. "All the more reason to throw caution to the
wind and have some fun, she'd said."

"And it *was* fun," Judy said, "until Daisy veered off the
main path."

Luke had shared this story with Devlin over the phone.
Daisy had turned onto a trail that went downhill, gaining
speed and managing to stay in control until the front tire hit
a rut and sent her skidding several feet over the grass and
into a tree. Similar to the snowmobile fiasco last winter, but
worse. This time she hadn't walked away.

"You should have heard her," Judy said, "whooping like a
kid as she sailed down the hill."

"We doubled back and saw the whole thing. She was in
her glory," Ethel said, "and I admit, for a minute I was envious."

"Until she crashed."

"It was awful."

"Dialed nine-one-one right away."

Now Gram was in the hospital with a broken ankle, frac-
tured rib, scrapes, bruises, and a gash on her forehead.

"She's lucky she's alive," Ethel said.

"Doc said it helped that she'd been drinking," Luke threw
in. "If you can believe that."

"Wine," Ethel said. "Just a glass."

"But enough that her limbs were loose. Could've been
worse if she'd tensed up. Instead she just sort of rolled with it.
Good news is by skidding through thick grass she lost most
of her momentum by the time she conked her head on the
tree."

"You should've seen the blood," Judy said.

"Shush," Helen said. "You'll worry her sisters."

They already looked plenty worried to Devlin. As did Rocky and Chloe. Before he could put anyone at ease, his phone rang. Seeing the caller ID, he broke away. "Yeah, Dad."

"Have you seen her yet?"

"Just got here." He'd called their dad en route. Devlin didn't want to add to his worries, but at the same time the man deserved to know his mother was in the hospital. "Luke said she's resting comfortably."

"I know. I spoke to him. He put me on with the doctor who assured me, barring unexpected complications, she'll be okay. Dammit, what was she thinking?"

"I don't know, Dad, but I plan to find out."

"I should fly up, but I'm worried if she . . . if she sees me like this . . . I don't want to make things worse."

"I understand."

"But the family will wonder—"

"I'll take care of it."

"How?"

"I'll think of something and let you know."

"All right." He paused, sighed. "Did anyone call Kelly?"

His dad's sister. Nash's mom. The black sheep of the family, she'd been living in Vegas for years. "I spoke to her briefly," Devlin said. "She won't be flying in."

"Of course not."

"But she did ask that we keep her updated."

"That's something, I suppose." He blew out a frustrated breath. "I'll let you go. Thanks for handling things, Son."

Devlin shook off a wave of emotion just as someone touched his arm. His senses told him it wasn't Rocky or one of his great-aunts, and sure enough, when he turned it was Chloe.

"I should've been there. She invited me along and—"

"But then she would've coerced you into that bike ride as well, and unlike her friends, you would have followed her down that hill." He grasped her hand, squeezed. "Come on." Trusting Luke had the others under control, Devlin guided Chloe down the hall. "I know the doctor said no visitors, but we can at least try to peek in."

"Look," Chloe said, nodding down the hall. "Vincent Redding."

Devlin spied the owner of Oslow's stalking toward them as fast as he could, given his chunky stomach and short, stocky legs. He remembered how Chloe had mentioned the possibility that Vince and Daisy were dating. From the harried look on the old man's face, Devlin could tell there was more to this visit than simple friendly concern.

Well, damn.

"Got here as soon as I could," Vince said, puffing to catch his breath. "Is she okay?"

"Worse for wear," Devlin said, "but she'll live. This time." Still holding Chloe's hand, he narrowed his eyes on the man who he now assumed could clear up a few mysteries pertaining to Daisy-I've-got-secrets-out-the-wazoo Monroe. He jerked his head toward an outdoor seating area. "I want to talk to you."

* * *

"It started with Jessup's illness," Vince said. "Yes, Daisy was brokenhearted when he passed, but what gave her nightmares, what tormented her soul, was watching him waste away."

Chloe felt Devlin's fingers tighten around hers. It was subtle but just enough that she knew he was bothered by Vince's words. She knew from Monica that Jessup had died from lung cancer. But that had been ten years ago.

"Not long after, she lost a brother. Over the next five years, she lost a few friends, a sister and a brother-in-law. Two years ago—"

"Sam's wife," Devlin finished. "Ovarian cancer."

Chloe hadn't known the cause. Had she lingered? Suffered? How awful for Sam and his children. Chloe looked at Devlin, but he was focused intently on Vince.

"It ate at Daisy," Vince said. "The death. The misery." He cocked a snowy brow. "Made her question her own mortality. The hereafter."

"I had no idea," Devlin said.

"No one did. She never talks about it."

"Except to you."

Vince shrugged. "Daisy's been shopping at Oslow's forever. One day not long after Jessup passed, she came in looking for the ingredients to make Chocolate Turtle Cupcakes—I'll never forget it because she brought me a sample the next day and . . . yowza. Anyway." He blew out a breath, spread his meaty hands. "We got talkin' and we've been talkin' ever since."

"Just talking?" Chloe asked.

"I wanted more. She didn't. I'm all right with that."

Devlin shook his head. "So you're telling me my grandmother's been flirting with death because she's *afraid* of death?"

"She's taking advantage of every opportunity," Chloe said, "every adventure. Because you never know when your number's up."

Vince clucked his tongue and shot her with a fat finger. "Bingo."

"I get that."

Devlin looked at her with a raised brow. "You do?"

"Yeah." She'd been doing the same thing for the last seventeen years, although her approach had been slightly different.

"Okay," Devlin said, "but she didn't take up this thrill-seeking agenda until last winter."

"The snowmobile incident. Mmm. Well." Vince cleared his throat and looked away. "This is where it gets sort of sticky, because I probably should've told someone in the family, but Daisy swore me to secrecy and—"

"Just spit it out, Vince."

"She'll understand," Chloe added with a tender smile.

"I doubt it," Vince said, "but it's gone too far, this derring-do crap." He scratched his beard, nodded, then reestablished eye contact. "Last November, I drove Daisy into Pixley to see the big Christmas tree lighting. Something we'd been doing for the last several years."

From Devlin's expression, Chloe could tell it was yet another thing he'd been unaware of.

"Daisy started feeling, well, not right. Shortness of breath, sweating, dizziness. I took her straight to the emergency room, here at this hospital. Mild heart attack."

Devlin jerked. "What?"

"It was so mild and caught so early, they treated it with medication. They emphasized her high blood pressure. Gave her a lecture about lifestyle changes and diminishing stress. They told her to consult her regular doctor right away. Only she didn't want Doc Worton to know, fearing he'd alert the family."

"For Christ's . . ." Devlin jammed a hand though his hair. "Why wouldn't she want the family to know?"

"Because you'd try to take control of her life," Vince said. "She'd had enough of that from Jessup, and then your dad started imposing his will. Hired that cleaning crew to invade her house every week. Lectured her about wasteful spending. Then you intervened, Devlin. Nagging her about her driving. Insisting she hire someone to do her cooking."

Chloe swallowed. "I feel awful."

"Don't," Vince said. "That's one thing she did have control over, choosing you, Chloe. She felt"—he shook his head—"*feels* good about that. About you."

"I'm glad."

Vince glanced at Devlin, frowned. "As for you—"

"I interfered," Devlin said, "because I was worried. She'd become accident prone."

"Short-term memory loss," Vince said. "Scattered thoughts, inability to focus. Side effects of the medication Doc Worton gave her for anxiety. Only he didn't know about the medicine she was taking for her heart. She refused to tell him, so I talked her into coming clean with Dr. Beane, her physician here in Pixley. I drove her here last week and Dr. Beane gave her the riot act about mixing meds, set her on a new course. I thought everything was okay. But I guess she's still got . . . issues."

After a moment, Chloe scrambled to break the tense silence. "At least we know what we're dealing with now."

Devlin nodded, extended a hand to the older man. "I appreciate the information."

"Just want what's best for Daisy."

Chloe squeezed Vince's arm, cast Devlin a supporting smile. "We all do."

Just then Luke poked his head out the door. "Gram's awake. Doctor said we can go in four at a time. No more than ten minutes." He glanced at Vince and Chloe. "Sorry. Family only."

Chloe wondered if Vince felt as crummy about that as she did.

His crestfallen expression said he felt much worse. "I'll be back tomorrow first thing."

"I'll be in the waiting room," Chloe said. She'd ridden over with Luke, although she could probably get a lift home from Vince.

Home.

She'd been here less than a month and she was already thinking of Sugar Creek in terms of home. Just like she thought about the Monroes as her family. Except they weren't.

"I'll have a word with the doctor," Devlin said close to her ear as he escorted her back inside. "Get him to make an exception."

"What? No," she said, realizing he'd misinterpreted her troubled expression. "I mean, I'd love to see Daisy, but I don't want to intrude on family time. If you're going to bend the rules, you should bend them for Vince."

"I'm not feeling particularly generous toward Vince right now."

"Breaking his promise to Daisy didn't come easily."

"He shouldn't have made that promise at all. If we'd known about Gram's fears, about the heart attack, for Christ's sake—"

"His intentions were good," Chloe said reasonably, her temples throbbing with her own questionable promise. "What would you do if someone you cared about asked you to keep a secret for what they considered good reasons?"

He glanced away, nodded. "I'll be out in a few minutes; then I'll drive you home."

There it was again. That word. That sentiment. As if she *belonged* in Sugar Creek. "It's going to feel strange, depressing actually, being in that big house without Daisy."

Devlin kissed her forehead, before trailing after his brother and sister. "Then you'll stay with me."

TWENTY-EIGHT

She should have told him no. Refused politely. Made an excuse. But instead, Chloe quickly packed an overnight bag, shoved her laptop into its tote, and, after locking Daisy's front door, hurried to rejoin Devlin in his rental car.

"That was fast."

"Yeah, well . . ." She shrugged, fiddled with her seat belt. Could she be any more anxious to spend the night with this man?

At the same time, she was nervous about the prospect of sex. She hadn't been with anyone other than Ryan for close to three years, and their lovemaking hadn't been all that great. Easy to blame on him, but what if it was her? What if she fizzled in bed? What if she lost her nerve? What was worse? Being considered a lousy lover or a tease?

"I know I already said this, but don't worry about entertaining me tonight." She patted her laptop. "I have a lot of work to do for Cupcake Lovers."

"And I need to prepare for tomorrow's meeting." He slid her a knowing look. "You don't have to sleep with me tonight, Chloe. I have an extra bedroom. No pressure. That said, I'm hoping like hell you'll jump my bones."

Chloe laughed, grateful for the tension breaker. "At least I know where you stand."

Smiling, he pulled back out onto the street.

Desperate for neutral, nonsexual ground, Chloe diverted the conversation by broaching Daisy's state of mind. Mostly Devlin had glossed over his visit—*She was only alert five minutes before drifting off*—focusing more on Vince's revelation as well as the doctor's prognosis. "I'm still having trouble believing Daisy agreed to a caregiver."

"Temporarily," he said. "I didn't bully her, if that's what you're thinking, although I might have if she'd been opposed to reason. The doctor was clear. She's going to need help for a while. Someone to assist with bathing and dressing. Monitoring medication."

"I could've done that."

"She didn't want you to. Said you're a cook, not a caregiver."

"That could've been the pain meds talking. You said she was groggy. Maybe she'll change her mind tomorrow, when her mind's more clear."

"Don't bet on it. She said she needs you in the field."

"What does that mean anyway?"

"I don't know. I asked, but she turned her attention to Rocky, offering to introduce her to Big Al, since you wouldn't need him anymore. Then she nodded off." He cast her another look. "Who's Big Al?"

"Not who. What. And I'd rather not say."

"Fine," he teased. "I'll ask Gram when I visit tomorrow. Rocky's curious, too."

"A vibrator."

"What?"

"Figured you'd rather hear it from me than Daisy."

He blinked, then laughed. "Gram tried to hook you up with a vibrator?" He shook his head. "That's so wrong. Not you and a vibrator. But Gram—"

"I get it." Chloe shifted, cheeks burning.

"Why—"

"She thought I was . . . you know, sexually frustrated."

"Now she thinks Rocky's sexually frustrated?"

"Do you really want to talk about your sister's sex life?" *Please don't make me pretend not to know about Adam and, for God's sake, Jayce.* Devlin had been angry that Vince had kept a secret about Daisy. How would he feel when he learned Chloe had been privy to a family secret as well?

"Point taken," he said, and she nearly wilted with relief. "Although sometimes I wonder if she even has a sex life."

Chloe barely contained a snort.

"So why does Gram call it Big Al?"

She raised one brow. "You really don't want me to go there."

He laughed. "Probably not. So, what do you want for dinner?"

"Oh, my God, *dinner.* I totally forgot. I could've packed the pork chops I marinated—"

"Don't worry about it. We'll order in."

"I'd be happy to whip up something on the fly."

"Except you won't find much to work with in my fridge and pantry."

"Oh, right." She flashed on the first day they met, sighed. "Don't you ever get tired of microwavable foods?"

"Sure. But it's easy and fast."

"And lacking in nutrients."

"Hence occasionally ordering in or eating out."

"That's not always healthy either. Except I have to say the Sugar Shack's menu offers plenty of low-fat and heart-healthy fare."

"Luke's idea. He wanted to offer his customers more than greasy burgers and buffalo wings. I suggested we interview and hire an affordable gourmet chef."

"What made you go into the restaurant business anyway?"

"Luke. He'd always wanted his own bar and restaurant. It's a social thing. He likes people, being around people, showing them a good time. He'd been bartending at the Sugar Shack, which used to be called Don's Bar and Grill, for close to five years. When it came up for sale—"

"He jumped."

"It needed a lot of work. He had big ideas and limited funds."

"So you invested. Co-owner. But you don't seem to spend a lot of time there."

"I don't want to step on his toes. It's his dream. Although I am hands-on with accounting. Luke's got vision and drive but, in the words of our mom, runs the Shack with his heart, not his head."

Chloe smiled.

"What?"

"It makes you feel good, watching out for your little brother's best interests."

"If only Rocky would let me do the same." Just then his phone rang. After glancing at the screen, he excused himself to take the call. "Sorry I hurried you off before, Jayce."

Not wanting to eavesdrop, Chloe focused on the passing scenery—a mixture of colonial and saltbox homes, their manicured lawns augmented with picket fences and various hardwood trees. Day by day the leaves turned more vibrant, various shades of red, orange, and yellow. According to Daisy, within two weeks Chloe would be privy to the full autumn spectacle. She could scarcely wait. But even as she tried to imagine the beauty, her brain fixated on the one-sided conversation between Devlin and the man who'd broken Rocky's heart.

"Banged up but in good care," Devlin said. "Absolutely. I know Gram would appreciate hearing from you, but hold off until tomorrow. . . . What? . . . When? . . . Well, hell. No, I . . . Sure. Talk to you then."

"Everything okay?" Chloe couldn't help asking.

"Jayce is flying back to New York. Said something came up with an old case and he has to get on it today."

For real? Chloe wondered. Or was he getting the hell out of Dodge, hoping to retain "the secret" for another ten years? "Wasn't he in the middle of doing something with his house?"

"Consulting with a contractor about renovations. Said he still hasn't decided whether to sell or lease."

"Would it bother you if he sold?" It would probably make Rocky delirious. Jayce Bello—out of her life for good.

Devlin considered Chloe's question, nodded. "It would.

Jayce and I go way back," he said as his own house came into view. "We're still tight except . . ."

Normally Chloe would've prompted him to continue with his thought, but she was pretty certain that would be inviting trouble.

He swung into his driveway, cut the engine, then shifted to face her.

She braced for . . . *something.*

"You spent a lot of time at Rocky's this weekend. How were things between her and Jayce?"

Oh no. "I couldn't really say." *How's that for a spin?* "I mean there were a lot of people around and mostly the men were immersed in cleaning up the crushed shed and erecting a new one. I don't think I ever saw her alone with Jayce." *True.* "Come to think of it, I didn't share more than five minutes with him myself." *Also true.* Knowing what she did about him and Rocky, she'd steered clear.

Instead of pushing the topic, thankfully, Devlin backed off. "Why am I burdening you with this? Enough drama for the day, right?" He squeezed her hand and swung out of the car. "If I learned anything this weekend, it's that there are some problems I just can't fix."

That made Chloe smile. "Oh, but you'd like to try."

"We all have our flaws."

Ain't that the truth? Chloe thought as Devlin nabbed their bags, then ushered her toward his front porch. *Like falling for controlling men.*

As she crossed the threshold, she bolstered her senses against a tide of emotions. She'd only been in this cozy colonial one time, but if she closed her eyes she could envision the kitchen, dining room, and living room in detail. She even knew where he kept his favorite coffee mug and the television's remote control. When he set aside the luggage and placed his hand at the small of her back, she felt like he was welcoming her, into not only his home but also his life.

For the second time in a week she experienced the sensation of floating, only this time her head was in the clouds.

She was high on this man's essential goodness and sexy charisma. Breathing was a chore and the warmth emanating from her heart and spreading throughout her body was so comforting yet exhilarating, she felt giddy with wonder.

Monica's voice trilled in her ear. *Are you in* love*?*

Blown away by the realization, she scrambled to pinpoint the when and why.

Maybe she'd fallen when he'd absolved her of blame regarding Daisy's accident. Or maybe when he'd offered to bend rules to make Chloe feel better or when he'd eased the minds of Daisy's friends and sisters. Or maybe Monica had nailed it and it *had* been love at first sight, only Chloe had been oblivious until now. All she knew for certain was that her heart had taken a serious tumble.

Which added a whole new frightening dimension to *jumping his bones.*

"Make yourself at home," Devlin said. "I'll take up our bags and be right back."

She grabbed his shirt before he turned. "I just want you to know . . ." She looked into his bluer than blue eyes and revealed her biggest immediate fear. "It's been a long time since I've been with anyone other than . . . well, you know. And we weren't that . . . It wasn't . . . spectacular." *What if I'm a dud in bed?* hung unspoken in the air. Voicing that insecurity would be lame. Especially when statistics suggested most men found *confident* women a turn-on. Not to mention she'd just brought up a past lover. *Way to go, Madison.*

But instead of backing away, Devlin pulled her into arms and claimed her mouth. *Bliss.* He kissed her long and deep, until her heart pounded in her ears and her legs went all noodly. Heat pooled to intimate places, and erotic images of them in bed together, naked, conjured a groan of pure ecstasy. When he finally broke off, her thoughts were dazed and her balance iffy.

Smiling, he palmed her butt and pressed his rock-hard erection against her lower belly, evidence of his desire, proof of her potency.

She smiled back up at him, senses zinging. "Or maybe I'll rock your world."

"I vote for the latter."

* * *

Rocky pulled into Jayce's driveway just as he was backing out. Like Dev, he was driving a rental car. Since she'd just blocked him in, he had no choice but to kill the engine. She walked to his car just as he was climbing out. Her gaze skimmed over his cargo pants, torso-hugging T-shirt, and the layered poplin shirt, unbuttoned and with the tails hanging out. Sexy casual. His longish blond hair was tousled and his killer eyes hidden behind aviator sunglasses. Regardless, she blushed under his scrutiny. Between Gram's accident and this impending showdown, Rocky felt somewhere between frazzled and sick.

"You all right?" he asked.

She started to get flip—*Do I look all right?*—but instead stated the truth. "No."

"Is it Daisy? Did she take a bad turn?"

"Gram's fine. Well . . . recovering. No, this is about this past weekend."

He glanced at his watch. "If you're going to give me hell about something, make it quick. I've got a plane to catch."

Her pulse tripped. "You were leaving without saying good-bye?"

He slowly pulled off his glasses, narrowed his eyes. "You kicked me off your property and now you're pissed because I didn't check in with you before getting back to my life?" He dragged a hand down his whiskered chin. "You're a piece of work, Dash."

She shored up against the emotions that nickname inspired. "It's just . . . we have unfinished business."

"How so?"

The nerve she'd worked up on the drive over started to fade. She nodded toward his parents' house. Funny, how he never referred to it as *his* house even thought he grew up there. Even though he owned it. She remembered sneaking into his room that night and . . .

"Can we take this inside?" It's not that she wanted to tempt memories, but she really didn't want to discuss something this private out in the open where anyone could drive by.

He worked his jaw, then made a call. "Yeah, Nash? . . . Jayce. . . . No, I'm not canceling, but I am running late." He shot Rocky an annoyed look. "Ten, fifteen minutes. . . . Right."

"*Nash* is flying you out?"

"Got a problem with that, too?"

She bit her tongue, channeled her energy. But by the time they crossed the yard and breached his front door, she'd moved on from nervous to angry. She'd come here to make peace and he was picking a fight. They squared off in the living room, the totally empty, devoid of everything including carpet and baseboards, living room. She knew his tenants had moved out. She knew he'd initiated renovations, but it still surprised her how the house lacked any semblance whatsoever to the powerful, charismatic man looming in front of her.

He crossed his arms over his chest. "You wanted to talk. Talk."

She swallowed the urge to sock him and clung to Luke's advice: Acknowledge his good intentions and move on. "I forgive you."

At first he said nothing. Just shifted his weight, angled his head. "What the hell for?"

"For ruining everything by doing the right thing." Okay. That hadn't come out like she'd rehearsed it. But, dammit, that's how she felt.

He bit back a laugh, shook his head. "Is this your way of putting the past behind us?"

Her back went up. "At least I'm trying."

"Let me ask you something, Dash. How do you feel about Adam?"

The question caught her off guard and caused her skin to burn because, just now, she felt awful about Adam. Or, rather, how she'd hurt him. "I like Adam. He's a good man.

Certainly someone who deserves better than me, so . . . I
broke off with him. I've got a lot going on. Issues I need to
work through. Problems I need to tackle. The Red Clover—"

"How do you feel about me?"

"I . . . I . . ."

"Let me put it another way."

The next thing she knew she was in his arms, under his
spell, being deeply, thoroughly kissed. She burned. And just
like that she was a seventeen-year-old virgin, melting under
the practiced touch of the man she'd pined for since she was
thirteen.

Heady, heady stuff.

When he broke off, she nearly lost her balance, her
thoughts and feelings a tangled, jumbled mess.

"Good-bye, Dash." He strode out the front door without a
second look. "For now."

* * *

Devlin couldn't remember the last time he'd felt this content.
Yes, he was sexually frustrated, but even that was sweet
misery. The kiss they'd shared earlier had promised fire-
works in bed, whenever they made it that far. He could've
pushed it then, but even after he assured her she had no worries about fizzling in the sack, he'd still sensed apprehen-
sion. He didn't think it was because of her ex-boyfriend but
couldn't be sure. So he'd backed off, allowing Chloe to adjust to his home and the thought of them together. When the
time was right to seduce her, he'd know. Yes, he was rusty in
the romance department but far from inept. It might not happen tonight, but it would happen, and when it did . . .

Devlin shifted and angled his laptop to hide a die-hard
boner. Frustrated, but content.

He glanced at Chloe, sitting at the other end of the leather
love seat, a mountain of research materials between them.
His. Hers. After pigging out on "a little bit of everything"
from Chang Li's, the only Chinese restaurant in Sugar Creek,
they had changed into sweats and tees and settled in with

their projects. They'd been working in companionable silence for over an hour, although once in a while she asked him a question about one of the members of Cupcake Lovers or for clarification on a charity event. Just now she surprised him with an enraged outburst.

"She has *got* to be kidding!"

"Anyone I know?"

"Tasha."

"Ah." Unfortunately, he knew *Mrs. Burke* better than he wanted to. "What did she do now?"

"I sent her an e-mail, asking if she'd heard about Daisy's accident and inquiring about the possibility of postponing the photo shoot until the end of the week at least. I worded the e-mail in a pleasant way and was mindful to stroke her ego, closing with: *I'm sure the editor won't mind a slight delay, since it involves a senior member.* And what response do I get to my thoughtfully worded half-page note? Three words: *No can do.* No salutation. No signature. Did she even think about it? Did she even try? How rude is that?"

"She has an agenda."

"Well, screw *that*."

"You're cute when you're riled." Devlin quirked a half smile. "Especially on behalf of my family."

"It's just so wrong. Daisy's in the hospital, for God's sake. What's a few more days? So what if she has a cast on her leg and a bandage on her forehead? There's such a thing as creative posing and airbrushing. Daisy's been a member of Cupcake Lovers longer than anyone else, even Ethel."

"I know."

"She deserves to be pictured in the recipe book."

"I agree. But remember," he said, seeking to lower her blood pressure, "this is just a proposal. A sampling." He flashed back on all the info Tasha had shared that night. "There'll be an additional shoot should the book go to contract."

"It doesn't matter. Daisy will be crushed. A major disappointment like that is the last thing she needs right now."

He couldn't argue with that. "Want me to call Tasha?"

"Yes. No. What did you ever see in her anyway?"

He raised a brow.

"Sorry. None of my business."

"It's okay. Well-known fact Tasha and I dated for a couple of months about a year ago. I was coming out of a bad relationship and she . . . made me feel good. For a while."

"The sex got boring, huh?" Chloe asked with a teasing smile.

"Let's just say, she was more interested in my money than me."

She studied him for a moment, then sighed. "I've said it before and I'll say it again: Tasha's a shallow pinhead."

He laughed at that, charmed that Chloe made light of a past affair, flattered that she didn't ask about his bank account. "Regardless, she still thinks she can weasel her way back into my bed."

"Even though she's married?"

"Annoying. But it does give me a modicum of control. If I asked her to call off the shoot—"

"So that she can expect something from you in return? Uh, no. Besides, I don't want you to fight my battles for me."

"Like you didn't want me to take on Deputy Burke in your defense."

She frowned. "I sort of forgot about that incident."

"I didn't." But he did keep his promise not to seek out Billy. That's not to say he wouldn't have a word in the future should the situation warrant. Devlin crossed his arms over his chest and studied the pretty woman sitting so close yet so far, her attention now riveted on her computer screen. "So why is that anyway?"

"Why is what?"

"Why don't you want my help?"

"Because I need to do things for myself, on my own. First Dad managed my life, then Ryan. Not that I really fought them. Okay. I didn't fight them at all," she continued, eyes averted. "Thinking back, I guess I considered them my safety net while I blazed through life taking risks and chances and bouncing wherever my passion sent me."

Because of Jayce he knew how many times she'd changed schools and careers. He'd attributed it to laziness or fickleness. The inability to finish what she started. Now he didn't know what to think. He remembered something she'd said at the hospital. "Taking advantage of every opportunity because you never know when your number's up."

"Exactly."

"Want to tell me why you relate to Daisy's fear of death? Is it the water incident in Florida when you were a kid?"

"Daisy told you about that, huh?" She shook her head, then looked his way. "That only pertains specifically to the fear of drowning. My overall need to cram in as much life as possible is connected to my mom. She died when I was fourteen. She was only thirty-five. Hit by a drunken driver. She was shopping in town, standing at the curb, waiting to cross the street. The driver lost control and . . . One minute she was there, the next gone."

"I'm sorry, hon."

"Every time I think of her, I remember her dreams and interests, big and small, most of them unfulfilled. She put everything on the back burner, devoted her life to Dad and me. She'd always say, 'I have plenty of time.'" Chloe frowned. "Only she didn't."

She turned back to her work, and Devlin assumed she'd shared all she wanted just now regarding her chosen lifestyle. Not that he needed her to elaborate. Coupled with the information supplied by Jayce, he now had a pretty clear take on Chloe Madison. The question was, would she finally settle down and commit to one passion? One career? One man?

That he was thinking in terms of long-term commitment was troubling. He'd known her less than a month, not that he'd fared well with women he'd known a long time. Still, unless Chloe licked her fear of death, along with Gram, he stood the chance of losing them both, albeit in different ways. A sobering thought.

"What are you up to?" he asked, intrigued by Chloe's intense expression and flying fingers.

"Sending an e-mail to every member of the club, well, at

least the ones with e-mails. Since it's so late, I'll have to call Ethel, Judy, and Helen in the morning."

"About?"

"I'm rallying the troops. I figure if everyone bands together and refuses to participate in tomorrow's photo shoot, Tasha will have to postpone."

Devlin powered down his laptop. "Don't underestimate Tasha's influence."

"They won't abandon Daisy." She glanced up as he set aside his laptop. "Are you finished?"

He was, in fact, as prepared for tomorrow's meeting as he would ever be. He'd also checked over his investments and juggled a few finances while she'd been organizing and formatting the proposal. "It's been a long day. Time to unwind. How about a bottle of wine and a movie?"

She looked up, smiled. "That sounds great. Just let me hit 'send.'"

After the drama-filled day and the somber talk of her mom, he figured Chloe would welcome a chance to lighten the mood. He needed a breather himself. His head was jammed with family crises—Gram, his dad, Rocky—the employee meeting, and erotic thoughts about Chloe. "I don't have much of a DVD collection, but check out that guide. Maybe there's something of interest on cable or pay-per-view."

"You should get Netflix."

"I don't watch a lot of movies." Winding down was almost a foreign concept. By the time he returned from the kitchen with a bottle of red and two glasses, Chloe had packed up her work and was skimming the movie guide. He lowered the lights, then sat next to her and poured. "Find anything?"

"I did." She smiled, pointed.

"Driving Miss Daisy." An old movie about an old woman and her chauffeur. He smiled. "I'd sort of hoped for a sexy thriller, but what the hell?" He handed her a glass of wine, proposed a toast. "To Gram's speedy recovery."

She clinked her glass to his. "To living in the moment."

TWENTY-NINE

Chloe woke with a crick in her neck, a bad taste in her mouth, and a dozen worries grinding through her rusty brain. Daisy's injuries, Rocky's secret, Tasha's obstinacy. The only nice thing was that she was cocooned in Devlin's arms. Even though she was only half-awake, she was fully aware of his signature scent, his warm body. She registered the caress of his hand, the weight of his thigh. Morning wood pressing into her backside. Unfortunately, the more aware she became of the intimate spooning, the greater the nauseous pounding in her head.

"Rise and shine, beautiful," he said close to her ear. "I'm late for work."

It took a minute for his words to compute and for her bleary eyes to adjust. They were still in the living room, but the flat-screen television was dark and the braided rug dappled with daylight. "We fell asleep on the couch?"

"I don't know who zonked out first, but I attribute it to the late hour and too much wine, not the company."

She squinted at the empty bottle and palmed her aching head. "I never overindulge like that."

"Easy to do with a good vintage on top of a stressful day."

She'd yet to turn and meet his gaze. Even though there was no censure in his voice, she was mortified. The goal had been to unwind, but throughout the movie her brain had obsessed on the day's crises and night's potential. Falling in love had intensified her expectations. The more she'd obsessed on sex, the more she'd imbibed to calm her nerves. Well, she'd calmed herself all right. "I feel like an idiot."

"How do you think I feel? Alone all night with a hot chick," he teased, "and what do I do? Pass out."

That coaxed a smile out of her. "Something tells me you were completely sober."

His lips brushed her ear. "A gentleman never kisses and tells."

"Very old-fashioned of you," she teased back, but truly she was charmed. The dating scene had been less chivalrous in New York. Going to bed with a man while buzzed was the norm, and last night had, in a way, been a date. She remembered cuddling, affectionate caressing, and one very long, sensual kiss. He could've taken advantage. Instead, he'd been sensitive to her anxiety and compromised senses. She rolled into him then and met his hypnotic gaze. "I'm sorry I didn't jump your bones. It's not that I don't want to. It's just last night . . ."

"Wasn't the night." He smoothed her hair out of her face. "But it wasn't a waste."

She lost herself in those blueberry eyes. "You say the most romantic things."

"Not by design, trust me. Not my style."

"You're not a player. I know. Which makes your actions and sentiments all the more appealing." She realized then that he was staring at her mouth. As much as she wanted him to kiss her, all she could think was morning breath—hers, not his. Plus it felt as if someone were driving a spike through her brain. Literally.

"If I weren't so rushed for time, I'd carry you up to my bed and make slow, hard love to you, Chloe."

Whether it was due to the use of her name or the sexy timbre of his voice, despite her hangover she tingled in all the right places. "Rain check?"

He sealed the deal with a kiss that melted what was left

of her brain cells, then peeled himself away looking rumpled and to-die-for sexy. "You could join me in the shower," he said with a wicked grin.

"Maybe next time," she said, feeling shy and queasy, not that she planned to admit either. "You're late for work, remember? Big day. Important meeting."

"I also want to check in with the hospital, check up on Gram and visiting hours."

"I wish we could drive over right now," Chloe said, "but I know she needs the rest."

"Not sure how to handle her *issues.*"

"Maybe if you embraced her spirit for living rather than addressing her fear of death?"

"Accentuate the positive."

"Something like that."

"Would it help if I took that approach with you?"

She blinked, then realized she'd confessed her own unique fear of death last night. "I'm not sure."

He reached down and tucked her hair behind her ears. "When you figure it out, let me know."

Which meant he'd understood and accepted her need to fight her own battles. Her smitten heart thudded, rivaling the obnoxious pounding in her head.

His gaze lingered, a silent bid of respect and affection, before he finally broke away and headed for the stairs. "There's a second bathroom down here if—"

"I remember. Thanks." Her stomach flipped and turned, a combination of being wonderfully lovesick and horribly hungover. *Get a grip, Madison.* When he was gone, she dragged herself off the sofa, nabbed the small toiletry bag she kept in her purse, then hurried into the downstairs bathroom. She intentionally avoided the mirror, relieved herself, then washed her hands and face with ice-cold water and brushed her teeth. "Don't puke. Don't puke." Last night she'd fretted over disappointing Devlin in bed. Now her biggest concern was resisting the urge to hurl into his toilet. Gulping air, she braced her hands and stared at her reflection. "*You* are pathetic."

She was not, however, beaten. Even though she looked like death warmed over, he'd initiated a kiss that still hummed through her noodly body. She managed a cocky smile. "He likes you," she told herself. "A lot."

It wasn't just sex. The tenderness in his gaze and touch suggested a deeper intimacy. Her heart swelled just thinking about the way he'd indulged her desire to sample various dishes off the take-out menu as well as her sentimental movie choice. The way they'd worked on individual projects side by side. His gentle expression when she'd opened up about her mom and her own reckless approach to life—something she hadn't realized until meeting Daisy. Underneath Devlin's controlling nature beat the heart of a sensitive soul. Last night they'd connected as friends. This morning as a couple.

She thought about him, standing in the shower, buck naked, steaming water sluicing over his toned muscles, and fought the overwhelming desire to join him. As much as she wanted to jump his bones, she didn't want to interfere with his big day at work. Knowing the employee meeting weighed heavily on his mind and aware he was already running late, she dragged her sorry butt out of the bathroom and into his kitchen.

"The least I can do," she told herself as she nabbed coffee and eggs from his fridge, "is send him off with a hearty meal."

After breakfast she'd check for e-mails from the club members and somehow, someway tackle Tasha and the photo shoot dilemma. Suddenly Chloe understood why Daisy wanted her "in the field." Daisy needed a champion. Someone to assure her place in the recipe book. In the same instant Chloe understood Devlin's sometimes-overbearing determination to protect his family and his willingness to compromise rather than alienate. Family, no matter how big or small, was precious. Family was messy. In search of perfection, she'd abandoned her own blood. Instead of mending wounds and bridges, she'd run.

Guilt ate at her gut worse than the hangover.

Flicking on the coffeemaker and lowering the heat on the skillet, she rushed into the living room and fished her phone out of her purse. Her heart sank a little when she got his answering machine, but regardless, she left a heartfelt message: "Hi, Daddy. Call me when you get this. We need to talk."

* * *

Devlin blew into J.T.'s at 9:30 a.m., a half hour after the doors opened for business, two and a half hours past his normal arrival time. Normally, he would have been on edge, pissed because he'd missed the additional time to cram numbers and review reports. Instead he was relaxed, optimistic, and heart over head for Chloe Madison. Luke was right. She wasn't Janna.

Yes, they were both reckless free spirits who courted trouble and both possessed irresistible sex appeal, but the similarities ended there. Janna had lacked depth and selflessness. Chloe was complex and sensitive to feelings and plights other than her own. She'd only been in Sugar Creek a short time and she'd already shown more genuine concern for his family than Janna had over their rocky two-year courtship and six-month marriage. Whereas Janna paid lip service, Chloe took action. Her devotion to Gram was just one of the things that seduced his cynical soul. The fact that Chloe cooked like Cat Cora of Food Network fame was a bonus. He wasn't sure which lingered in his mind more, the sight of Chloe making herself at home in his kitchen this morning or the incredible taste of the full breakfast she'd made utilizing what little he'd had in the fridge.

Nodding and smiling to the employees who greeted him, Devlin breezed through the nearly deserted first floor of the department store counting his blessings, including this morning's encouraging phone calls with Gram (*Doc said he'll spring me in two days!*) and his dad (*At this rate, I'll be home by Christmas*). Not even the present rainstorm, the fourth in a week, or the gloomy expression on his approaching assistant manager's face could dampen Devlin's spirits. "Good morning, Chris."

"I don't know about good," the man said as he fell in beside Devlin. "Although it could be worse."

"What's wrong?"

"For one, the toilets in the public ladies' room overflowed. I put an *Out of order* sign on the door, sent in the janitor-on-duty, and called the plumber."

"Perfect. Next?"

"Gemma's Bakery bailed on catering the employee meeting tonight."

"Why?"

"Closed for business."

"Since when?"

"Since this morning."

"No advance notice?"

Chris shook his head. "I don't know what's going on."

Curious but nonplussed, Devlin scaled the stairs to his second-floor office. "Don't worry about it. I'll call Luke, get the Shack to send over desserts and coffee. Anything else?"

"Yeah."

Devlin placed his briefcase on the desk, shrugged out of his drenched jacket, and fired up his laptop. Meanwhile, his second-in-command hovered on the threshold, weighing his words. "Just spit it out, Chris."

"Ceiling leak, third floor, men's department."

"Water damage?"

"Moderate. I've got a crew on it."

Devlin's first impulse was to rush to the scene and evaluate. Instead he sat down and opened his briefcase. "Sounds like you've got everything under control."

"Yeah, but . . ."

"What?"

"Don't you want to supervise?"

Devlin glanced up. "Do you need me to?"

"Not really, but that's never stopped you before."

He laughed at that. "True."

Hands on hips, Chris shifted his weight, angled his head. "You're awfully . . . relaxed. You get laid or something last night?"

"No. But I did get a life."

"Meaning?"

"Meaning I trust your judgment and skill." Not that he'd exhibited that trust over the past few months. No, as was his style, and just like his dad, Devlin micromanaged even the most capable people. His most irritating quality, according to friends and family, and part of the reason he had no social life. Who had time? If he'd learned anything this past week, it was that life was too short. "Thank you for troubleshooting this morning, Chris."

The man puffed out his chest and smiled. "Just doing my job." He turned, then paused and looked back at Devlin. "But you are going to check in later. Assess the damage control."

"If I didn't I wouldn't be doing *my* job."

Chris nodded. "Just wanted to make sure getting a life didn't entail leaving J.T.'s. I know you've been at odds with your dad."

"I'm not going anywhere." At least not until his dad returned and took back the reins. Devlin would gladly step aside when that day came. The sooner, the better. Mostly because it would mean his dad was in good health. Partly because it would enable Devlin to pursue alternate opportunities and maybe an adventure or two. Preferably with Chloe.

Although . . . he wouldn't be doing anything or going anywhere until he'd secured the loyalties of J.T.'s crack sales and management team. He'd reviewed the file listing the various health and wellness packages offered by VT Med and he'd sold his dad on offering employees the chance to personalize their benefits package—at minimal cost to J.T.'s. What Devlin had failed to do was gain his dad's approval regarding incentive bonuses, something he said the company couldn't afford.

But Devlin could. He'd set those wheels in motion days ago. Curious as to the present status of his strategic planning, he'd signed onto the Internet and into his stock portfolio.

At the same time his door creaked open and Rocky stepped in. "I need to talk to you."

Something personal, he assumed, since she actually shut the door behind her. Something troubling, because, instead of flopping into a chair, she paced.

"If this is about Jayce—"

She stopped cold, fists clenched at her sides. "Why would you think that? What did he say about me?"

"Nothing. Other than telling me you run a damn nice inn. You're the one who's been bent out of shape since he came to town. Not him." As Devlin noted her flushed cheeks and anxious tone, something itched at the back of his brain. He stepped out of his sibling shoes for a second and regarded Rocky as a woman, remembered how Jayce had described Chloe from an outdated picture—blond hair, kick-ass curves. His typical type. Rocky to a T. Was it possible? Had Jayce made some sort of unwanted advance? Paid her a colorful comment? Or maybe it had been the other way around. Maybe Rocky had expressed interest and Jayce had rejected her advances. That made more sense, since Devlin couldn't imagine his best friend taking advantage of his little sister. He couldn't pinpoint it, but something told him Rocky's current distress revolved around sex. Feigning nonchalance, he leaned back in his chair. "Something you want to tell me?"

"I've been having an affair with Adam Brody."

Well, hell.

"Okay, not an affair exactly. More like a fling. Although that sounds too passionate. We weren't in love or anything; it was just, you know, casual sex."

Devlin's first thought was, *Thank God it wasn't Jayce.* Then Devlin zoned in on the "casual" aspect. He would've preferred a passionate affair. Yes, his sister was a grown woman. Yes, she was single and available. But thinking about her indulging in ongoing *casual sex,* as in friends with benefits, with a guy Luke had gone to high school with no less, made Devlin's head ache. "So, what? Jayce caught you two together and gave you some sort of lecture on responsible sex?"

"What? *No!*" Her eyes blazed as she resumed her heated pacing. "Would you forget about Jayce? This is about me and Adam. I'm only telling you because things got weird, not in a bad way, but I ended up breaking off with him."

"Because he was a jerk?"

"Because he was a nice guy."

Devlin searched his drawer for a bottle of Tylenol.

"I wouldn't have said anything at all, but I spoke to my lawyer and loan officer about entering into a possible partnership with Adam, although I don't think I mentioned his name, and, given this is a small town and you've got big ears, I figured you'd hear about it and grill me, so I decided to get it out in the open and over with."

Did she even breathe during that daylong sentence?

"Bottom line: The Red Clover's *my* dream. I don't want to share it with Adam or anyone else, but I do need help." She finally stopped and looked Devlin in the eyes. "Your help."

Just when he'd made a personal pledge not to interfere with his friends' and family's lives.

The irony.

His brain burst with ideas on how to steer Rocky toward a more lucrative and stable future. Instead, he invited her to sit down and absorbed her fierce though wounded spirit. "How can I help?"

THIRTY

Being summoned to Tasha Burke's home had caught Chloe off guard, but she'd readily agreed, determined to champion Daisy on any battleground. What Chloe hadn't counted on was a thirty-minute rural drive through yet another torrential downpour.

Fingers aching from the white-knuckled journey, she pulled the Caddy into the long and winding private lane of the huge and majestic Burke country estate, beyond relieved that she'd finally reached her destination.

Rolling back tense shoulders, Chloe squinted through the veil of silvery rain at the rolling meadows, spectacular mountains, and what looked to be an apple orchard. Beyond a rippling pond and an elegant white gazebo, she noted stylish stables and fenced pastures. She easily imagined thoroughbred horses tucked in their stalls, protected from the storm. The house itself was more of a sprawling mansion—a modernized farmhouse surrounded by rambling stone walls. Clearly, Burke Farm (*established in 1891,* as was advertised by the sign at the entrance of the drive) was worth millions.

Now Chloe understood why Tasha had insisted on meeting in person as opposed to discussing the photo shoot over the phone or through texts or e-mails. She hoped to intimidate Chloe. Thing was, she had never been intimidated by wealth or prestige. She'd grown up the daughter of a rich and influential man. And since her mom had been down-to-earth, Chloe had never considered herself superior to those who had less. People were people in her book, and Tasha Burke was just another character in her colorful life.

Still, she took a moment to gather her wits, reflecting on the whirlwind morning and bracing for the unknown.

Breakfast with Devlin had been quick but invigorating, full of meaningful looks and sexually charged silence, ending with an agreement to dine at the Sugar Shack later that night. An honest-to-God *date*. The anticipation had worked like a miracle drug on her hangover, buzzing through her veins even now.

After he'd dropped her back at Daisy's house, Chloe had showered and changed into a cheery dress in protest of the dismal weather. Not even a fourth day of rain could dampen her elated spirits. Refreshed and ready for battle, she'd checked her texts, phone messages, and e-mails. To her disappointment, her dad had yet to return her call, but she'd heard back from most of the members of Cupcake Lovers, catching up with Ethel, Helen, and Judy via early-morning phone calls. Everyone agreed that they didn't want to send off the proposal without a professional shot of Daisy. Unfortunately, Tasha had countered with an e-mail specifying an urgent rush from the editor, something about a window of opportunity. Tasha had said not to worry. She had a plan for including Daisy in the photo portion of the submission. Tasha had followed up with a personal e-mail to Chloe, which had led to this moment.

Wary, Chloe eyed the house. "What do you have up your sleeve, Madam Prez?" The rain eased from a downpour to a drizzle, and she seized her own window of opportunity. She pocketed the car keys, snapped shut the rain slicker she'd borrowed from Daisy's coat closet, pulled up the hood, and dashed for the front porch.

She half-expected a maid or a butler to greet her, but it was Tasha who swung open the door. Perfectly coiffed, dressed in skinny jeans, a crisp white shirt, and red heels, she noted Chloe's soaked and colorful appearance with an amused smirk. "Nice getup."

Chloe just smiled. "Thanks." In addition to the blue and yellow polka-dot slicker, she'd also borrowed her soul sister's neon-pink rubber boots. Daisy couldn't be here, so Chloe had brought a bit of Daisy with her.

Tasha opened the door wider and beckoned Chloe inside.

Chloe pushed back her hood, swiped her muddy, treaded souls on the welcome mat, then moved into the spacious farmhouse. In addition to the prestige Tasha had won by marrying an influential and obviously wealthy man, she'd also inherited this incredible home. Chloe tried not to gawk at the warm and stunning interior. She'd expected stunning, but the warm aspect was surprising, since Tasha was pretty much a cold fish. Maybe the house had been decorated by the previous Mrs. Burke. Maybe Randall Burke, thirty years his new wife's senior and set in old ways, had stonewalled any renovations. Why else wouldn't Tasha make her own mark?

"I'd offer to take your coat, but you won't be staying long."

Chloe blinked at the woman's rudeness.

"Time is of the essence," she went on.

"So you said in your e-mail."

"You were a fashion photographer, right?"

"Who told you that?"

"Dev."

Chloe shifted, bothered by the intimate way Tasha spoke his name. Bothered because she didn't recall telling him about her short stint as a *fashion* photographer. Maybe he'd learned about that from Monica or Daisy?

"Are you or aren't you proficient with a digital camera?" Tasha asked.

"Depends on the camera."

Tasha moved into the next room and returned seconds later with a bells-and-whistles Canon Digital SLR. "Randall bought this for me for Christmas. Don't break it. I'll get the cupcakes."

What? "Wait—" But the woman was already gone. Clueless and chilled, Chloe stood in the foyer, mere inches from a cozy, inviting living room, dripping rain and holding a cold fish's camera.

"Indulged in any joyrides lately?"

Her already-goosepimply skin crawled. "Deputy Burke."

He'd appeared out of nowhere and now leaned against the doorjamb of the dining room. Decked out in full cop uniform, wearing a self-assured, smarmy expression, he ignited a firestorm of injustice within Chloe. This man had humiliated her, *violated* her. It had been easy to bury her feelings when he'd been out of sight. Just now she itched to voice her outrage.

Instead she breathed and considered.

Did she really want to make a scene within Tasha's earshot? A woman who'd no doubt twist things to her own advantage? Not to mention he still had it in his power to make Daisy's and Devlin's lives difficult.

Swallowing her pride, she held his gaze. "Nice weather we're having."

He frowned, annoyed or confused by her sarcasm. His IQ, as far as she was concerned, was up in the air.

Tasha returned holding a small cupcake carrier and the camera's case. "I see you've met my stepson Billy."

Chloe simply nodded, surprised Tasha had referred to a man close to her own age as "son," even if it was technically true. Adding to the *ick* factor, Billy actually *leered* at his dad's wife. Did the man have no shame? Worse, Tasha didn't seem to mind. Chloe wasn't sure what she'd stepped into, but she couldn't wait to get out.

Apparently, Tasha was just as eager to show her the door. She instructed Billy to pack up the camera, then thrust the dessert container at Chloe. "Lemon Blueberry Cupcakes with Lemon Cream Cheese Frosting and a Twist."

"Wasn't this recipe featured on *Cupcake Wars* last week?" Or maybe it was the week before. Chloe had recently watched multiple episodes online with Daisy.

Tasha sniffed. "It's a variation. Mine's better."

Chloe lifted the lid and smiled. "Strawberries and red licorice." She imagined the flavor, admired the presentation. "Creative."

"There's a reason I'm the president of Cupcake Lovers," Tasha said by way of a thank-you. "Take these and the camera and get a few imaginative shots of Daisy holding a cupcake. Then get the camera back to me pronto. Larry—"

"Who?"

"The local photographer we've booked for the shoot. He has an advanced version of Photoshop. He'll work magic with the pictures you take of Daisy and we'll incorporate them into the submission."

"Why can't we just include a photo from a previous charity event? I'm sure someone in the club—"

"That's already covered. In addition, we need a current professional shot, one that matches the tone of the group's studio photos. All you have to do is snap a few images of Daisy holding these cupcakes and Larry will do the rest."

"Sounds more complicated than it needs to be."

"Only because you're making it so." Tasha raised a challenging brow. "We could just as easily move forward without Daisy and add her into the mix later."

"Forget it."

"Then you'll have to act now. If you drive straight to the hospital—"

"I don't know how to get to Pixley from here . . . unless I backtrack."

"Why tack on an additional thirty minutes when you can cut through the mountainside?"

Tasha spewed directions while Billy hovered, his obnoxious smirk pushing Chloe's buttons and causing her blood to boil. If she didn't leave now she'd blow.

"Once you hit One-Eighteen it's a straight shot south," Tasha finished while guiding Chloe toward the porch.

"Call if you have any trouble," Billy said.

As if she'd want his help. If she got lost, she'd consult the GPS on her phone. Or call Devlin or Monica or Rocky. Reeling, Chloe left the house with camera and cupcakes in hand and a creepy feeling in her gut. She'd swear that was the strangest ten minutes of her life, except, given her colorful existence, it wasn't. Part of her couldn't wait to get away from the Burkes. Part of her couldn't wait to see Daisy. It all added up to Chloe dashing to the Caddy and making haste for Pixley.

Thankfully the rain had eased to a fine mist. Visibility was clear even though the skies were grey. Chloe placed the cupcakes and camera on the passenger seat next to her purse, then wiggled out of the slicker and tossed that in the backseat. She replayed Tasha's directions, jotting them on a piece of paper she found in the glove compartment. Since they were pretty straightforward, she didn't think she'd forget, but better safe than sorry. When she'd first moved to the city, she'd constantly braved the unknown in order to get just about anywhere. She eyed the distant wooded slopes, telling herself if she could navigate Manhattan's subway system she could handle a few winding roads.

It occurred, however, that she might lose her already-weak phone signal once she drove into the thick of the woods, and since she'd promised to check in with Monica . . . Chloe dialed her friend, frowning when she rolled over to voice mail. "Hey, Mon. It's Chloe. Just now leaving Tasha's place. On my way to Pixley to take pictures of Daisy. I'll explain later. Please call everyone in the club and tell them not to worry. Daisy *will* be in that photo submission. Depending on weather, I might be a little late for the official shoot at the studio, but I'll be there. See you then. Bye."

Then she called Daisy.

"Hello?"

"I can't believe I actually got you," Chloe said as she steered the Caddy toward the main road. "What a relief."

"What's wrong, kitten?"

"Nothing. Everything's great. I'm on my way over with cupcakes and a camera. Ask and see if one of the nurses will help you primp. You're going to be part of the photo submission for the book proposal."

"I *knew* I could count on you!"

"How do you feel?"

"Sore but photogenic."

Chloe smiled. "I should be there by twelve thirty. I'm taking a shortcut via Thrush Mountain."

"What do you mean, shortcut?"

"I'm already a half hour on the opposite side of Sugar Creek. Tasha said if I took—"

"Took what? Breaking up . . . I . . . Chloe?"

"Hello?" *Silence.* She glanced at her phone. No signal. "Damn." She would've been upset, except reception had been iffy ever since she'd arrived in Vermont. Two miles down the road she might register four bars. Then two, then none, then four. She told herself not to worry. The closer she got to Pixley, the stronger the signal.

THIRTY-ONE

Rocky swiped her muddy sneakers on a mat before crossing the polished planked floors of the Sugar Shack. Even though the restaurant served lunch from 11:00 a.m. to 4:00 p.m., the dining area was practically deserted, no doubt due to the weather. Streets and parking lots were flooded, and though the rain had stopped, there was talk of another storm blowing in. Most people had hunkered down at home, preferring to stay safe, warm, and dry, but Rocky wasn't most people. She had things to do and problems to tackle. If she drove home now, she might not make it back in time for the photo shoot, and no way in hell was she going to miss that. The flurry of e-mails initiated by Chloe regarding Daisy's exclusion had put Rocky on guard. She could feel Tasha manipulating the situation but couldn't guess where it was going. Maybe she was the only one, but she'd just about had it up to her eyeballs with the damned recipe book project. Yes, they'd mailed out care packages to two separate troops this month, but discussions regarding the club's next big charity function had fallen through the cracks. Although Tasha would argue the book *was* their next charity project, Rocky disagreed. As far as she was concerned, this quest for fame diluted the club's core objective.

"Look like you could use a drink," Luke said when she plopped on one of his stools.

"Looks like you could use some customers." Even the bar was deserted, except for two guys at the other end nursing beers and watching ESPN on the corner-mounted plasma screen.

"Mondays never kick in until happy hour," he said, pouring her a cup of coffee. "Not to mention the weather sucks. Nash is stuck in New York because of this latest front."

"I'm sure Jayce will keep him entertained." She hated that she sounded so bitter, but dammit, that *good-bye* kiss irritated the hell out of her. What did it . . . *he* mean? *For now.* What the hell?

"I wasn't going to ask," Luke said, pouring a cup for himself, "but considering Jayce split town in a hurry I'm guessing your talk didn't go so well."

Blood burning, she heaped sugar into her coffee. "All I can say is I did my part. It's not my fault he's an obnoxious ass."

"Mmm."

"What's that supposed to mean?"

"Nothing. So what happened with Adam?"

"He took the high road, which made me feel like a total shit."

"Ah."

"What?"

"Nothing. You met with Dev this morning, right? How'd that go?"

"Better than I expected." She'd expected some sort of *I told you so* or *I tried to warn you* when she confessed the extent of the renovations needed at the inn and the depth of her financial woes. She'd expected Dev to dominate the conversation. Expected him to advise her to cut her losses and sell. Instead he'd listened patiently while she'd explained her dilemma, ultimately saying, *Let's see what we can do to make your dream come true.*

"Essentially, I agreed to loosen up," she continued, "and he agreed to back off. He's putting together the terms for a personal loan—I insisted on paying him back—and a proposed business plan."

Luke raised a brow. "You're letting him manage your finances?"

"With the stipulation he teaches me the ropes. I don't want to go to school for business like he did, but I *do* want to be successful and self-sufficient. Eventually. I'm surprised you haven't asked him to teach you a few tricks instead of relying on him to handle the Shack's accounting."

"We're partners, remember? Have to give him something to do so he doesn't horn in on my managing style. Besides, numbers bore me."

"Mmm."

"What does that mean?"

She grinned. "Nothing." Just then her phone rang. After a glance at that screen, she answered. "Hi, Monica."

"Have you talked to Chloe?"

"Not since yesterday. Except for the e-mail exchanges about the photo shoot. Why?"

"She left me a message. She's on her way to the hospital to take pictures of Daisy. Has something to do with the book submission. Said she was leaving from Tasha's, so I guess it was Tasha's idea. I don't know. I just . . . the roads are bad and Chloe's a nervous driver. I tried calling, but it keeps rolling over to voice mail."

"I'm sure she's fine," Rocky said. "She may be a nervous driver, but she's a capable person. She survived New York City all those years, didn't she?"

"That doesn't make me feel better."

"I hear you." Although Rocky wasn't worried so much about Chloe losing control of the car as taking a wrong turn. What route had she taken? If she ended up on one of the logging roads in this kind of weather, chances of getting stuck and stranded in mud were high. "Do you have a time reference?"

"She left the message just shy of noon. I just now heard it."

Rocky glanced at the time. Twelve forty p.m.

"I called Daisy's hospital room to see if Chloe was there. She wasn't."

"She's probably taking her time because of the weather. Do you know which route she took?"

"Not exactly. But Daisy said she mentioned Thrush Mountain."

An area comprised of winding roads and prone to flooding. Suddenly Rocky's own concerns ratcheted a notch. "Let me make some calls. I'll be in touch."

"What's wrong?" Luke asked when she disconnected.

"Nothing," she said without humor. "I hope."

* * *

Devlin ventured up to the third floor of the store around 12:45 p.m. He'd wanted to check on that ceiling leak earlier, but he was determined to demonstrate his trust in Chris and crew. Employees who felt appreciated rather than second-guessed or dominated were more likely to stick around rather than jump to a competitor's ship.

Devlin also had been waylaid by Rocky. Given her pride, he knew it had cost her to ask for his financial help and guidance. Sensitive to the downside of his controlling nature, thanks to Chloe, he'd treaded lightly, offering options. His gut still sided with selling that money pit, but he'd finally absorbed a facet of his sister's stubborn determination. This was about more than clinging to a childhood dream. This was about making her own way, her own mark on the world. A notion he well understood.

His only regret was that she hadn't left his office in a lighter mood. He suspected that was because of her breakup with Adam, but when Devlin had tried to pry further she'd shut him down. The same way she cut him off every time he brought up Jayce. Next time Devlin saw Luke, he'd have to pick his brother's brain. He had a theory about the rift between their sister and Jayce. Devlin wanted to hear it.

"As you can see, we roped off the affected area," Chris said. "Moved racks and covered merchandise with plastic. We lost about four dozen casual shirts, due to water damage, and the ceiling tiles need to be replaced."

"Could've been worse."

"The day's still young. I've got Cal Perkins booked to locate and repair the leak, but he's backed up with two other clients. Been a lot of damage due to the heavy wind and rain."

"And we're due to get hit with another storm later this afternoon," Devlin said.

"If it rolls in before Cal works his magic, could get ugly in here."

"I'll call my cousin Sam. He reroofed his house last summer. Maybe he can run over and do a temporary quick fix." But just as Devlin went to dial, his phone chimed with an incoming call.

"Devlin, I'm worried about Chloe."

"Gram?"

"She said she'd be here before twelve thirty and she's not. I sensed trouble the moment she mentioned Thrush Mountain."

"Wait a minute." He held up an apologetic hand to Chris and swung away. "Chloe told you she was driving over via Thrush Mountain? That's out of the way."

"Not if you're coming from Tasha and Randall's house."

Devlin massaged his temple. "What was she doing over there?"

"Something to do with the photo shoot."

Christ.

"It's been raining here in Pixley all day. Chloe's a nervous Nelly behind the wheel on a clear day. What if she got lost? What if she spun off the road?"

He glanced at his watch. Close to one. *Shit.* "She's probably taking it slow." Although it didn't sit well that she was a half hour overdue, he didn't want Daisy to panic.

"I've been trying to call her for an hour."

"She gets sketchy reception up here." He'd been meaning to talk to her about another server. Especially if she was going to stay on in Sugar Creek, which he realized he'd been assuming for more than a week now. He *wanted* her to stay.

"I know that, Devlin," Gram snapped. "Even worse. If

she's in trouble, she won't be able to call anyone. And it's not like there'll be a lot of traffic so that she can wave someone down. Most folks steer clear of those roads when the weather's bad. I blame that pinhead Tasha!"

So did Devlin. Directing anyone, especially a Flatlander, to that route during inclement weather had been thoughtless.

Or calculated.

"I'm sure everything's fine, Gram," he said, even though he wasn't.

"I have a bad feeling."

So did he, dammit. Simply because Chloe had proven herself a lightning rod for disaster. He thought about his grandma's fragile condition, her previous heart attack. "I need you to calm down. I'm on this."

"What was Tasha thinking?"

"I don't know." But he'd find out. "I'll call you with updates. You call me if Chloe shows."

"Deal."

He disconnected, then accessed his contacts, but before he could dial Tasha, Rocky called.

"Spoke with Monica a few minutes ago. She had a voice mail from Chloe. Said she's cutting through Thrush—"

"I know. I just got off the phone with Gram."

"So that's why I couldn't get through to her. Is Chloe there?"

"Not yet."

"She's a half hour late, Dev."

"I know."

"I checked the weather service and there are some road closings due to flooding. Maybe she took an alternate route or maybe she turned back. I'd feel better if I knew which road she took to begin with. I tried calling Tasha but keep getting her voice mail. Bitch is probably ignoring my calls."

"She won't ignore mine. Relax, Sis. I'm on it." He disconnected and dialed the woman who'd slithered her way under his skin for two full months before he'd seen through her scheming seduction. Sure enough, she answered on the first ring. "You sent Chloe to Pixley via Thrush?"

"Well, good afternoon to you, too, Dev," she answered in a husky drawl.

"Birch Road or Route Two-Oh-One?"

"Birch Road, of course. It's the most direct."

It was also the more remote of the two. Hoping Chloe had miscalculated her estimated arrival time, he pressed for more specifics. "What time did she leave?"

"I don't know why you're being so rude, Dev. Chloe's the one who insisted Daisy be included in the photo submission. I came up with a way. I even loaned her my expensive camera and baked a special batch of cupcakes."

"And provided her with the most dangerous route to Pixley."

"That's ridiculous."

"When's the last time you took that road during a rain- or snowstorm?"

"If you're insinuating—"

"What the fuck time did she leave?"

"Around noon," she snapped.

He cut her off before telling her off. She wasn't worth the time or energy. At least not now. He turned and saw his diligent right hand maneuvering a bucket beneath a new steady drip of rain. *Dammit.* "Do me a favor, Chris. Call Sam. See what he can do about the roof. Then call and light a fire under Cal's ass."

Chris raised a brow. "Trouble elsewhere?"

"Maybe." He quickly processed his options. Chloe hadn't been missing long enough to call the police. Nor did he have proof that anything was seriously wrong. Still, he couldn't shake an ominous feeling and waiting and worrying had never been his style. "I need to leave for a while and there's a possibility we might need to reschedule the employee meeting."

"Considering all the planning you put into tonight, must be urgent. Is it Daisy?"

"No. But it does concern family." Similar to his feelings about Jayce, Devlin felt connected to Chloe in a way that went beyond blood. Temples pounding, he thought about the road conditions, considered the rental sedan he was driving because Rocky's Jeep was still in the shop and she had his SUV. He called Leo. "I'm desperate for a four-wheel drive. What've you got?"

THIRTY-TWO

On any other day . . . Strike that. On a clear, sunny day Chloe would've enjoyed the scenic drive through the slopes of Thrush Mountain. The dense wooded area popped with fall foliage. Or rather it would have popped on a dry, sunny day. Just now the bold leaves were dulled by a silvery mist. Between the oppressive black clouds and the leafy canopy, daylight was practically nonexistent. She guessed the temperature was in the low fifties and had even cranked up the Caddy's old heater. She wasn't sure if she was chilled because of the weather or because of the stressful drive. Though it was a decent, paved road, there were several sharp curves, and since the ground was saturated from several days of rain low-lying sections were flooded. She'd slowed to a crawl, worrying about stalling the engine, every time she pushed through one of those pools of water.

Then there was the wildlife. So far she'd spied several deer grazing amongst the trees. What if one darted in front of her? The thought of harming an animal made her stomach turn, and she wasn't crazy about dinging up Daisy's car either.

At one point Chloe had considered turning back for Sugar Creek, but the road was just as ugly behind her as ahead and she was actually closer to Pixley, so she'd sucked it up and forged on. Plus, she was anxious to see Daisy. Not just because she needed to take her picture but also to make sure she was truly okay. Although they'd spoken on the phone, Chloe hadn't seen her since the accident.

Speaking of phones, Chloe glanced down and, for the hundredth time in the past hour, took stock of her signal. One bar. Better than zip, but it didn't mean she'd get through. She'd tried at least five other times. Still, she tried again. Daisy was no doubt worried because Chloe was running late. The call failed. She blew out a frustrated breath, gave it another few minutes, then tried again. This time she dialed Devlin. For some reason she was desperate to hear his deep, confident voice. It rang once, twice . . . —"Come on, come on"— . . . warbled, then silence. "Dammit."

She tossed the phone on the seat, then repositioned the pillow under her butt, trying to raise herself up for the best view over the dash. Not for the first time, she wondered if Daisy would consider buying a newer car, a smaller car, something with electric adjustable seats and a shorter hood. That's the kind of car she'd get if she stayed on in Sugar Creek. Not to mention a different phone server with better reception!

Rolling back tense shoulders, Chloe tried to fend off the creepy feeling of isolation. Was she the only person brave or stupid enough to take this route? She hadn't seen another car for twenty minutes. She reached for the dial on the old-fashioned radio. At least she had music to keep her company, although she was sick of mellow rock. She skimmed over static, heavy metal, and disco, hoping to find a news channel and mention of the weather. The winds had picked up and she'd swear those black clouds looked as if they were about to explode. *Again.*

Just then something caught her eye. Squirrel? Chipmunk? A small furry thing with a fluffy tail darted halfway across, then back, then changed his mind again.

She screamed and swerved at the same time, losing control as the tires slid over mud and rain-slick asphalt. The back end whipped around and in the moment her brain raced to remember which direction to turn the steering wheel the front end lurched down a small slope and slammed into a tree.

Chloe lurched forward as well, and though she was wearing a seat belt, her chest and shoulders slammed into the steering wheel—no air bag. Then she bounced back and left, smacking her head against the driver's window.

Dazed, she closed her eyes and resisted the urge to puke. Her pulse hammered and her lungs burned. After what seemed like forever, the panic subsided and she slowly took stock. No blood or broken bones. She didn't know about the squirrel.

The hood of the Caddy was buckled and steam hissed from the engine. Heartsick, she put the car in reverse and tried to back out onto the road; the wheels spun and the engine ground. She paused, then tried again. More spinning. More grinding.

Head throbbing, she pushed open the door and stepped outside. Her pink boots squished into thick mud and a fierce gust of wind whipped her hair from her clammy face. Rubbing her goose-pimpled arms, she inspected the damage. The front fender was crushed and the hood half-mangled. All four tires were mired in thick mud.

The car was stuck and so was she. In the freaking middle of nowhere. Temples throbbing, she climbed up on the road, looked both ways. No cars. No houses.

Don't panic.

Hoping against hope, she reached back into the car and nabbed her phone. One bar. She slogged through the mud, a little to the left, then two steps north.

Two bars!

As she looked at the mangled car all she could think was, *Devlin's going to kill me.* Still her first instinct was to call him. Her heart raced as the phone rang . . . once . . . then . . .

Silence.

"Are you kidding me?" She sloshed through more mud, hoping to reestablish the signal, and suddenly the ground gave way and she was on her back sliding down a muddy slope. Knocked breathless, she clawed at brush to slow her descent. She didn't slide far, but with enough force that her left foot jammed and lodged beneath a fallen tree trunk. No matter how hard she tugged, she couldn't free her ankle.

She fell back in the soggy muck, trying to catch her breath and wits. She'd lost her phone in the tumble. *Great.* And her foot was wedged tight. *Trapped.*

Her mind blurred and she had an awful thought. What if this was it? Alone in the wilderness, trapped, vulnerable to the elements, to wildlife. Other than deer and squirrels, what other creatures roamed these woods?

What if my number is up?

She'd followed all her passions and whims, pursued all of her dreams. She'd crammed a boatload of life into thirty-one years. Nothing was left undone.

Feeling more nauseous by the moment, Chloe pushed herself up and shoved at the tree trunk, only it wouldn't budge. She clawed at the ground, trying to dig her foot free, except thick, slimy mud kept seeping in and slowing her efforts.

Panicked, her mind grappled for something left undone.

Fixing things between her and her dad.

Marriage. Children.

Devlin.

Her disoriented brain flashed on an image. Driving through Sugar Creek this morning, the huge sign in the window of Gemma's Bakery: *OUT OF BUSINESS.* She had a fleeting vision, latched onto another dream.

Goals!

A wave of dizziness overwhelmed her digging efforts. Light-headed, she wilted. Flat on her back, breathing in the pungent scents of nature, she pondered her condition. She'd hit her head twice. Concussion? She struggled to stay alert.

That's when she felt it. Fat, cold raindrops.

And heard it. The thunderous rumbling of another storm.

And sensed it. Someone watching her.

Bleary-eyed, she craned her head to the left. *Holy . . .*

She recognized it from the special display at J.T.'s. The mugs. The ball caps and socks.

A moose.

Only he didn't look cute as much as intimidating.

Twelve-hundred-odd pounds of furry wild animal. And he was headed straight her way. She didn't know whether to laugh or cry. At least her death, she thought as consciousness faded, like her life, wouldn't be boring.

* * *

By the time Devlin spotted the Cadillac, it was nearly three o'clock, although it looked closer to dusk. Visibility sucked. Driving the Hummer he'd borrowed from Leo's personal collection, Devlin had hauled ass until hitting Birch Road; then he'd slowed for two reasons. First, he was eyeing every logging road, rest stop, and inch of Thrush, hoping to spy the Caddy. Second, it was raining buckets and there were several flooded areas. He'd barely gotten through.

Up until now he'd been calm, focused on the drive, focused on finding Chloe. Seeing the wrecked car rattled his composure. Pulling the Hummer to the side of the road, he eyed the damage, assuring himself it didn't look that bad. Chloe was probably shaken but fine, taking shelter in the car until another motorist happened by. Willing his heart to settle in his chest, he zipped up his fleece-lined rain jacket and stepped out, his waterproof hiking boots sinking into ankle-deep mud.

Squinting against the pelting rain, he hurried to the Caddy and opened the door. No Chloe. "What the hell?" Her purse was on the front-seat floor, along with a camera case and cupcake container. Probably slid off the seat when she hit the trees. Her slicker was on the backseat. Either she was walking around in the storm without a coat or someone had picked her up. The thought of her alone with a stranger, possibly someone unscrupulous, sent his pulse into overdrive. He nabbed the polka-dot coat and slammed the door. "Chloe!"

Goddammit.

He searched in all directions, cursing the rain, the situation. *Tasha.* "Chloe! Where are you?"

"Here! Down here!"

Her voice was shaky and muted by rolling thunder but loud enough to give him direction. He made his way down a slope, grabbing onto branches to steady his footing. When he saw her, his heart pounded like a mother.

She was sitting on the ground, huddled over, arms wrapped around her knees as if trying to keep warm. No wonder. All she was wearing was a thin flowery dress and a short little sweater, both soaked through and clinging to her shivering body. She looked up and met his gaze, smiled in relief, then faltered. "I'm sorry I wrecked the car."

"I don't care about the car, hon." He knelt beside her, gently draped the slicker over her hunched shoulders. Then he smoothed her drenched hair from her face. He ached to kiss her but held back, putting his own needs aside. "Are you all right?"

Teeth chattering, she slowly nodded. "I'm stuck."

He glanced down, noted she was wearing Gram's bright pink rain boots and that the left one was half-hidden beneath a felled tree. "Does it hurt?"

"Only when I pull or twist too hard," Chloe said while shoving her arms into the slicker.

Her movements were sluggish, her voice weak. *What the hell?* He pulled a compact, high-intensity flashlight from his pocket, shedding some light on the situation.

"Tried to dig under, but then I got light-headed. I think I passed out. Not sure how long."

He glanced over his shoulder, shined light near her face. He saw it then, a goose egg on the left side of her forehead. "You *are* hurt."

She gently fingered the bump. "Must've happened when my head smacked against the driver's window. Or maybe when I fell up there. It's just sore. I'm fine. Well, except for my foot."

Anxious to free her, he squatted with the tree trunk at his back. "When I tell you, scoot back." She nodded and he put his weight into it. Between his adrenaline and leverage, it didn't take much. "Now."

She shifted and as soon as he saw the flash of pink toe he let go. Next he pulled off that boot, her thick sock, and inspected her ankle, her foot. Gently probing, twisting. She swiped rain from her eyes. "I'm fine," she called over a crack of thunder. "Just tingly. Foot fell asleep."

There were scratches on her legs and a sizable bump on her forehead, but other than that and the fact that she was chilled and wet, outwardly she seemed in decent shape.

He stood and pulled her up, saying, "Just lean into me," and half-carried her up the hill. When they reached flat ground, he lifted her into his arms and carried her to the Hummer, opened the door, and placed her in the passenger seat. Reaching over, he nabbed a thick blanket and wrapped it around her.

She burrowed into the dry warmth. "The Caddy . . ."

"I'll send someone later."

"Purse and c-c-camera," she said, teeth chattering.

He shut the door, retrieved everything loose in the car—purse, camera case, cupcake carrier, pillow—then returned to the Hummer. Sliding into the driver's seat, he shut out the storm and placed the goods in the backseat while keeping a close eye on Chloe. Conscious of her shivering, he started the four-wheel drive and cranked the heat. Idling on the side of the road, he used the weather app on his Android to check the latest forecast. Unfortunately, they looked to be in the thick of it for at least another hour. Which meant the roads would only get worse.

He dialed Daisy first. "Rest easy, Gram. I've got her."

"Is she okay?"

"Shaken, but fine. Roads are bad. Don't know when we'll get to you."

"Don't worry about that. Just keep safe. And tell Chloe not to worry about the photo shoot. I don't give two figs."

He smiled at that. "I'll let her know." He signed off and repeated Daisy's message, to which Chloe replied, "She's lying. She c-c-cares."

"Maybe so. But she knows you did your best. Far more than most would've done," he added.

"But not good enough." She palmed her forehead. "There was a moose."

"You swerved to miss a moose?" In these parts it wasn't unusual for a moose to meander across the road, and hell yeah, at upwards of two-thousand pounds it could do a lot of damage to an oncoming car.

"No. Squirrel. Or maybe it was a chipmunk. Darted out of nowhere."

He wasn't sure where the moose fit in. Then again, she didn't seem to be thinking straight. He raked her matted hair from her face, sighed. "Honey, never risk your safety—"

"Can't stomach hurting anything."

"I get that, but . . ." He shook his head, dialed Rocky.

"Did you find her?"

"Yeah."

"Is she okay?"

He glanced over. "Car slid off the road. Some bumps and bruises, but other than that, fine. Do me a favor. Let Monica and Leo know."

"They're right here. We gathered at the Shack. Sam, too. He came over after fixing the leak at J.T.'s. We've been waiting to hear from you or Chloe. Feels like that scene out of *A Perfect Storm*. You know? The one where the women gather in the local bar waiting for news about their fisherman husbands lost at sea?"

He hadn't seen the movie but understood the sentiment. It also occurred to him that he wasn't the only one who thought of Chloe as family. That she'd warmed her way into their lives in such a short time said a lot about her character. To think, after hearing Jayce's report, he'd instantly assumed the worst. What did that say about *him*?

"Tell her not to worry about the photo shoot," Rocky said. "I contacted everyone in the club. We're pretty sure Tasha sent her on that mission knowing she'd be delayed by the weather. Sam put it simply: She's threatened by Chloe and didn't want her offering her professional advice at the session."

"Makes sense." Thinking Tasha had merely wanted Chloe

out of the way was more palatable than assuming she'd intended physical harm. Then again, she'd fooled him before.

"Let Chloe know we're boycotting the shoot. That should make her feel better."

"Will do. Is Luke handy?"

"Hold on."

"I knew she was all right," Devlin's younger brother said into the phone. "Chloe may be a sweet city girl by circumstance, but she's a tough country girl at heart. What's up?"

"Roads are bad and I need to get Chloe warm and dry. What's the latest news on conditions? Should I return to Sugar Creek or push on?"

"Where are you exactly?"

He relayed their location.

"Road's closed ahead of you, Dev, and you'd be crazy to utilize one of the logging routes. I'd say turn back, but there were reports a few minutes ago about Sugar Creek swelling and overflowing. By the time you get that far, roads might be impassible. Best advice: Hunker down for the night."

He racked his mind for the nearest resorts or vacation homes. "Suggestions?"

"Closest, safest bet? Backtrack half a mile, make a right at the sign marked *Private,* and muscle the Hummer up the gravel drive. You'll come to a cabin owned by the Brody brothers. Mostly they use it during the winter, snow excursions. Although I think Kane said he was up there just last week."

"Electricity? Hot water?"

"You won't be roughing it. I've been there a couple of times. Small, but comfortable. They keep a key under the mat. I'll let them know you're crashing for the night. As long as this storm passes, the roads should be clear by tomorrow."

Devlin glanced at Chloe, who looked like she was nodding off. "Sounds like a plan, Luke. Thanks." He pocketed his phone, then smoothed his fingers over her chilled, muddy cheek. "How's a hot bath sound?"

She quirked a shaky smile. "Like heaven."

THIRTY-THREE

It only took a few minutes to reach the cabin Devlin had told her about. By that time, Chloe was thinking straighter, but her muscles ached and she couldn't seem to shake the chill that had seeped beneath her skin. She was still unclear how long she'd lain in the mud and rain before regaining consciousness. And she had no idea what had happened to that moose. Although she supposed it was possible Bullwinkle had been a hallucination. The shock of the wreck, the bumps to her noggin. Not to mention the bone-jarring fall and slide down the hill. She'd only roused a few minutes before Devlin's arrival. Seeing him standing there, like some superhero savior, had been one of the happiest moments of her life. But in the next second she'd felt like an idiot and maybe even a little resentful.

"What made you come after me?" she asked when he cut the engine.

"Concerned calls from Rocky, Monica, and Gram, along with my own gut feeling that something was wrong."

"That's the second time you've rescued me from a dicey encounter. First the river. Now this."

He met her gaze. "I kind of like being your hero."

"I don't." She furrowed her brow. "I mean, I'm grateful. Of course. I just don't want you to think I'm helpless. I would've eventually dug myself out. I would've survived just fine even if I'd been alone all night."

"I believe you."

"Do you?" She licked dry lips, searching for the right words, and instead blurted her mind. "I need you to know that I can take care of myself. That I don't need you emotionally or financially." Putting herself in that position again would be disastrous and, with someone as competent and controlling as Devlin Monroe, all too easy to do.

He angled his head and studied her hard. "I have every confidence in your abilities, Chloe. Spinning out, falling down that mud-slick hill, could've happened to anyone in this weather."

"I don't just mean—"

"I know. I get it. I get you."

Her heart thudded against her aching chest. She quirked a small smile. "There you go again with the romantic talk."

He smiled and tugged at her blanket. "Pull that jacket hood over your head. We're bravin' the storm." With that he slid outside and rounded the hood of the Hummer.

By the time he opened her door, she'd organized her thoughts. "I just realized something. You're going to miss your employee meeting."

"I had Chris reschedule it."

"But it was important."

"So are you."

"But—"

"I'm exactly where I want to be, Chloe." He put his arm around her waist and together they sloshed through the mud and downpour, finding shelter beneath the roof of the cabin's porch. "I can hear your wheels turning. Stop worrying about it. Everything's under control."

But of course it was. Devlin was one of those people proficient at juggling a lot of balls. She had to admire that, and she wasn't too proud to acknowledge that she was glad he was here. Yes, she could have survived the night alone, but this was so much better.

He reached under a mat, produced a key.

Chloe scoffed at the obvious hiding place. "They may as well have left the door unlocked."

"Welcome to Vermont." He ushered her inside and, though it wasn't overly warm, it was dry.

"Are you sure they won't mind us staying here?"

"The Brodys are good guys," he said, feeling along the wall for a light switch. "Especially Adam. Just ask Rocky."

"She told you about the two of them?" Chloe blurted.

He switched on a table lamp and caught her gaze. "You knew?"

"Only recently. She was troubled about . . ." Did he know about Jayce, too? Then Chloe remembered how adamant Rocky had been about keeping that secret. *Oh yes, that damned* secret.

"About?"

"About blurring the lines of their relationship. He offered to invest in the inn."

"She decided not to go that route. In fact, she broke off with him altogether."

"That I didn't know." But it didn't come as a surprise. No matter what Rocky said, Chloe believed she was still in love with Jayce.

Devlin looked around, frowned. "Do you think Adam ever brought her up here?"

She smiled a little at his big-brother tone. "Rocky's a grown woman."

"Right." He blew out a breath, then focused back on Chloe, angled his head.

"What?"

"How do you feel?"

She clutched at the blanket still wrapped around her shoulders and counted her blessings. Daisy had sustained far worse injuries in her bicycle accident. "Achy. Cold. But considering, okay."

"Good." He moved in, trapping her between his hunky, soaked body and the pine-knotted door. "There's something I've been wanting to do ever since I found you in the woods."

She felt his sizzling kiss to her toes, even before his mouth touched hers. Those expressive blue eyes telegraphed his desire. His tender touch, as he cradled her face, initiated a fire in her belly. When he brushed his lips across hers, sane thoughts turned to ash.

Chloe loosened her hold on the blanket, allowing it to fall away as she wrapped her arms around Devlin and leaned into an openmouthed kiss. Hot yet tender. Possessive. *Sexy.* Delicious sensations stole throughout her body, causing her to shiver with delight.

He eased back and regarded her with a concerned expression. "We've got to warm you up."

She caressed the side of his gorgeous face, traced her thumb across his sexy lower lip. "I was getting there."

He arched a playful brow. "I'm ahead of you," he said, and pressed his lower half against her.

Feeling bold, she palmed his arousal, scraped her thumbnail over his zipper. "There are perks to being stranded in the middle of nowhere with you."

"Lots of perks," he said, sliding off her rain slicker. "But first, a hot bath."

Noting the mud on her clothes and legs and the ache in her muscles, she didn't argue.

He took her hand as they explored the cabin together. Small, rustic, but clean and comfortable. The highlight of the living room—an oversized couch and a wood-burning stove. She eyed a steel basket full of logs. *Thank God.* A compact kitchen and two bedrooms—one with a queen-sized bed, the other with two twins—and finally the bathroom.

Devlin flicked on a dim wall sconce, then stepped away from her to turn on the faucets of the claw-footed tub. "Might take a couple of minutes to heat up."

She hugged herself, missing the warmth of his body. "My purse. I have a travel kit. Toothpaste and deodorant."

"I'll get it. As soon as that water's warm, slide in." He glanced over his shoulder, before leaving. "You okay?"

She resisted the urge to palm her aching head. The bump had started to throb. "Fine."

He didn't look like he believed her, but he left anyway.

Suddenly weary, she pulled off her muddy boots and socks and inspected her filthy, already-soaked clothes. Shut off the tub faucet and instead moved to the corner shower stall and turned on the water full blast. As soon as she saw wisps of steam, she stepped in and under the showerhead. Bracing her hands on the tiled wall, she bent her head and allowed the pulsing water to pound her body, clothes and all. She watched, half-exhausted, half-mesmerized, as dirt washed to the tiles and swirled down the drain.

She stood there quite a while soaking in the heat, knowing she should move but not finding the strength. A knock on the door caused her to at least lift her head. "Come in."

"Here's your purse," he said as he entered. "I started a fire in the . . . What are you doing?"

She *felt* the moment he spied her through the transparent stall. Her body hummed from the intensity of his gaze. Her compromised senses danced. "My clothes were dirty and I'll have to wear them again tomorrow."

"We could have washed them in the sink."

"This seemed easier."

"There's a warped logic to that." He eased open the glass door. "They look pretty clean now, honey."

"I know, but . . . the water's so relaxing. I feel like if I let go of the wall I'll wilt."

He stepped in with her, fully clothed. Mostly. He'd shed his rain jacket and shoes.

"Your clothes aren't dirty," she remarked as he pressed against her and placed his hands over hers.

"Maybe not," he said close to her ear, "but my thoughts are. Does that count?"

She laughed. It was weak and a little nervous, but it felt good.

"Let me help." He eased her hands off the wall, absorbed her weight.

First he peeled her sweater off, draping it over the top of the stall. Then he unbuttoned the front of her dress, slowly easing her arms from the sleeves, then pushing the bodice to her waist. One more tug and the dress fell in a soaked heap at her feet. She found the strength to kick it aside. Which left her in her bra and thong.

"I've spent several sleepless nights fantasizing about you in your underwear. Got my first glimpse at Oslow's. The first day we met. Pink."

She groaned with embarrassment.

"Then that day at the river. Pink and red flowered bra. Matching thong. Almost distracted me from your perfect body."

She melted more with every word.

"Now," he said, unclasping the hooks of her lacy black bra, "you're killing me."

She felt the straps brush off her shoulders, felt the bra fall away, leaving her breasts exposed. Even though the water was ultrawarm, the air steamy, her nipples puckered and an erotic shiver stole through her nearly naked body. She closed her eyes and moaned, relaxing against Devlin as his palms stroked her arms and his mouth grazed her ear.

"How do you feel?" he asked gently.

"Like I'm going to die if you don't touch me." She felt his smile, her breath catching when his hands caressed her breasts.

"Like this?"

"More," she whispered.

His fingers skimmed her nipples, then plucked and rolled. At the same time he nipped and suckled her earlobe, igniting a firestorm of lust.

She could scarcely breathe. "More."

Her belly coiled even tighter as one hand continued to fondle her breast and the other slid south, his fingers teasing the waistband of her thong, then dipping lower, touching her intimately.

The hot water pelted and excited. His fingers probed and played.

Chloe quivered with need, with anticipation. She'd fantasized about Devlin touching her like this. The reality trumped her wildest imaginings as she felt an orgasm building . . . building. . . . "Dying here."

"Can't have that." Increasing the pressure, the intensity of his touch, he incited a heady rush of sensations, blurring her thoughts and blowing away even the most high-powered, jet-pulsing, masturbating showerhead.

Chloe cried out with an explosive climax. *Heaven.* Stars imploded behind her closed lids. Her body quaked, then wilted. "Oh, my God."

"You okay?" he asked with a smile in his voice.

"Yes. I mean wow." She laughed a little as pure bliss and relief surged through her blood. "Just need to catch my breath."

"Feeling a little light-headed myself," he teased while holding her steady. "Pleasuring you is an intense turn-on."

She willed her legs steady as he brushed aside her long, drenched hair, then kissed the back of her neck. Her pulse refused to settle as he kissed and licked his way down her spine, his hands sliding over her wet curves, his fingers hooking the waistband of her lacy thong. He peeled away the wisp of fabric, nipped her butt, then, in a heartbeat, was again standing and silently soaping up her body.

"Wait." She knew he was taking it slow because he was worried about her injuries, but just now a sensual ache outweighed all others. She turned in his arms and unbuttoned the drenched shirt that clung to every muscle of his toned torso. "I've been fantasizing about you, too."

She also thought back on that moment at the river. How amazing he'd looked in his soaked clothes. The intensity of the erotic thrill when he'd peeled off his wet shirt. But the biggest turn-on had been before that, when he'd dove in and rescued her. Yes, she was being hypocritical. She didn't want to be saved and yet, with Devlin, it had been the ultimate aphrodisiac. She couldn't imagine Ryan diving into a river fully clothed or braving flooded roads to rescue her. She couldn't imagine Ryan at all.

She pushed Devlin's shirt off of his broad shoulders, reveled in hot, bare skin, but only a moment before unzipping his pants.

"Chloe . . ."

"When I was trapped in the woods, all sorts of insane thoughts went through my head. But mostly I focused on things undone. Things I very much wanted." She shoved his pants down his legs. "I want you."

He grasped her forearms and pulled her to her feet, face-to-face. "You . . . are dangerous."

She smiled a little as she wrapped her soapy hand around his erection and stroked. "How do you feel about that?"

Groaning with pleasure, he met her lusty gaze, "Bring it on."

* * *

Making love with Devlin was as close to perfection as Chloe had ever experienced. No moment rushed. No sensation spared. She'd felt cherished, in the shower and after when he toweled her dry, then carried her to the bed. She'd been hot, slick and ready and she knew she'd driven him to the edge minutes before with her hand, but instead of entering her right away, he'd turned her onto her stomach and trailed his fingertips over her shoulders and back, her sides and hips, a feather-soft touch that tickled and excited. Her butt and inner thighs. Her calves. Her feet.

Sensuous delirium.

Then he flipped her onto her back and started on her front. Could a person die of want? "Devlin," she panted. "Please."

"Savoring the moment," he said in a husky voice.

"But—"

He silenced her protest with his deep kiss, then continued his feather-light assault, skimming his fingertips and mouth over her neck and collarbone. Her breast and stomach. Then . . .

"Oh, God." She arched her back and moaned as he pleasured her with his mouth. So thrilling. So intimate. Suddenly he was there, his palms on her thighs, his tongue flicking over her most sensitive place, and she was helpless to resist. She almost climaxed twice, but each time he eased away, prolonging a delicious agony. Now . . . now her body quaked beneath his touch, his teeth and tongue as he drove her closer . . . closer . . . Lungs burning. Heart pounding. Muscles quivering. Chloe cried out with her second orgasm, certain she'd died and gone to heaven.

Only it got better.

Devlin shifted on top of her, cradled her face, and, while gazing intently into her eyes, slid deep inside. The friction, the rhythm, the erotic and overwhelmingly tender sensations . . . She climaxed within seconds. Breathless, embarrassed, she whispered, "Wow. Sorry."

"Wow. Lucky me. Are you always this—"

"Easy?"

"Responsive."

She palmed his face, then threaded her fingers through his hair. "This is a first. The multiple-orgasm part, that is."

He smiled at that and her heart did a crazy happy dance. *This is love. This is love.*

"Let's go for more," he said, resuming his lovemaking at an even slower pace.

To her amazement, even though she thought she was spent, satiated, her body responded, springing back to life, anxious for more. "I'm not sure I can survive this."

"I was thinking the same thing."

His hands skimmed her bare curves and in turn she explored the sinew of his shoulders, his back, gripping his tight butt and pulling him deeper. It was as close as she'd come to aggressive since she'd undressed him in the shower. Once he'd taken control, she'd crumbled with her own wants and needs.

"Not normally so passive," she said softly as he dominated, pleasured. "Selfish."

"Sexy."

She couldn't imagine why. Then again, her brain was short-circuiting. *Harder. More.* She tensed, quaked.

"Come for me, baby."

His words seduced; his body tempted. *Burn. Soar.* She reveled in his physical intensity. Lost herself in a kiss that turned the world inside out. Delirious with lust, her stomach knotted with the beginnings of another orgasm. Amazed at the erotic sensations zinging throughout her body, she dug her nails into his biceps, holding tight as another earth-rocking climax slammed her senses and soul.

She called out and he followed, his own body shuddering with a powerful release. The passionate kiss lingered, then turned tender as he gently rolled off her trembling body, taking her with him, holding her close.

Her heart thudded against her chest, in her ears, almost muting his playful words. "I'm not normally so quick," he said.

"That was quick?" She smiled against his neck, thinking, even at her most passive, she hadn't been a dud in bed. Not with this man. Knowing she'd pleasured him without even trying was an incredible rush. As for her multiple orgasms, she'd been right: Devlin Monroe was a sexual paragon.

He brushed his lips across her forehead, then slipped away and into the bathroom. He returned moments later and pulled her into an embrace that warmed her far more than the down comforter.

Rain pelted the roof and windows, lulling Chloe closer to an exhausted sleep. Sated and happy, she snuggled closer, his lovemaking resonating throughout her weary body. Next time she'd give as good as she got. "Next time I won't be so easy on you," she promised in a drowsy voice.

He curled into her, smoothing a strong hand down her back. "If that was easy, I'm in trouble."

THIRTY-FOUR

Devlin didn't remember falling asleep. He remembered Chloe naked. Chloe driving him insane—her kisses, her touch, her throaty sounds of pleasure. He remembered incredible sex.

Not that he was a stranger to satisfying sex, but in addition to her mind-blowing responsiveness there'd been an added element. An emotional connection that had blindsided him.

Love.

He was savvy enough to recognize it. To acknowledge it. Voicing his feelings, however, would take time. Unlike Luke, who'd been in love several times, so he professed, for Devlin losing his heart didn't entail losing good sense. Logic told him, he and Chloe barely knew each other. Logic said she was on the rebound and he had yet to maintain a healthy romantic relationship for more than a few months. On top of all that, he was feeling edgy because of his dad's questionable health. Because of Daisy's personal and physical crises.

At a moment when Devlin yearned to embrace life, to experiment and experience, to *embellish,* what if he declared his love only to scare Chloe away?

Or what if he put everything he had into the relationship, only to learn two months down the line she was returning to New York? Or home to her dad? Or that her passion for him—*I want you*—was as fleeting as her passion for photography? Or acting? Or publicity? The longer he lay there, staring into the darkened room, listening to the silence, the more he questioned her ability to commit long term. How long before she tired of Sugar Creek? Of his complicated, in-your-face-and-life family? Of cooking for and driving Miss Daisy? How long before she tired of his workaholic and controlling nature?

When did you become such a skittish pansy-ass? he could hear Jayce say.

Devlin realized suddenly that he was pushing Chloe away before she could run—*like Janna*. Needing to shake off his present frame of mind, he gently disentangled his arms and legs from the woman who'd seduced his heart with her unique spirit, reminding himself that she wasn't his ex-wife. And he sure as hell wasn't a pansy-ass.

* * *

"Are you people *crazy*?"

Rocky turned in her seat to see Tasha stalking across the bar, taking wicked delight in the fact that her designer boots and coat were splattered with mud. Best guess: A car had driven through a puddle and splashed her big-time. Rocky smiled. "Won't you join us for a drink?"

"Happy hour," Monica said.

"Two-for-one," Sam said.

Rachel held up a margarita on the rocks. "You can have one of mine if you want."

Red-faced, Tasha made angry-eye contact with each of the people seated around the two tables they'd pushed together. Every core member of Cupcake Lovers with the exception of Daisy. "We were supposed to meet at the photography studio over a half hour ago. Instead you're here at the Shack getting sloshed."

"Speaking for myself," Ethel said, after a sip of white wine, "I'm just getting started."

"If you don't want a drink, maybe you'd like an appetizer," Helen said. "We just ordered. Sit."

"I'm not—"

"Sit," Sam said, pulling out the empty chair beside him.

"It's not as if we stood you up," Rocky said reasonably. "I texted you we weren't coming. Even told you where to find us."

Red-faced, Tasha huffed. "I didn't believe it. Why would you all blow a chance to sign with a New York publisher?"

"Take a seat," Casey said, motioning for a waitress, "and we'll tell you."

Tight-lipped, Tasha sat.

"What would you like?" Nell, the newest waitress on Luke's payroll, asked.

"An explanation."

"Not on the menu," she said with a meek smile.

Tasha glared. "An Apple Martini. Now get lost."

"Is that what you'd hoped would happen to Chloe?" Rocky asked, getting straight to the point.

"I don't know what you're talking about," the woman said as she peeled off her ruined coat and draped it on the back of her chair.

Sam leaned in, his big body overshadowing Tasha with implied menace. He rarely lost his temper. He didn't have to. Rocky attributed his intimidation skills to his years in the military. As much as she didn't want to, she had to give Tasha credit for not shrinking back.

"Let's cut to the chase," he said. "You didn't want Chloe at the shoot, so you found a way to detain her. Don't bother," he said, cutting Tasha off when she opened her mouth to lie.

"Were you afraid we'd want her included in the pictures?" Judy asked.

"She would look awfully pretty on the cover," Rachel said. "Could mean higher sales."

"You tricked her by sending her off to take photos of Daisy," Monica said.

Tasha glared. "*You're* the ones who didn't want to send off the proposal without a shot of Daisy! If Miss Big-City-Know-It-All got lost on a simple drive through Thrush, then *you're* to blame."

"She didn't get lost," Rocky said. "She spun off the road. Hit a tree. She's fine, not that you care, but here's the deal: The recipe book project's off."

Tasha's beautified head nearly exploded. "What?"

"Unless . . . ," Casey started, then took a lazy pull off her longneck.

"Unless what?" Tasha snapped.

"Unless you step down as president," Monica said, then took a sip of her own drink.

They'd reasoned it out prior to Tasha's arrival, come to a unanimous decision. Rocky watched Tasha's face as the ultimatum sank in. In the long history of Cupcake Lovers, no president had ever been asked to resign.

Judy cleared her throat and took a somewhat gentler approach. At least her tone was kind. "The only reason you're president to begin with, Tasha, is because it was a deathbed wish of your mother's and Della Harper, rest her soul, was a good woman who deserved some peace of mind."

"I'm sure she thought," Helen added, "as we all did, that between the shock of her death and your marriage to an older stable man you'd mature into a more grounded and, well, generous soul."

"Instead," Ethel said, "all that new power went to your head."

"And being the dynamo you are," Rachel said, "you sucked us all into your big plans, which, at the time, sounded noble."

Sam raised a brow. "Now we know better."

Rocky reveled in a morbid bit of satisfaction as Tasha gritted her insanely white teeth. They'd been at odds for years, and most of the time Tasha came out on top. Mainly because she was conniving. Rocky didn't play dirty. Not usually, anyway.

Before Nell could set the dual martinis on the table, Tasha nabbed one of the glasses out of her hand and drained the drink in one long swallow. She glared at Rocky. "This is your doing."

"No, it's all yours."

"So you're kicking me out of the club?"

"Just asking you to step down as president."

"I suppose *you're* going to step up."

Monica spoke for her. "We all voted."

Still glaring at Rocky, Tasha spewed, "You can't even make a success of a rinky-dink inn, yet you think you can handle negations with a big-time publishing house?"

The insult hit its mark, but Rocky simply balled her fists beneath the table. Due to Tasha's raised voice, suddenly everyone in the now-crowded bar was looking their way.

"No need to get ugly," Ethel said in a hushed voice. "You'll still be the go-between with that editor man," she said to Tasha, "but Rocky will be the club's official leader. We need to refocus on our core objective."

Ignoring the older woman, Tasha downed her second martini, then slammed the glass to the table. "You're jealous of me. You have *always* been jealous of me! Take the damned presidency, Rocky. You are and will always be a pathetic *loser!*"

That last taunt burned to Rocky's toes and gave her feet wings. She flew out of her chair, sailing over Monica, and knocked Tasha, chair and all, to the floor.

"Whoa, whoa!" Rocky heard Luke bellow as the rest of the crowd gasped and hooted.

Straddling her longtime enemy, Rocky smacked Tasha hard for fifteen years of insults. Only Rocky's hand was balled so it was more like a punch.

"Bitch!" Tasha fought back, grabbing one of Rocky's braids and yanking so hard, Rocky yelped and lost her balance.

Keeling sideways, she conked her head, shouted, "Fuck!" then kicked out just as Tasha lunged. They whaled on each other, rolling into a table. Drinks flew and plates of food crashed to the planked floor. Cheering patrons gave a wide berth.

Out of the corner of her eye, Rocky saw Luke coming their way. "Break it up, dammit!" Only he tripped over Sam's big foot (*Thank you, Sam!*), allowing her to get in another swing.

At the same time Tasha shoved Rocky's face into a glob of artichoke dip.

Rocky saw red, white noise roaring in her ears when the freak tried to shove an olive up her nose. As she retaliated, the last thing Rocky heard before scooping up a handful of maple cream pie was, "Ten bucks on Rocky!"

* * *

Chloe's eyes flew open. She stared into the dark, heart pounding, confused about her whereabouts and the spooky silence. Then her brain engaged and she realized the storm had abated. No rain. No thunder. She reached out. No Devlin.

Her nostrils twitched with an acrid smell, a familiar smell. Kitchen fire!

Clutching the comforter to her naked body, she rolled out of bed, wincing as her feet hit the ground. Her ankle throbbed along with her head. Ignoring the pain, she limped toward the stink. She spied Devlin moving a smoking pot from the stove to the sink, heard him cursing under his breath. Confident he had the situation under control, she breathed easier and bit back a smile. He looked pathetically inept in the kitchen, but he was trying, which struck her as oddly sweet. Waving her hand in front of her nose, she asked, "Are you okay?"

"Better than these baked beans," he groused, dousing them with water and igniting a fresh burst of sizzle and steam. "I only turned my back for a couple of minutes."

She moved forward and glanced at the stove. "You had the heat set too high."

"I'm used to nuking everything in the microwave." He looked over his shoulder then.

For a moment, time ceased as he took in her disheveled state. Her heart pounded in slow, desirous thuds. A heady mix of lust and affection heated her cheeks and blood. She opened her mouth, then shut it when he cocked his head and smiled.

"I'd planned on serving you supper in bed," he said, "but you brought the bed out here."

She glanced down, noting she'd not only wrapped herself in the comforter, but the top sheet was half trailing behind her as well. She laughed, welcoming his lighthearted tone. Then she noticed *he* was wearing clean, dry sweats and a T-shirt. "Hey, where'd you get those?"

He nodded toward the bedroom. "The five-drawer dresser."

"Be right back."

"Be right here," he said, scraping charred beans into a pail.

Chloe limped back inside, ecstatic things weren't weird between them since they'd had sex. Sometimes sex changed everything, and not always for the better. When he'd dragged his gaze over her just now, she sensed the same raw desire, a deeper regard. Lost in her own firestorm of emotions, she'd been tempted to speak her heart. Right there in the kitchen. A charred pan of beans between them. But in the next second she questioned her timing.

He knew she'd lived with Ryan for two years, suggesting a serious relationship. What if he didn't believe she was over Ryan? What if Devlin thought she was on the rebound and didn't know her own heart? Or thought that she was fickle and fell in love at the drop of a hat?

"Too soon," she whispered to herself as she switched on a small bedside lamp. "Take it slow." For once in her life she wasn't going to rush into something, only to muck it up. She heaped the blankets on the bed and quickly rooted through the drawers. She didn't feel right about pulling on a pair of whatever brother's briefs were in the top drawer, but she did pull on a thick pair of socks. Chilled, she a nabbed a flannel shirt. Made for a tall man, the sleeves were too long and the shirttails hit her mid-thigh. Long enough that she didn't have to worry about going commando. Twisting her damp, clean hair into a knot, she returned to the kitchen to find Devlin looking through the limited cabinet space. "So what are our choices?"

"Beans, beans, and more beans. A can of crushed tomatoes, bag of popcorn, Scotch Broth Soup—"

"Let me see."

He passed back the can while still looking through the cabinet.

" 'A traditional everything-in-a-pot barley soup,' " she read from the label. "I like the sound of this. What else?"

"Quaker Oats, brown bread in a can—"

"What?"

He passed that back, too. "A throwback to old New England," he said, scouring the next cabinet. "You've never had it?"

"No." She read the description. " 'Moist and dense. Natural ingredients. Rich molasses taste. Serve right out of the can, or toast, bake or microwave.' Given the latter, I assume you've had it?"

He laughed. "Yeah."

"Good?"

"Surprisingly, yes."

She moved on to the fridge. "Not much here. Beer, jar of pickles and . . . oh no. For real?"

"What?"

"An unopened package of Vermont smoked summer sausage."

Looking over, she could tell by the hot spark in his eyes that he, too, was thinking about their first sexually charged meeting in Oslow's. "Expiration date?" he asked.

She looked, smiled. "We're good to go."

"I know I am."

Flustered by his intense stare, she blushed. "What?"

"Just thinking how sexy you look in that shirt and wishing it were mine."

She sighed. "Romantic notion number . . . I've lost count."

"Trust me," he said, devouring her with a hungry gaze. "Romance is the last thing on my mind just now."

Noting the not-so-subtle bulge in his sweats, her intimate parts tingled and a dozen racy scenarios played through her head. Doing it on the sofa, bent over the sofa, burning up the rug in front of the wood-burning stove, and nailing him up-right against the wall. As much as she wanted to jump his bones here and now, her throbbing ankle and various body aches proved an irritating distraction. Starting something she couldn't finish wasn't an option. She wondered if the Brodys kept a stash of Tylenol.

Mind racing, Chloe lightened the sexually charged moment with a playful wink. "Yeah, well, let's get some food into you first, mister, because the next time we . . . tango," she teased, "you'll need all the strength you can get."

"Promises, promises."

She waggled her brows as she ambled to the stove. "I am a woman of many talents."

"You're also limping." And just like that the playful moment was gone.

"It's nothing."

"Let me see."

"Devlin . . ." She broke off as he knelt, grabbed her foot, and rolled down her sock.

"It's just a little swollen," she said of her ankle.

"And bruised."

Because of the force of the impact when she'd collided with the trunk. A freak accident that still blew her mind. "I'll live." Speaking of freaky things . . . "Do you know anything about dream animals?"

"What?"

"When I was in the woods, I thought I saw a moose; then again it could have been a hallucination."

"Plenty of moose inhabit Thrush and the surrounding area," he said as he rolled her sock back up.

"So maybe he *was* real. Still, he inspired these . . . visions."

Devlin regarded her with a raised brow.

Since she wasn't ready to talk about marriage, babies, and her plans for Gemma's Bakery, she laughed off her ramblings as though they were whimsy. "That's what a head conk will do to you. Do me a favor and open up that soup, please."

"How's your head?" he asked while pushing aside her hair and inspecting the bump.

"Honestly."

"Chloe."

"All right. It's throbbing a little. And my chest . . ."

"What?"

"I think it's because I hit the steering wheel so hard when I crashed. No air bag."

He unbuttoned the top three buttons of the flannel shirt and pulled it wide. "Jesus."

"What?" She looked down but couldn't really see.

"You're bruised."

"Is that all?"

"You're getting a head-to-toe checkup when we get to the hospital tomorrow."

"Fine. Can we have supper now? I'm starving."

He shook his head, rebuttoned her shirt. "Luke was right about you. Sweet city girl by circumstance, tough country girl at heart."

She knew Luke was a player; still . . . "What a sweet thing to say."

"In case you haven't noticed, my brother's enamored with you."

"According to Daisy, Luke's enamored with most women."

"In your case," Devlin said, brushing a kiss over her lips, "his appreciation is justified."

Her heart swelled as Devlin eased away to open the can of soup, then the canned bread. Chest fluttering with joy and contentment, Chloe adjusted the heat on the stovetop as well as the oven. She poured the soup into a pot, asking Devlin to search the cabinet for spices. They worked in tandem, her lip twitching when he mocked a wince while slicing up the summer sausage. After arranging their appetizers on a plate, he popped the tops of two beers and passed one to her.

She sipped and stirred the aromatic soup.

He sipped and moved in behind her, wrapping a possessive

arm around her waist. "I could get used to this," he said, nuzzling her ear.

Taking that as her cue to give up at least a hint of her true feelings, she snuggled back against him. "So could I."

THIRTY-FIVE

Silk. No, *feathers.*

And velvet.

Devlin stirred from a heavy sleep.

Chloe.

She was straddling his body, teasing his chest with whisper-soft kisses. Her long, soft hair tickling his skin as she worked her way down his torso. Sweet torture.

"Good morning," she said in between playful nips.

"I'll say."

She continued working her way south—lips, tongue, teeth.

Judas Priest, if she put her sexy mouth around him, he'd lose it before they even got started. Shifting, he clasped her arms and deftly maneuvered her beneath him. Now he was on top. Brushing tender kisses over her bruised collarbone, suckling her breasts. She moaned and arched as he worked his way lower, intent on making her come with his mouth. He loved her scent, her taste, her passionate response to his touch. The need to vanquish her memories of ex-lovers, of possessing her body and soul, resonated with raw intensity.

"Wait," she whispered. "I wanted . . . I want . . ."

Her words faded as he lingered, increasing the pressure and pace of his tongue until she shattered, an explosive orgasm that sent shock waves of lust to his core. He moved over her, reaching for a foil packet on the nightstand.

"Not yet." She nabbed his wrist, finessed him onto his back. Impressive. Exciting. "Told you I'd have my way."

Well, hell.

Devlin summoned calm and stamina as she straddled him and kissed her way down his body. *Holy shit.*

"My turn to savor."

Her fingers scorched his skin as they skimmed over his bunched muscles, as they kneaded, tickled, tempted. Her mouth, *ah, Christ,* so soft, so demanding. When she closed her lips over his cock, he tensed with erotic euphoria. Even though she was an adventurous, passionate soul, she still struck him as old fashioned and sweet. As a result, going down on him was a magnified turn-on. On the brink of losing it, he nabbed her forearms and pulled her up his body. "I'm going to fuck you blind."

Instead of shying away from his coarse declaration, she smiled, an ornery grin that amped his desire. "Sorry," she rasped. "My turn." She nabbed the condom from the nightstand.

He watched as she rolled on the Trojan—no coy tricks or looks, just a straightforward process, which was somehow sexy as hell. He drank in her curves, her flawless skin, and that sweet face. "You're beautiful, Chloe."

"Even with the bumps and bruises?"

"Badges of honor," he gritted out as she lowered herself onto him. "You were on a noble mission."

"On a mission now, too," she teased. "Although I wouldn't call it noble."

"What would you call it?"

She rolled her hips, riding him slow, driving him crazy. He groaned and she smiled. "I'd call it selfish." Hands braced on his shoulders, she continued her sexy assault.

He let her have her way, her pace, even though it was killing him. He refused to climax before her, and damn, unlike last night, she had unbelievable restraint. She picked up the rhythm, her face heated from passion and exertion. He gripped her hips, reveled in her dominance. "Let me have it, baby."

"Come for me," she demanded.

"You first."

When she grasped his wrists and pushed his arms over his head, holding him captive, he nearly lost it. His heart pounded like a jackhammer in his ears. Then he heard his name, only it wasn't Chloe.

She stilled.

He listened. The pounding sounded again.

Not his heart.

The front door.

He closed his eyes, cursed. "Luke."

Flustered, Chloe rolled off of him and wiggled under the blanket. "What's he doing here?"

"What time is it?" Devlin reached for his Android. "The battery died." He nabbed his wristwatch, blinked. "Shit."

"What?"

"It's almost noon."

"You're *kidding*!"

It's not like they'd had marathon sex last night, but they had kept late hours and they had fooled around. A lot. Still, he hadn't been *that* exhausted. Content, maybe. Shaking off a barrage of thoughts, he rolled out of bed. "Who knows how long my phone's been dead and how long they've been trying to call." He slipped into the bathroom, flushed the condom. "We were expected at the hospital this morning."

"And I lost my phone back in the woods. Crap."

She scrambled into the bathroom as he emerged, shoving his legs into his shorts and pulling on his pants. He glanced over his shoulder, saw Chloe hooking her bra, and mourned their stolen orgasm. Luke pounded on the door again and as Devlin stalked out of the bedroom he seriously thought about killing his brother.

The timing of the morning was royally screwed. Bad went to worse when Devlin wrenched open the door just as Chloe limped into the room pulling down her dress and asking, "Where did you put my underwear?"

It wasn't Luke's raised brow that bothered Devlin as much as the mottled face of the stranger standing just over his shoulder.

King of the understatement, Luke said, "This is awkward."

The other man pulled him aside and Chloe gasped. "Daddy."

Hell. "I can explain, sir." Although Devlin wasn't sure exactly how to address the obvious.

The older man glared. "I'd rather hear it from my daughter."

Luke cleared his throat, looked back and forth between the two men. "Dev, this is Mr. Madison. Mr. Madison, my brother . . . uh . . . right." His other brow shot up. "Could I have a word with you outside, Dev?"

Devlin looked back at Chloe—standing there in her wrinkled dress, no underwear, twisting her bed-mussed hair into a knot—and kicked himself a thousand times for making things worse between her and her father.

"It's okay," she told Devlin as the steely-faced man shouldered his way into the cabin. When she bolstered her shoulders and faced her disgruntled parent, Devlin ached to be her champion—whether she liked it or not.

Luke yanked him over the threshold and shut the door. *What the fuck?* he mouthed, dragging Devlin off the porch and away from the cabin.

"Why did you bring him here?"

"Why didn't you answer my calls? Or Rocky's? Or Gram's, Chris's, or Monica's? Between all of us, we've been trying to call you and Chloe since nine a.m."

"My phone died," Devlin explained while buttoning his shirt. "No charger. And Chloe lost her phone in the woods."

"All the more reason to haul ass to Pixley first thing this morning. You had to know we'd be worried."

"We just woke up."

"It's noon."

"I know."

Hands on hips, Luke stared. "You've been getting up at the butt crack of dawn every morning since we were teens."

"I know."

Luke jammed a hand through his shaggy hair. "So what?

You overslept, then decided to indulge in a roll in the sack before a leisurely drive to Pixley? Who are you and what have you done with my pain-in-the-ass, ultraresponsible brother?"

"It wasn't like that, and get your mind and mouth out of the gutter when referring to Chloe." He hadn't meant to sound so brusque, but damn.

"Oh, hell." Luke did a double take. "Are you serious?"

Devlin swung away and looked toward the cabin. What was going on in there?

Luke moved into his line of vision. "I knew you were hot for Chloe. We all saw the sparks, but . . . Are you in *love*?"

He didn't answer.

Luke shook his head, whistled low. "I don't know whether to celebrate or worry."

"What are you talking about?"

"I mean love at first sight or first . . . uh, hookup, well, that's fine. But you being you . . . You're not going to do something foolish—"

"Like?"

"Like asking her to marry you just because her dad caught you two, well . . ."—he waved a hand in the air—"you know. First of all, that's fricking old fashioned. Second, you barely know her."

Devlin tempered his anger, angled his head. "Not sure you're the best person to dole out advice on meaningful relationships."

If the insult registered, Luke didn't show it. "Just don't want to see you making the same mistake twice."

"You're the one who reminded me Chloe's nothing like Janna."

"I'm talking about rushing into marriage because of your overdeveloped sense of duty."

Stomach cramped with fury and regret, Devlin leaned in and lowered his voice. "She was pregnant with my baby. What would you have done?"

"Since you're asking, first I would've made sure the baby *was* mine."

Devlin clocked his little brother with a swift uppercut.

Luke stumbled back, then, finding his balance, massaged his jaw. "Damn."

"Sorry." Really he was. His brother had simply voiced what a lot of people had thought. Yes, Devlin and Janna had been involved on and off for two years and, yes, she'd dated other guys in between, but when she'd come to him sobbing, when she'd told him she was pregnant . . . just knowing the child was very possibly his and that her parents were throwing her out . . . that had been enough for him to postpone attending college in favor of settling down.

Luke horned in on his thoughts. "That was uncalled for," he said. "My taunt, that is. Sorry. I just . . . I want you to be happy, Dev."

Instead of a hug or handshake or, God forbid, a philosophical discussion, Devlin breezed over the altercation with a cocked brow, something he knew his brother would understand. "I need to check in with Gram and Rocky."

Luke tossed him his BlackBerry, then leaned back against his SUV and crossed his arms. "This should be good."

* * *

As soon as the door shut, as soon as it was just Chloe and her dad, she broke down and rushed into his arms. Three years. She hadn't seen him for three *years*. It hadn't seemed that long until this moment. Life had whizzed by and distance had muted the intensity of their disconnection. As she saw him, touched him, all the strife she'd felt, the resentment and disappointment, melted away. Overwhelmed, tears slipped down her cheeks as she regressed to the little girl who'd once worshiped her daddy. No matter their baggage, he was her blood. If she'd learned anything from the Monroes, it was that family was messy. But with love and respect anything was fixable. She hugged her dad with all of her might, her heart breaking when he didn't hug back.

"I know this looks bad," she said.

"It will look slightly better when you're fully clothed."

No underwear. Right. Mortified, she eased back and disappeared into the bedroom, then the bathroom. She looked harder and found her clean, dry thong inside the shower stall. She pulled it on and, addressing her pitiful reflection in the mirror, pulled herself together. "He's never been the touchy-feely type," she reminded herself. Even if she'd been decently dressed, he would've tensed when she assaulted him with that teary hug.

She dried her eyes, then unknotted her hair, allowing it to hang loose in order to hide the discolored bump near her temple. Taking a deep breath, she pulled on her green socks and Daisy's pink boots, smoothed her cheery dress, then calmly made her way back into the living room. Her dad had settled on the edge of the sofa. Skittish now, she didn't sit beside him but across from him in a mismatched club chair. "I—"

"Let me speak."

Except he fell silent for a good two minutes. She supposed he was contemplating his words. She contemplated his appearance. An old-fashioned businessman, he'd always worn a shirt and tie and he wore one now, only the shirt was wrinkled and the tie crooked. He looked unkempt, tired. He looked older. She mourned the time lost.

At last he dropped his greying head. "I don't know where to begin."

"I do," Chloe said. "I'm sorry my fear of dying pushed us apart."

His head snapped up.

She swallowed hard. "I want to talk about Mom."

* * *

Devlin had just disconnected with Rocky when Chloe and her dad emerged from the cabin. He passed Luke his phone, watched as the father and daughter shared a brief, stiff hug. According to Jayce's report, Roger Madison was a highly successful car dealer who owned a small franchise. Considering his occupation, Devlin would have guessed him to be charismatic, gregarious—a people person. Granted this was a tense situation, but the man didn't exhibit an ounce of warmth. Conservative, uptight, judgmental, and, according to Chloe, controlling. No wonder she was estranged from the man.

"Brace yourself," Luke muttered under his breath as Madison left the porch and strode toward them.

Devlin braced, although he wasn't sure for what. A lecture? A smackdown? A punch in the gut?

"Could I trouble you for a ride back to Sugar Creek?" Madison asked Luke.

Luke shifted. "Actually I was hoping . . ." He sighed, shoved a hand through his hair. "Sure." He looked to Devlin. "Tell Gram I'll visit later today." He waved to Chloe, flashed Devlin a baffled look, then turned for his SUV. "Ready when you are, Mr. Madison."

"Hurt her," the man said to Devlin, "and I'll find a way to hurt you."

The threat should have made him angry. Instead it gave him hope that the man actually loved his daughter.

Devlin sure as hell did. In spite of his hang-ups. In spite of his history with women. He'd accepted the fact last night while she'd stirred spices into their canned soup. Not exactly a hearts and roses moment. But one that had seduced him heart and soul.

Just now she looked both vulnerable and strong. An intoxicating mix. He waited until Luke pulled away until he approached. "You okay?"

She tilted her face to the sun, closed her eyes, and breathed deep. "Living in the moment."

THIRTY-SIX

"Are we going to talk about it?"

Chloe shifted in the passenger seat of the Hummer. She'd wondered when Devlin was going to pry. The whole time they'd tidied the cabin, she'd expected him to interrogate her about her dad, but Devlin had held silent, assumedly waiting for her to broach the subject first.

It wasn't that she didn't want to talk about it. She just needed time to put her thoughts and feelings in perspective. Now that they were on the road to Pixley and the heartfelt conversation with her dad was twenty minutes behind her, she felt calm enough to share her thoughts without deteriorating into an emotional basket case.

"I know he didn't make the best impression," Chloe started, "but considering what he walked in on—"

"Trust me. That part I understand."

She shifted her glance from the passing scenery—vastly different on a sunshiny day—to the man navigating the winding road with ease. So confident and caring. Her love for him grew with every beat of her heart. Suddenly she ached for Devlin to know as much about her family as she knew about his. Even though her immediate family only consisted of two.

"My dad was never an overly demonstrative man," she explained. "It's not that he didn't love Mom and me; he was just uncomfortable with displays of affection. Mom was the warm and fuzzy one. Dad . . . he showed his love by buying us things and taking us places. I don't think I've mentioned this, but my dad's stinking rich. He owns a car dealership. A franchise actually."

"Self-motivated," Devlin concluded. "Driven."

"Yes." She'd always been proud of those qualities. "But also controlling and obsessed with the business."

"A workaholic."

"It got worse after Mom died. She used to push family time, Sundays were our special day, and although he always groused at first, once he relaxed into it . . ."—she reveled in a hundred memories, smiled—"we always had a great time. Anyway, after . . . he withdrew. From me, from life. I spent more and more time with my Grandma Madison, who was nice, but kind of distant and conservative. As for me, instead of withdrawing from life, I attacked it with a vengeance. As I got older I spent the majority of my time at friends' houses, especially Monica's. I joined every club imaginable—Girl Scouts, Four-H, choir, drama. I took extracurricular classes—dancing, horseback riding, ceramics."

"Squeezing as much into life as possible. No dreams or goals unachieved."

"Exactly."

"And your dad indulged your activities because it kept you busy and scarce and because it's how he showed love—by buying you things. Instead of affording you his time and affection, he supported you financially."

She was surprised by how well Devlin understood and pleased that he didn't seem to be taking sides. "It became our way of life. Totally dysfunctional really, because we were both hiding from our fears instead of addressing them. I know why I kept my emotional distance."

Devlin arched a brow. "Because every time you tried to get close, he pushed you away?"

"Right again. What I didn't know was *why* he kept me at arm's length. No special trips together. No family time at all. He even made it a point to work every Sunday. I assumed he wasn't interested in being a single parent. That, without Mom around, he didn't know what to do with me, how to *be* with me.

"Today, after I shared my fear of dying with him and explained about the compulsive need to explore every passion, he confessed that the reason he pushed me away was because he couldn't stand the thought of losing me the way he'd lost Mom. Emotional disconnect was his lifeline to mental stability."

"There are few things that rank with the loss, or fear of loss, of one's child," Devlin said in a thoughtful tone.

"That's very tolerant of you. Most people would call his behavior cowardly or at the very least selfish."

"I'm not most people."

"So I'm learning." She studied him a moment, conscious of a wisp of melancholy. Did this subject conjure painful memories relating to his own life? Again she wondered about the former wife no one talked about. Did he lose her in an accident? To disease? Childbirth? For his sake, she prayed deep down that they'd simply divorced.

Maybe she was pushing, but she couldn't help giving him the opportunity to reveal his past marriage and the lingering effects. "Do you know my dad still mourns my mom to this day, as in he can't imagine remarrying? *Ever?*"

"He must've loved her very much." Devlin reached across the seat and squeezed her hand. "Something tells me he loves you just as deeply—in spite of his efforts not to."

Okay. So maybe he wasn't taking this conversation personally. Just now he seemed entirely focused on her and her dilemma. Relaxing a little, she smiled at his observation because today she'd come to the same conclusion. "He flew out here because our last phone conversation had ended so badly. Like you with your dad, he wanted to confront the situation face-to-face. You can imagine how upset he was when he arrived and couldn't reach me by phone, nor could he find me at Daisy's. That's when he reached out to Monica, who put him in touch with Luke. Knowing I'd been in an accident and then stranded . . . he wanted to see for himself that I was all right. He didn't expect to find us . . . you know."

"Awkward for everyone. So," he said, glancing over. "What did you tell him about *us*?"

"I told him we click." Which was true, but her actual words had been, *I think he's the one, the man I'm destined to be with*. She'd confessed that her father had been right about Ryan—a lapse of judgment on her part but not a total mistake. Because of Ryan she'd enrolled and graduated from culinary school, an accomplishment she cherished and one her dad applauded as well. "And I promised I'd take it slow."

"A challenge for someone who attacks her passions with reckless abandon," Devlin teased.

"Yes, well, that was the old me. The new me intends to hone the art of savoring."

He cast her a look that spiked her libido. "Sounds like we're on the same wavelength."

Meaning he intended to cut back at work? To slow down and smell the roses? To commit more time to his personal life? To her? She knew he wanted to pursue their relationship, but to what level? Could he imagine marrying a second time? Did he ever want children?

She buzzed with a dozen questions, only she didn't know which one to ask first. Asking him if he loved her wasn't exactly taking it slow, and it wasn't fair. He'd known her less than a month. Just because she'd fallen head over heels in the blink of an eye didn't mean he had.

Just then the wilderness gave way to civilization, saving her from bobbling the conversation. Devlin took the lead as they hit the main highway and neared town. "You realize that between what Gram saw of us in the backseat of the Caddy last week and what Luke and your dad saw today we are now, like it or not, an item."

Another cryptic insinuation. "As in a couple? As in . . . dating?"

"Sounds kind of archaic, but yeah."

"Exclusively?"

"I'm old fashioned that way." Staring straight ahead, he added, "Do you mind?"

She sensed vulnerability in his tone. Did it have something

to do with his former wife? *Dammit*. The longer he kept that part of his life quiet, the greater her curiosity. "I think it's sweet," she said. "For what it's worth, I'm not keen on sharing you either."

That coaxed a smile out of him.

Heart skipping, she thought about them stepping out in Sugar Creek as a committed couple. "Tasha won't like it," she blurted.

He clenched his jaw, brushed aside her hair. "I'll handle Tasha," he said, frowning at the discolored goose egg. Then he noticed the stubborn set of her own jaw and laughed. "Right. *We'll* handle Tasha. Although she's already taken a beating from my sister."

"What?"

"Touched base with Rocky this morning and got an earful."

Chloe settled back in her seat, absorbing the story, wondering what effect this fallout would have on the ongoing Monroe/Burke feud, and having an epiphany about Cupcake Lovers. By the time she and Devlin reached the hospital, she couldn't wait to run her idea by Daisy.

Unfortunately, Devlin steered Chloe straight to the emergency room. "My girlfriend was involved in a minor car accident," he said to the nurse. "Just some bumps and bruises, but I'd feel better if she was examined."

Without looking up, the uniformed woman passed them a clipboard. "You'll have to fill out these forms."

Knowing it was useless to argue, Chloe nabbed a pen and took a seat.

"What are you grinning at?" Devlin asked as he eased down beside her.

She leaned over and, feeling like a besotted teen, brushed a playful kiss across his lips. "You called me your *girlfriend*."

* * *

While Chloe was being checked out by a doctor, Devlin had words with Daisy's attending physician, Dr. Beane, then slipped into her room. "Hi, Gram."

"It's about time you got here," she grumbled, pressing a button to raise the top half of her bed. "Where's Chloe?"

"I asked a doctor to look her over."

"Is she all right?"

"Seems to be. Just wanted to make sure. What happened to your hair?"

"Is that your way of saying you don't like it?"

"It's purple."

She smiled. "A candy striper did it for me."

He pulled a chair up to the edge of the bed, smiled back. "I don't think they're called candy stripers anymore."

"Whatever. She was young and peppy and had bright purple stripes in her hair. I asked if she could make me look hip. Told her I needed to look glitzy and special for a publicity photo. She left and came back with a can of spray-on hair color and a bunch of sparkly makeup. I looked fabulous, if I say so myself."

"I'm sure you did." He pointed to the yellow headband with purple stars, strategically placed over her bandaged forehead. "She bring you that, too?"

"Clever way to hide the bandage, I thought. I washed the makeup off last night, after I knew Chloe wasn't coming. But I'm thinking about keeping the hair color for a while. What do you think?"

Purple curls. Pink eyeglasses. He thought she looked ridiculous. "Does it make you happy?"

"Delirious."

"Then I love it."

Her smile widened. "Rocky said the same thing. She's around here somewhere. Ran down for some coffee. Did you hear about how she beat the stuffing out of Tasha?"

"I did." He reached for his grandmother's hand, trying not to fixate on how fragile she looked, hooked up to an IV, a cast on her ankle and a camouflaged bandage around her head. "Gram, I know about your heart attack last year. I need to talk to you—"

"So what's going on with my son?"

He froze, blindsided by the change of subject. "What do you mean?"

"You told me he and your mom booked a spontaneous Caribbean cruise and that's why he didn't fly straight up after hearing about my accident. Because he's in the middle of the ocean."

The lie hadn't come easily, but it had come from the heart.

"He's called numerous times to check up on me," she continued. "In two days he's sent a flower arrangement, a plant, and a basket of baked goods."

"I'm sure he's feeling guilty—"

"Guilty, schmilty. I suspected something when he retired early. Jerome's a chip off his father's block. J.T.'s is in his blood. He lives and breathes that store and he wouldn't walk away—not at his age—unless something was terribly wrong. At first I thought it was a midlife crisis. Maybe he'd had an affair and he and your mom went away to work things out in private. But now . . . I think different." She squeezed Devlin's hand and looked him dead in the eyes. "What's wrong with my son?"

Christ almighty. Devlin's heart cracked with the knowledge, the burden.

"Lie and I'll know, Devlin. I always know with all of my grandchildren."

Dammit. "I promised I wouldn't tell."

"Then I'll guess. Affair?"

"God, no."

"Financial problems?"

"No."

"Heath issues?"

He didn't answer.

She licked her lips. "Your mom?"

"No."

"Your dad then."

"I can't—"

She squeezed his hand harder. "It's serious then. Terminal?"

Jesus. He couldn't take it. "He's seeing a specialist, Gram. The prognosis is promising." She didn't gasp or cry or fall apart in any way. She merely opened her scrawny arms to him. Weary with the secret, the fears, Devlin, a grown man, a man who always assumed the role of caretaker, took solace in his grandma's embrace.

THIRTY-SEVEN

Chloe had raised her knuckles to announce her arrival just as Daisy's door swung open and Devlin stepped out. They looked at each other, asking at the same time, "Are you okay?"

"Fine," they answered in unison, then laughed.

Shaking his head, Devlin lowered his voice, "Why would you ask me that?"

"I don't know. You look a little . . . wiped out. Did Daisy give you a hard time?"

He scraped a hand over his stubbled jaw. "Actually, she went out of her way to make me feel better."

"So she agreed to ease up on her Errol Flynn escapades?"

"I didn't ask. Instead I invited her to join us for a hot-air balloon ride with Nash as soon as she gets out of here."

Chloe smiled. "Seriously?"

"Dr. Beane assured me he'd made Gram understand about mixing meds and I decided to broach her fondness for cocktails subtly, after she's home. As for the reckless stunts, I took your suggestion about nurturing the positive. Figured if she's desperate to experience some thrills in life, why not join in so I can at least ensure a modicum of safety?"

"That's almost contradictory," Chloe teased, "but I get what you mean. It's a sweet gesture."

"Yeah, well, I haven't been spending as much time with

family as I should. I intend to change that. According to almost everyone I know, I need to get a life." He gazed into her eyes. "Last night was a start."

"Keep looking at me like that and I'll have to find a private place and . . . take advantage of you."

"Tempting." He moved in just as two interns pushed a cart past them, short-circuiting the charged moment. Expression intent, Devlin brushed her hair from her face. "So what did the doctor say about this head bump?"

"He saw no reason for concern. Came to the same conclusion regarding my other bruises. He did, however, give me pills and instructions to reduce the swelling of my ankle." She smiled. "I won't be running any races this week, but other than that, I'm fine."

"Good to know."

"So, is it okay if I visit with Daisy?" Chloe was anxious to see for herself that her friend was on the mend. She was also bursting to share her new dream. If anyone could help to put her vision in perspective, it was the woman who shared her love of cooking and had a long history in Sugar Creek.

"Sure. In fact, she's anxious to see you. I need to step outside, make a call. Rocky's in the building, so don't be surprised if she drops in."

"Okay. Thanks." She coordinated her thoughts as she moved quietly inside, hoping she could run her idea by Daisy before Rocky or any other family member showed. As Chloe peeked around a partially closed curtain, the first thing she noticed was the cast that covered Daisy's foot and rose to mid-shin. At least it was colorful—pink—which made Chloe smile. She would've been bothered by the IV drip, but she knew it was helping to ease the woman's discomfort. Knowing she'd suffered a gash to the forehead, Chloe had prepared herself for ugly stitches or a bloody bandage and instead saw a bright headband with stars.

Daisy opened her eyes and, seeing Chloe, grinned. "Hi, kitten."

"Oh, my God," she blurted, loving the whimsy of it all.

"Who did your hair? I love it!" What she loved was this woman's confidence and, dammit all, her sense of *derring-do.*

"I *knew* you would," Daisy said, eyes sparkling behind her pink blingy glasses. "Hey, are those my boots?"

"Hope you don't mind. What with the weather—"

"Speaking of, what did the doctor say about your injuries, kitten?"

Blushing, Chloe raised a hand to her bruised temple. "I'm fine. Which is more than I can say for the Caddy. I'm so sorry, Daisy."

"Bah. It's just a car. If Leo can't fix it, I'll get a new one." She patted the edge of the mattress. "Sit. We need to catch up. Did you hear? Rocky's the new president of Cupcake Lovers!"

Chloe nodded. "Heard she gave Tasha a black eye."

"Yes, well, Rocky's got a shiner, too. But it was worth it, she said. Now the club will get back on track with our charity efforts."

"About that," Chloe said, her stomach fluttering with nerves. "Did you hear Gemma's Bakery went out of business?"

Daisy's bandaged face lit up. "I *did.* Don't tell anyone yet, but I'm thinking of buying it."

Her fluttery stomach dropped. "What?"

"I've always wanted my own business."

"J.T.'s—"

"My husband's passion. My son's. Not mine."

Chloe noticed she didn't mention the store as Devlin's passion, but didn't comment. Her brain was stuck on Gemma's.

"Anyway," Daisy said, "it's the perfect venture for us."

"Us?"

"You and me. The Soul Sisters. Can't you see it? Our own bakery!"

Her enthusiasm danced back to life, albeit an altered life. Going into business with Daisy? There was something fantastically inspired about that. "I was envisioning more of a coffeehouse café. I mean . . . You're not going to believe this, but *I* was thinking of buying Gemma's."

"Really?" Daisy's eyes grew wide with amazement, then crinkled with humor. "Adventurous minds think alike. It's a sign!"

Chloe laughed. "It has to be."

"I toyed with the idea as soon as I heard the news, which was this morning. What about you?"

"Yesterday, when I was stranded in the woods, pinned under that tree, I racked my brain for new goals, a new dream. One of the things that popped into mind was Gemma's. I could see it. Sugar Creek's first Internet café, with a twist."

"A what?"

"A place with wireless Internet access. Where people can come in with their laptops and PDAs and go online. Check their e-mails, the news, and weather. Surf blogs and Web sites. Cybershop."

"Greek to me, but go on."

"This is a tourist town and yet there's no public place for visitors to go online except the library. And no one offers wireless. Another thing: How do people function around here without a Starbucks? A place to hang out and drink gourmet coffee? To enjoy specialty snacks and sweets while reading a book or newspaper. Picture it, Daisy. A quaint café with oversized cushy chairs and maybe a sofa. Mismatched antique tables with unique collectibles and art."

"I can see it!"

"Maybe some sort of logo that goes with an overall theme. A mascot. Like . . . a moose."

Daisy scrunched her silvery brows. "A moose?"

"I saw one when I was in the woods and . . ." She shrugged. "It inspired me."

"A moose makes sense," Daisy said. "Indicative of the area. Tourists love them. We've got a whole table allotted to moose souvenirs at J.T.'s."

Chloe smiled. "I know. I saw. Oh! And I was thinking . . . why not have a special display featuring cupcakes made by members of Cupcake Lovers? All proceeds for those sales could go to a charity of the month. Also, if anything ever happened with the Cupcake Lovers recipe book, we could sell copies in the café." She fidgeted, feeling as though she'd maybe overstepped. "Bad idea?"

"Swell idea. In fact, your entire concept is impressive, Chloe."

"Really?"

"Far more imaginative and hip than a plain old bakery."

"I didn't mean—"

"I know you didn't." She grinned ear-to-ear. "So we're going to do this?"

"I want to. I hope so. But . . ." She glanced away, embarrassed. "I need to look into a loan."

"Why?"

"There will be significant start-up costs," she said reasonably. "Leasing the space, redecorating and refurbishing, advertising, utilities . . ."

Daisy snorted. "I have enough in my savings to cover all that."

Chloe flushed. "All my life someone, mostly my dad, has supported me financially. I can't . . . I won't ask you for money, Daisy."

"You're not asking. I'm offering. And it's not charity. It's a partnership. I have the money. You have the vision and know-how. A culinary arts degree, a background in publicity, experience with various eateries, and so much more."

Chloe swallowed hard, her hands trembling with excitement. "It's like everything I've ever done in life has led me to this moment. This is what I'm supposed to do." *Click.* "Still, I don't feel right about the money."

"If it makes you feel better, you can invest later, paying me back half when you have the funds."

"That would work, I suppose."

"Of course it would. Think about it." She patted Chloe's hand. "Remember, it's my dream, too."

"All right, I'll think about it. I mean, I'm in." How could she rob this incredible woman of her dream? Chloe wouldn't do that to anyone, especially not Daisy. "I just want to look into some financial options, so don't . . ." She licked her lips. "Can we keep this secret for now? Just between you and me?

I especially don't want to bring it up to Devlin until we have everything thought out."

"Good idea," Daisy said. "Otherwise he might try to nix the idea, claiming it's a risky investment."

"Or try to take control," Chloe said. "With the best intentions of course. Still."

Daisy offered her scrawny hand and they shook, agreeing to organize a plan before breaking the news.

Rocky pushed into the room, carrying a vase of beautiful flowers and looking downright cranky. At first Chloe thought maybe Rocky was cross because of the nasty shiner under her left eye. It did look pretty painful. But then Chloe learned better.

"Who are those from?" Daisy asked.

"Jayce."

"Such a sweet boy!" Daisy exclaimed.

"For a bastard," Rocky grumbled under her breath as she set the arrangement alongside several others.

Chloe was quickly reminded that though Rocky had set the club on a better path and though she'd struck an agreement with Devlin to save her inn, her relationship with Jayce Bello was still shaky at best. At worst, a shambles.

Chloe also struggled with the guilt of keeping Devlin in the dark about Jayce and Rocky's *affair.* At least she wouldn't be keeping her plans for Gemma's secret for more than a day or two. Not that Devlin didn't have a couple of secrets himself.

Before she could question the wisdom of beginning a relationship with so many skeletons in the closet, Rocky broke in on her thoughts. "So, Chloe," she said with a wicked grin, "*please* let me be the one to tell Tasha that you and my brother are . . ."—she glanced at her grandma and tempered her language—". . . *together.*"

THIRTY-EIGHT

Chloe bounced around Daisy's kitchen preparing what she considered to be her most important meal since that first Sunday dinner for the Monroes. She'd invited her dad over, wanting to impress him with what she'd learned in culinary school. She also hoped to further mend their relationship, although she wasn't expecting miracles overnight, and to maybe pick his brain about starting up a café. Who better to ask than someone who'd built a successful business from the ground up?

Meanwhile Monica, who'd already interrogated Chloe about her night with Devlin, lazed against the counter, sipping herbal tea and going on in detail about the bar brawl between Rocky and Tasha. "I'm telling you it was like something out of a movie. They did some damage to the Shack and each other."

"I can't believe Luke didn't break it up."

"He tried. Sam intervened." She snickered. "Guess he wanted Rocky to get her swings in. Apparently, Tasha's been torturing Rocky in some way or another since high school. Anyway, needless to say, those two aren't talking just now. Should make for an interesting meeting Thursday."

"You think Tasha will still come?" Chloe asked as she stirred crushed garlic into the caramelized onions. "I mean she's been stripped of her crown, so to speak. Won't her pride keep her away?"

"You'd think. But she's still the liaison between the club and that editor dude and she still wants to push the book through. I think it's all tied into some pathetic need to be famous in some way or to achieve something on a grand scale. Something that will have her rubbing elbows with the elite. You know, publishing execs, newspaper reporters, TV talk show hosts."

"Everyone's entitled to a dream," Chloe said, almost sympathizing with the woman.

"Absolutely. Don't get me wrong, the rest of us aren't immune to the prospect of a little excitement, but not at the risk of stepping on any member's toes or over any bodies in our quest to land the contract."

"If the book catches on and sells well," Chloe said, "it *could* generate considerable income for the designated charity."

"Which is in keeping with our core mission."

Chloe checked on the roasting chicken, then returned to the stovetop, adding vinegar and salt and pepper into the onion/garlic mix. Next, chopped sundried tomatoes.

Monica moved in beside her, pushed her glasses up her nose. "Are you sure I can't help?"

"I appreciate it, but I sort of want to impress Dad on my own."

She breathed deep, smiled. "Oh, he'll be impressed. How long's he staying in town?"

"Just a couple of days, I think." Two days to make up for three lost years. Two days to convince him that her future was here in Sugar Creek.

"Surprised he's not staying here with you. I mean Daisy won't be home until Thursday and there are so many bedrooms."

"Yeah, but it's the private home of someone he doesn't know. He wasn't comfortable, so I didn't press."

"So instead he's staying at the Red Clover."

Chloe smiled. "Luke's idea. I'm glad. Rocky could use the money. Plus, maybe he'll get a glimpse of Devlin through his sister's eyes. See that he's really a good guy."

"You realize you're the only one around here who refers to Dev by his full name."

Chloe blinked. "I am?" She hadn't noticed.

"It's kind of cute. Although I can't imagine calling Leo Leonard." She shook her head. "Nope. Total turnoff. Anyhow"—she gestured to Chloe's work—"remind me what's on the menu?"

"Baby Spinach Salad with Vidalia Onions, Sundried Tomatoes, and Goat Cheese, to start. Crunchy Roasted Lemon Chicken as the main dish. Wild Rice with Mushrooms, and Brussels Sprouts with Bacon, as the sides. And for dessert—Double Dark Chocolate Cupcakes."

Monica released a dreamy sigh. "Heaven."

"I'd ask you to stay, but—"

"I know." She glanced at her watch. "He'll be here soon. I should get going, but—"

"What?"

"You gave me the rundown about everything that happened with Dev yesterday and this morning."

"Mostly." She grinned as she divided baby spinach into two bowls. She'd glossed over the sex details, but they were crystal clear in *her* mind.

Monica nudged Chloe and grunted. "I'm not talking about that part. I'm curious about . . . Did Devlin say anything about his first marriage?"

Chloe's smile faltered. "No." The only reason Monica knew there had been a marriage was because Rocky had slipped. "I don't know any more than you do."

"Hmm. Well, I'm sure he'll get around to it. I wonder—" The doorbell rang.

"Crap," Chloe said. "Dad's a little early."

"Don't worry. I'll let him in, show him into the living room, and then I'll be on my way. Remember the keys to Leo's loaner are here on the counter. All gassed up. You're good to go."

"Tell Leo I really appreciate it," she said while Monica kissed her cheek, "and thank you for listening."

"Dev's a great guy, Chloe. And it means you'll be staying

on in Sugar Creek. I couldn't be happier. Well, except if I were preggo."

"How's that going?"

"Still working on it." Monica winked before slipping out. "Everyone's entitled to a dream, right?"

Her own dreams burning bright, Chloe lowered the oven's temperature. She checked the rice and Brussels sprouts and dressed the salad. Her heart swelled with pride. As varied as her interests were, she didn't excel at a lot of things, but damn, she shined in the kitchen.

If she did say so herself.

She looked forward to cooking a meal like this for Devlin, looked forward to the next big Sunday dinner. Her racing brain touched on some of the specialties she'd thought of for her Moose Café or whatever the heck she ended up calling it. Just as she was contemplating how to approach the venture with her dad, he poked his head into the kitchen.

He looked slightly refreshed—different shirt, different tie. "Smells great."

"I hope you're hungry."

"Starving." He moved closer, glanced into the steaming pots. "Brussels Sprouts with Bacon." He smiled. "One of your mom's specialties."

Tears burned Chloe's eyes as he loosened his tie, just like he used to do when he came home from work and found her mom cooking in the kitchen. "I know."

* * *

"Dammit." Devlin stared at his computer screen, torn between anger and shock. "Unbelievable."

After leaving the hospital, he'd dropped Chloe at Daisy's, then returned to J.T.'s. He'd spent two hours catching up on the previous day's business. Another half hour listening to the irrational complaints of a disgruntled customer. Another freaking half hour sorting out an accounting glitch. Then Mitzi Hall, in all her overglammed glory, had paraded into his office and complained about another male employee taunting her with lewd remarks. Given her past behavior, Devlin suspected she actually enjoyed the attention, if it was even true, but to be fair he'd had to call the poor accused guy into his office. The man had been clueless and Devlin had ended up having a second discussion with Mitzi—stretching his patience and diplomatic skills.

Finally, after four hours on the property, very late in his normal day, he'd opened his stock portfolio. He'd been watching so closely, had estimated and anticipated when to sell. But these days, more than ever, the market was unpredictable, and he'd been out of it for a good day and a half. It didn't take long to lose a bundle. He hadn't lost a fortune by any means, not factoring in his savings and various investments. But he *had* lost the cash he'd earmarked for the employee incentive bonuses. If he'd been paying closer attention like he usually did, he would have seen the signs, would've gotten that itch. He would've cashed out before taking a huge hit. Now . . . *Christ.*

He couldn't dip into his other accounts to fund the bonuses. He'd promised to help Rocky, for one. He also had Luke and the Sugar Shack to consider, not to mention his own personal ventures. *"Fuck."*

He glanced at his watch. If things had gone according to plan, Chloe was in the midst of entertaining her dad. Devlin had promised to stop by later in the evening, after her dad had left. The notion still appealed, but Devlin knew he'd be lousy company unless he reorganized his agenda for the employee meeting, which Chris had rescheduled for Friday. Even with this latest development, Devlin felt confident about boosting morale and fostering loyalty by introducing the new healthcare options. Since no one knew about the incentive plan, not even his dad, it wasn't like Devlin was taking anything away. The only disappointed party was himself. And he had no one to blame *but* himself.

He refused to dwell on the amount of money he'd lost. Instead he focused on how to make it back. It would take some time and imagination, but he'd do it.

Stretching his body and clearing his mind, he nabbed a bottled water from his office fridge and drank deeply. As a thought occurred, the part of him that was fascinated by investments and securities overshadowed the part overseeing daily operations at J.T.'s. At some point, he hoped to launch his own financial-planning firm. Something small and specialized. The rush of strategic financial planning was only exceeded by the satisfaction of seeing a client reach his financial goals. If it weren't for having to commit so much time to the store . . .

Tensing again, Devlin shook off the thought and, after pulling up the site for the New York Stock Exchange, settled back in his chair. Before losing himself in the market, he opened his bottom drawer and took out the file he'd prepared for the employee meeting.

At the same time his eyes landed on the smaller file Jayce had hand-delivered to him a week ago today. The in-depth background report on Chloe. He grimaced, thinking how hurt she'd be if she ever learned about this file, remembering how he'd been so quick to assume the worst. A manipulator, a gold digger. Someone who'd come to Sugar Creek and wormed her way into his family's life for ulterior, selfish reasons.

He opened the folder, intending to shred the contents. Instead, he read. Some sort of morbid fascination with her colorful, chaotic past. Two pages in, he came across the pictures. He hadn't seen them before, hadn't opened this file since Jayce had given it to him, listening to the man's verbal report instead.

One of the photos was a professional headshot, something Devlin assumed she'd used when she'd been training as an actress, working as a model. Chloe, a little younger and blond. Striking. Another was a full-body shot, bathing suit, *bikini*— also professional. Also striking. *Sexy.* No wonder Jayce had raved about her kick-ass curves.

A surge of jealousy warped his thoughts. How many other men had drooled over this photo? What other kind of modeling had she done? He thought about her reckless abandon and history of poor judgment. The way she attracted trouble.

Then came a candid photo of her with another man, an older man. Ryan Levine or someone else? She had her arms around his neck, her head on his shoulder, and she was smiling. Friends? Lovers? Why did he care? Everyone had a sexual history. *He* had a history. She hadn't given him a hard time about Tasha. Why was he so bothered by the thought of her with someone else?

Because it conjured memories of Janna—the only other woman he'd loved. Because it pressed hot buttons and clanged warning bells. Chloe had the power to crush his heart.

"Christ."

He shoved the photos and report back into the folder and tried blotting it all from his mind. None of it mattered. That was then; this was now. Not to mention, nothing in that file, aside from the shoplifting charge, was scandalous. Chloe had an artistic nature, and artistic people marched to the beat of a unique drummer. So far removed from his ordinary world. Not bad. Just different.

Feeling like a stodgy jerk, Devlin turned his thoughts to the stock market. Something he understood.

Before he knew it, he'd lost himself in the financial world. When he next thought to check the time it was two hours later. "Damn." He dialed his grandma's landline.

"Hello?"

"Hi, Chloe."

"I was beginning to wonder about you," she said. "Everything okay?"

"Been troubleshooting some issues at work. How was dinner with your dad?"

She sighed. "It was . . . amazing. Not perfect, but really nice. He was impressed by my cooking."

"Who wouldn't be?"

"Are you hungry? Should I have something waiting? No trouble," she said with a smile in her voice. "Plenty of leftovers."

Her sweet voice flowed through his blood, igniting visions of their first meeting in Oslow's. He couldn't help wondering how things would've developed between them if he'd never asked Jayce to dig into her past. In wanting to protect his family, he'd compromised his own peace of mind. That damned report tainted his relationship with Chloe on several levels. He couldn't decide whether to bury or address it. He realized suddenly that he needed to think things through, reassess his personal life with the same logic and calm as he'd employed with the glitch in his financial plan.

"Sounds great, but . . . I need to work late, Chloe."

"Is that your way of saying you won't be coming over?"

"I wouldn't be good company."

"What's wrong?"

"Nothing I can't fix. Just need some time."

"I understand. Must be daunting, juggling as many business interests as you do. Maybe you'll be able to pare down someday."

"Maybe." He wasn't concerned with paring down as much as shifting his main focus from J.T.'s to his own investment firm, but that depended on his dad.

"Should I pack up some food and drive it over?"

"That's okay, hon. I'm good. Just need to push through this thing."

"If you're sure."

"I'm sure. Sorry to bail on our plans."

"Don't worry about me," Chloe went on as if sensing his distraction. "I've been busy moving some of Daisy's things into the downstairs guest room."

So Gram wouldn't have to worry about the stairs. "I thought we were going to attack that together tomorrow. What about your own ankle?"

"It's not that bad. Besides, I took it slow. Stop worrying. Remember, I'm a tough cookie."

With a soft center. Instead of obsessing on that damned report, he'd do better to remember the kindness she'd shown Daisy and the rest of his family since arriving in Sugar Creek. He smiled. "All right, cookie. So you'll be fine on your own tonight?"

"Absolutely. In fact, I'm going to take advantage of the time alone to do some research. I've got plenty to keep me busy."

Since he assumed her research had to do with the club's

recipe book, his smile broadened. Monica had bragged about how, once intrigued, Chloe poured limitless energy into a project. He knew she championed the club and their mission and appreciated her attention as the group explored a new venture. "See you tomorrow?"

"With bells on. Or something. Ooh. Maybe *nothing*."

"Something to dream on," he said with a smile. "Good night, Chloe." He hung up, then, on a whim, plucked Jayce's report from his drawer. If he took half the risks in his personal realm as he did in the financial world, he'd double his chances of enriching his life. Without a second look, he shredded the file, photos and all. "Living in the moment."

THIRTY-NINE

Chloe woke at the break of dawn feeling as though today were the first day of her life. Or at least a new phase. A better relationship with her dad, a healthier attitude regarding life and death, a business venture with a friend, and, she hoped, a happily-ever-after with Devlin Monroe. A girl could dream and a girl could also think optimistically. All her life she'd been waiting for that "click": *This is where I'm supposed to be. This is what I'm meant to do.* She'd never felt more secure in her choices than this moment.

Brimming with enthusiasm and joy, Chloe attacked the morning with gusto. She showered and dressed, paying special attention to her makeup and hair—understated perfection. She also agonized over her clothing, deciding on slim-cut black pants, a long-sleeved pleated floral tee, and a funky black scarf creatively looped around her neck. Since it was chilly outside, she'd top it all with her vintage leather jacket. Her goal was to appear professional but down-to-earth. Approachable. Someone who'd fit into the quaint business world of Sugar Creek.

Her dad had agreed to meet her at Gemma's at 9:30 a.m. They'd contacted the Realtor and arranged for a tour of the defunct bakery. Chloe's father wanted to get a look at the interior, to help her gauge the condition as well as start-up costs, in order to estimate the amount of money she'd need to borrow in order to invest equally with Daisy. Even though Daisy was willing and able to fully cover the financial end and even though she'd been willing to allow Chloe to "buy in" at a later date, Chloe was adamant about paying her own way from the get-go. Even though her dad had agreed to cosign for a loan, she had no intention of ever missing a payment. She could and would hold up her end.

Since she had time to kill, she breezed through the house, making sure everything was in order for Daisy's return tomorrow. Then she hopped on her computer, checking e-mails, her heart pounding as she read one from Rocky saying Chloe's dad had spent the evening raving about her cooking and bragging about some of the triumphs of her youth. And here she'd thought he'd been oblivious to her sporadic achievements. She'd half-expected an e-mail from Ryan, because it would be so like him to ruin a perfect day. Thankfully, she was spared. Of course there was the chance he'd called or texted, but since she'd lost her phone . . .

Another thing she meant to tackle later today: New phone. New cell service. She'd also thought about asking the Realtor about the rental situation around town. Since Chloe intended to move to Sugar Creek permanently and since she was going into business with Daisy, it might be wise to have her own home rather than living under Daisy's roof. Chloe realized then that they needed to discuss and revisit her role as personal chauffeur and cook. Partnering to run the Moose Café, or whatever, complicated their previous arrangement.

Her brow furrowed as she contemplated the matter. *Well, damn,* and here she'd thought she'd had most everything figured out.

The phone rang, stirring her out of her musings. "Hello?"

"We've got a problem, kitten."

Daisy's urgent tone set Chloe's nerves on edge. Assuming her friend had had a medical setback, Chloe prayed it wasn't serious. "What is it? What's wrong?"

"I thought about our venture all night long. Couldn't help myself this morning and started the ball rolling. Called the bank, the Realtor handling Gemma's—"

"Okay." Chloe had done much the same. She couldn't blame Daisy for her enthusiasm. Plus it gave her something to dwell on other than her injuries. "Is there a problem regarding the initial investment? You don't have to cover it on your own, Daisy. I—"

"Devlin knows."

"What?"

"He's friends with Vernon Rusk, president of the First Fidelity Bank. Apparently, Vern was concerned that I was making a rash and risky decision with my funds, so he alerted Devlin. Why is it folks in this town can't mind their own beeswax? Why does everyone think I'm incapable of acting responsibly?"

Chloe could've offered an opinion on that last question, but she was too worried about the apparent fallout. Knowing Devlin's fierce commitment to his family's welfare, she could fairly guess his reaction to the banker's news. "Let me guess: Devlin called and grilled you about your potential investment and you told him about our proposed business venture."

"He made me so danged mad, as if I don't know how to handle my own danged savings, I rallied by pelting him with all our great ideas."

Chloe's stomach dropped. She could imagine Daisy giving him an enthusiastic sales pitch without backing their vision with grounded business aspects. "He's angry."

"He's a conservative killjoy!"

Someone knocked on the door. Every molecule in Chloe's now-tense body said it was Devlin. "I'll take care of it, Daisy. Please don't fret anymore." She meant to calm the woman and at the same time herself. "I think he's here. I'll call you later."

"Give him what for, partner!"

She disconnected with a shaky smile. Everything would be fine. She'd just sit him down and calmly explain why this was going to be a great investment for both her and Daisy. If Chloe's dad, a longtime businessman and operator of a successful franchise, had gotten it, so would Devlin. Now that he was here, she'd even invite him along to Gemma's so that he could be privy to specifics. A show of good faith on her part, faith that he'd trust her instincts and wouldn't try to take control.

She opened the door, her confidence faltering after she noted the look in his expressive eyes. She'd expected anger but not . . . betrayal. "I can explain," she said as he pushed inside.

"Looking forward to it." He turned and faced her, angled his head. "It's fascinating, actually, how you continually charm people into financing your whims."

His words struck like a knife to the heart.

"At least I assume this risky prospect was a whim, because you couldn't have known when you arrived in Sugar Creek that the bakery would be going out of business. According to Daisy, you two had an epiphany at almost the same *magical* moment."

His sarcasm plunged the knife deeper. "I know it sounds crazy, but . . ." Reeling, Chloe planted her feet and crossed her arms. "What are you saying? That you think I proposed the idea out of the blue yesterday and talked Daisy into financing this venture lock, stock, and barrel?"

He shook his head, looked away, then back. "I don't think it was calculated. I think you can't help yourself. You get an idea in your head, an impulse, and you act on it without thought. Daisy adores you and shares your impulsive spirit. I can imagine her offering to back you—"

"She did."

"And you didn't refuse."

"Not entirely. For your information, she brought up the idea first. Expressed interest in buying Gemma's, and then when I said I'd had the same idea she suggested partnering up. I couldn't imagine stepping on her dream in pursuit of mine. Partnering sounded like the perfect solution, and I don't mean just because she has money and I don't. Daisy brings a lot to the table, as do I, dammit." Furious now, she jabbed an angry finger at him. "You are . . . I can't believe you. . . . I had *no* intention of letting your grandma foot the bill. I asked my dad—"

"This from someone who was so adamant about doing everything on her own."

"An ass. That's what I started to say before. You are an infuriating, cynical *jackass*." Just now all she could see was shades of the man who had initially thought the worst of her based solely on the fact that she was a stranger moving in with his grandmother. "I didn't ask Dad for money. I asked if he'd consider cosigning because I knew I'd be unable to acquire a loan on my own."

That shut Devlin up. For a minute anyway. He dropped his head as if retooling his thoughts, seeking composure. When he refocused, his expression had softened, but his attitude still sucked. "What do you know about operating a business, Chloe? Do you know how much time and effort is involved in getting a new business off the ground? Do you know how long it takes to turn a profit? How could you? You've never held a job for longer than six months and your schooling is all over the place, not that you ever followed through with any of your studies. Culinary school notwithstanding."

She stared, shocked by his insensitivity. Stymied by his knowledge.

"Not to mention," he plowed on, "if you open a café you'll be in direct competition with the Sugar Shack."

"No, we won't," she said, feeling coldcocked. "Two different animals." She blinked. "How did you know about my education? And my work history? I never said . . ." She thought back on previous conversations. "You knew about my expunged police record, too. I assumed Sheriff Stone . . ." When Devlin broke eye contact, she sensed something else. Some other force.

Jayce.

"The friend who rarely visits Sugar Creek who just happened to arrive in town soon after me. A private detective based in New York." Her chest and eyes burned with the realization. "You had me investigated."

He at least had the decency to look embarrassed. "Considering the circumstances—"

She slapped his face.

Palm tingling, heart breaking, she spun away. "No wonder you thought the worst of me," she said while searching for her purse. "You pried into my background, my life, and without knowing specifics, without knowing *me,* you formed an opinion."

"Chloe—"

"Even after . . . our truce. After this past week . . . You said you believed in me, but you don't. You implied you care, yet . . ."

"I do care, dammit." He reached for her, but she stalked away, into the kitchen.

She nabbed the keys to Leo's loaner.

"Where are you going?"

She didn't answer, just plowed past him, toward the front door.

"You told me you'd changed," he said, hot on her heels. "You implied you care, yet instead of working this through, you're running away. If you walk out that door—"

The threat only accelerated her exit, the ultimatum hanging in the air as her heart imploded. Cursing her crappy judgment, for allowing herself to fall for Devlin when she absolutely knew they were a disastrous mix, she floored the borrowed two-door, destination unknown.

* * *

Devlin had suspected midway through the argument that he'd severely overreacted, but instead of stepping down he'd allowed his doubts and concerns to flow unchecked. No matter where the money was coming from, launching any new venture was a risk, and in spite of her culinary expertise and diverse background, Chloe had no experience with finance and business administration. In addition to the start-up costs and the day-to-day operations, there were legal and tax considerations.

He couldn't imagine his grandma had thought about any of that. She was just high on an idea, another thrill-seeking adventure. Except this one could end up costing her upwards of fifty thousand dollars. When Vern had called saying Daisy had inquired about the complexities of sinking her savings into a trendy café, Devlin had been stunned. After speaking directly with Daisy, he'd seen red. Between Rocky's flagging inn, Luke's burgeoning payroll, J.T's competition, and his stock loss, he was up to his eyeballs in financial unrest, and now *this*?

In a heartbeat, he'd reverted to his old self—protect the family at all costs—and because Jayce's damned report was still fresh in his mind, Chloe had been in the direct line of fire. He'd thought the worst. And, as accused, he'd behaved like an ass. He gave her that. But then she'd tweaked his deepest misgivings by walking out. In the past, whenever things had gotten tough, she'd moved on. All he could think as she'd stalked to that car was if she didn't have it in her to brazen out an ugly quarrel, to work out their differences face-to-face, what could he expect when they really hit a rough patch?

Pissed at the present situation and influenced by the wounds Janna had inflicted years before, he'd let Chloe go. Now he was sick with worry because she'd sped off in a fury. Unfocused, what if she got into another accident? He couldn't even call her to talk her down, because she didn't have a goddamn phone. Where had she run to? Monica? Her dad? Daisy? Rocky? Stalking toward his Escalade, he started making calls.

* * *

Chloe didn't know where she was driving until she arrived.

Gemma's Bakery.

She glanced at her watch. Nine twenty a.m. The Realtor and Chloe's dad would be here any minute. She couldn't think straight, so she put herself on automatic, checked her makeup, tempered her expression and left the car to wait in front of the store.

She couldn't remember ever feeling this hurt, this *angry*. Even the crushing breakup with Ryan paled. The scariest part was that the anger wasn't fully directed at Devlin. She was furious with herself. He was right. If she had truly changed, she would have stayed and ridden out that argument until they'd both cooled off and been able to talk reason. Instead, she'd let his angry words dent her newly won confidence. As if she didn't have what it took to run her own café. She knew she had a lot to learn, but she was smart and capable and, dammit, driven. But instead of giving Devlin what for, she'd shown him her backside.

Just like with her dad. Rather than enduring their tattered relationship or fighting harder to save it, it had been easier to move to New York City. The same could be said of her breakup with Ryan—rather than facing, fighting, or enduring, it had been easier to escape to Sugar Creek.

When she'd stormed away from Devlin, her first thought had been to call Nash. When was the soonest he could fly her out to . . . Indiana? New York? But nothing clicked. Sugar Creek clicked. She looked up and down the main street of the picturesque town and beyond to the rolling mountains now fully vibrant with the bold colors of autumn. She breathed in the crisp, fresh air and felt at home. That she could feel so content and comfortable, so confident, in such a short time was astonishing, and yet deep down she believed some things were just meant to be.

She turned and peered through the plate-glass window, into the bakery formally known as Gemma's. She envisioned the décor she had discussed with Daisy, imagined them bouncing between the kitchen and counter. Tourists and locals alike would flock to their unique café in search of snacks, java, delectable cupcakes, Internet access, and an old-fashioned sense of community.

She felt a hand on her shoulder, recognized her dad's aftershave.

"Second thoughts?" he asked softly.

"Yes."

FORTY

Devlin had always considered himself the good guy. Always doing the right thing, or at least making a grand attempt. Although he knew his family often cursed his meddling, they knew his intentions were pure.

By midday Wednesday he was certain most of them, including and perhaps foremost his sister, Rocky, and Chloe's friend Monica were having serious problems with his sensitivity chip. Being the in-your-face caring people they were, no one, including Nash and Sam and especially Luke, would accept Devlin's concerns about Chloe's safety and whereabouts without details. Which universally led to, *You accused her of taking advantage of Daisy?* As if it was the most repulsive assumption he could make. Never mind that it was.

Through the grapevine he'd learned Chloe was okay. She'd met with her father; she'd visited Daisy at the hospital; she'd touched base with Monica and Rocky. Unfortunately, she'd yet to call him, even though he'd spread the word that he needed to speak with her. Obviously she wasn't talking to him, and no one else would divulge her present mind-set or future plans. If he heard *It's not for me to say* one more time, he'd explode.

Desperate for distraction, he'd buried himself in work at J.T.'s. Finally, at 4:00 p.m., he got the call he'd been waiting for all day.

"We need to talk, Devlin."

"The sooner, the better."

"Meet me at Grenville's Overlook," she said.

"The covered bridge?"

"I'll be waiting."

* * *

Confrontation had never been her strong point, but over the course of the day Chloe had determined her new life, her happiness, was worth fighting for. Whether or not that pretty picture included Devlin remained to be seen, but she had every hope. She'd known from the beginning that he was controlling by nature and quick to attack when it came to protecting his family. Intimidating, infuriating, and, when angered, irrational. Some hefty faults. But she'd also learned that his admirable qualities—sense of humor, generous soul, kind heart—by far overshadowed his darker sensibilities. He was a complex man. Then again, she wasn't exactly a piece of cake. Maybe Monica had been right all along. Maybe they could balance each other out.

When he joined her on the bridge, her senses simultaneously rejoiced and panicked. Even though they'd parted on angry terms, her first impulse was to throw herself into his arms. The love she felt for this man was fierce and deep and filled her with an overwhelming sense of wonder. In spite of their many differences, in spite of their short association, in her heart of hearts she felt they were destined to be together . . . forever. Tempering her reckless optimism proved a challenge, but she dug deep, breathed deep. Even though she ached to rush blindly and blissfully forward with their relationship, she played it cool.

Take it slow.

"I'm sorry I pulled you away from work," she said as he moved in beside her.

"I'm not."

She smiled a little. "I'm sorry about this morning. I should have . . . Old habits die hard."

"No one knows that better than I, Chloe. I did you a disservice by comparing you to someone in my past."

Instead of being coy, she seized the chance to yank at least one skeleton out of the closet. "Your wife?"

"You know about Janna?"

"Not really. Just that she . . . was."

He leaned against the old wood railing and looked out over the sparkling river, swollen from the previous rains. "She was a free spirit, for lack of a better term. My first love. Young love, teenage lust, immature emotions—a powerful mix."

Rocky and Jayce came to mind—another skeleton—but Chloe held silent. Not her secret to out.

"We dated on and off for two years during high school," he went on. "I think, no, I know my feelings ran deeper than hers. Regardless, I was there whenever she wanted or needed me. I can't tell you how many times I bailed her out of a bad situation."

"Sort of like me." She indicated the river, thought about the reckless-driving arrest, the shoplifting incident, the car accident on Thrush.

"Yes and no." He met her gaze, smoothed windblown hair from her face. "The difference is, she manipulated me, used me. You wouldn't even let me confront Billy Burke or Tasha on your behalf."

Chloe furrowed her brow. "Are you saying Janna manipulated you into marriage?"

His expression clouded. "Just after I graduated from high school, just before I went off for college, Janna informed me she was pregnant. Her parents had disowned her and she was earning minimal money selling her handmade jewelry at one of the local shops. She was an emotional and financial wreck."

"The baby was yours?"

"So she said. Definite possibility."

"So you felt responsible, for the baby, for her. You offered marriage, sanctuary."

"Janna wasn't built to be a single mother and I'd nixed the alternatives. Regardless of what my family may think or say, I wasn't fooled into believing she married me because she loved me. I didn't care. I loved her. And I loved that baby. But then five months into the pregnancy, she miscarried and everything changed."

Chloe reached over and squeezed his hand. She didn't have to ask to know he'd been crushed by the loss of that baby—whether he was the biological father or not.

"Instead of overcoming the loss and moving on with me, Janna left me, and the life she never wanted, for a new life on the West Coast."

Chloe fidgeted, thinking about her own inclinations to run.

"Logically, I know it was for the best. Our relationship was dysfunctional to say the least. But I've never gotten over how *easy* it was for her to walk away." He turned now and faced Chloe full on, his heart in his eyes. "The hardest part about falling in love with you, Chloe, was accepting your free spirit."

She understood now why he'd been so angry when she'd walked away from their argument. In her next breath, she absorbed his admission. "You love me?"

"At the risk of moving too fast and scaring you off, yes. I love you, Chloe. I love your sweet face, your kind heart, your reckless passion. I love the way you worry about my family, your righteous fury." He quirked a tender smile. "The way you always twist your hair in a messy knot. You fascinate and infuriate me. You color my dull-ass world."

Her heart hammered in her chest as his sentiments echoed in her brain. He adored her and all of her quirks—good and bad—and that was amazing. A first. But would he support her dream? Instead of responding to his romantic declaration, she risked igniting his disapproval. "Daisy and I spoke," she blurted. "We're going forward with our plans to buy Gemma's."

"I'm not surprised."

She licked her lips. "We could use some advice."

"I'll help in whatever way I can. I'm hoping we can make a fresh start, Chloe."

Pulse racing, heart full, she eyed the water below. Sunlight danced on the soft ripples. Derring-do surged through her blood. *What would you do, how far would you go, for love?* Swallowing hard, she peeled off her leather jacket, toed off her shoes.

"What are you doing?"

"You're too conservative. I'm too impulsive. We need to meet halfway. Daisy said you used to cannonball off this bridge with Luke. When's the last time you did anything carefree and reckless like that?"

"Not since . . . Janna."

She pulled off her socks. "Come on. Take off your jacket and shoes. We'll take the plunge together. It's symbolic," she said with a crooked grin. "Get it?"

"But you're afraid of water."

"No, I'm not. I'm afraid of drowning. You won't let me drown, will you?"

"Chloe—"

"In the words of Daisy, 'if you live life ruled by your fears, you're not really living.'" Heart bursting with joy, she palmed his cheek and bared her soul. "I love you, Devlin Monroe. I love your handsome face, your generous spirit, and your obsessive, overprotective nature. I love the way you worry about your family, about me, your righteous fury, and the way you always smooth my messy hair from my face. You challenge and inspire me." She brushed her lips over his sexy mouth. "You set my colorful world on fire."

He kissed her deeply, fiercely, sealing their heartfelt declarations, and somehow managing to shed his clothes in the process.

Finessing under the railing, they balanced on the edge, their future bright with trust and reckless passion. Smiling into her eyes, he offered his hand. "Don't let go."

"Never."

Stripped down to their underwear, stripped free of their pasts, they held hands . . . and jumped.

HONORARY CUPCAKE LOVERS
Submitted Recipes from On-Line Members

CHLOE'S CARROT CUPCAKES
(submitted by Gina Husta of New Jersey)

Ingredients
2¼ cups of flour
2½ tsp. cinnamon
¼ tsp. nutmeg
1 tsp. baking soda
1 tsp. baking powder
⅛ tsp. salt
½ tsp. allspice
1 cup granulated sugar
½ cup light brown sugar
2½ cups shredded/ grated carrots
3 eggs
1 cup vegetable oil
1 cup raisins (I prefer golden)
¾ chopped nuts
1 20 oz. can crushed pineapple
1 cup coconut

Cupcakes

- Heat oven to 350°. Grease and flour cupcake pans or use cupcake liners.
- Mix flour, cinnamon, baking soda, baking powder, salt, and Allspice in a bowl.
- Beat sugars, oil, eggs in a second bowl.
- Stir in carrots, pineapple, and coconut.
- Add flour mixture, add raisins, and nuts.
- Fill each cupcake to half with filling baking for 25 minutes (or until an inserted toothpick comes out clean). Cool before adding frosting.

Frosting

8 oz. cream cheese
1 cup butter
2 tsp. vanilla
2½ cups confectioners sugar

- Beat cream cheese, butter, vanilla until well blended. Gradually add sugar until creamy.

WHITE CUPCAKES

(Submitted by Tammy Yenalavitch of North Carolina)

Ingredients

1 cup white sugar
½ cup butter
2 eggs
2 teaspoons vanilla extract
1½ cups all-purpose flour
1¾ teaspoons baking powder
½ cup milk

Directions

- Preheat oven to 350 degrees F
- Line a muffin pan with paper liners.

- In a medium bowl, cream together the sugar and butter.
- Beat in the eggs, one at a time, then stir in the vanilla.
- Combine flour and baking powder, add to the creamed mixture and mix well. Finally stir in the milk until batter is smooth.
- Pour or spoon batter into the prepared liners.
- Bake 20 to 25 minutes. Cake is done when it springs back to the touch.
- Frost with your favorite frosting.

HARVEST CHEATER CUPCAKES
(Submitted by Beth Bliss of New Jersey)

These cupcakes cheat in nearly every way: made from a mix, frosted from a can . . . The only thing honest about them is the homemade whoopee pie cream hidden inside.

Makes 20 nicely-domed standard-size cupcakes—because I cheated and filled them ¾ full instead of ⅔.

Cupcake
1 box "moist" style yellow cake mix (15.25 oz. box)
⅓ cup vegetable oil
1 cup canned pumpkin (not pumpkin pie filling)
½ cup water
3 eggs
1 tsp. cinnamon
½ tsp. allspice
½ tsp. powdered ginger
¼ tsp. cloves
¼ tsp. nutmeg

- Bake at 350° for 20-24 minutes. Done when they spring back to the touch, or when a cake tester or toothpick inserted in center comes out clean.

Secret center (Whoopee Pie) Filling
A little dab of these goes a long way; only about a teaspoon goes in, but the sweetness offsets the spices and pumpkin nicely.

1 cup vegetable shortening, such as Crisco (butter-flavored shortening might work, too)
1 cup powdered sugar
2 cups (one 7-oz. container) marshmallow fluff (aka marshmallow crème; often found near ice cream section of grocery store)
2 tsp. vanilla extract (not "flavoring"—only extract will do!)
Small pinch table salt

* Blend in mixer until light and fluffy.
* Using a paring knife or apple corer, cut out a plug from the center of each cupcake.
* Using a silicone spatula, shovel filling into a pastry bag with large-opening tip, or into a ziplock baggie and snip a hole in the corner.
* Pipe about a teaspoon into each cupcake. Don't fret if it spurts out a little. That's life.

Kick-in-the-Pants Frosting
1 can milk or dark chocolate frosting
1 tsp. cinnamon
¼ tsp. chili powder (more, if you want a serious kick)

* Mix using hand-held or stand mixer until spices are incorporated.

PUMPKIN CUPCAKES
(Submitted by Chris Behrens of Florida)

Ingredients
2 ¼ cups all-purpose flour, sifted before measuring
1 tablespoon baking powder

1/2 teaspoon baking soda
1/2 teaspoon salt
3/4 teaspoon ground cinnamon
1/2 teaspoon ground ginger
1/2 teaspoon ground nutmeg
1/2 cup butter, softened
1 1/3 cups sugar
2 eggs, beaten until frothy
1 cup mashed cooked or canned pumpkin
3/4 cup milk
3/4 cup chopped walnuts or pecans

Directions
- Sift together the flour, baking powder, baking soda, salt, ginger, cinnamon, and nutmeg into a bowl.
- Cream butter and sugar until light and fluffy; beat in eggs.
- Blend in mashed pumpkin.
- Stir in the sifted dry ingredients alternately with the milk, blending until batter is smooth after each addition; stir in chopped walnuts or pecans.
- Spoon batter into well-greased and floured or paper-lined muffin pan cups. Fill about 2/3 full.
- Bake at 375° for 25 minutes, or until a wooden pick or cake tester inserted in center comes out clean.
- Frost with cream cheese frosting or whipped cream.
- Makes about 24 cupcakes.

LIDA'S HOT MILK SPONGE CAKE
(Submitted by Mary Stella of Florida)

Ingredients
4 eggs
2 cups sugar
2 cups flour
2 tsps baking powder
1/2 tsp salt

1 cup milk (heated just to boiling)
1 tbl butter
1 tsp vanilla

Directions
- Beat eggs, then add sugar and beat well together.
- Sift flour, baking powder and salt. Stir into egg mixture.
- Heat milk to boiling, remove from heat and melt in butter, add vanilla.
- Beat liquid into flour/sugar/egg mixture until blended. Do not overbeat.
- Pour into prepared tube pan, two 8″ layer pans or one 9″ × 13″ pan.
- Bake at 350 degrees for 30 to 45 minutes. (Do not look to check cake before 30 minutes.)

- NOTE: The above is for the 'cake' version. For 'cupcakes' use standard size cupcake tins and check for doneness a few minutes earlier than stated for the cake recipe.

Buttercream Frosting
3¾ cups powdered sugar
½ cup softened butter
3–4 tablespoons milk
1 teaspoon vanilla

- Combine all ingredients, beat at medium speed until creamy.

STRAWBERRY DELIGHT CUPCAKES
(Submitted by Dawn A. Jones of New Jersey)

Ingredients
1 box Strawberry Premium Cake Mix (Pudding in the Mix)
1 small jar strawberry jam
1 can milk chocolate frosting

Cake Directions

- Preheat oven according to cake mix.
- Line a muffin pan with paper liners.
- Follow directions on box.
- Pour or spoon batter into the prepared liners.
- Bake according to cake mix. Cake is done when it springs back to the touch or when a cake tester or toothpick inserted in center comes out clean.

Center Directions

- Using a steak knife cut out a plug (piece of cake) from the center of each cupcake and put it aside, then use a teaspoon and add a small amount of strawberry jam. Then replace the plug (piece of cake) and frost with milk chocolate frosting.
- Makes about 24 cupcakes depending on cake mix.

Read on for an excerpt from

The Trouble With Love

—the next Cupcake Lovers Novel from
Beth Ciotta:

Jayce shook off the past and focused on the woman who emerged from the hotel bathroom. Curvier than the girl he'd bedded thirteen years prior. He'd gotten a prime view of Rocky's bodacious figure three weeks ago when they'd faced off in her bathroom at her inn. At the time she'd been wearing a sheer cami and skimpy underwear. Now she wore a long-sleeved, knee-length, black-and-white patterned dress and tall black boots. Nothing racy about this ensemble, yet his pulse revved.

"How do I look?"

I'd like to lick you head to toe. "Not bad."

Rocky frowned. "This meeting is important. I need to look great." She unknotted the sash-belt and tied it in a bow. "Better?" She turned before he answered, kicked shut the bathroom door to see for herself in a full-length mirror. "Too frilly. Maybe it's supposed to tie in the back."

"It was fine before."

"Then what?" she snapped, fixated on her reflection. "Too short? Too long? Too clingy? Not clingy enough?"

Okay. This was a side of Rocky he'd never seen. He'd never heard, let alone witnessed, her fretting over her appearance. Never known her to ask anyone's opinion. Unlike most of the women Jayce knew, Rocky didn't obsess on fashion. She opted for comfortable. Casual. Jeans and T-shirts never looked so good. Sneakers never so sexy. He chalked it up to confidence. One of Rocky's most alluring and irritating qualities. She was definitely off her game.

Jayce remained seated, although he did lean forward, bracing his forearms on his knees. He locked onto her nervous energy, her uncharacteristic insecurity, and considered that gash on her forehead. She'd just been mugged, then hit by a car. Rocky was tough but was she really up for a corporate meeting? What if she got dizzy? Or sick? Though she'd downplayed the head wound there'd been a lot of blood on her shirt. Enough to stop his heart. He'd spoken to the doctor who'd declared her fit enough to leave. But that overworked resident had also been dealing with various other crises. Could he really trust the man's, *She'll be sore, but fine*?

The more Jayce thought about it, the less inclined he was to let Rocky out of his sight. "Maybe you should call Tasha and ask her to postpone the meeting."

"Seriously? I look that bad? Dammit!" She fussed with the deep-V-neckline, frowned. "Chloe said this wrap-around style was a good fit for my figure and business appropriate. I called her from Macy's and . . ."

"It's not the dress."

"Is it the boots? Too clunky? Should I go with the pumps?" She bent over, flashing her generous cleavage as she unzipped the boots and kicked them away, treating Jayce to her shapely calves. The woman had kickass runner's legs and she accentuated them by slipping her pretty feet into a pair of pointy-toed, three-inch-spike-heeled pumps. *Christ.*

She straightened. "Better?"

Jayce shifted to hide a boner. "Only if you want the marketing department to be distracted by your legs." He dragged his gaze from her killer gams to those lethal eyes. "Sexy."

She flushed, holding his gaze for a second before grunting in exasperation. "I don't want to look sexy. I want to look stylish. Tasha said . . . Oh, what does she know?" Rocky turned her back and rooted through her shopping bags. "I bought a new blazer. Maybe I should just wear my jeans—"

"The dress looks great, Dash." Jayce pushed out of the chair. "Go with the boots. Business appropriate. Stylish."

"You sure?"

"Positive. Although if you're opting for stylish over sexy you might want to reconsider your hairstyle." The tousled mass of soft blond curls looked just-rolled-out-of-bed enticing. He should know. She'd rolled out of his bed after that one night of lovemaking, backlit by moonlight and looking like a young and sassy version of the legendary bombshell who shared her last name.

Boots zipped, Rocky whirled back to the mirror. "I'd go with a ponytail, but I don't want to expose my forehead. That butterfly strip looks like a freaking badge of stupidity and the bump is starting to discolor."

"Let me see." Jayce turned her around and gently inspected the wound. "It's swollen now, too." Plus, flecks of dried blood caked one edge of the butterfly strip. *Damn.* "How do you feel? Dizzy? Achy?"

"Stressed." She batted away his hands and glanced at her watch. "I'm supposed to meet Tasha in forty minutes and I look like freaking Frankenstein."

"Not quite that bad," Jayce teased. "And I'll get you there in plenty of time." He moved into the bathroom, inspected the vanity strewn with toiletries. Powder, deodorant, lotions, hairbrush, blow dryer, elastic bands, hair clip. "Where's your makeup?"

"Why? Aren't I wearing enough? Jesus. I'm going for a book, not a modeling, contract. There's something to be said for understated, you know."

"Relax. Just looking to camouflage that bruise."

"Oh. Right. Well, I don't wear foundation, if that's what you're looking for. Just mascara and tinted lip balm."

A natural beauty, Rocky didn't need makeup to enhance her looks. Still, most women he'd known kept an array of beauty products even if they only used them for special occasions. Rocky wasn't most women. He spied a nail file and a pair of manicure scissors. "How do you feel about bangs?"

"What?"

He rounded the corner—comb, towel, scissors, and hair clip in hand. "I dated a hair stylist once."

"That qualifies you to cut hair?"

"Let's just say I was subjected to enough fashion hype to know what qualifies as stylish."

"You're kidding me, right?"

"Sit." He motioned her into one chair, placed the towel over her lap, then pulled over the other chair and sat across from her. "Lean forward."

She blew out a breath and did as he asked. "Fine. Chop away. Just . . . not too much."

"Just enough." Jayce concentrated on the task, thankful that Rocky lowered her lids so he didn't have to gaze into those feisty baby blues. Breathing in the tantalizing scent of her shampoo and body lotion was torture enough.

Rocky blushed when he brushed the pad of his thumb over her cheek. Shivered, when he lightly blew wisps of cut hair from her face.

Time froze as Jayce focused intently on the woman he'd set his sights on. A woman he'd known all his life yet barely knew. Jayce had spent years waiting for Rocky to grow up and address their history, to banish the secret that had distanced Jayce from the town and people he loved. He was tired of waiting. Fuck waiting.

Sitting stock still, gaze lowered, Rocky licked her lips. "Are you done yet?"

His cock twitched at the nervous catch in her voice. *He hadn't even begun.* As always a raw sexual heat burned between them. She was as turned on as he was, not that he'd act on it. Not now. *Let it simmer.* "Good to go."

She cleared her throat, eased away. "How do I look?" she asked, forcing her gaze to his. "If you say: *Not bad,* I'll sock you."

Good enough to eat, would at the very least earn him a glare, so instead he went with, "Almost perfect." He raked his fingers through her silky curls—yeah boy, *heaven*—then twisted and secured an up-do with one of those hair gadgets that reminded him of a potato chip clip. "There."

Even though Rocky scrambled toward the mirror, the heat lingered. The air sizzled. Visibly shaken, she focused on her reflection, blinked. "Wow. I never considered bangs. They not only cover the bump, but they're . . . flattering. And this style . . . nice. How—"

"Man of many talents," he said, coming up behind her. They locked gazes in the mirror and Jayce felt something beyond the heat. A shift. An added element. Swimming in Rocky's vivid blue eyes, alongside resentment, lust, and hurt, he spied curiosity.

"It occurs to me that I really only know the Jayce Bello of my youth," she said, breaking eye contact. "I'm still pissed at that man. I'd like to get past that, move on. Maybe we could do something about that while I'm in town."

"Meaning you're ready to talk about the infamous morning after?"

"No," she said while nabbing a baker's box from the mini-fridge. "Meaning I'd like to know more about the big bad private dick who just cut and styled my hair like a seasoned pro."

Fuck waiting. Primed for the challenge, Jayce glanced at his watch, then formulated a plan as he helped Rocky into her coat and out the door. "It's a start."